Coming Swoon

Sarah Estep

ISBN: 979-8-9880770-7-7 (print)

ISBN: 979-8-9880770-6-0 (e-book)

For my hopeless romantics who never give up on love...Don't use this as an excuse to call your ex. He's not Peter.

Author's Note

Before you begin Coming Swoon, I wanted to give a few content points to be aware of, should you need them. Keep in mind this is still a Brunch Bros book, so despite the nature of some of these points, Coming Swoon is still a warm, cozy read.

I tried to take great care to treat these subjects with as much sensitivity as possible, as some of them may be upsetting to some readers. Please take care of yourself.

Content warnings:

- Parental Abandonment/Neglect
- Car Accident (Deer Dies)
- Pregnancy (side character)
- Alcohol Consumption
- Explicit Open Door Scenes
- Thwarted Sexual Assault (Past, non-descriptive, not POV character)

Prologue
London, Twelve Years Ago

Peter Parker-Green didn't know why he picked the bookshop with the blue door, except that maybe it reminded him of the one from *Notting Hill*. It wasn't remarkable in the slightest beyond the cheerful door and the tabby cat sleeping in the window, obscuring part of the display. Parts of the gold lettering on the window had peeled off, making it a "Boo s op", but Peter had time to kill so he went inside. He needed to buy a birthday present for his mother anyway.

The shop was dark, the light disappearing the further back he walked, as overstuffed shelves of used books crowded out the sun filtering in from outside. Used bookshops all had the same smell to him, a unique combination of dust, paper, and old binding glue. The organization was always a bit different, and this one fell into the "non-existent" category, which was actually the best kind. Treasures hid in shops where no one could tell you exactly what the inventory was.

Peter crouched down in front of a shelf. His parents had taught him to start from the bottom and work his way up, since casual browsers were more likely to only look at what was eye level or above. Book thrifting was a family hobby, hunting for specific covers or out-of-print books in the cities they visited. Both of his parents were such voracious readers that their production company specialized in adaptations. And his mother collected Jane Austen novels specifically. Charlotte Parker had enough money that she could have hired someone to find them for her, the way some of their friends had art buyers, but she liked to find them herself or get them as gifts so each one had a memory attached. That was what he was hunting for: an Austen his mom didn't already own.

A pair of cheap, knock-off Doc Martens caught his peripheral attention. The owner of the boots was stretched up on their tiptoes, reaching for something, but he was fixated on their feet. The heel on the right boot was separating from the sole, and it took every ounce of self-control Peter possessed to not see which of his fingers would fit in the gap. People didn't like having fingers randomly shoved into their gaps.

Focus. He needed to focus. He tore his eyes away from the derelict boots and trained them firmly on the shelves in front of him. There was something special in this shop. He could feel it. It made the skin on the back of his neck prickle and his toes clench in his shoes.

Peter's eyes trailed upward, quickly scanning spines, pausing on the ones that were almost too cracked to read. Spine-cracking was a sin, according to his mother. When he spied the red leather spine, with the title engraved in gold letters, his heart quickened. He had seen this edition of *Emma* before, but never in such good condition. If the rest of it looked like the spine, he'd found a diamond in the rough.

His fingers collided with someone else's as he reached for the copy of *Emma*. Electricity shot up his arm and sparks crackled in his blood.

He turned his head to tell the person that he'd seen the book first, but the words evaporated on his tongue like water splashed into a scalding pan.

Peter believed in true love the same way other people believed in religion. Love at first sight was akin to a miracle, a sacred thing that could happen if the soul was open to the possibility.

It was like he'd left his sepia-colored life and stepped into bright, jarring technicolor. Warm brown eyes stared up into his, narrowed and unblinking. The light caught her red hair just right, setting it aglow in a deep, fiery copper. Dozens of gingerish freckles stood out against a rosy pink blush.

So this was it. The moment he'd waited for and dreamed about his entire life. He'd finally met the other half of his soul.

His heart beat truly for the first time and the sound filled his ears. *Tha-thump. Tha-thump. Thu-thump.*

"You a big Jane Austen fan, buddy?"

Her snarky tone jolted Peter out of his haze.

"More than a fan," he said, imbuing all the serious reverence of a priest into his voice. "This isn't just a book. It's a sacred text of Our Lady Most Ardently."

She suppressed her smile, but the amused twitch in the corner of her mouth encouraged him.

"I'm Peter," he said, and for some unknown, god-forsaken reason added, "Like the rabbit."

"And I need to get this book and leave," she said, tugging it off the shelf. She frowned when he didn't release the hold he'd had on the copy. "A devotee like yourself doesn't own a copy of *Emma?*"

"I do."

She tried to tug the book away from him, but he gripped it tighter. "If you already own it, why aren't you letting go?"

"Because it's not for me. It's a birthday present for my mother."

"You're getting her *this* for her birthday?" She frowned at him. "Why?"

"Because she collects Austens," Peter said. "Why do you need this copy so badly?"

"It's a gift for my sister."

Peter raised an eyebrow, and she rolled her eyes.

"I want to bring home something special for her, not a Big Ben keychain."

"I'll let you have the book," Peter said, "if you go out with me."

"A guy that needs to hold a book hostage to get a date? I don't think so."

"I guess we'll have to stand here and get to know each other, then, because I'm not letting go."

She tugged on the book again, but he didn't budge.

"I knew I should've gone to Waterstones. But no, I saw the blue door and thought, 'That looks like Hugh Grant's place in *Notting Hill.*'" She frowned, and added under her breath, "Last time I ever watch a rom-com."

"This is fate. You were going to go to Waterstones, but you came here instead. We reached for the same copy of the same book that's been out forever for the same reason. We were supposed to meet today."

"There's no such thing as fate," she told him.

An idea lit up his mind like a lightbulb.

"If I can convince you that fate is real, will you go out with me?"

She sighed heavily and shifted her weight onto her right foot. "I can't wait to hear how you're going to prove this."

"Easy. London is a big town. We don't know anything about each other. If we run into each other again, it's clearly fate that we're supposed to get to know each other." He looked at the book clasped in their hands. He could find his mother something else for her birthday. "You can have the book as a gesture of goodwill."

She looked at the book, sighed, and let go. "No. You take it. My sister probably wouldn't appreciate it anyway." She took a few steps back. "We won't be seeing each other again, by the way. Fate isn't real."

"Maybe you'll change your mind the next time I see you."

She shook her head while she rolled her eyes, then turned and made her way to the front of the store. Peter watched her stop to give the store cat some pets before she left, and he let the image sear itself into his brain.

He'd be seeing her again. They were meant to be.

Chapter One

Sybil Morgan was not a chitchatter by nature. There was too much to do, and she was of the opinion that most people were as shallow as a bird bath. She enjoyed a good conversation with her small handful of friends, but that was about it. Almost everyone got the hint that she wasn't interested in talking to them outside of the amount of time it took them to order a cup of coffee from her by her monosyllabic answers.

Then there was Arthur Green.

Being impervious to her unresponsiveness must be genetic; his son was exactly the same.

Sybil wasn't sure exactly what a movie producer did, but if Arthur was anything to go on, it involved a lot of coffee in the morning and tea in the afternoon. Occasionally she saw him take a phone call or use his laptop to supposedly answer some emails, all on her Wi-Fi. It wasn't like he didn't have somewhere to go. The movie people had rented out the Crane Hotel, and the hotel had *excellent* Wi-Fi. Graham Thatcher, the owner and her best friend's husband, had made sure of that, and since in his previous life he'd been the founder and CEO of a tech company, Sybil assumed he knew what he was doing.

Not that she would ever, *ever* tell him that.

Despite having a room at the hotel and access to their excellent Wi-Fi, Arthur Green had chosen to spend his first two weeks in Crane Cove sitting in her coffee shop, using her mid-level Wi-Fi, and drinking enough cups of her coffee to give a man half his age heart trouble, talking to her and anyone else who made the mistake of entering his orbit.

Before she'd known exactly who he was, Sybil had thought that Arthur reminded her of Peter. They had the same easy way of talking to strangers so they became friends within minutes. Hell, if he wasn't a British citizen, Arthur could have run for mayor of Crane Cove after his first week in town and won. The residents of her sleepy coastal town probably would have ignored the glaring legalities if his name should magically appear on the ballot in November.

Because of who his son was, she was determined not to like him. The fact that she did like him made her feel like an abject failure.

"Another cup, dear," Arthur said, putting his ceramic cup on the counter. It was a beautiful iridescent blue-green glaze that he'd purchased from the shop next door during its going-out-of-business sale.

Sybil picked up his mug. "If you have a heart attack, I'm not reviving you," she warned as she headed for the urns of brewed coffee.

He snorted. "It'll take more than a little coffee to do me in. I'm made of stronger stuff than that."

"I'm switching you to decaf."

She glanced over her shoulder in time to see Arthur clutch his chest with a wounded expression on his face.

"You wouldn't do that to me."

"It's for your own good." Sybil filled half the mug with

decaf, and the other half with regular. "You have more coffee in your veins than blood."

"It's like petrol. Keeps me going."

It was Sybil's turn to pretend to be offended. "Did you just compare my coffee to gasoline?"

"Never." Arthur accepted his mug back. "Maybe the high-grade petrol they use in Formula One cars."

The mischievous sparkle in his blue eyes made her heart twist painfully in her chest. Arthur was a tall, slender man whose limbs had retained the gangly quality of boyhood. By American standards he wasn't so much handsome as "interesting." Peter had gotten his unearthly good looks from his movie star-turned-director mother. But his eyes and his smile he'd gotten from his father. Every time she made Arthur grin, she wondered if she was looking into a future she'd only see from afar.

"Don't insult your dealer," Sybil warned.

"Wouldn't dream of it." Arthur winked at her and went back to the same little table he sat at every day. She might as well order a brass nameplate for the spot.

Stardust Coffee, the coffee shop she owned and ran, was empty except for Arthur. Fall was in full swing in Crane Cove, and with it came the low season for tourism. Locals stopped in at predictable intervals, but her profit margins were considerably narrower outside of long school breaks and the summer months. So, despite the disruption to local life, this movie came at a great time for the community. The movie people would spend their money at local businesses. The Crane Hotel was fully booked for the duration of the film shoot. And maybe the notoriety of having a movie directed by Charlotte Parker would attract more tourism, particularly in the off-season.

The front door flung open and the bell overhead clanged instead of jingled. Like merely thinking about her could summon her, Peter's mother Charlotte stormed inside with murder written on her face.

"That mother*fucker*," she bellowed, fighting with the zipper on her coat before yanking the expensive blue raincoat off and throwing it on the floor. "That fucking motherfucker promised me those tweets were a one-time, Ambien-induced anomaly. His agent promised me. His manager promised me. Everyone but his mother promised me it would never happen again. So what did I do? Against my better judgment, against my gut feeling this was a bad idea, I caved to the studio and approved his casting. And how does that motherfucker repay me?"

There were a million tasks Sybil could be doing in the back, from inventory and ordering to preparing her quarterly taxes, but instead she picked up a bottle of sanitizer and a rag and went to work wiping down her counter.

Arthur seemed unfazed despite all the shouting and a record number of "motherfuckers." He sipped his coffee and asked, "What did he do this time?"

"In the middle of the night he got on his stupid fucking phone"—Charlotte mimed typing on a smartphone—"and managed to insult and offend just about every protected class in the country."

"Was he really that thorough?" Arthur asked, and whatever look his wife gave him prompted him to say, "What do you want to do about it, my love?"

"I want to fire his ass. I want you to tell me that legal will approve me livestreaming the burning of his contract. I want to tap-dance on his grave."

"You know I support all of your endeavors," Arthur began in a diplomatic fashion that made Sybil want to duck for cover. She'd tear someone's head off if they used that tone with her. "But there are a lot of factors to consider before you go scorched-earth, darling. The first being that your actors are due to arrive *tomorrow* to begin their read-throughs and rehearse. Not only do we have to find someone available on such short notice, we need to find a name big enough that the studio will be willing to take it in the teeth when he sues. Plus there's the money we'll have to pay him even if we fire—*when* we fire him—and then whatever astronomical amount someone's agent is going to bend us over the barrel for because they know we're desperate."

"We're not *desperate*," Charlotte said, the obvious lie laced into every syllable. "*Someone* has to have time in their schedule. Projects fall through. People think they want family vacations and they're wrong. Someone has to be sitting at home, twiddling their thumbs, wondering why the damn phone doesn't ring anymore."

"Yes, but we'd need to be very careful about *why* no one is ringing them, love," Arthur pointed out. "Don't want to end up in this spot again."

Charlotte groaned and pushed her hands through her gray hair, knocking her rain-specked reading glasses off her head. She looked at the floor in surprise and cursed, stooping to pick them up.

"I've been looking for these for an hour." She tried to dry them on the hem of her sweater. "Can you think of anyone off the top of your head who's got star power, a good to excellent public image, is fucking competent, and available?"

Arthur picked up his coffee cup and blew the steam off the top. "I can, but you're not going to like it." He sipped his coffee, then said, "Peter."

"No."

It wasn't until Arthur and Charlotte looked at her that Sybil realized she'd said the thought out loud in unison with Charlotte. Mortification burned her face, and she searched for a quick lie to cover her tracks.

"I, uh, forgot to order milk," she said, turning quickly and knocking over a stack of cups she needed to stock. Luckily they were still in their plastic sleeve.

"I won't hire Peter," she heard Charlotte say as she hid in the backroom, listening at the door.

"He fits the brief. Competent, excellent public image, and he's meant to be headed this way on holiday."

"Isn't that convenient?" Charlotte retorted. "Did you two plan this?"

"I'm going to ignore that because you're under stress."

"I meant—" Charlotte let out a frustrated groan. "You know I never wanted this for him."

"I know, love," Arthur said gently. "But it's what he wanted. At some point you do have to accept that this is his career."

Charlotte sighed heavily. "Pretend to be a producer for the day and round me up a list of potentials by four o'clock. If I hate all of the options, we can call Peter."

Sybil exited the backroom as casually as she could, though she felt like she had the subtlety of a Mardi Gras parade float. She came out in time to see Charlotte give her husband a tender peck on the lips and wrestle herself back into her coat.

"Did you walk or drive?" Arthur asked.

"I walked. I don't need another speeding ticket from the Barney Fife wannabe they've got in this town," Charlotte said bitterly. "Plus, the walk calmed me down."

"That was you calm?" he teased. "Do you want a ride back to the hotel?"

"No. I think another walk and I should be back to my standard level of ghastly."

"Be safe. Don't walk into the ocean," Arthur said as Charlotte exited, holding up her middle finger over her shoulder. He chuckled, then said to Sybil, "There goes the love of my life."

"The movie isn't going to be cancelled, is it?" she asked, the cost of the extra supplies she'd ordered in anticipation of increased business hovering in the back of her mind like a vengeful ghost.

"No, it's not," he assured her, and Sybil let hearing those words in his accent soothe her. There was something incredibly comforting about a British accent. Everything sounded better. "My son is a wonderful actor, and he's been trying to be part of one of Charlotte's projects for years."

Except for that.

At eight p.m., Sybil turned the sign in her door from open to closed and locked the door from the inside.

Another fourteen-hour workday in the books.

"Sadie, I'm going to count the till in the back. Don't worry about doing refills, just do the cleaning list," she said to her seventeen-year-old employee, who gave her a mock salute. "You can have the tip jar. Thanks for showing up tonight."

Normally she had two closers, in addition to herself, but a last-minute callout left them shorthanded. If Sybil got home before ten, she'd be happy.

It didn't matter if a sales day was good or bad, doing the books gave her heartburn. The day had been middling, almost exactly what Eloise's magical spreadsheet had predicted, down to the penny. Sybil didn't know how her friend did it, or why she *liked* doing it.

She needed to call Eloise. Or show up at her door with a bottle of wine and, as casually as possible, ask her when the fuck she was going to divulge that Peter was coming to town for a vacation.

Sybil put down the stack of five-dollar bills she'd been counting because all she'd actually done was move the money from one hand to the other without a single number floating through her head.

Peter wasn't even in town yet, and she was a fucking disaster.

If she'd known the first time Graham Thatcher had come into her business that his best friend was her ex, she'd have run him out of town. No thinly veiled protective hostility because Graham was involved with Eloise. Full-scale warfare. She would have made Graham thankful he'd left Crane Cove, and he would have told anyone who crossed his path to never, ever visit.

But because she'd been mildly pleasant to Graham, Peter had delivered a ballgown to her house, walked her down the aisle at Graham and Eloise's wedding, and switched the place cards around at Thanksgiving so they were sitting next to each other.

And then there were the flowers.

Every week for the last year and a half, a floral arrangement had been delivered to Stardust Coffee. She didn't know how he did it, but they always arrived when she wasn't there or had stepped into the backroom so she couldn't refuse the delivery. But they were all so beautiful, she didn't know if she'd have had the heart to refuse them, even if they left her with complicated feelings she thought were finally dead and buried.

This week's arrangement was small enough to fit on her desk: orange, yellow, and red roses in a black, square vase. Perfect for the beginning of fall. That was almost what the note had said.

Happy you season. In my mind you'll always be
falling leaves, warm tea, and stolen sweaters. I miss the

*way your cheeks turned pink when you got cold and the
way you cursed the rain that got into your boots.
Yours, PAPG*

The note, along with seventy-seven others, was hidden in the locked drawer in her desk. Another thing of Peter's she couldn't bear to throw away.

"Sybil! I'm heading out!" Sadie shouted from the front of the store.

Sybil startled, hastily swiped the tears that had formed in her eyes away before they had a chance to fall, and shouted back, "Have a good night! Be safe!"

How long had she been staring at those damn roses? She needed to learn to blink so her eyes wouldn't water.

She finished the deposit and put it in the safe, then went out into the front of the store to finish the closing duties. It was tempting to call the job Sadie had done good enough, and the person opening could deal with the rest of it, but Sybil was the one opening in the morning, so one way or another it was one hundred percent her problem.

So she checked the perishable products to make sure nothing was about to expire, restocked the dairy fridge under the counter, got new bottles of syrup out and ready to replace the ones that were running low, and finished with the cups and lids.

Her never-ending day was over.

Almost.

The back door needed to be locked and the alarm set, because she'd always reasoned if anyone was going to break in, they'd break in through the back door. Not that Crane Cove was a hotbed of criminal activity. Most of the work the local police force did was writing speeding tickets to tourists and people passing through. But it made her feel better.

She turned the deadbolt, and curiosity tickled the back of her mind. Slowly, she unlocked the door and opened it just a crack. Over the summer she'd seen a stray cat near the dumpsters. For years she'd joked about getting a cat to complete her status as Crane Cove's least eligible—or least desirable—bachelorette. The black-and-white cat would watch her, but never come to her, no matter what she did. So she put food near the back door of Stardust, hoping someday it would trust her.

The food dish was still full. Sybil knew there was a chance that the cat would move on or possibly die, but she hoped it was empty by the morning so she knew the cat was okay. Either that or she was going to unintentionally become Queen of the Raccoons.

The deadbolt relocked and the alarm set, Sybil turned off the lights and left through the front door, locking it behind her. Like most nights she stood in front of her business, trying to practice gratitude and pride for what she'd built on her own. She'd hustled, scrimped, saved, begged, and bullied to make Stardust Coffee a reality. But no matter what she accomplished, she found it hard to sit still in the warmth of her successes. There was always more to do, more to accomplish. She never reached a goal because she kept moving the goalpost further away. Sybil didn't have time or money to spare for therapy, but she'd read books hoping to find the answer to why she just couldn't be fucking happy. The books told her it was okay to be proud, grateful, and happy, but only half of her brain agreed. The other half said it was all a crock of shit and the advice only applied to *other* people.

Stardust was successful. She was proud of that. It supported her and about a dozen part-time employees. She was grateful for that. But she wanted more.

The storefront adjacent to hers was empty again. Originally

she'd dreamed of Stardust being a coffee shop and bookstore, but the overhead was too high and the margins too thin to justify the leap of faith. Coffee was a safer bet than books. But the dream remained, always slightly out of reach.

Maybe it was for the best that she'd never been able to make the bookstore a reality. There were times over the last twelve years, especially the last seven, when she would have wanted to burn it to the ground to escape herself. The scent of ground-wood paper was too strongly associated with unhurried kisses, effortless intimacy, and being young and in love with a golden-haired boy that could crack her heart open with a smile.

She needed to go home and go to bed. It had been a long day, which would be followed by another long day, and standing on the sidewalk drowning herself in memories wasn't helpful. Whether she liked it or not, Peter was coming to Crane Cove, and if Arthur got his way, he'd be there for *weeks*. She couldn't avoid him for weeks.

Was it too late to skip town?

Chapter Two

"I HAVE TO THINK ABOUT IT" was not the response Peter ever thought he would give his agent if presented with the opportunity to work alongside his mother.

"What do you mean, you have to think about it?"

Peter used the celery stalk in his Bloody Mary as a spoon, stirring his drink until it made a little tornado, and then he let go of the vegetable, letting it spin around in the glass.

"I have to think about it," he reiterated, hardly believing the words coming out of his mouth. "I'm supposed to be going on vacation. I haven't had a proper vacation in...so long that I can't actually remember."

"You're the one that wanted to chase the EGOT," Cleo reminded him, her sullen displeasure that he wasn't ecstatic about her call loud and clear over the phone. "You wanted to be booked and busy, I got you booked and busy. If you want to sunbathe with models on a yacht in Saint-Tropez, I can stop giving you scripts. But Peter, this is what you've *wanted*. This role is Oscar fodder. This story is Oscar fodder. The entire PR campaign would be an easy layup for Inger. Getting to work with your parents, swooping in at the last minute to save the production, and the book it's based on—"

"I know what book it's based on. I've read it."

He'd purchased that book while waiting for Sybil in the bookshop where they'd met. After reading it, he thought it was perfect for his parents' production company and gave it to his mother. Well, not so much gave as snuck it into her luggage before they went on vacation. If he'd handed it to her outright and said, "I think this should be a movie," he didn't know if she would have read it.

Their relationship around work was...complicated.

"Why are you being so resistant? You can reschedule your vacation."

He plucked the leaves off the celery stalk. Technically he *could* reschedule his vacation. But he didn't want to. He'd been waiting twelve years to be with Sybil again, and the last year and a half had been excruciating knowing exactly where she was and only having a few scattered hours to fit in all those years of paused conversations. If he was working, he couldn't focus on her. Shoot days were long, and if they'd stuck close to the source material, he'd be emotionally exhausted at the end of the day. How was he supposed to juggle the role he'd wanted for his entire life with convincing the love of his life to give him another chance?

"If you don't want it—"

"I never said I didn't want it," Peter interjected. "I said I needed to think about it."

"I can give you two hours," Cleo said, "then I need to get back to them so they can move on down the list."

"Ah, so there's a list." Jealousy stung like a bee. Even if he didn't take it, he didn't want anyone else to have it either.

"This isn't *The Invisible Man.* Someone has to do it." Cleo sighed dramatically. "I thought this would be the easiest call of my career. All these years and they never considered you for one of their movies, even when your mother wasn't directing. All these years of submitting you anyway, over and over, in case they'd changed their minds. Now they come crawling, and you have to *think* about it. When is this chance ever going to come around again? What if it never does?"

Peter sank down in his chair, the weight of indecision heavy on his shoulders. What if the chance to work with his parents never came around again? But what if the chance to make things work with Sybil never came around again? Could he do both? Either way he was going to be in Crane Cove. At least if he was there for work he seemed a little less desperate. But non-desperate men didn't send flowers every week for a year and a half without so much as a *thank you* or a *back off, you fucking creep.*

Across the small airport lounge table, Dempsey tapped their wrist to remind him that they had a plane to catch.

Fuck it. He could do both.

"Fine. I'll do it. Whatever number they offer, just take it."

"Wonderful. Can you be there the day after tomorrow?"

"I can be there this evening," Peter said, pushing back his chair. "I'm getting on a plane right now. Have a nice day, Cleo."

"You're not going on vacation, are you?" Dempsey asked after Peter hung up his phone.

"It's a working vacation," he said. "A workcation."

Dempsey rolled their eyes and shouldered their backpack. "Does this mean my Peter-free weeks are canceled?"

"I don't see why. How much trouble can I get myself into?"

"You bought me a plane ticket so I could fly with you to Portland, only so I could turn around and come home the same day. It's not how much trouble, it's *when.*" Dempsey dug their phone out of the front pocket of their jeans. "I'm booking myself a flight for next week. Some poor production assistant can probably babysit you until then."

"Am I ruining your plans?" Peter asked, guilt twisting his stomach.

"Not really. Only ruining my delusion that I could have plans to ruin." Dempsey shrugged. "Have someone in production email me the call sheets so I can upload them into your calendar...Actually, no. I will email production."

They walked with purpose to their gate. When discussing travel plans with Graham—or more specifically, watching Dempsey and Graham plan his trip in their group chat—there had been a lot of back and forth about the merits of private travel versus commercial. Obviously private was much more expensive, but it would have taken less time and removed a lot of the hassle of being in public. Peter didn't mind saying hello to fans, taking photos, and signing random bits of whatever was thrust under his nose. The problem was that he didn't know how to stop interactions. He could feel the awkward nervousness radiating off of people and he wanted to put them at ease, so he talked...and talked and talked. Dempsey was his assistant and not a qualified bodyguard, but one of their duties was to ensure Peter made it from Point A to Point B on time, so they often acted as a quasi-protection specialist, marching him through airports across the world. Besides the financial aspect, the issue with private travel for this trip was that the so-called airport they would have landed at close to Crane Cove didn't have any rental cars.

So, commercial travel it was for this trip. Los Angeles to Portland, and then a few hours driving down the Oregon coast to Crane Cove where his best friend and former roommate Graham owned a hotel with his wife Eloise.

Boarding was almost complete when Peter and Dempsey arrived at the gate. Dempsey handed the agent their boarding passes, and then they went down to the airplane. The flight attendant greeted them, and then did a double take, which Peter pretended he didn't see. Dempsey pointed to the empty seats in the second row of first class, and Peter took his seat by the window. He always sat in the window seat because it made him less inviting to talk to and he wouldn't distract the flight attendants from their duties.

At least until he got up to use the bathroom.

The moment the plane was airborne, Dempsey had their headphones on and their laptop open, typing thirteen miles a minute. Peter shifted in his seat, never more restless than when he was required to stay put. He could read or watch a movie, but instead he stared out the window, watching the southern California coastline slip away as the plane climbed into the clouds.

Sharp, cold spikes of anxiety pierced his stomach and dug deep. What if this was the time Sybil told him to stop coming around, to never contact her again? He couldn't slink off to lick his wounds or walk into the ocean because he'd accepted a job. A job that required him to stay within a five-mile radius of the woman who held his heart in the palm of her perfect hand.

Peter gave Dempsey an unanswered glare. Wasn't it their job to keep him from making rash decisions? Technically decisions about his career was Cleo's job, but she had a financial interest in keeping him working. Dempsey got paid whether Peter was working or not.

"Mr. Parker-Green, I'm sorry I didn't get a chance to take your order before we closed the door. Can I get you anything to drink?"

The flight attendant stood in the aisle next to their seats, pen hovering over a small tray, with a bright smile plastered on her face, but she was flushed and he noticed her hands were trembling. She was very young, probably no more than twenty-three. Wasn't it odd that after he'd crossed thirty he'd started to consider anyone too young to rent a car as "very young" and anyone under thirty as "young"? Was this a universal experience? Or did other people perceive time in a different way?

The plane hit a small bump, and it jostled Peter back into focus.

"A sparkling water, please, with just a tiny splash of cranberry juice," he said, and held up his hand like he was holding a box or a glass. "Just a little flick of the wrist with the cranberry." He demonstrated. "And they'll have a Diet Coke with lime. Thank you."

She wrote down the orders, then took in a soothing breath. "I do have a light breakfast today, but choices are a bit limited—"

"Whatever you have left over is fine," Peter interjected with a reassuring smile. "We're not picky."

Her face was bright red as she nodded, then turned so quickly to the pair of seats across the aisle she almost tripped over her own feet.

Dempsey moved one of their headphones off their ear. "Did you order for me?"

"Diet Coke with lime and whatever they've got on hand for breakfast."

"Do you want to switch jobs? I could get paid to look pretty and you can make coffee runs."

Coffee. Peter's heart rate kicked up a notch. "I don't mind making the coffee runs on this trip."

"Because running to crafty is *so* hard," Dempsey deadpanned.

"Actually there's a great coffee shop in town—"

"No." Dempsey took off their headphones. "You can't just run into a coffee shop while you're working. You'll be in there for a minimum of forty-five minutes. If you want coffee from there that badly, I will get it."

He needed a different approach. "Should I sponsor a food truck to say hello—oh, maybe a coffee cart."

"You really have coffee on the brain." Dempsey opened up a notepad on their laptop and typed up the ideas. "I can start doing some research. What's the name of this coffee place you're obsessed with?"

"Stardust," he answered, then added, "You don't need to research this. I can ask Graham. He has to know who in town could do mobile catering."

"If you can get me some names, I will set it up."

Peter bit his tongue to stop himself from arguing. Sometimes Dempsey's ruthless efficiency was a curse. If they had their way, he'd lose a perfectly innocent excuse to go talk to Sybil.

The flight attendant came back with her tray, this time filled with drinks. She held out a rocks glass with barely pink bubbly liquid inside to Peter, her hand shaking. He quickly intercepted the drink before any of it spilled and she expired on the spot. Her hand trembled less when she gave Dempsey their Diet Coke.

"Thank you," he said with a warm, friendly smile. Her face turned a concerning shade of red and she rushed back to the galley.

Dempsey inspected their Diet Coke. "She forgot my lime," they said and reached for the call button. Peter pushed their hand away.

"Don't."

The last thing he wanted was to be labeled as a high-maintenance asshole. He never knew who was taking photos or recording, and negative headlines got a lot more traction than good ones. It wouldn't take a lot to twist something as innocent as asking for a lime into a discourse that could conquer four different social media platforms with ease.

"When she comes back with our trays, ask for another lime. Don't tell her she forgot," Peter whispered.

When the flight attendant brought them their breakfast trays, Dempsey politely asked for another Diet Coke with lime because they'd guzzled down the first one, and when it came back, there was indeed a lime included this time.

Peter scrolled through the onboard movie selection while he picked at his yogurt and granola. Two of his films were in the library, but he wasn't in the mood to watch himself. Then a thumbnail caught his eye. It was the first film his parents had ever done together, the one where they met. The classic British mystery had a large cast and their characters were never alone on screen together, let alone romantically involved, but there was a strange, crackling chemistry between them. Or maybe he imagined that because he knew how their real-life story ended. He selected the film and put on his headphones.

Most people would only ever see young versions of their parents in photographs or a few grainy home movies. If he wanted to, Peter could see his mother from her childhood through adulthood. This film was his father's first major film after cutting his teeth on the London stage. Arthur had been twenty-five and Charlotte a fresh-faced nineteen with world-weary eyes. She played a loud, brash American heiress, which Arthur always teased her as having been typecasting at its finest, and he played a vicar with a checkered past, which couldn't have been further from his actual person.

It would take fifteen years from the time they met for his parents to get together. They didn't work together again until after they were married, but they'd run into each other every few years at events. When his mother went to rehab, his father wrote to her to tell her that if she ever needed a friend he was always around. She didn't answer that letter. But two years later when they quite literally ran into each other on a London street, she asked him to have dinner, he blew off an important meeting with the Bond producers, and two months later he called her on a rainy Tuesday afternoon and asked her if she wanted to get married. She said yes, and since then they'd never spent more than two weeks apart.

A lump formed in his throat, as it always did whenever he watched this film, because this film was the reason he was alive. It was the start of his parents' epic love story. Then hot tears welled in his eyes because maybe someday his children would watch the movie he was headed to make and they'd say, "This is why Mommy and Daddy are together."

It was drizzling when they touched down in Portland. The gray, gloomy sky was a far cry from Los Angeles. As soon as the aircraft was parked and the door was opened, Peter's day went into fast-forward. An airport representative met them in the jetway and took them down to the tarmac where a black SUV was idling. His two large suitcases were being loaded into the back.

"Not letting me loiter in baggage claim?" Peter teased Dempsey as they buckled up in the backseat.

"No, because I have a plane to catch," they replied, digging around in their backpack. They produced a folder and handed it to him. "There's printed directions, non-emergency numbers, roadside assistance, and a copy of your insurance cards."

"You worry about me too much," Peter said, taking the folder and leafing through it.

"I worry the correct amount. If I didn't do this and something were to happen, it would be my fault. This is exactly what you pay me for."

It was exactly what he paid Dempsey to do. Very early on in his career he'd recognized that he was a professional disaster human and needed help. Dempsey had been a production assistant on a TV show he'd done a guest spot for, and he'd poached them very quickly.

"Did you know it's almost our ten-year anniversary?"

"Don't remind me. You were supposed to be a bridge job to a real career."

"But you just can't quit me?"

"I feel responsible for you. You're like a baby duck that imprinted on me. Plus you pay me too well, and I don't know where else I'd ever get the kind of vacation time you give me."

Their SUV pulled into the private plane terminal adjacent to the airport and parked. The driver got out to unload Peter's bags.

"I rented you a mid-level sedan. Very safe, good gas mileage, and it won't make me cry if you scratch it." Dempsey opened their door and got out. Peter followed. "Please call me when you get there so I know you didn't die in a ditch."

"Because if I die, where else will you ever find a job this good?"

"Exactly." Dempsey shouldered their backpack. "Can you behave yourself until next week?"

"I'll try to only create those minor messes you love to clean up," Peter promised with a wry grin. Dempsey rolled their eyes, and he broke into a full smile. "You miss me when I'm not around and you know it."

Dempsey reached up and put their hands on his shoulders. "You are the reason I have gray hairs. I cannot wait until you find someone to love you so we can share responsibilities and talk about you behind your back."

Warmth rolled through Peter's body as his brain quickly concocted a supercut of a feature-length fantasy about how wonderful and cozy a life with Sybil would be, but all the heat pooled in his cheeks in what was probably a brilliant blush.

"Don't hold your breath. I've been told I'm only tolerable in small doses."

Once his rental car, a sensible black sedan, had been sorted and his bags loaded into the trunk, Peter hugged Dempsey tightly.

"Do you need a ride back to the airport?"

"No. I've got it covered. You need to get on the road so you can get there before it gets dark. Call me after you're settled. I mean it."

"Aye, aye, Captain," Peter said in a goofy pirate voice and saluted like a drunken sailor, triumphant at the slight smirk that hitched up the side of Dempsey's mouth.

Chapter Three

THE DRIVE to Crane Cove was long, but outside of a few patches of road construction, blissfully traffic-free, at least by his Angeleno standards. Cities and suburbs dissolved into pastures and farmland. Occasionally he'd pass through towns along the highway that he would've missed if he'd sneezed.

It wasn't his first time making this drive. Three years ago he'd come here for the first time with Graham on their way to save his fledgling relationship with his now-wife. Then he'd made it again for their wedding, and then last year for Thanksgiving. On the plus side, at least he wasn't jetlagged this time.

He set his cruise control for ten miles over the speed limit and tried to relax, but the two topics at the forefront of his mind that he had to choose between were Sybil and his mother's movie. Neither one of those was a relaxing thought. So he let the scenery roll over him, let his mind flit around from topic to topic like a hummingbird confronted with a mountain of flowers. Movie quotes, song lyrics, what it might be like to own a farm with cows, what farmers did all day, the time he'd played a farmhand in that period romance, how *The Princess Bride* was a perfect film and they should never remake it but if they did he wanted to play Westley.

There were pockets of rain—from drizzles to intense downpours—and one vibrant rainbow that kicked off a train of thought about *The Wizard of Oz* and all its adaptations and variations that lasted until the thick trees thinned and he saw a small glimpse of the lighthouse that Graham and Eloise had purchased to be a vacation rental. Where Jordy and Annie had fallen in love.

Had he missed the turn to Sam's house? He knew it was somewhere outside of town, but his borderline reclusive friend wouldn't tell anyone where he'd built his home. Except for Lacey, who'd gone from being his fake girlfriend to his real wife.

Peter pressed on his sternum, trying to muffle the ache that had begun last year. Thanksgiving, specifically, when he'd met Lacey and knew Sam had found his person. His best friends were growing up and moving on without him. He'd never expected to be the last man standing. He'd never *wanted* to be the last man standing. As far as he was concerned, he'd been a done deal twelve years ago.

His eyes flicked to the time on the dash screen. Quarter after five. Graham and Eloise would likely still be at the hotel. They were always at the hotel. If Peter called and Graham's cell phone went to voicemail, he tried the hotel before calling their house number.

The Crane Hotel was a gorgeous building that had been lovingly and expensively restored by the Thatchers. It was their pride and joy, followed by their house that Graham had egregiously overpaid for because it was Eloise's favorite house in town. As far as Graham was concerned, Eloise got whatever she wanted, though she would never ask for it. And if she did ask for something, it usually came with a tabbed and color-coded binder presentation that gave Graham heart eyes and made his heart beat comically out of his chest. It was how she'd gotten the "good towels" for the hotel.

Peter parked his rental car and pretended he hadn't seen that he was partially in another spot when he got out. He wouldn't be there too long; he just needed to get the keys to their house. He knew where they hid the spare, but he was pretending he didn't know about that either. Did hotels have hide-a-keys? Were hotels ever locked in quiet places like Crane Cove?

The lobby was already decorated for Halloween. Every year Eloise lost more and more ground on that front to Kiki, the assistant general manager. He tipped an imaginary cap to Clarence, the life-sized skeleton they dressed up as a bellhop and propped against the front desk. Did Kiki move him around at night like an Elf on the Shelf? If she didn't, he was going to suggest it.

Peter tapped the old-fashioned brass bell, and a satisfying *ding* filled the lobby. He waited and was about to ring it again because it was fun when Graham emerged from the managers' office.

"Peter?!" The combination question mark-exclamation point hung in the air as a stupefied smile spread across his best friend's face.

"Did you forget I was coming? Because I know how careful you and Eloise are with that calendar after the Annie-Jordy debacle."

"No. I just assumed you'd go straight to the house." Graham ran a hand through his dark hair like he was trying to subtly fix it, when what he needed to fix was his tie and the bit of his wife's lipstick he'd missed wiping off.

"I couldn't remember where you hide the spare key," Peter

lied, meeting Graham halfway between the office and the front desk for a tight hug.

Graham chuckled. "We don't usually even bother locking the door." He grasped Peter's shoulders and held him out at arm's length. "I can't believe you're really going to be here for longer than forty-eight hours."

"It's all he's talked about for *weeks*," Eloise chimed in as she appeared behind her husband. She drew Peter in for a gentler hug. "We're so excited you're here. We've missed you."

"I've missed you too," Peter said. He noted, but did not comment on, the button Eloise had missed when she'd buttoned up her blouse. He gestured to the empty front desk. "Where's the crack staff of the Crane Hotel?"

Eloise blushed. "We were covering their dinner break. Needed to get something done in the office."

His dubious snort was easily covered up with a cough.

"We're going to be here for another hour," Graham told him. "Do you want to go to the house or you could hang out around here until we're done?"

"I could go pick up dinner," Peter offered, "or make a coffee run, if you need a little pick-me-up—"

"Peter!" His father's voice boomed across the lobby like jolly cannon fire. When he turned to look, Arthur was all smiles, but his mother, trailing a few steps behind, had a blank expression carefully painted on her face. Without a smile, or even a frown, Charlotte looked tired, and maybe she was. It couldn't have been an easy twenty-four hours for her.

The hug from his father was bone-crushing, like always. For a man entering his late seventies, he was surprisingly strong.

"Thank you," his father whispered in his ear, and squeezed him again before loudly asking, "When did you get here?"

"About five minutes ago," Peter answered.

Charlotte stood a few feet away, studying him hard, a tiny

frown creasing her forehead. Finally she sighed and said, "I guess I'll have to wait and see if you make more sense once you're in wardrobe." She gave him a much more tepid hug than his father. "You're too nice for this role. Your face is too sweet."

From any other mother, this would have been a doting compliment. But Charlotte had grown up in the entertainment industry. She honestly meant that she didn't like how he looked for the part.

"Beggars can't be choosers," he reminded her. "And the brilliant part about acting is the *transformation* from who I am to the character."

"Maybe makeup can rough you up a bit."

"Charlotte, maybe you should give him his script so he can get to work," Arthur said gently, prying the green book from her tight grasp and passing it to Peter.

"We were just talking about what we were doing for dinner if you wanted to join us," Eloise offered.

Sweet Eloise. Peter had adored her from the moment he met her. She was always thinking about the people around her and how to make them feel comfortable. Could she feel the tension rippling through his family? Of course she could. People three miles away could probably feel it.

"We were going to eat at the hotel restaurant," Charlotte said.

Graham grinned. "Would you believe I have a standing reservation there?"

If Charlotte noticed the joke, she ignored it. "I guess Peter can get settled into his room and then we could all meet at the restaurant in about half an hour? Or do you need longer?"

Peter frowned and cocked his head slightly. "My room? I don't think I want to drive into town just to drive back."

It was Charlotte's turn to look befuddled. "Why would you drive into town? Get a key, go to your room, wash the airplane off you, and come to dinner." She looked at Eloise and put a hand on her arm. "Your water pressure is fantastic, by the way. Hotel showers usually have a hard time penetrating my hair."

Eloise blinked. "Oh. Thank you."

"Mom," Peter said slowly, "I'm staying with Graham and Eloise. Their house is in town. I know it feels like they live here, but they don't."

Charlotte's face hardened into an expression he was very familiar with from his childhood. "If you're going to be part of this production, you're going to stay where the production is staying. If you have a problem with that, you can take it up with the producer."

Arthur looked between them, and there was an awkward silence before he realized he'd missed his cue.

"It's, um…" he began, rocking forward onto his toes and back onto his heels. "Well, it would be helpful to have you nearby. To know where you are. At least for this first bit of production while we bring you up to speed."

"Give me a call sheet, and I'll show up when and where I'm supposed to," Peter said, more to his mother than his father.

"You'd probably see us more here than if you stayed at our house," Eloise pointed out.

Peter took a deep breath, pursed his lips, and looked at the ceiling. Eloise was only trying to help, but she was going to ruin part of his plans. If he stayed at Graham and Eloise's house, he increased his chances of casually running into Sybil. They had wine night every week, and Eloise hosted a lot. And Sybil's house was nearby. He could easily run by it several times before anyone thought it was weird. But if he stayed at the hotel, he may as well still be in Los Angeles because his good reasons for going into town hovered right above nil.

Charlotte teetered on smug. "See. Simple."

"Fine," Peter ground out from between his teeth. "Eloise,

may I have a key please?" He drummed his fingers on the hard-cover of his script. "I will get settled and see you all down here in an hour for dinner."

Dinner was not the disaster he'd imagined it would be.

There was something magical about good food that got people to relax, and Graham's chef Amara was a wizard in the kitchen. The appetizers eased some of the tension at their table, and by the time entrées were finished, it was like the movie wasn't happening at all. It helped that they avoided talking about work—or movies—and stuck to safer topics, like politics and religion.

"I don't have any room for dessert, but it sounds fantastic." Charlotte held her menu out at arm's length because she'd forgotten her reading glasses.

"Get it now. Amara is changing the menu on Friday," Graham warned.

"No!" Arthur protested. He'd wiped his plate clean with the last piece of bread from the basket, vowing more than once that he was going to leave his wife for the mushroom sauce.

"Not the entire menu." Eloise laughed. "She likes to rotate some options monthly. Keeps everyone interested."

Arthur placed a hand over his heart and sighed dramatically. The table laughed.

Peter placed his napkin on the table and pushed out his chair. "Send in the clowns for me. If I eat another bite, I'll fall asleep."

"You don't have to eat," Charlotte said. "Stay."

Peter snuck a surreptitious glance at his watch. It wasn't as late as he thought it was. He could stay for another twenty minutes.

"Okay, okay. I'll stay."

. . .

It was longer than twenty minutes. Once Arthur Green got to telling stories, there was never an easy way out. Peter didn't know if Graham somehow texted Kiki from under the table or if that magnificent goth had a sixth sense, but she came and whispered something in Graham's ear and it was enough to finally break up the dinner party.

Peter went up in the elevator with his parents and went to his room, but only to get his jacket.

The short drive into Crane Cove was dark. It was almost nine o'clock, and the clouds covered the moon. He should have checked when Stardust closed. Coffee shops stayed open late, didn't they? At least in the Pacific Northwest. There was a chance she was still at work. He could see her. Say hello. If not, he could...drive by her house and not stop because that would be weird.

Peter continued to tell himself that dropping by her business unannounced after dark was normal the entire time he parked his car, put his hood up to shield himself from the rain, and walked down the dimly lit sidewalk with his hands in his pockets.

There was still a light on in Stardust.

And then it turned out.

"Damn," Peter cursed under his breath.

There was movement inside, and he stepped into a shadow, trying to blend into the building. Two women came out—teenage girls, actually. Neither one of them was Sybil. They were too tall. They walked down the sidewalk away from him, and Peter breathed for the first time in thirty seconds.

Stardust was closed, but they hadn't locked the door behind them. Was she still in there?

Peter waited until the teenagers were a long way down the

sidewalk before he left his hiding spot and walked up to the coffee shop. His heart was beating so fast as he tried the door that he could feel his jugular vein fluttering in his neck.

The door opened, and a bell tinkled overhead. He stepped inside, closed the door gently behind him.

"Did you forget something?" Sybil called from the backroom.

Peter swallowed several times, trying to make some moisture in his mouth which had gone drier than the Atacama Desert in Chile.

"Sadie? Georgia?"

Say something, he urged himself, but his tongue refused to move.

Sybil came around the corner, a baseball bat in her hand, and froze when she saw him.

The world ceased spinning and time slowed to a crawl. It was a phenomenon that needed to be studied because it happened every time he saw her. It was like his brain knew she was the most important thing there had ever been and ever would be and it was determined to memorize every minute detail.

Her thick red hair was in a loose French braid, like she'd gotten sick of it being in her face and didn't want to deal with it anymore. It didn't knot that way, unlike in a bun. He remembered. And there was a mystery smear on her gray T-shirt, right across her midsection.

And she was wearing the sweater. *His* sweater. The sleeves were pushed up to her elbows and it had dropped off her right shoulder, but it still looked better on her than it ever had on him.

Then time sped back up to normal speed, and Sybil found her voice.

"What are you doing here?"

Chapter Four
Twelve Years Ago, London

"My round," Peter declared, tipping the final foamy dregs of his beer into his mouth. "Give me your empties, you animals."

He climbed out of the booth and gathered the empty pint glasses, pinching the rims between his fingers so he wouldn't drop them on his way to the bar. Quiz night was always busy in The Hare and Thistle, and the sound of broken glass followed by a resounding "Oy!" from the assembled patrons was part of the soundtrack.

"You're a pretty barmaid, Peter," Blair teased, his rolling Scottish accent starting to slur around the edges. Getting pissed before the start of the quiz was half the fun of quiz night.

"Up yours," he said to hysterical laughter from the lads. It wasn't that funny, but they'd all beaten him to the pub so who knew exactly which round they were on.

Peter put his arms above his head, glasses held tightly between his fingers, and weaved through the crowd. The Hare and Thistle was a popular pub with students, artists, and other flat broke young people because it was dirt cheap and on quiz nights they discounted the beer.

Movement at the door caught his eye. It shouldn't have, but

it did. And for the second time that day, the world stopped spinning and his vision tunneled like he was living in a movie. His heart flipped, flopped, and did a double pirouette. He watched as she squeezed through the crowd to get to the bar. Peter left his polite British heritage behind and accessed his pushy American roots to get to her.

"Fancy seeing you here," he said. It wasn't smooth at all, but she made him stupid. He was quickly coming to terms with that.

She looked up at him, her expression transforming from bored and annoyed to startled. "Are you following me?"

Peter smiled. "No, I'm not." He pointed to the empty pint glasses he'd just placed on the bar. "I've been here for ages. So maybe I should ask why *you* are following *me*?"

She rolled her eyes. "I'm not. I'm bored. I saw a flier."

He leaned against the bar. "Do you know how many pubs there are in London?"

"No, but I have a feeling you're about to tell me."

"Depending on how you define London, there's between two thousand to four thousand pubs. What are the odds we'd end up in the same pub on the same night?"

"About one in four thousand?" she deadpanned.

He snapped his fingers. "Exactly. It's fate."

She rose up on her tiptoes to look for the barkeep, and he narrowly resisted the urge to step on the heel that had separated from the rest of her boot.

"When you find a line you really stick with it, don'tcha, buddy?" she asked, trying and failing to make eye contact with the man filling pints.

"It's not a line," he insisted.

"Fate doesn't exist. This is simply a coincidence. Or you're a really excellent stalker who guessed the plans I only made twenty minutes ago"—she looked at the empty pint glasses and frowned—"hours ago. Are you okay? That's a lot of empty glasses."

"These aren't all mine. I'm here with some friends." Peter pointed to his booth. "We do quiz night here every week. You should join us. It's fun."

"How do I know you're not all blithering idiots?" she asked, raising an eyebrow. He smiled and she blushed.

"We are all blithering idiots," he said, and put a hand on his chest. "Especially me. So really you'd be doing us a favor by joining."

"Why would I want to join a quiz team full of admitted idiots?"

"Free beer?" Peter suggested.

She considered that while Peter finally got the attention of the barkeep.

"Can we get another round, please," he asked, pointing to the empty glasses, "plus one more?"

"I haven't said yes yet," she reminded him as the barkeep left to fill up fresh pint glasses.

"I know," he said, leaning in so they didn't have to raise their voices above the low-level din, "but I'm an optimist. What do you have to lose?"

She regarded him with skepticism, and he held his breath. Finally she said, "My dignity." Then the barkeep returned with their pint glasses, and she picked hers up to take a sip. "But I guess I can debase myself for an hour."

Peter was so thrilled he could have floated away like a runaway balloon, but he didn't want to scare her away. He carefully modulated his face into a satisfied smile and picked up three of the pints.

"Can you grab the others?" he asked.

"Are there tips at the end of this?"

"If we make it to your round, I'll spot you a tenner."

She picked up the pint glasses. "Sold."

As they waited for a group to pass them, he leaned down close to her ear and said, "You do have to tell me your name, though. I can't introduce you as This Girl I Met at the Bookshop."

She peered up at him, and for a moment he got distracted trying to find shapes in the freckles on her nose. "Sybil."

It fit her, in a strange, mystical way. He couldn't imagine her as a Brittany or an Ashley. Sybil held secrets, and he wanted to discover all of them.

"My name is still Peter." *Idiot.*

Sybil grinned. "Like the rabbit. I remember."

So he was never going to live that little incident in the bookstore down, but he was okay with that. He'd been memorable. And he'd made her smile. He wanted to do more of that.

They weaved through the crowd, Peter constantly checking to make sure Sybil was still right behind him—he understood why Orpheus had to look—and made it to the booth without spilling any beer.

"Lads, this is Sybil. Sybil, these are the lads." He put his pint glasses on the table and pointed as he named his friends. "Blair, Aarav, Lewis, and Stuart."

There was a chorus of bewildered hellos as they sat down.

"So how do you know Peter?" Aarav, one of his flatmates, asked. "He's never mentioned you, and he mentions everything. Literally. He's scared that if he stops talking, he'll stop breathing."

"I noticed that," Sybil said. "And we just met."

"And he got you to go with him in under ten minutes?" Aarav let out a low whistle. "Normally it takes him *hours* to get a pretty girl to go anywhere with him. What did he say?"

She held up her pint glass. "Free beer."

That got an uproarious laugh from the group. Peter slid down in his seat and considered hiding under the table.

"And technically it did take him hours. We met in a book-shop earlier."

Lewis leaned forward. "So is that where the pretty girls hang out? Bookshops?"

"You'd have to learn to read," Peter told him. He didn't want Lewis moving in on Sybil because Lewis was slick. It wasn't fair.

"I can read," Lewis protested.

"Yeah, but you're not going to find anyone age-appropriate in the children's section," Blair said, and the group erupted in laughter again.

There was a screech of feedback over the speakers, followed by the quizmaster half-heartedly apologizing over the mic. She explained the rules and format to anyone who had never partici-pated before and kicked the evening off with a geography section.

"This desert is the driest place on Earth."

The group hunched together.

"It's the Sahara, right?" Stuart said, looking around the group for confirmation.

"Bugger if I know. It's the only desert I can think of," Blair said.

The answer—or what he hoped was the answer—appeared in Peter's mind. "It's the Atacama Desert in Chile."

No one questioned his answer, and when the quizmaster gave the answer, Sybil narrowed her eyes at him suspiciously.

"I thought you said you were a blithering idiot."

Peter draped his arm across the back of the booth and leaned in like he was going to tell her a secret. "I am. I'm completely useless outside of quizzes."

"Head full of Snapple facts?"

"Pretty much."

His head full of Snapple facts kept them in third place, which didn't win them any money or free drinks, but it did win Blair the right to taunt their quiz night rivals over their fifth-place finish.

Lads' Night Out normally dispersed after the quiz finished, but they all stayed on, buying another round to keep Sybil around. And the more cheap beer they drank, the closer Sybil sat to him, until she was leaning against him, her head occasionally resting on his shoulder.

It was Stuart who broke up the fun because he had to work in the morning. That caused the cascade of leaving excuses, so while everyone else scooted out of the booth, Peter jumped on his last chance to ask her out.

"Would you like to go out with me?"

He expected her to give him a hard time, so when she asked, "When?" he blurted out, "Right now."

A puff of air could have blown him over when she smiled and said, "Sure."

Chapter Five
Crane Cove, Oregon

"WHAT ARE YOU DOING HERE?"

The bat was heavy in her hand. The temptation to swing it at Peter's head or drop it and run into his arms were equally strong. Which about summed up how she'd felt every other time she'd seen him over the last few years.

How the fuck did he look *better* since they'd gotten older? It shouldn't have been possible since he'd been inhumanly gorgeous when they'd met, but the proof that life wasn't fair and men got all the luck stood a measly fifteen feet in front of her.

"I, um..." Peter did the verbal equivalent of a drunk stumbling out of a bar and down the sidewalk, doing a succession of useless oral pauses until he finally said, "Work."

The visceral disappointment caught her off guard, like putting salt instead of sugar into her coffee.

"We're closed," she told him, tapping the toe of her shoe with the bat.

"The door was unlocked and—"

Her sweater slipped further off her shoulder and she adjusted it, and then she realized why Peter had stopped talking.

She was wearing the damn sweater.

His sweater.

Her sweater.

Their sweater.

The red cardigan he'd loaned to her and she'd kept borrowing until the actual ownership became questionable.

Why the hell had she kept it? Why had she kept any of the things that reminded her of him?

"The lights are off," Sybil pointed out tersely. "Most people can take a hint."

Peter had taken several slow steps toward her, and the closer he got, the harder it was for her to take a full breath.

"I need to talk to you, and historically you won't talk to me on the phone."

"I don't like talking on the phone."

In the golden glow of the streetlights, she saw the corner of his mouth twitch. "Should I have been sending letters? Carrier pigeons? Morse code with a flashlight?"

She bit her tongue to stop a smile. She refused to be charmed by him. Again.

"What do you need to talk to me about so badly that you needed to do some questionable breaking and entering?"

"The door was unlocked, so I think it was only entering," Peter pointed out. "Is that a crime in Oregon?"

"Focus, Peter."

When he was about three feet away, Sybil held out the bat to stop his progress, the end resting on his sternum. He sighed and gave her the good natured, boyish grin that made her heart flutter.

Used to make her heart flutter.

"I want to host a coffee cart for the movie," he explained. "Is that something you do? Catering?"

Disappointment reared its ugly head again. It really had been about work.

"I might be able to do that, but it won't be cheap," she said. "Why not open a tab here for a day?"

There was a brief flash of panic on his face. Peter had an expressive face; it was part of what made him such an excellent actor. He tried to keep his face carefully neutral, but when he slipped, his emotions projected on his face in CinemaScope.

"It's hard for people to get away from the set. I wouldn't want anyone to miss out."

"So leave the tab open for a few days."

"You're making it very hard for me to give you money."

Sybil held out her hand. Peter laughed, and she hated what the sound did to her insides. She was warm all over like a human cup of tea on a foggy morning, and it made her miss those naive palpitations of a simple crush. This kind of comfort could only happen after being in love.

She should have hit him with the bat while she had the chance.

Sybil dropped her hand, lowered the bat, turned, and started to walk back to her office. Standing near Peter for too long was dangerous. She'd fall into his gravitational field and want to orbit him like a small, insignificant moon around a brilliant sun.

The sound of Peter's steps synced with hers.

"Depending on the cost, we could run the cart for more than one day," he suggested, following her into the cramped office. Sybil gently prodded him back into the doorway with the tip of the bat.

"What's this 'we'? Are you going to be in there with me pulling shots?"

It was the wrong thing to say because under the bright office lights she could see the twinkle in his eyes.

"You could teach me," he said, leaning against the door-frame. "I'm a fast learner."

A different kind of warmth spread through her body, the kind that crackled like electricity. Her body remembered what a fast learner he was. It remembered what it was like to have him between her thighs diligently taking directions and putting all his hard studying to good use.

Sybil sat in her chair and stowed the bat in its hiding place before she was any more tempted to use it. The odds of "I had to hit him, he made me horny" working as a defense when Willis showed up to arrest her for battery were slim to none.

"My equipment is expensive, and you could burn water," she said as she logged into her computer. "When did you want to do this?"

"Whenever it works for you."

Sybil started to try and build a quote, but it was impossible with Peter lounging in her doorway looking at her while he looked like he'd stepped out of an ad for raincoats.

"You got my flowers."

"I do. Every week." She focused on her computer screen even though she wasn't doing anything. "I think the local florist will be sending you a gift basket for Christmas."

"Probably just a nice card. Do you like them?" he asked, the earnestness around the edges of the question making her heart twist.

She loved them, but she wasn't going to tell him that. He'd get *ideas,* and he didn't need any help in that department.

Sybil shrugged. "They're pretty, I guess. But they're such ephemeral things, and now I've got a bunch of vases I don't know what to do with."

Peter sighed. "You know what Scrabble words do to me."

They got him all riled up. If she managed to use all her tiles in one go, he'd practically faint. It was one of the many quirks that had been so endearing all those years ago.

"Can I get this estimate to you tomorrow? I open in the morning, and I don't think you can be quiet long enough for me to finish my closing duties."

"I'd love to see you tomorrow," he said. "When should I come back to go over everything?"

"I'll take it to the hotel when it's finished." Maybe she could drop the estimate off at the front desk and run away before he knew she was there.

"Are you sure you don't want me to stay? The front door is unlocked and anyone could walk in—"

"Peter, I have a bat. And everyone in this town knows I'm not afraid to use it."

"What about someone who isn't from around here?"

"They'll find out I'm not afraid to use it. Good night, Peter."

There was an unusual amount of silence from the doorway, and finally curiosity bested her survival skills. She looked. Peter was still there and he looked like he wanted to say something, but he finally tapped his fist against the doorframe and gave her a tight smile.

"Good night, Sybil," he said, and took a few steps back. "I missed you, by the way."

Then he left, and the tinkle of the bell over the door ripped her heart out. How was she supposed to survive the next few weeks if he insisted on coming around and then leaving her hollow?

She should take her bat and go smash Graham's car for bringing Peter back into her life. If Graham had never showed up, if he'd just given Eloise the money to fix up the hotel without ever coming to Crane Cove, Sybil could still feel only minorly off-kilter when she saw tabloid photos of Peter at the checkout stand at the grocery store.

Sybil clenched her jaw and refused to acknowledge the tightness in her throat. She finished her spreadsheets for the night and turned off her computer.

Tomorrow she'd drop off the estimate at the hotel and find someone else to cover the coffee cart if Peter was serious about coughing up the money. A guaranteed revenue stream wasn't a bad thing. Her old cart from before she had the storefront was stored at the McMahon farm, so if she borrowed a truck she could set up almost anywhere.

Sybil had never been much of a silver-lining kind of person. Life was tough; she was tougher. But if she couldn't find the good parts of this situation she was going to talk herself out of money that she could put towards her bookstore fund.

The bookstore. Books. Peter reading a book. The way his finger would slip between the pages to turn them. He had such great hands.

Sybil pushed back from her desk quickly and jumped to her feet. She needed to go home and get some sleep because she clearly wasn't in her right mind if she was fantasizing about her ex-boyfriend turning the pages of a book.

Tomorrow she'd find a way to put some distance between herself and those hands.

Chapter Six

Peter barely slept.

None of his usual tricks worked. Not listening to an audiobook, not cognitive shuffling, not visualizing the ocean coming into the shore to take his worries out to sea while he took deep breaths. Progressive muscle relaxation did nothing but make him hyperfixate on an ache in his left hip. He made himself a cup of chamomile tea from the little coffee station in his room and began to work on his script, hoping that trying to pick up a task he was *supposed* to do would make him sleepy out of spite.

With half his brain he highlighted his lines and things relevant to his character, making notes in the margins of the script on arc and motivation, while the other half of his brain replayed his interaction with Sybil over and over and over again.

Compared to the last two times he'd seen her, that had gone swimmingly. She hadn't pretended he wasn't in the room, and she'd talked *to* him instead of *at* him. But he'd dropped the ball. The setup couldn't have been more romantic: alone in the glow from the streetlights, the rain pelting the pavement outside, and they hadn't seen each other in months. He should have started by telling her how much he missed her, how he thought about her all the time, how he didn't understand what had gone wrong between them but whatever it was he wanted a chance to fix it because they'd been so good together it had ruined him for anyone else. He should have told her that he had never stopped loving her.

It had always been like this with her. If they were in the same room, his brain became absolutely useless. He was hanging on for dear life from one sentence to the next. Sometimes it worked out in his favor, but most of the time he forgot to do and say important things.

At least he'd remembered to talk to her about the coffee cart.

Sleep had barely settled over him before it was cruelly ripped away by the shrill ring of the phone in his room. His script hit the floor with a *thud* when he rolled over to answer the phone.

"What?" he grumbled and put the clock face down because he didn't want to know how many hours of sleep he hadn't gotten.

The voice on the other end was so chipper it was like he'd woken up in a cartoon. "Good morning, Mr. Green. This is the wake-up call you requested."

Peter groaned. He'd requested the wake-up call after he'd seen Sybil the night before, back when he was optimistic about getting a good night's sleep. He'd get up early and sit in the lobby with his script, waiting for her to show up. If he gave her the chance, she'd drop the estimate off at the front desk and bolt.

"Mr. Green?"

"I'm awake. I'm awake," he groaned, and pushed himself into a sitting position.

"Do you want me to call you back in twenty minutes?"

He sighed. "Yes, please."

Peter did almost his entire morning routine with his eyes closed, too tired to care if he put the shampoo or conditioner in his hair first. Maybe he could take a nap in one of the big chairs by the fire in the lobby while he waited for Sybil to show up.

The phone rang again twenty minutes later.

"Hello?"

"Rise and shine, pumpkin pie!" a different but still cheery voice chimed in his ear.

"Who is this?"

"It's Kiki, you dolt. Hurry up and come downstairs and say hi before I leave for the day."

"Do you have coffee?"

"I could be persuaded to find you a cup if you talked me up to any cute single ladies you happen to know on the movie."

Peter rubbed his eyes with the heel of his hand and grinned. "Don't you think Graham will have a problem with you fraternizing with the guests?"

"Considering I have enough dirt on Graham to bury him, I think he'll keep his mouth shut," Kiki said. He could hear the self-satisfied smirk on her face.

"I'll be down in a couple of minutes. Coffee with cream, unless it's the powder stuff, and then I'll choke it down black."

Kiki, bless her dark, creepy soul, had a steaming mug of coffee waiting for him on the front desk when he came downstairs.

"Graham got Crane Hotel-branded mugs?" he asked, taking a cautious sip.

"He did for the staff so we would stop walking off with the ones for the guests," Kiki said. She picked up her own unbranded mug.

Over the last three years Kiki had metamorphosed from regular goth to corporate goth chic. Black jacket, black silk shirt, black wide-leg trousers, burgundy lipstick, and a wing liner sharp enough to cut someone. Chillingly professional.

"How's it been going with the movie here?" Peter asked.

"Charlotte is your mom, right?" Kiki asked, and he nodded. "Yeah, I'd let her hit me with her car and thank her for it. I found some of her old movies, and not to be weird, but your mom was a stone-cold fox."

Peter shuddered dramatically. "That was not something I needed to hear before breakfast."

"Your dad is cute in a goofy, British grandpa way, but you definitely got the bulk of your looks from your mom."

"I will be sure to thank her if I ever win Sexiest Man Alive," he assured Kiki. "What other gossip do you have?"

"Garden-variety noise complaints, questions about weird sounds—per Eloise's request, I have not told anyone it's a ghost even though we both know..." She gave him a meaningful look. Kiki believed in ghosts the way kids believed in Santa Claus.

"I hope Eloise enjoys her one week of peace and quiet before ghost tour season starts."

"That's what I told Graham, and then I had to talk him out of canceling them entirely this year. He's trying to keep Eloise's stress to a minimum."

Peter raised an eyebrow. "But those two run on stress. Trying to minimize Eloise's stress is like trying to mop up a flood with a...mop. Or a sponge."

"Exactly. So if you find out what's happening there, report back." She tapped her long, black fingernails against the side of her rebellion mug. "What else...what else...Oh, Madelyn Penn asked me what time the grocery store opened and then puked in one of the potted plants by the elevators."

His other eyebrow shot up in surprise. "She puked? Is she okay?"

"I think so," Kiki said. "She went back to her room. The

plant is living outside until someone either puts it out of its misery or changes the soil."

The adrenaline spike pushed the lingering sleepiness from Peter's mind. Madelyn was an old friend and a fellow nepo baby. She was a slightly reformed party girl, and there was no doubt that wasn't the first potted plant she'd thrown up in, but where in Crane Cove could she have located a party? And why did she need the grocery store?

"What's her room number?" Peter asked. "I'll go check on her."

Kiki wrote down Madelyn's room number on a sticky note for him. "If Graham or Eloise ask, you didn't get that from me."

Madelyn's room was on the same floor as his and only five doors down. He knocked gently.

"Mads," he said through the door, "it's Peter. Are you okay?"

A toilet flushed, and then the door opened. Madelyn's signature red hair was gathered on top of her head in a droopy messy bun, and her fair complexion was ghostly with a hint of green.

"You look like crap." The words fell out of his mouth without ever having stopped at the decision-making part of his brain.

Tears filled Madelyn's eyes. "I think I'm in trouble."

That was how Peter ended up buying three pregnancy tests at the grocery store shortly after it opened because when he got to the pregnancy tests, awkwardly situated between the condoms, lube, yeast infection medication, and the menstrual products, he didn't know which one he was supposed to buy and panicked and grabbed one of each kind Hudson's Grocery stocked.

When he got back to Madelyn's room, her eyes were red and puffy from crying and the acrid smell of vomit hung in the air.

"Can you stay?" she asked, taking the grocery bag from him. Her arm drooped at the unexpected weight, and she frowned at the bag. "Why is this so heavy?"

"I grabbed you some ginger ale and Pedialyte while I was there. Oh, and some crackers."

She stared at him. "How the hell are you still single?"

"A real mystery," Peter answered and steered Madelyn toward her bathroom.

When she came out of the bathroom, he was sitting in the desk chair, leafing through her script to look at her notes.

"I'm scared to look," she said, pacing the length of the room.

"From what I read on the box it takes a few minutes to process." Peter closed her script. "Why did you say you're in trouble?"

"How am I *not* in trouble? I can't be pregnant right now. I'm shooting this movie, and then I'm supposed to start a brand campaign, and then I'm supposed to do a guest arc on *Dr. Philadelphia*." Madelyn wrung her hands to the point where Peter worried she was going to twist off one of her fingers. "And Mac and I had a huge fight. I don't even know if we're still together."

"Do you want advice, or do you want sympathy?"

She sniffled. "Sympathy."

"If you are pregnant, this sounds like super shitty timing."

Her chin wobbled. "Where's the 'but'?"

Peter gave her a soft, reassuring smile. "But if you don't want to be pregnant, you don't have to be. And if you do want to be pregnant, all of the things you listed can be worked around. Plus, you've got two more minutes before you can officially panic."

"Can you go look?" she asked and sat down on her bed. "I'm too scared to look."

"I think it's too soon," Peter warned her, going into the bathroom. "I don't think I'm going to see any— Oh shit."

Two pink lines on one very positive pregnancy test.

"Peter, what does 'oh shit' mean?"

"It's, um, positive."

"Are you sure?"

He looked at the test again. There was no mistaking that result for anything but positive. "Very sure."

"I think I'm going to be sick."

Madelyn was sick again, and when she came out of the bathroom, Peter handed her a cup of Pedialyte.

"Anything I can do?" he asked.

She shook her head. "Your mom is going to fire me when I tell her. I'm already so sick. I'm a liability to the schedule."

Peter sat her down on the bed and put an arm around her shoulders. "My mom isn't going to fire you for being pregnant. Does this mean you've decided to keep the baby?"

Madelyn shrugged. "I don't know yet. It doesn't really feel real."

"When are you going to tell Kitty?"

Peter had introduced Madelyn to her boyfriend, Los Angeles Phantoms lineman MacKenzie Kitten. Most people called him Mac or Big Mac because he was huge. With a name like MacKenzie Kitten, he really didn't have any choice but to grow up to be a 6'6" professional football player. But Peter called him Kitty. It had just rolled off his tongue one day, and his brain refused to think of him as anything else.

"I don't know. I'm not ready to tell him yet. I think I want to have a better idea of what I want to do before I drop this on him." She swiped at her eyes with her hands. "I don't think there's enough ice in the world to de-puff me today."

Peter squeezed her shoulders. "Don't worry about being puffy. That's what post-production is for."

That got a laugh that ended in a hiccup.

"Will you come with me to tell your mom? I'd rather get fired sooner rather than later."

It took some searching, but Peter and Madelyn found Charlotte in her makeshift office. She'd taken over a small conference room and was surrounded by stacks of binders and papers, and was flanked by two rolling whiteboards covered in a rainbow of dry-erase marker. On the walls she'd hung storyboards, location scouting photos, and enough sticky notes to keep the local office supply stores in business for the next year.

Charlotte looked at them over the tops of her glasses balancing precariously on the end of her nose. Her other set of glasses were on top of her head, but Peter didn't think it was a good time to ask her why she had both sets on.

"What's wrong?" she asked without any attempt at pleasantries.

Peter waited for Madelyn to say something, but she was petrified. He put a reassuring hand on her back. She took a deep breath.

"I'm pregnant."

Charlotte stared at them, then fixed a fiery glare on Peter. "Peter Alan Parker-Green, what did you do?"

Peter put his hands up and took a big step away from Madelyn. "It's not mine."

"It's not his," Madelyn quickly agreed. "He's just being a good friend."

Charlotte took off the glasses on her face and rubbed her forehead. "How pregnant are you?"

"I don't know. I just took the test."

"Did you just miss your period, or have you not had one for a while?" Charlotte asked.

"It's a week late," Madelyn said. "I'm so sorry."

Charlotte frowned and then softened. "No, no, no. Don't be sorry. I'm just trying to figure out if we need to adjust anything. Sit down. Please." She gestured to one of the chairs. "How are you feeling?"

"Like shit," Madelyn answered frankly as she sat. "I puked in one of the lobby plants this morning."

Charlotte winced sympathetically. "I was sick as a dog with Peter. Arthur couldn't breathe in my general direction without me getting nauseous."

"Are you going to fire me?"

"Jesus Christ, of course not. Do you want to keep working?"

Madelyn nodded vigorously.

"Then we'll figure it out," Charlotte assured her. "You're not going to feel this bad every day. It might not even be an issue. Go back to your room and rest until you feel better."

Madelyn gave her a weak smile and left the room. Charlotte waited twenty whole seconds after the door shut to groan loudly.

"This fucking movie," she complained. "If it's not one thing, it's another."

Peter took the chair Madelyn had vacated. "It'll make for a great story when the press tour rolls around."

That got a small smile from his mother, then she fixed him with a hard stare.

"You're really not the father?"

Most men his age would've thought their mothers were angling for grandchildren, but his mother's tone was downright accusatory.

"I am definitely not the father." Peter crossed his heart.

Charlotte sighed and pushed her hair back with her hands,

and he had to bite his tongue to keep from laughing when her expression shifted from glum resignation to befuddled surprise when she found the glasses on top of her head.

"Maybe we're getting all the bad stuff out of the way early and the rest of the project will be smooth sailing," he said.

"You sound like your father. Always a bright side."

"Keeps our blood pressure low." Peter glanced at the clock and hopped up from the chair. He'd lost track of time and didn't want to miss Sybil. "Well, got to run. I'll be in the lobby if you need me."

"No," Charlotte corrected, leafing through some papers until she found one and held it out. "You have meetings with hair, makeup, and wardrobe, plus I want you to run your script notes past Michelle so we're all on the same page about your performance."

"I didn't know Michelle was your assistant director on this. Michelle Yost, right?"

"Yes. You're meeting with her at four. Don't be late."

"But what if I had plan—" Peter's protest was cut off by a withering glare. He looked at the packed schedule and sighed. "I will see Michelle at four with my script notes."

Chapter Seven

Sybil stared at the Crane Hotel through windshield wipers that were working overtime, even though she was parked. The heavy rain would pass soon, and then she'd be out of excuses not to go inside.

All she had to do was drop off the estimate at the front desk and leave before Peter, Eloise, or Graham saw her. Peter because he'd want to talk to her, and Eloise or Graham because they would waylay her and give Peter an opportunity to talk to her.

Talking to Peter was dangerous because she started to forget all the reasons she shouldn't talk to him.

The rain let up as abruptly as it had started, and she took a steeling breath. She could do this. In, out, and on with life. The money was too good to pass up, especially since she'd jacked up her usual prices. Or what her usual prices would have been if she did catering.

Sybil walked quickly through the parking lot, her boots splashing through the puddles that had formed. As she stepped onto the curb, the door opened and her heart stopped, but when the two people who exited weren't Peter, she breathed again.

The Crane Hotel looked stunning all year-round, but she loved it best at Halloween. Fake cobwebs, fake bats "flying" out of the fireplace, and Clarence the skeleton dressed as a bellhop, hat and all. She gave a small salute to Clarence as she passed him.

The front desk had acquired a large crystal ball this year, and she could imagine Kiki pretending to use it in the middle of the night when guests asked her questions.

The front desk was also unoccupied. Panic spiked her heart rate. Kind of hard to drop and run if there was no one to drop to.

Sybil tapped the bell. Kevin popped up from behind the desk like an overcaffeinated Jack-in-the-box, and she jumped.

"Kevin!" she yelped, leaning against the front desk for support while she got her breath back. "Don't *do* that."

Kevin held up a ballpoint pen. "I lost my pen."

Sybil pressed a hand to her chest and glowered at him. She'd babysat him a few times when she was a teenager and he was in elementary school, and he'd always been such a weird kid. Now he was a semi-awkward adult who'd dropped out of college because he didn't know what he wanted to do with his life and his parents had said if he was going to live in their house he had to get a job. So Kevin had gotten three part-time jobs: the hotel, the ice cream shop, and the movie theater.

"Don't jump up like that," she reprimanded him. The paper had gotten crushed in her hands when he'd startled her, and Sybil tried to smooth it out on the counter. "I need this paper delivered to a guest. Or left for them. I just need it to get to someone, okay?"

"Who's it for?" Kevin asked as he located a pad of sticky notes and poised his pen over the bright paper.

The words stuck to the roof of her mouth. Kevin wasn't a gossip on purpose, but he loved small talk and worked all over town. Since everyone's favorite topic was the movie, Sybil Morgan leaving Hollywood heartthrob Peter Green a piece of paper at his hotel was bound to come up.

"I'm so glad to see you up and about."

A hand on Sybil's shoulder gave her her second mini heart attack in under five minutes. She whirled and came face to face with Charlotte, who looked as surprised to see her as she felt to be touched.

"I'm sorry, I thought you were...Has anyone ever told you that you look a remarkable amount like Madelyn Penn from behind?"

"No, no one has ever told me I've got the ass of a movie star," Sybil said before she could stop herself.

Charlotte didn't seem to have heard her or was choosing to ignore the comment. She was too busy scrutinizing Sybil.

"Have you ever wanted to be in the movies?"

"Nope." She didn't need to think about that for a second.

Charlotte stared at her. It was probably incomprehensible to her that someone wouldn't want to do what she'd devoted her life to.

"Let me put this another way," she said once she'd regrouped her facial expressions. "Would you like to get paid two hundred dollars a day to stand around?"

"I own a business. I make more than two hundred dollars a day doing that." Sybil neglected to add that was before expenses because it definitely dampened her argument.

"I know. You own that coffee shop in town. The one my husband is obsessed with." Charlotte looked at the estimate that was lying on top of the front desk. "Who ordered a coffee cart?"

A blush burned Sybil's cheeks. If anyone else had asked, it wouldn't have mattered. But this was Peter's mom. What if she was like her son and could look at a person and *know*.

"Um, Peter did."

Charlotte asked Kevin for a pen and then wrote a few things on Sybil's paper.

"You can charge him at least ten percent more. I adjusted some of the figures for you." She slid the paper back toward Sybil. "You could do both things and double your income while we're here."

Yes, it did appear that the ability to find someone's buttons and push them was genetic. Money was the bottom line, and the bookstore loomed large in her mind. She shouldn't turn her nose up at an extra couple thousand dollars.

But that couple extra thousand dollars came at the expense of being near Peter for his entire visit. Could she put a price tag on that kind of prolonged heartache?

"I don't know..."

"Think about it," Charlotte encouraged her and wrote down her phone number on a blank corner of the paper and tore it off. "Call me at this number. Or at the hotel. Or you can tell Arthur."

"You are really gung-ho about this," Sybil said, tucking the scrap of paper into her back pocket. "Is it really that important?"

"I am on a very tight, non-extendable schedule. I'd rather be over-prepared than fucked up the ass without lube."

Sybil's eyes almost popped out of her head, and she had to clench her teeth to keep her jaw from falling open. That phrase coming out of Peter's mother's mouth hadn't been on her bingo card.

"I will, uh, let you know," she said. Sybil handed the crumbled, torn estimate to Charlotte. "Can you give this to Peter? I don't want it to get lost."

There was an offended grunt from Kevin's general direction.

"I will do my best," Charlotte said. "The sooner you can get back to me, the better."

"Are you sure you want to put dirt in front of these headstones? Someone might think you actually buried bodies here." Connor wiped the sweat off his forehead with the back of his wrist but still managed to leave a streak of dirt behind.

"Less talking, more shoveling. We've got an hour before it gets dark."

Sybil grasped the lip of her rain gutter tightly in one hand while she stretched her body and her other arm as far as she could reach to attach the leg of the giant spider decoration to the hook she'd installed years ago for this purpose. The spider was a pain in the ass to put up, but it looked cool—like it was climbing up her house—and her neighbor across the street, Edith Nelson, hated it, which made it even better.

Decorating her house for Halloween was a task she should have put off until Sunday when she had an entire day to devote to it, but after the last twenty-four hours, she was restless and itching to do something productive. Maybe if she kept moving, she wouldn't dwell on Peter or his mother's offer.

So she'd called Connor, her best friend since high school, and told him to come over once he was done coaching high school cross-country practice to help her. They'd hung lights and fake cobwebs and a witch riding a broomstick from a branch of the big tree next to her house. Together they'd lugged the solar-powered witch's cauldron down from the attic and, like every year since she'd bought it, complained loudly that they were idiots for storing it up there. But she'd never get rid of it because it glowed green and bubbled fog all night.

"Why did we have to do this *right now?*" Connor asked, imitating her urgency on the phone.

"Because it's not supposed to rain until tomorrow afternoon. Did you want to do this in the rain?"

"We live on the coast. We do everything in the rain." He shoveled some dirt into an even mound in front of one of the plastic headstones she'd jammed into her lawn. "Does this have something to do with the movie?"

Sybil's foot slipped, and she grabbed the top of the ladder to catch herself. She blamed her racing heart on the near fall and not Connor's question.

"What does me decorating have to do with the movie?" she asked in her best I-don't-give-a-shit voice.

"I didn't know if they were filming on your street."

"Not that I know of." She climbed down the ladder before she fell off. "Are they filming on your street?"

"They're using my house."

Her foot missed a step but luckily hit solid ground.

"Your house? Why?"

The idea that Peter and Connor were going to be in close quarters for more than a handful of hours turned her stomach into an angry sea of cold dread. They'd met before, but their interactions had been limited to casual, large-group small talk. Or as much small talk as Peter was capable of. It was inevitable that she would come up as a topic of conversation and Connor was too smart to not fill in the blanks about her two trips to London. Sure, she'd threatened Peter within an inch of his life at Graham and Eloise's wedding to never, under any circumstances, talk to anyone in Crane Cove about their relationship, but she'd also witnessed firsthand his ability to talk first and think later.

"Because it's a construction zone. Over the summer I was cutting some lumber in the front yard when a location scout drove up and asked if I'd be interested in having my house in a movie." Connor rolled his shoulders. Sybil didn't know if he was shrugging or stiff. "They offered me a lot of money to leave my house as it was and then rent it for two weeks during the shoot.

School was about to start so I was going to have to slow down work anyway, and now I can afford to hire out some of the projects I didn't want to do anyway."

"You didn't *want* to do any of those projects," she reminded him. "You're just poor."

Connor had purchased a large Victorian home on Lilac Lane, the same street that Graham and Eloise lived on. The income disparity between Connor, a high school English teacher, and the Thatchers, who owned a hotel and had money from when Graham had owned a tech company, was comical. Connor had lived with his parents for years, saving every spare penny for a down payment, and even though he said it was his dream house, she didn't understand why he'd bought it. It was too big for a single man and needed a ton of work. The place was a money pit.

"And for once my poverty has worked out in my favor." He finished the last of the fake graves. "If I hadn't needed to go so slow, they wouldn't have wanted the house and it would've taken longer."

She cocked her head to the side. "It would've taken longer if you had more money? Is that English teacher math?"

He rolled his eyes and put the shovel into the wheelbarrow. "It's the end of my day. I used all my brain power on teenagers."

"How much did they offer you?"

"Thirty thousand dollars."

If she'd still been on the ladder, she would have fallen off.

"Thirty grand? Are they nuts?"

Connor grinned. "Probably, but I wasn't going to point that out. I got that number in writing quickly."

"Fuck." The size of the number had dazed her. She shook her head. "I thought Charlotte was offering me a lot of money."

"Did the movie people want to use your house too?" he asked.

"No, my body," she answered.

"They want to use your *what?*"

Sybil mentally slapped herself. "No, not like however you're thinking," she reassured him. "The director asked if I want to be a double because I guess I look like Madelyn Penn if you squint hard enough."

Connor narrowed his eyes. "Huh. Yeah, I guess you're the dollar-store version."

Sybil picked up a plastic pumpkin off the porch railing and threw it at him. It bounced harmlessly off his shoulder and he laughed.

"How much did they offer you?"

"Two hundred dollars a day. Which sounded great until you opened your big mouth."

"It's not bad," he said, taking hold of the wheelbarrow handles and lifting. "What would you have to do?"

She shrugged. "I don't know, I didn't ask. I don't see how I can take the gig. Stardust takes up all my time."

"Did you know," Connor began, pushing the wheelbarrow toward the backyard where her shed was hidden, "that you have these people called employees and you pay them money to work at your business? I've heard a rumor that you don't even have to *be* at your business for it to operate."

"Stardust is open and I'm here now," she reminded him, crossing the lawn to pick up the pumpkin she'd thrown at him.

"Yeah, but as soon as we're done, you're going to go back there and work. You close early on Mondays for Wine and Whining." He stopped to open her gate and then called over his shoulder, "Psychologists call that having control issues."

"I don't have control issues," Sybil mumbled, moving some dirt with her foot.

"So you bury the bodies on your front lawn? Bold."

Her head snapped up so fast she got dizzy. Peter stood

next to her mailbox, dressed for a run and artfully disheveled. She knew she didn't look that good when she was sweaty. Her entire face turned cherry-tomato red when she got hot, but Peter had perfectly pink flushed cheeks and glistening sweat on his forehead. His plain, nondescript green sweatshirt wasn't even damp under the armpits.

"One of those isn't for me, is it?" he asked, taking a few steps up her front walk.

"Could be." She picked up the pumpkin from the damp grass. "What are you doing here?"

"I was out for a run and saw your street," he said innocently as he moved toward her slowly, like she was a baby deer that would run away if he made a sudden move. "Any chance you give passing joggers water?"

"Only from the hose."

There wasn't enough menace or malice in her voice because he smiled at her, and her traitorous heart had the nerve to have palpitations.

He stopped a few feet from her, put his hands on his hips, and surveyed her house. "I've been on movie sets with lower production value. This is really impressive."

She blushed so hard she worried there was steam rising from the top of her head.

"Peter, why are you here?" she asked again.

He looked at her and his face softened. "Because—"

"Did you want to set up the hands before I go home? The ground is soft." Connor half shouted as he came out of the backyard. He stopped when he saw Peter. "Oh, hey, man. How's it going?"

Peter gave him a small wave. "Hey, Connor. It's good. Just out for a run, saw the house, and had to stop and say how impressive it looks."

"Can you settle something for us?" Connor asked. "Is there such a thing as too much fake cobweb?"

"No, but there is certainly such a thing as too *little* fake cobweb."

Sybil smugly stuck her tongue out at Connor, then her face froze as she realized she'd said the exact same thing to him when he'd complained about how much fake cobweb she had.

"What are 'the hands'?" Peter asked, holding up his own hands and wiggling his fingers.

"She got these skeleton hands last year, and we installed them along the walkway so it looks like they're trying to grab your ankles," Connor explained. "They looked pretty cool."

Sybil's forehead reflexively creased into a frown, but she corrected it quickly. Connor wasn't the biggest fan of her Halloween decorations. He was more the "carved pumpkins are more than enough" type. Either he was lying to Peter for some reason that was only clear to him, or after sixteen years of friendship he'd finally come around to her way of thinking.

"Do you need any help?" Peter asked.

"No," Sybil answered quickly before Connor could open his mouth. "We were wrapping up for the night. Connor has papers to grade, and I have to get back to the shop."

Cinematic disappointment crawled across Peter's face. "Well, if you ever want help, you know where to find me."

"You're at the hotel with the movie people, right?" Connor asked, and Peter nodded. "That reminds me. Sybil, can I sleep here while they're using my house for the film?"

"I guess so?"

Connor was acting weird, and Peter's face was blank with a cheerful smile painted on top. She hated that she knew what he looked like when he was pretending to be happy. She hated more that she wanted to run her hands over his face to wipe that expression away.

Peter looked up at the sky. "I should get back before it gets too dark."

"Yeah, you should really wear reflective gear. Someone might hit you with their car," Connor said.

Peter nodded and then went down the walkway a lot quicker than he'd come up it, and walked toward the stop sign at the end of the street with his hands in his pockets.

"Someone might hit you with their car?" Sybil repeated. "What the fuck?"

Connor shrugged, his eyes still trained on Peter's retreating form. "It's true. Someone might hit him with their car if they don't know he's there. Kids these days text and drive."

"Yes, with all the glorious cell service we have in Crane Cove, texting and driving has become endemic," she said sarcastically. "What's your problem with Peter?"

"You mean Peter Alan Parker-Green?"

Her face burned. That lovely intimate knowledge slip up had happened at Graham and Eloise's wedding when Connor was filling out the witness information for the marriage license. He'd tried to ask her about it after the fact, but she'd stonewalled him.

"I don't have a problem with him," Connor continued, "but you do, and I don't like how he comes around even though it makes you uncomfortable."

She crossed her arms. "I don't have a problem telling someone if I want them to go away and stay away."

He leveled her with the kind of skeptical look he reserved for his students, but when she didn't back down or cave, he sighed and said, "Fine."

They headed toward her house so Connor could wash his hands. Halfway up the front steps, she stopped. "Do you actually want to stay here while they're filming in your house, or were you bluffing?"

Chapter Eight

"Peter? What are you doing here?" Graham asked when he opened his front door. Concern creased his forehead, and he stepped out of the doorway to let Peter in.

Peter didn't feel entirely attached to his body. He floated through the door, his brain humming with white noise. He was vaguely aware that he'd walked from Sybil's house to Graham's house, but he had no idea how to retrace his steps. And he didn't exactly remember ringing the doorbell, but he must have because Graham had answered it.

"I was in the neighborhood," he answered.

"Why?" It was an abrupt question, but Graham recovered quickly. "I mean, don't you have rehearsals or work? I thought you were always super busy on set."

"I just had random stuff today." Peter looked at his feet. Should he take off his shoes? Was he staying? "I got done and decided to go for a run."

"Where's your reflective gear? You're going to get hit by a car."

It wasn't menacing when Graham said it. It had been menacing when Connor said it. But why? He and Sybil weren't together. Peter had asked. A lot. In soft, subtle ways he'd made sure that there wasn't anything going on between the two. But maybe something had changed in the last year and...

His stomach pitched and twisted, and nausea rolled through him like a wave.

Sybil would have said something if she was seeing Connor. It would have been blunt so he couldn't misinterpret it, willfully or otherwise. Plenty of people thought Sybil was mean, but she wasn't cruel. She wouldn't have strung him along, allowing him to have a glimmer of hope, for a year if her relationship status had changed.

Graham put a hand on his shoulder, and Peter nearly jumped out of his skin.

"Are you okay?"

"I'm tired," he admitted. "I haven't been sleeping well."

The frown returned. "Is something wrong with your room? Is it a problem with the hotel?"

Peter put a shallow smile on his face. "No, the room is great. The bed is fantastic. I'm just..." He wiggled his fingers near his temple because the words weren't coming to him. "In my head, I guess."

"Do you want a glass of wine?"

"Yes, please."

Peter followed Graham to the kitchen, where his best friend presented him with a bottle of red and a bottle of white to choose from. He picked the red because it felt more melancholy.

"Where's Eloise?" he asked, opening the fridge to look for a snack.

Graham twisted the corkscrew into the bottle. "Tree lighting committee meeting."

"Like a Christmas tree?" Peter located a cheese stick. Wine and cheese went together, didn't they?

"Yes, the town Christmas tree. It's a big deal and she's *thrilled* to have been asked to join the committee, so if she brings it up, please feel free to ask her a million questions."

"That sounds lovely."

"Does it?" Graham shook his head, utterly bewildered. He poured two glasses of wine and picked his up. "I don't think you could pay me to be in that room."

Peter unwrapped his pilfered cheese stick. "But without the people in that room, a beautiful community tradition dies. Community is such an important thing, but it's also so fragile. You're so lucky to live in a place where people still care. Apathy is everywhere."

Graham grunted into his wine glass. "Well, now I feel guilty for not being more excited."

"After I die, I'm going to submit my résumé to be a Ghost of Christmas Past. Or Christmas Present. Don't think I could hack the future bit."

"Don't sell yourself short. You're an excellent warning."

That made Peter smile. "What else is new?"

"Well." Graham took another large sip of his wine. "We're trying to have a baby."

That was exactly the news he needed to hear. Joy and hope warmed him from the inside out, like his veins were filled with sunshine.

"That's amazing!" He threw his hands into the air and his cheese stick flew out of his hand and hit the ceiling. "Oops. Sorry. You're going to be a dad! Which means I get to be an uncle. That's not too presumptuous, is it? Because I don't have any siblings so you're kind of the closest thing to a brother that I have and—"

"Don't get too excited," Graham warned. "It's taking a lot longer than we planned on. If we haven't gotten pregnant by Christmas, we're going to talk to a fertility specialist again."

"Again?" Peter frowned. "You already talked to one?"

Graham sighed. "Yeah. We did a few months ago. They ran tests, and nothing is wrong. Did you know you only have a twenty-five percent chance of getting pregnant each month? And then we watched a video and holy shit, how does *anyone* get pregnant?"

"So what are you supposed to do in the meantime?"

"Relax. Have fun with it. Track Eloise's cycles and temperature."

"Ah yes. Relaxing and having fun. Two things you two are famous for doing." Peter sipped his wine. It was smooth and had a buttery finish. "Wait, is that why you're still fucking in your hotel office?"

A pink blush rose on Graham's cheeks, but he seemed more smug than embarrassed. "Yeah. We're trying to keep it interesting. Baby-making sex can get a little..." He searched for the word. "I don't want to say monotonous, but the pressure takes some of the fun out of it."

"Is there a spreadsheet?"

"Of course there's a spreadsheet."

Peter chuckled and threw away his projectile cheese stick. "I only have one request for my little niece or nephew. I don't want to be called Uncle Pete or PeePee."

"Why not, PeePee?"

"Oh, shut up." Peter rolled his eyes and took another deep drink of his wine. "So, I stopped by Sybil's house earlier to talk to her about doing a coffee cart for the movie, and Connor was there. Did they start dating?"

Graham's laugh filled the room.

"So that's a no?"

"Unless you caught them in the act of doing something obviously couple-y, no, they're not dating. Why? What was going on?"

"He was helping her put up her Halloween decorations."

"The *scandal*. And in broad daylight too?" Graham *tsked* several times like a disapproving Southern grandmother. "Any particular reason you wanted to know?"

Peter shrugged, adopting an air of nonchalance. "I was curious. You know me, nosey as can be." He paused, then added, "He did ask to sleep over at her house while we're using his house for filming."

"Are you protecting Sybil's virtue now?" Graham added more wine to his glass.

"Sybil doesn't need anyone's protection, but it is one of the oldest romantic plots in the book. Boy meets girl, boy and girl become friends, years later boy and girl become lovers."

Graham shuddered. "I hate that word. Lovers."

"But what if you've missed this love story brewing right under your nose?"

"I will have Eloise do some snooping if you're this invested," Graham promised. "Have you had dinner yet? We could order a pizza."

"Pizza sounds great."

Peter nursed his glass of wine and hoped the alcohol would slow down his brain. Visions of Connor and Sybil doing couple things swirled in his head, and it was making him motion sick.

Chapter Nine
Twelve Years Ago, London

Sᴙʙɪʟ ᴇxɪᴛᴇᴅ her economics class and blinked in the harsh sunlight. The chill in the air bit her cheeks, and she wrapped the cardigan Peter had lent her tighter around her body. Wool, soap, and some kind of warm, spicy cologne tickled her nose, and she surreptitiously sniffed her shoulder to get a lungful. Heat traveled down her body and pooled in her core. The phantom pressure of his lips still lingered on hers.

Maybe she shouldn't have been so coy with him. No, not coy. Obstructive. If she'd merely been coy, she would've given him some actionable hints about her whereabouts. No, she had to tempt fate after the best kiss of her life.

It was his fault. He'd talked to her about fate and soulmates, and he'd pretended to read her palm and then kissed her in a phone booth while they hid from a downpour.

"You're going to have an epic love story," he'd said, tracing the line that ran from her index finger to the base of her palm. It tickled and made her want to squirm. "And a beautiful life." He traced the next line over. "And you're going to give Peter your phone number so he can take you out on a proper date."

"I don't have a phone."

"Everyone has a phone."

She'd shook her head. "I pay my own bills, and a phone is not in my budget."

"Where do you live?" he asked, his finger still tracing the lines on her palm in the most deliciously distracting way.

"Nope. I don't know you, so you don't need to know where I live."

"Not even a hint?"

"You believe in fate, right?" He nodded. "Well, if this is fate like you keep saying it is, then we'll run into each other again. The universe can't help but put us together, right?"

Stupid, stupid, stupid. She should've given him a hint. She should've—

He was sitting on a bench, drinking from a paper to-go cup.

"Peter?" she said, like he could ever look like anyone else.

He turned his head toward her and smiled. It was like staring into the sun. "There you are. I was wondering when I was going to see you."

"What are you doing here?" she asked, stopping a few feet away from him. "You can't expect me to believe you just wandered onto campus."

Peter stood and closed the few feet between them in two steps. "It's fate, remember?"

She gave him a look that made most people she'd met tuck tail and run. He smiled again.

"And I saw your university ID last night when you were looking for your Oyster card."

"So you're a stalker."

"I prefer to think I used my outstanding detective skills in the best British tradition of Sir Arthur Conan Doyle and Dame Agatha Christie."

"How did you know which building I'd be in?" Sybil asked,

and crossed her arms. She tried to push to the back of her mind that she was wearing his sweater in front of him.

"You mentioned you were studying business. A quick-ish internet search gave me the most plausible buildings, and then I picked one. That part was pure fate." He gently touched her elbow. "This looks really good on you."

The blush that inflamed her cheeks had to match either her hair or the sweater.

"Did you track me down to get it back?" she asked.

"No, not at all. In fact, as long as we're seeing each other, you're welcome to keep it. You can't keep it indefinitely, though, because it is my favorite." The roguish smile returned and turned her insides to molten goo. "I wanted to take you on a proper date, remember? I needed to know where to send the pigeons."

"The pigeons?"

"Since you don't have a phone. I'm also amenable to telegrams, Morse code, and smoke signals, but I think the old-fashioned post will take too long."

Sybil rolled her eyes even as her heart fluttered. "You're ridiculous."

"Does that mean you'll go on a date with me?" Peter asked, the earnest, hopeful look on his face baffling her.

It didn't make sense. He was gorgeous and sweet and funny. If last night was any indication, he was thoughtful and romantic too. What the hell was wrong with him that he was chasing after her so hard? It couldn't be the thrill of the chase. She wasn't satisfactory enough prey for that to be true. Did he have a wife he'd locked in the attic? Or a portrait in the attic that was getting progressively older and uglier while he stayed perfect?

Or maybe he just...liked her?

No, that couldn't be it.

But her curiosity was piqued, and she wouldn't mind

another kiss like the one they'd shared in the phone booth. That had been the kind of kiss she could live off for months. A few more, and she'd be set for life.

"Fine, but only so I can keep the sweater," she said.

The smile that broke on his face was enough to break her heart. How could anyone possibly be so excited about her? And how disappointed were they both going to be when he realized that she was, well, *her?*

Chapter Ten
Crane Cove, Oregon

THE LOBBY of the Crane Hotel was bustling with activity, but Charlotte somehow spotted her.

"Sybil!" she shouted. Sybil was tempted to act like she hadn't heard her but the woman was fast. Charlotte was within acknowledgement range before Sybil had made a decision.

"It's busy here," Sybil said in lieu of a greeting, putting her hands in the pockets of her corduroy overalls. Why had she worn overalls? She looked like Pippi Longstocking.

Charlotte glanced around like she hadn't noticed the chaos. "Oh, yes. Move-in day for the rest of the production. Speaking of the production, did you have any time to consider my offer? I checked with accounting, and I can bump up your pay to two hundred and fifty dollars a day."

Sybil spied Eloise working at the front desk, but her friend was too absorbed in work to notice she was in the room. She wished she had Eloise with her. Or that she was negotiating for Eloise instead of herself. It was easier to be brave for other people.

"I've thought about it," Sybil began, "and I've checked in with some of my employees that would be covering my absence. Two fifty a day is nice, but if you only need me twice, I've lost money putting people on the schedule that don't need to be there. So I need some kind of guarantee. A minimum amount of days I'm getting paid for even if I don't get called in."

Charlotte arched an eyebrow, and Sybil understood why she'd played princesses and queens.

"Most people are just grateful for the opportunity to be on a film set."

Sybil shrugged one shoulder, even though her stomach was churning at the possibility she'd pushed too far. "Based on our conversation yesterday, you need me more than I need you."

Charlotte stared her down, and it took every ounce of self-control Sybil had to steel her backbone and not squirm. Then, Charlotte sighed, defeated.

"It's a deal," she said and held out her hand. Sybil shook it and was surprised by the iron grip. "You'll need to talk to the production manager and coordinator, and their office is...Oh, fuck, I forgot."

A nervous laugh bubbled out of Sybil's mouth. She would have never expected a foul word to come out of someone that looked like Charlotte Parker.

They were rescued from their mutually awkward moment by Arthur, who joined them looking every inch an English Literature professor emeritus on holiday. All he was missing was a pipe.

"Sybil, dearest, I didn't think you ever left your charming cafe," he said. "Speaking of, you didn't happen to bring any coffee, did you? I'm hankering for a cup."

"You've already had three cups," Charlotte reminded him. "I don't understand how your heart hasn't exploded yet."

Sybil tried to keep her face neutral, but the smirk tugging at the corner of her mouth was strong.

"No coffee today," she told him, "but Peter is sponsoring a coffee cart soon."

"I knew having children would pay off some day," Arthur said. "I'm glad my son has excellent taste."

"Could you help her find the production office? She's going to be standing in for Madelyn."

His face, which was already cheerful, brightened considerably. "Splendid." He offered her his arm. "Shall we off to see the Wizard?"

Sybil understood right then that Peter had never stood a chance at being normal with a father like Arthur. It was somewhere between strange and comforting that in forty-some-odd years, his antics would still be adorable and charming.

She threaded her arm through Arthur's and was relieved when he didn't try to skip through the lobby.

Velda and Verna were like bookends at the ends of the table they occupied. The paperwork was long and boring, they took a picture of her that amounted to a mugshot, and then was told at the end of it all that she needed to stop by the office Friday at four to pick up her call sheet for Monday. When she enquired about email, she learned that Velda and Verna preferred paper copies and didn't trust email because emails got hacked.

"That explanation could've been an email," Sybil muttered as she and Arthur exited the temporary office.

"An office supply store loves to see them coming," he said with a wry grin. "They're a bit stuck in their ways, but their ways work."

"I will not question the process again," Sybil promised. "Mostly for my own sanity."

Arthur pushed back the sleeve of his sweater and checked his watch. "I am about to be late for a conference call. Do you know your way out?"

"It's a hotel, not Ovid's labyrinth. I think I can find a door that leads out."

Arthur examined her with intense curiosity. "You know Ovid?"

"You're going to be late," Sybil reminded him. If he pried hard enough, she might have slipped and told him she'd happily listened to Peter ramble about how *A Midsummer Night's Dream* was an adaptation of Ovid's *Metamorphoses* during one of their long walks where he'd had an arm around her shoulders and she'd had a hand in his back pocket.

"If I don't see you for coffee soon, I will see you on Monday," Arthur said and, after a moment's hesitation, squeezed her shoulder affectionately.

Sybil watched his rangy form disappear down the hallway and around a corner. She wished she didn't adore the old man so much.

She turned to go the opposite direction, even though the shorter way was the way Arthur had gone, and there was Peter, maybe twenty feet away. He looked as surprised to see her as she was to see him.

Then a smile dawned on his face, bright as a new day.

"I was wondering when I would see you again."

There was something she'd seen once about how bodies remembered—or maybe how they kept score—except her body didn't just remember, it had cataloged with librarian efficiency every single feeling Peter had ever caused. Every ache, good or bad, was filed away neatly and recalled in their entirety. Her body remembered in equal measures the lightness of love and the crushing weight of heartbreak.

"Are you following me?" she asked, unable to force the necessary irritation in her voice to keep him away. Peter closed the distance between them while her feet remained rooted to the floor.

"I would've needed to know you were here to properly stalk you," he said, his voice pitched low so his words were for her ears only. Goosebumps grew on her arms as her stomach fluttered. "Believe it or not, I was looking for the gym."

"Graham didn't tell you?"

"He did...and I forgot." Peter put his hands in the pockets of his joggers. "I *can't* ask him again. I'll never hear the end of it."

"It's across from the pool," Sybil told him. "Follow the smell of chlorine."

"You always were clever."

The twinkle in his eyes scrambled her ability to think coherently, so she fumbled for a topic.

"Did you really just happen to be running by my house yesterday?"

Peter took a hesitating half breath and his mouth opened to speak, but then Velda or Verna exited the production office.

"Peter!" one of the Vs exclaimed. "How are you?" She didn't wait for an answer and instead turned to Sybil. "I've known him since he was hip height and under foot. He's a good egg." And then she did the universal matchmaking eyebrow wiggle, like Peter and Sybil were even in the same universe of eligibility.

"Don't listen to her," Peter said, and wrapped his knuckles on his head. "I'm a little cracked. Velda, where are you headed?"

"The dining room. Verna and I are a little peckish." She patted her stomach and laughed. "Don't be a stranger, Peter."

She left in search of food, but then two more people wandered down the hall, and Sybil had enough. Once the most recent interlopers were out of sight, she grabbed Peter's sleeve and tugged him into the nearest cleaning closet. The motion sensor light flickered to life as the door closed.

The closet was small, stocked with disinfectants, wood polish, and garbage bags. The bigger ones were upstairs, on the floors with the guest rooms. But a couple of vacuums made the space tighter than she'd anticipated so that she was toe-to-toe with Peter, her sense of smell overwhelmed with cleaner and his cologne. It made her nerves fray around the edges.

"Why were you at my house yesterday?" she demanded.

Peter was reading a label behind her head so she snapped her fingers in front of his eyes to get his attention. He sighed.

"I heard you," he said, looking down at her with the kind of calm, gentle patience that made her want to scream. "I was trying to organize my thoughts."

"Don't make up a story."

"I'm not," he promised, and crossed his heart. "I wanted to see you. I miss you. And I needed to talk to you about the coffee cart."

Talking business was good. Business was safe. Business popped her hopeful heart like a balloon.

"I left the estimate for you with your mom. Was there a problem?"

He shook his head and a little piece of blond hair fell out of place. Sybil clenched her hands into fists so she wouldn't brush it back into place.

"No problem. I'm fine with the numbers. Curious about what happened to the paper, though." He raised an inquisitive eyebrow. "Crumpled, torn, and a small splash of coffee."

"The coffee wasn't me, and the tear was your mother."

"But the crumpling was you?"

"Your mother startled me," Sybil explained. A nagging worry she'd had since Arthur first set foot in Stardust rose from the back of her mind. "Do your parents know about us?"

Peter pursed his lips thoughtfully, and then cautiously said, "Yes and no. They know bits and pieces about us, but not that the 'us' in question is you and me. I—" He paused, and looked down at where the tips of their shoes were touching. "I used to think you'd be able to fill in the blanks yourself. Someday."

Why the fuck did she pick a closet? There wasn't enough space to run away and there wasn't enough air to breathe. She knew from her time volunteering as an accident victim for the Crane Cove Volunteer Fire Department that her chest wasn't supposed to hurt this much.

"Everything I said before Graham and Eloise's wedding is still true," she said. "As far as anyone else is concerned, there was never an 'us.' They don't need to know about London." Sybil drew in a breath that was like trying to inflate concrete. "The next few weeks are too important for me. When I'm here, I'm working. I don't need you trying to distract me."

"I can keep us a secret," Peter said in a low, velvet tone. His fingertips brushed her forearm, and Sybil felt that tantalizing touch between her legs. The body remembered. "But if I'm distracting you, it's because you want to be distracted."

Her mouth and throat were dry, so her words caught as they came out. "I can't afford to be distracted."

"What's so distracting?" he asked, tucking her hair behind her ear. It took the entirety of her willpower not to lean into his touch like a cat starved for affection. "Are you wondering if we'd still be good together? Or remembering how good we were?"

Her body remembered, and so did her mind. The closet melted away to a red London phone booth, rain bouncing furiously off the top. Her heart beat in time with the twenty-year-old version of herself she barely recognized, racing so fast she thought she'd faint before he kissed her. Unable to breathe because she wanted him to so badly, scared that an inhale would break the spell. She put her hand on his chest, not to hold him back but to see if he was as affected she was. *Tha-thump. Tha-thump. Tha-thump.* Forceful and rapid under her palm. He cupped her cheek, his long fingers able to grip the back of her neck and then—

The door swung open and Sybil jumped backward, her back colliding with the metal shelves. Cleaning products rattled.

"Fuck!" Kevin shouted like he'd seen a mouse.

"Kevin!" Sybil bellowed. "Don't *do* that. Jesus."

"Do what? I opened a door to get a barf kit and almost had a heart attack."

She squeezed around him and out into the hall. There was air out there. She could think straight if her brain had oxygen. Too much Peter and bleach had confused her.

"Sybil!" Charlotte's voice from the end of the hall jolted her like she'd touched a live wire. "I'm glad I caught you. If you have a few minutes, wardrobe can squeeze you in to see if you fit into Madelyn's costumes."

"Don't you mean they can fit me in to see if I can squeeze into Madelyn's costumes?" Sybil deadpanned half-heartedly. She walked quickly toward Charlotte, not wanting her to catch sight of Peter if she hadn't already. "Where is wardrobe?"

"I have an overeager PA who is dying to take you," Charlotte said, putting a gentle, guiding hand on Sybil's back.

Chapter Eleven

PETER HAD JUST EXITED the steamy confines of his bathroom after his post-workout shower when his room phone began to ring. He groaned.

It had been nonstop rehearsals and meetings. Mentally, he was spent. Physically he was tired too, but he'd done that to himself. Exercising almost helped with his pent-up frustration surrounding Sybil.

"Hello?" he said, pinning the phone between his ear and his shoulder so he could at least put on some underwear. Talking on the phone naked was awkward.

"Hey, bud!" Jordy's cheerful voice barked in his ear. "How's it going?"

The weight that lifted off his shoulders made Peter feel like he could float to the ceiling.

"It's going," he said and sat on the edge of the bed. "Stepping into a production at the last minute is not for the faint of heart. How are you? How's Annie?"

"We're good," Jordy said, and there was a hesitation there that told Peter to keep his mouth shut and let his friend fill the silence. "I need your advice."

"About what?"

"Proposing to Annie."

"You haven't done that yet?" Peter teased. It wasn't a secret that Jordy wanted to marry Annie. He'd technically already proposed once when he was high on painkillers after his motorcycle accident. Every time Jordy sent him a picture, Peter half expected it to be a ring on Annie's finger.

"She didn't want to get engaged until after we went to her ex's wedding this summer. And then I wanted it to be a surprise so I've been waiting to throw her off the scent. Like, I *wanted* to propose on the car ride back to the hotel after the reception, but this is the story we'll tell for the rest of our lives. We're going to tell this story to our kids. It has to be perfect. And I thought, who knows romance better than Peter?"

"You've come to the right place," Peter said. "Let's brainstorm. What places are special to the two of you?"

Jordy listed off a few places, included the hospital room he'd initially proposed in, and then said, "And the lighthouse, obviously."

"Call me sappy, but my vote is for the lighthouse. It's where you fell in love."

"It's where she almost stabbed me," Jordy said wistfully.

"I don't know if I want to know what the two of you get up to in the bedroom."

Jordy laughed. "No, when we met. Or, re-met. I was taking a shower and Annie thought I was an intruder and surprised me with a knife."

"Kinky."

"You don't think the lighthouse is too obvious?"

Peter sighed softly. "It's okay to be obvious. Though when you tell your love story to your kids, I think you should leave out the knife play."

Jordy plowed on, ignoring the joke. "How do I make a trip to Crane Cove not suspicious?"

"Are you coming here for Thanksgiving again?"

"I don't know if I can last a month and a half. Or is it a month and three quarters? I haven't looked at the calendar yet."

Peter checked the calendar on his phone. "It falls on the last week of the month. How do you feel about Veterans' Day?"

"That's not really a romantic holiday."

"Neither is Thanksgiving, but with Annie's teaching schedule you have to plan around school breaks. Not everyone is an old, retired man like you."

"Maybe I could charter a private jet and cut a lot of our travel time. I'm starting to see why Sam does it," Jordy mused. "But what's the occasion? I can't say Veterans' Day."

Peter stood and paced as far as the phone cord would allow. "Is there any sort of birding event she might want to see or take part in?"

There was a pause and then, "Fuck, you're good at this. I will do some research. I know you're busy and working, but can I call or text you about this some more?"

"Any time. Let me know what you figure out."

"Thanks. Love you."

"Love you too," Peter said and hung up.

It was easy to give other people advice. It all seemed so clear when it was someone else's love life. He could read the map and see the path they were supposed to take. It was so easy that he always assumed he would know exactly what to do when he reunited with Sybil.

He knew he'd have to clear up a few things about the last twelve years, but all of that could have been solved with a simple conversation, right? He never expected to Wile E. Coyote into the brick wall she'd erected between them over and over and over again. She didn't want to talk about them. She didn't want to acknowledge there had ever been a them.

But she kept the flowers he sent. She'd kept the red sweater. And when he'd almost kissed her in the supply closet, she hadn't pulled away or punched him in the throat.

She'd told him that he was a *distraction*.

That buoyed him more than it should have buoyed a reasonable person. But Peter had sped past reasonable years ago.

If he distracted her, that meant the door wasn't shut. There was still a small glimmer of hope, like spotting a lost ring in a storm drain.

How the hell did he get the door to open again?

His phone rang again. He wasn't this popular on a normal day.

"Hello?"

"Hi, is this Peter?" asked a soft, sweet female voice.

"Yes. Who is this?"

"It's Dahlia, the intimacy coordinator. I'm sorry to bother you during your down time, but I had some questions for you. Is now a good time to talk?"

"It's a good time. What did you need from me?"

"Well, I had a meeting with Charlotte today to go over what you, Madelyn, and I discussed in our meeting about the intimate aspects of the production," Dahlia began. "And Charlotte is concerned about potential delays because of Madelyn's morning sickness. She told me that she's hired a photo double for Madelyn, and she brought up the possibility of the photo double filming some of the intimate aspects. I know this isn't a particularly racy production, but we do want everyone to feel comfortable. Keep in mind you can absolutely say no, but would you be comfortable potentially kissing Madelyn's double if that became necessary?"

Peter had zoned out a little while Dahlia had been talking,

but the part of his brain that was tuned in to any potential mention of kissing Sybil grabbed his attention. He took a deep breath and concentrated on sounding casual.

"I don't mind. A kiss is a kiss, and the schedule is important," he said, his heart racing. "Have you spoken to Sybil about this?"

"No, I haven't. She's my next call." There was a beat of silence, and then she asked, "Have you two met already?"

"Oh, uh, yes." Peter winced. He hadn't meant to slip up like that. The suitable, innocent explanation was on the tip of his tongue, but all he could think about were the nights—and days—they'd spent in bed together. With an effort, he forced out, "Our best friends are married to each other. We were in the wedding together."

"That's so sweet," Dahlia cooed. "Are you sure you're comfortable kissing her? If it's weird, we can always find another way."

"It's fine. Really," Peter insisted.

"Okay." Dahlia didn't sound convinced. "If you're really sure, I'll go ahead and give Sybil a call to see how she feels about the arrangement. I'll see you on set. Have a nice rest of your day."

"Thanks, Dahlia," he said and hung up.

It had to be a sign from the universe. How else could he explain the timing of Dahlia's call? He needed a way to shift things with Sybil, and one had been provided to him.

Was it wrong to call Madelyn and beg her to pretend to be too sick to kiss him?

Yes, yes, it was very, *very* wrong. But extremely tempting. He needed to keep trusting that everything was going to work out.

Chapter Twelve

Sybil had gone to eight new schools before moving to Crane Cove. Her mother moved her and her sister Mallory to wherever that year's model of stepdad lived or wanted to live. She was used to being an outsider, to not fitting in. Never once had she been as nervous as she was when she showed up to the set of *The Light Below*. It was surreal seeing the title of a detective thriller she'd read on the black T-shirts the production assistants wore.

She showed her badge to a security guard and then one of the black T-shirt-wearing production assistants whisked her off to hair and makeup. The whisking was wholly unnecessary because she had to sit in a chair and wait for them to be ready for her. Sybil didn't have any games on her phone, but she wished she did. Someone should have told her to bring a book.

"Here." A book appeared under her nose, and she jumped, startled. She took the mass-market paperback and held it so she could read the title. *Night Watch* by Terry Pratchett. "I just finished it."

Sybil looked up at Peter, who towered over her from her seated position. He'd been transformed into the quintessential

Pacific Northwest Man. Hiking boots, jeans, a blue-and-green flannel, and a Columbia Sportswear rain jacket. Either he'd already been to wardrobe or he'd embraced method acting.

"You're still reading Terry?" she asked, turning the book over to read the back cover.

"I love Sam Vimes. He's my favorite literary copper," Peter said, continuing to stand instead of taking the open seat next to her. "I'm trying to get into that suspicious bastard headspace."

A muffled chuckle made her shoulders jump. "You're too nice to be a suspicious bastard," she said, and immediately wished she could take the words back. Not because they were mean, but because they were *nice*. Friendly. He was going to think she wanted him hanging around, smiling at her, making her heart beat like it was trying to break out of her chest to get to him.

"It's called acting. I've been told I'm quite good." He had the audacity to wink at her.

Sybil averted her gaze and saw Madelyn Penn swan out of hair and makeup. She understood now how Charlotte could have mistaken her for Madelyn. It was eerie to see someone she resembled walk toward her and stop next to Peter. Except she was the knockoff version of Madelyn Penn. Not quite as thin, not quite as pretty, more freckly, and her hair wasn't lusciously silky. Hopefully hair and makeup was staffed by actual fairy godmothers.

"Do you think crafty has any potato chips? I read online— Oh, hi! You must be my double." Madelyn caught sight of Sybil and smiled like a pageant queen greeting commoners.

The urge to stand overwhelmed Sybil, and she rose, clutching the small book to her chest. "I'm Sybil."

"That's such a pretty name," Madelyn gushed, but then her smile vanished. She was perfectly still for three seconds, and then she walked off quickly without saying goodbye.

"That was like looking into a funhouse mirror, but instead of looking weird, I looked prettier," Sybil said.

Peter frowned, but she didn't get to find out if he would have argued with her because hair and makeup beckoned her into their lair of foundation and hairspray.

There were Polaroid pictures of Madelyn taped to the mirror she was sat in front of, and two women immediately went to work on her like she was an F1 car and they were her pit crew. It wasn't a collaborative process. At one point they measured the length of her ponytail and then teased her hair to make it a little shorter.

When they stepped away, the effect was astounding. She could never be an exact match for Madelyn Penn, but she could easily win a look-alike contest. They smoothed out her complexion, made her eyes look bigger and more doe-like, and had somehow managed to get her hair into a ponytail that looked good and not like she was a colonial drummer boy who had fallen through a rift in time.

"Wow," Sybil breathed, wanting to touch her face but not daring to disturb their handiwork. "Do you offer classes on how to do this?"

"Maybe on a more relaxed day we can give you some pointers," the makeup artist said, and then studied Sybil's face. "But this isn't how I would do your makeup if I was doing it for you and not to make you look more like Madelyn."

There wasn't a chance for Sybil to ask any follow-up questions because another black-clad production assistant showed up to collect her. She was hustled to wardrobe where they put her in the exact same outfit as Madelyn: gray slacks, black belt, white blouse with the first three buttons undone. Professionally sultry. Her gift from props were a badge and fake gun.

"It's not loaded," the props person told her, and showed her that it was empty. "So even if you want to shoot someone, you can't."

Sybil stood still while they adjusted her gun and holster. "Have we met before?"

"Because I showed you it wasn't loaded?" They grinned. "Peter told me to tell you so you wouldn't be tempted to point it at him."

"It's day one, and my reputation has already preceded me."

"I worked with him on a western. He teases a lot, but he's a really nice guy. Don't be nervous."

"A western? Someone handed him a loaded gun?"

The prop person chuckled. "Not loaded. Okay, you are good to go, my friend."

"Where am I supposed to go?" Sybil asked.

The prop person frowned. "That is a great question." They looked around and pursed their lips. "I swear the PAs have a sixth sense for when I need them and hide from me— Oh! Hey!" They grabbed a passing PA. "This is Madelyn's double. Can you take custody of her?"

"Am I a prisoner now?" Sybil asked the PA as she was hustled off, her book—*Peter's* book—clutched tightly in her hand.

"By the end of the day, this all feels very Hotel California," the PA told her. "So, in a way, yes."

The PA took her up the magnificent staircase in the lobby of the Crane Hotel, and then to a hallway stuffed with people, lights, and cameras.

"Holy shit," she muttered under her breath.

"Yeah, it's a lot," the PA agreed.

So maybe not as under her breath as she thought.

Sybil saw Charlotte talking to two other women, one with a thick binder, and one with a clipboard. Charlotte glanced up briefly, then did a double take when she caught sight of Sybil, and the relief on her face was clear.

The PA deposited her with the trio and managed to slip away without being given another task.

Charlotte put a gentle hand on Sybil's shoulder. "Sybil, this is Michelle, my assistant director, and Ayesha, my second assistant director. They are my brains outside my body. And this is Sybil, who is going to be standing in for Madelyn until she feels better."

"Wow." Ayesha looked her up and down. "The resemblance is uncanny. You really found her in the lobby?"

"Coffee shop, actually," Sybil corrected. "I own Stardust downtown."

"And we've used up our time for chitchat," Michelle said after a look at her watch. "Tick-tock."

"So, we do need you to have another conversation with Dahlia, the intimacy coordinator," Charlotte began once her assistant directors had dispersed to make sure everyone was doing their jobs. "Madelyn is currently indisposed, so we're very grateful for you. We're going to shoot as many of Peter's shots as we can, but there is a kiss on today's schedule."

Sybil's stomach flipped anxiously and her palms became embarrassingly damp. "But we might not get to that part?"

"I'm hoping Madelyn will be back with us before lunch," Charlotte said, "because fuck, I do not want to be behind on day one."

From the corner of her eye, Sybil spotted Peter down the hall, talking to a tall woman with electric blue hair and a yellow dress that looked like something out of Eloise's closet. That had to be Dahlia, the woman who had called the night before to talk to her about kissing Peter. It had sounded like such a remote possibility twelve hours ago.

"I will go talk to Dahlia, then," Sybil promised.

"And then we need to do lighting and focus checks," Charlotte added. She looked down at Sybil's hands. "You can leave your book on Madelyn's chair."

Sybil picked her way down the hall, carefully trying to avoid stepping on cables or being in anyone's way, but she came a hair's breadth away from being smacked in the face by a boom mic. By the time she reached Peter and presumably Dahlia, the book cover was slick with sweat from her palms and her pulse was ragged. Then Peter looked at her with a friendly smile that faltered, and she tossed the book like a frisbee onto the nearest chair.

"Sybil, this is Dahlia. I was just telling her how"—he paused ever so imperceptibly, but she noticed the rest and how his smile faded further—"Graham and Eloise's wedding was at the hotel. Are you okay? You're very flushed."

"I'm fine," she insisted, dodging his hand when he tried to check her temperature. That kind of casual intimacy was akin to cruelty because the only people who would have dared were her very close friends and the only person in her history who had logged the man hours to know exactly how to make her legs shake uncontrollably. "There's just a lot of fucking people around here."

"It's normal to be nervous," Dahlia interjected, "but everyone here is a professional. To them, you're a moving part."

"Was that supposed to make me feel better?" Sybil put her hands on her hips because she didn't know what else to do with them. "Is it always this hot?"

"Kind of," Peter answered cautiously.

"We can get you a fan for between takes," Dahlia said. "So, yesterday I spoke with both of you about the possibility of a kiss, and you both said you were okay with that. Does that still stand?"

Peter nodded stoically, and that small gesture set her teeth on edge. Then her knee-jerk reaction to be frustrated that he wasn't jumping up and down with excitement to kiss her made her more frustrated, and it wasn't until Dahlia repeated her question that Sybil realized she hadn't answered.

"Yeah, it's fine."

"So this is supposed to be a very passionate kiss. You've had feelings for each other for a long time, you're finally reunited, you've been pushing those reemerging feelings aside because of the case you're working on, but it's finally too much," Dahlia explained.

Sybil dared a glance at Peter. He was studiously listening to Dahlia's rundown of how she saw the kiss playing out, but then his eyes flicked to hers and she quickly focused back on Dahlia.

"Boundaries are very important so everyone feels safe and comfortable. Peter, is there anywhere you don't want to be touched?"

Peter shrugged nonchalantly. "I'm up for seeing where the mood takes us."

Dahlia looked at Sybil expectantly, waiting for her answer. What was she supposed to say? That she still had dreams about Peter's hands and the paths they'd forged across her body? That she was anxious and terrified that he still could find his way without a map—or worse, that he'd forgotten his way entirely?

Her clothes were too tight. She wanted to tear them off, run outside, and jump into the ocean. Her skin was so hot she'd sizzle when she hit the frigid waves.

"Yeah, it's, uh, fine," Sybil said. "It's just acting, right?"

"Don't be surprised if your body has a different reaction than your head," Dahlia warned. "It's not uncommon for actors to become physically aroused during intimate scenes, even when they're not emotionally aroused. Our bodies don't always listen to our brains."

Dahlia was preaching to the choir.

"I'll be on set all day if you have any questions or concerns," Dahlia promised. "If you're uncomfortable talking to each other, or to Charlotte, I am a neutral third party here to make sure everyone feels safe and heard."

"Thank you, Dahlia." Peter smiled sincerely.

"Sybil, I'm going to go hunt you down a fan." The intimacy coordinator gave a small finger wiggle wave and headed back to the mass of crew further down the hall.

"If you grab my boob, I will punch you in the throat," Sybil said.

Peter stifled a laugh by pretending it was a cough. "Didn't feel comfortable saying that in front of Dahlia?"

"I didn't think she'd approve of justified violence."

"I'm not going to maul you. It's a kiss. We're professionals."

"*You're* a professional," she reminded him. "I was in the wrong place at the wrong time."

"Why does it feel like you're going to blame this on me?"

"Because it is your fault. If I hadn't been dropping off your stupid estimate for the stupid coffee cart, your mother never would've realized I look a little bit like Madelyn Penn and I'd be at work right now instead of playing dress up in front of"—Sybil tried to get a headcount of the crew in the hall but gave up—"too many people. I don't even understand what I'm supposed to be doing. Do I stand there while you talk at me?"

Peter put his hands on her shoulders, and the tornado of terror swirling inside of her slowed to a sedate dust devil. "It's a lot like how you used to help me rehearse. You're going to do great. The camera will be focused on me. They might catch some of the back of your head." He gently tugged her left ear lobe. "Maybe your ear will be famous."

"I don't want to be famous," she said in a voice just above a whisper.

A few feet away, a PA cleared her throat. "They're, um, ready for you."

Any calmness Sybil had achieved vanished. Peter squeezed her shoulders.

"You're going to be fine," he promised.

"I'm not. But I'll get through it."

Inside the hotel room they were filming in, they got a brief rundown of what they'd be shooting, while at the same time someone else pointed a light meter at her face, and a PA—they were all blending together now—put some papers in her hands.

"Those are your sides. We highlighted the lines you need to read. Look over those real fast, and then we'll get rolling," Charlotte said. "And Sybil, you don't need to give an award-winning performance, but a little oomph when reading helps your scene partner a lot."

Sybil's head swam with all of the directions she'd received. Could she get fired on the first day? *They should have hired a real actor for this*, she thought, then remembered technically they had, but were making do with her.

Her next self-pitying musing about why they couldn't just wait for Madelyn to feel better to get started soon became clear to her. Charlotte's version of "real fast" was another fifteen minutes for everything to get adjusted. Multiply this by however many scenes they had to shoot, and she could see how waiting around for Madelyn wasn't going to work.

Then it was time for her to open the door to let Peter in so they could start the scene. Except when she opened the door, she didn't let in Peter. She let in Glenn, a detective with the sheriff's department of a rural county. The transformation was jarring. But Peter had been right: it was a lot like helping him prepare for auditions, except she had to move around the room instead of laying on the bed reading lines while he did all the actual work. He'd been so good back then, in his small bedroom in his dingy flat that he shared with a few of his mates, but now he was incredible. She didn't know how he remembered the little adjustments Charlotte made to his performance, how he managed to repeat his performance exactly for every take after they'd repositioned the camera, but he did.

It cracked her heart right down the center, but they'd made the right choice to break up. Peter never could have done this if they'd stayed together. That wide-eyed hopeless romantic in him would have prioritized her over his career. He'd have passed on opportunities because it interfered with her birthday or their anniversary. She never could have survived in LA or New York, where he could find work as an actor, and he'd have withered and died in Crane Cove, resenting her a little more every year for not wanting to live anywhere else.

"Cut!" Charlotte shouted from her chair in the hallway.

The mask fell, and Peter was Peter again.

"You're doing great." He'd told her that after almost every take.

Charlotte poked her head into the room. "Madelyn's here, so Sybil, you can go have a seat. Peter, we're going to shoot her sides and then hustle into the kiss before we break for lunch."

He nodded. "Sounds good."

Sybil slipped out of the room and down to the empty chairs reserved for Madelyn and Peter. Madelyn was seated in her chair getting a last-minute touch up from one of the makeup artists.

"How did it go?" she asked, glancing at Sybil as she got her under eyes powdered.

Sybil picked up her book and sat in Peter's chair. "It was fine, I think?"

"I know it's your job, but thank you for being here." Madelyn fumbled blindly for Sybil's hand, and squeezed her forearm instead. "I appreciate it."

Sybil didn't know what to say. It was her job, technically, though two hundred and fifty dollars didn't feel like enough money anymore. It had been hours, and they'd produced maybe one half of five minutes of film.

"You're welcome."

The makeup artist finished with Madelyn, and then Sybil was alone. No one cared that she was there, but she wasn't allowed to leave yet. So she read the book Peter had handed her. Or tried to read it. She couldn't see what was happening in the room, but she could hear Madelyn and Peter delivering their lines. They sounded spectacular. She could imagine the emotions playing across their faces from just their voices. It was a good thing she wasn't an actress or she'd have developed a complex.

"Let's get this kiss in and then we can go to lunch," Charlotte hollered from her chair. "Quiet on set!"

Peter was outside the door again. Sybil's stomach twisted sharply. He was going to kiss Madelyn like he meant it. Logically she understood it was his job, and Dahlia had said they were professionals and it didn't mean anything, but she'd also said that arousal happened. There was an immense amount of pressure on her sternum and Sybil couldn't breathe right. A selection of her worst imaginings from the last twelve years paraded through her mind. Peter kissing other people. Peter undressing someone else. Peter in bed with other people, making them buck, and writhe, and whine like she did back when she was his. Bile rose in her throat when Peter began to deliver his lines of longing and regret, and she shut her eyes tightly so she couldn't possibly accidentally glimpse—

The sound of Madelyn puking might as well have been music to her ears.

"Cut," Charlotte groaned. "I need air freshener, a glass of water, and someone to take Madelyn back to her room." She took off her glasses and rubbed her eyes. "Sybil, you're back in."

Sybil jumped to her feet, dropped the book she'd barely opened on the chair, and was down the hall in a flash. Hair, makeup, and wardrobe appeared like fairy godmothers to give her a quick once-over while the crew reset. Peter lingered in the doorway, glancing between her and Madelyn, who refused to go back to her room and stood behind Charlotte's chair, sipping delicately at a bottle of water.

The helpers vanished as quickly as they'd appeared, and then Charlotte was in the doorway with Peter.

"Sybil, you'll start behind the camera back by the desk, and then answer the door after he knocks. He's going to say some stuff, the kiss cue is going to be 'please.' Are you good? Are you ready?"

Sybil nodded. "Let's get this over with."

"Quiet on set!" Charlotte bellowed as she hustled back to her seat behind the monitors.

Sybil went to her spot by the desk, and the door to the hallway was shut. Charlotte's next set of commands were muffled, partly by the door and mostly because her pulse was pounding in her ears.

"Action!"

Even though she was expecting it, the knock at the door made her jump. She concentrated hard to keep her steps slow and even because her first instinct was to run to the door to get this over with before she lost her nerve. Her palm slipped on the door handle, but she managed to cover that up by looking through the peephole. She opened the door, and there was Peter as Glenn, looking tortured and wretched, visibly struggling with his inner turmoil.

"Did you forget something?"

"I didn't come here to talk to you about the case, Honor.

That was just an excuse. I came here because—" He gave a small, uncomfortable, rueful chuckle, his eyes following the line of the doorframe. "I've never stopped thinking about you. I've never stopped *wanting* you, Honor. I know you don't want me or this town or the life we almost had, but my heart doesn't understand what my brain knows. I can't sleep because I know you're close and I'm not with you. I don't think I can keep doing this—being so close to you and not being able to touch you. It's fucking torture. I couldn't go another minute without you knowing that it kills me to pretend that I don't want you on the off chance that you want me, too."

Reality and fiction blurred because the pain in his eyes crushed her soul. The hope that lingered in the shadows breathed life back into her.

"Say something. Please."

"Fuck it." She grabbed the collar of the white cotton undershirt under his flannel and twisted the material around her fist, pulling him to her. She didn't know who kissed who first, but when their lips met it was like dropping a match into a pile of fireworks that had been doused in gasoline. Her world exploded and heat consumed her body. She didn't dare release her grip on his shirt, but her other hand gripped the hair on the back of his head, and she felt the rumble of approval against her lips.

And then she tried to gasp for air and Peter's tongue slipped into her mouth and slid against her tongue and Sybil lost whatever sense she had left. One of his hands cradled her cheek, his long fingers burying themselves in her hair, and his other hand trailed down her spine to the curve of her ass and pulled her flush against him.

She caught his bottom lip between her teeth and drank in his full-body shudder like top-shelf liquor. Peter plunged his tongue into her mouth once more and then broke away, leaving her breathless and reeling. She put up no resistance when he backed her into the wall and then scraped his teeth against her neck like he meant to bite her. Her pussy clenched uselessly around nothing, and she would have begged for some relief if she had the ability to marshal her brain cells into any semblance of order to make speech possible.

Then his hands were on the backs of her thighs and he lifted her enough so she could wrap her legs around his waist. He kissed her again, lips warm and firm. She shifted and his belt rubbed against her clit, but he swallowed her gasp.

Something hard and cold hit his side and bounced off her thigh. They both started, mouths breaking apart, and her legs reflexively tightened around his waist. Peter's pupils were blown so wide he looked like he was high. Sybil looked down to see what had hit them.

It was a water bottle.

"I said cut!" Charlotte shouted from the doorway. Sybil hadn't heard her open the door. Dahlia stood behind her, eyes wide with surprise. Charlotte looked at her. "What exactly did you tell them to do?"

Chapter Thirteen

"I heard you almost had your mother making a very different kind of film today." Arthur fell into step with Peter as they made their way to the elevator. "I got a peek at the dailies. That kiss might skew the MPAA rating."

Peter sighed and pushed the down button with his thumb. He'd gotten variations on his father's comments all day from anyone who had been on set to witness his kiss with Sybil. Especially from Madelyn, who was finally able to work in the afternoon.

"Not a lot of gusto there, sport," she'd teased after their kiss. *"Use up all your energy this morning?"*

It was all in good fun and he was used to it, but Sybil wasn't, and the second she got the go ahead to leave, she was out of there so fast she left smoke trails. They hadn't gotten a chance to talk about it. He needed to talk about it.

He hadn't been prepared for that kiss. Peter had imagined a kiss that started slow and built in passion as it went on. He hadn't planned on her grabbing his shirt and pulling him to her. "Fuck it" wasn't even in the script. That kiss wasn't a slow burn, it had been a wildfire, and she'd charred him to a crisp. If his mother hadn't thrown that water bottle...

"We got told to go for it, so we went for it," Peter explained.

He'd never lost his head like that before at work. Peter prided himself on always being professional, always being in control of himself, especially in intimate situations. But as soon as their lips had touched, the rest of the world ceased to exist.

Nothing had changed there.

The elevator announced its arrival with a ding, and Peter and Arthur stepped inside.

"Where are you off to this evening?" his dad asked, pushing the button for the lobby.

"Graham's house. He promised me takeout and a decent enough glass of wine. You?"

"There's supposedly a stunning little restaurant in another little town called Salty—isn't that so charming?—and I'm taking your mother there for a romantic night to celebrate a successful first day of filming and narrowly avoiding becoming an adult entertainment director."

"It wasn't *that* bad," Peter insisted, and Arthur snorted his dissent.

The elevator slowed to a halt and dinged. The doors slid open to the lobby.

"I've spent a lot of time with Sybil since we've been here," Arthur said as he stepped out of the elevator. "Remarkable young woman. Strong, independent, cutting sense of humor. I felt like I'd known her for a long time when we met. It's a miracle and a tragedy that she's still single."

"She's...something," Peter said in a vain attempt to be evasive. There was a suspicious twinkle in his father's eyes that sent a shiver of cold dread down his spine.

Arthur smiled fondly. "Yes, she is. Now I suggest you scurry out of here before your mother leaves her production meeting and starts interrogating you about that kiss."

Peter took his father's advice and hightailed it to his rental car, running through the parking lot as rain pelted him. His zip-up hoodie was uncomfortably damp by the time he turned on the engine.

The great part about a small town like Crane Cove was that it was almost impossible to get lost. If he missed a turn, it didn't take too long to realize it, and there were only so many directions to go. Peter had a feeling he'd be able to get from the hotel to Graham's house with no problems in about a week.

The rain had graciously subsided to a drizzle, but he still bounded up the front walkway like he might melt if he got too wet. Peter opened the front door and went inside.

"Honey, I'm home!" he called, his voice carrying in the foyer.

Eloise appeared in the entrance to the front living room with a large glass of red wine in her hand. When he'd met her, he'd told her that she and Graham were going to make beautiful babies. In a different century, she would have been an artist's muse with her thick, brown curls and big blue eyes.

"Hey, Peter. Graham went to go get pizzas. Do you want to have a glass of wine with us until he gets home? We're just drinking and complaining about our days."

"I could absolutely use a glass of wine." He took off his shoes and placed them carefully on the shoe rack. When he'd lived with Graham they'd had a similar shoe storage system by the door, but his shoes never found their way in that one. He liked Eloise enough to make the effort here. "Who is we?"

"Connor and Sybil," Eloise answered as they entered the living room. Connor overwhelmed an armchair and Sybil was on the couch with her feet tucked under a blanket and his red sweater wrapped around her body. Their eyes met, but Sybil quickly looked away, her cheeks flushing. She drained her wine glass and reached for a bottle on the coffee table.

"It's Monday night. We drink wine and whine about our weeks. Do you want red or white?" Eloise asked.

"Either is fine."

Eloise went to find him a wine glass, and an awkward silence choked the room like smoke. Sybil wouldn't look at him, and he was avoiding eye contact with Connor, though he could feel the other man glaring at him.

Peter rocked back on his heels, then up on the balls of his feet. "So..."

"So...fancy seeing you here," Connor said, his tone bordering on hostile, right on the edge of plausible deniability. Sybil shot him a warning look.

"Just waiting on Graham," Peter assured him and took a seat on the couch next to Sybil. "How's the school year going so far? It's cross-country season, right?"

Peter couldn't remember where he put his keys most of the time, but he did have an uncanny knack for remembering details about people. Connor taught high school English and coached long-distance runners. He was also so anal-retentive about baking that Sam, an infamous kitchen hog, would actually let him help cook.

"The only thing my students care about right now is home-coming," Connor answered. "It now takes an entire Broadway production to ask someone to a dance, so if I can cobble together twenty minutes of their attention in a fifty-minute period, I'm having a good day."

"Nice to know the grand gesture isn't dead yet," Peter said, which earned him an obvious glare from Connor. Instead of letting the subject drop, he carried on. "I mean, we complain about how kids today are lazy and unmotivated, but when they do get excited about something, we put it down and say it's stupid. And some of it is, undeniably, stupid, but the creative spark is there. It needs to be channeled."

"Well if you ever want to come teach, the school district is always looking for subs." It wasn't a nice offer. It was a thinly veiled "I'd-like-to-see-you-do-better."

Sybil was doing her best to make it to the bottom of her wine glass, and Peter wished he had one of his own so he had something to put in his mouth besides his foot. It was clear enough that Connor didn't like him, and though he didn't know why, he did know that he needed the big blond grump on his side if he wanted to get Sybil back. If her best friend didn't like him, he didn't stand a chance.

Mercifully, the front door opened and Graham came inside carrying two pizza boxes stacked on top of each other.

"Peter!" He smiled, surprised. "You're early for once."

"Am I?"

Next to him, Sybil stifled a laugh. If only she knew all the things he'd do to make her laugh. He'd become a clown and throw a pie in his own face to get a giggle.

"Oh thank god, you have food." Eloise intercepted Graham in the hallway and took a pizza box from him. She came into the living room, handed Peter a wine glass, and put the pizza on the coffee table. She started to open the lid, then hesitated, looking between Graham and Peter. "Um...did you two want to join us?"

It was an offer she wanted turned down, so Peter gave up his precious spot and stood.

"No. Graham promised me boy talk. Gotta dish about cars and sports."

Graham frowned. "Neither of us cares about cars, and all the cares we gave about sports retired with Jordy."

Peter shrugged. "So we'll talk about action movies using monosyllabic words."

"Don't ever play Scrabble with him," Graham warned. "He acts like an idiot, but he's got an overinflated vocabulary."

"Doesn't mean he can spell," Connor stage-whispered to Sybil.

"Is pizza allowed in the breakfast nook?" Peter asked, choosing to ignore the comment.

"Pizza is an any time of the day food, so yes," Graham answered, took two steps down the hall, then stopped and looked at Sybil. "Do you know when Mallory is coming home? We could use her at the bar. The movie people drink. A lot."

"No clue," Sybil said. "She doesn't give me an itinerary."

"Can you call her?"

"I am not your secretary. If you want Mallory to come home, you call her and ask."

"Fine," Graham grumbled, and it was Peter's turn to stifle a laugh as they walked to the back of the house.

The wine Graham had paired with their pepperoni and olive pizza was divine. Peter wanted to drink it straight from the bottle and not share.

"How was your first day of work?" Graham asked, grating fresh parmesan cheese over the slices he'd put on his plate.

"Not bad. Long, but not bad," he replied, and took a bite of his pizza. The salt and fat kissed his taste buds, and he moaned. "I love pizza."

"Long but not bad," Graham repeated suspiciously. "I've never gotten less than a ten-minute answer when I risked asking you about your day, and when I'm genuinely interested I get 'long but not bad'?"

"It was..." Peter searched for something non-incriminating to talk about, but the only part of his workday his brain recalled was kissing Sybil. It wasn't just the highlight of his day, it was the highlight of his decade. That kiss was better than any award he'd won or role he'd landed. But if he talked about it, he'd gush, and gushing was a slippery slope to telling Graham everything Sybil wanted kept secret. "A day."

"What was it like working with Sybil?"

"She did a good job," Peter answered diplomatically. "Very good at following directions."

"Good kisser?"

"Very— How'd you find out about that?"

"Your gossips talked to my gossips, and my gossips talk to Kiki, who reports to me." Graham grinned and wiggled his eyebrows. "I heard it was so hot the film combusted."

Peter's face got so hot he worried his hair would catch on fire. "Reports have been greatly exaggerated. It was professional."

Graham's grin grew. "So your mom didn't have to throw a water bottle at you two to get you to stop?"

"She was in the hallway. We didn't hear her yell cut. Where did you get this pizza from?" Peter closed the lid to investigate the logo.

"Didn't hear or didn't *want* to hear?"

"Is there a point to this line of interrogation, or have you become exceedingly bored by your provincial life and need to dramatize mine?"

Graham laughed so hard he wheezed, then snorted, which made him laugh more. Peter rolled his eyes and sighed.

"I'm going to the bathroom, you anthropomorphic hyena."

He pushed back from the table and headed for the first-floor powder room. The door was closed, and he stared at it for a moment, trying to remember if Graham and Eloise were a closed-door or open-door household. He reached for the handle to see if it was locked, and the door swung open.

Sybil jumped, her brown eyes wide in shock.

"Oh. Sorry." Peter sidestepped out of her path to let her pass.

Except instead of shooting him a dirty look and leaving, Sybil grabbed his wrist and pulled him into the bathroom, locking the door behind them.

"We need to talk," she whispered, crossing her arms.

He tried to figure out what she meant by her tone and body language, but came up with a few too many possible answers to safely guess. So, he went with an old improv standby. "Yes, we do."

When in doubt, say yes.

"Look, this"—she gestured between them emphatically—"cannot happen. It *won't* happen again. You're you and I'm me, and we don't work. But...maybe I didn't hate kissing you today."

Peter squeezed his eyes shut and opened them quickly. No, he wasn't dreaming. If this had been one of his vivid fantasies, Sybil would be miraculously naked.

"And maybe"—her cheeks were a shade of red somewhere between her hair and his sweater—"I wouldn't hate doing it again on a strictly casual basis."

A strictly casual basis wasn't what he wanted, but it was a starting point. It got his foot in the door, which was more than he'd had that morning.

"For the record, I'm not objecting, but why?"

Curse his mouth for opening before his brain could take control. Never look a gift horse in the mouth. Don't ask questions, just say yes please and thank you very much.

Sybil became very interested in her socks. "Because I think I've mythologized you in my mind. Made you into something you can't possibly have ever been. I need proof you're just a man so I can stop wondering what I'm missing out on. So, casual."

"What does casual look like to you?" he asked, not adding that his version of casual included not so casually marrying her.

"We fool around while you're here filming and then we cut it off. A clean break this time with no stupid plans or promises."

There was a distinct irascibility to the latter portion. "We never tell anyone because no one needs to know."

"You want me to be your dirty little secret?"

Curse his fool mouth.

Sybil's eyes flicked to his groin. "I wouldn't say little, but yes. You'll be my secret and I'll be yours, and we'll take this to our graves."

There was something undeniably poetic about that. Not the reference to his penis, which became rapidly engorged as soon as fooling around had been suggested, but the secrecy and graves. Peter filed the thought away to text Sam later, in case he could use it for a song.

"How exactly are we supposed to sneak around if Connor is staying at your house?"

She frowned in confusion and then rolled her eyes. "He's not. He just doesn't trust you and wanted to scare you off. Thinks you're up to no good."

"If you get your way, I won't be up to any good." He put his hands on her waist and brought her close. "Do I have to climb in through the window, or am I allowed to use the front door?"

She touched his chest and goosebumps erupted all over his skin. "The tree *is* right by my window," she mused, her hands sliding up to his shoulders.

"I would've scaled the drainpipe."

She wrapped a hand around the back of his neck and pulled his face down to hers. The first brush of her lips was electric and sent sparks down his spine. He'd missed her lips, so soft and warm, yet always insistent and eager, like kissing was a battle she could win. Her tongue gingerly caressed his bottom lip, and he opened to her sweet invasion.

Peter lost all sense of time while they kissed. What else mattered? Nothing. Just her. Always only her.

Sybil melted against him with a soft sigh, her hold on the

back of his neck still iron, like she was afraid he might possibly pull away. There was zero chance of that ever happening, but he wasn't going to tell her that because he liked her clutching at him, holding him, wanting him maybe half as much as he wanted her.

His cock was a hard, insistent rod against his thigh, fighting to break free of his jeans. The pressure was building, and he clenched, trying to hold back. He couldn't come in his pants. It was the epitome of embarrassing in adolescence when it was more acceptable, but after thirty?

She sucked on his tongue gently and it was over. He'd have had better luck stopping a bullet train with his pinky finger. A shudder wracked his body, and he whimpered into her mouth. The relief of release was awkwardly coupled with panic at how he'd hide the evidence. Already the hot, viscous liquid was trailing down his leg.

"Peter?" Graham knocked on the door. "Are you okay?"

Sybil jumped back abruptly like Graham could see her through the door.

Peter took a breath and called back, "You know how I like cheese, but cheese doesn't always like me? I'd back away while you still can."

Sybil pursed her lips to keep from laughing, and he shrugged sheepishly.

"Use the air freshener."

There was a breathless thirty seconds while they waited for him to go away, then she whispered, "You should probably get out of here."

"Um..." Peter was scared to move. Nothing had soaked through his pants yet, or ended up any further down than his knee, but if he so much as sneezed it could be a different story. "I still need to go to the bathroom."

"Sybil?" This time it was Eloise delicately knocking at the

door. Peter looked up at the ceiling in dismay. "Are you okay? You've been in there a while."

Her eyes grew wide with panic. "I, uh, had to poop. A lot."

"Oh god." Eloise sounded concerned and sympathetic. "Do you need anything?"

"Some privacy. I'm almost done."

"I'll grab you some Pepto from upstairs," Eloise said and another thirty-second silence ensued while they waited to be sure she was gone.

Sybil let out the breath she'd been holding. "That was too close. We can't do this where we'll get caught."

"Do you want me to come over when I'm done here?"

She shook her head. "No. I have to go to bed when I get home. I've got an early morning."

"I could go to bed with you," he offered.

"I need to *sleep*, Peter."

"Fine," he acquiesced. "I'll see you tomorrow?"   .

"Whether I like it or not." She checked her appearance in the mirror before sliding around him to get to the door. "I'll bring the invoice for the coffee cart tomorrow."

"Hey." He put his hand over hers on the doorknob, and she looked at him quizzically. "I still love you."

Any warmth in her brown eyes disappeared. "I know," she answered softly, then carefully exited the bathroom.

It wasn't as bad as it could have been. She didn't tell him to go to hell or call off their arrangement. But it wasn't "I still love you too."

Peter looked down at his pants. How was he going to clean himself up without making a bigger mess?

Chapter Fourteen
Twelve Years Ago, London

PETER'S FINGERS followed the length of her spine from neck to tailbone while he kissed her bare shoulder, his eyes drinking her in, half hooded with languid satisfaction.

Peter had no problem being naked, though if Sybil looked like he did, she wouldn't have a problem being naked, either. She could see the places where he was still exiting the lankiness of his boyhood and entering the lean musculature of manhood. It was like seeing one of the great marble statues while it was still being carved, and she wished they had more time for her to see the rest of the transformation.

"You're so beautiful," he murmured, his voice prayer quiet.

Sybil rolled her eyes, hoping the act of nonchalance would balance out the hot blush spreading from her face to her chest.

"You're only saying that because I have sex with you."

He brushed a few sweaty curls away from her temple. "No, I really mean it. You look like you stepped out of a Rococo painting."

"Putting that art museum date to good use."

"What was it you said? Free is more fun?" He grinned at

her, quiet laughter making his blue eyes sparkle. "I feel like the luckiest guy in the world that I get to be with you."

Sybil pulled the sheets up and held them tightly to her chest. "I dare you to say that again now that my tits are covered."

"Sybil..." Peter growled playfully and curled an arm around her waist, pulling her against him. His skin was warm, soft, and a little sticky from drying sweat. They should shower, but the bed was too beguiling. "You're the most beautiful thing I've ever seen. And I can't even see your tits right now."

"But your hand is on my ass," she pointed out, and he groaned and flopped onto his back dramatically.

"What is it going to take for you to accept a compliment?"

"Some originality."

Peter sighed, then rolled back onto his side so he could look at her again. He touched her cheek, caressing her skin with his thumb, then slid his fingers down to her shoulder, following the curve down the length of her arm.

"I love your freckles. They remind me of spending summers at our house in the Cotswolds when I'd lay outside at night, the grass tickling my skin and the earth still warm from the sun, and I'd look up at the night sky in wonder, unable to fathom the beauty of the stars. Because these"—he linked their fingers and moved her arm so they could both look at it—"remind me of those stars. You're covered in stardust, Sybil, and I cannot comprehend how I got so lucky to hold a galaxy in my arms."

There wasn't enough space in her ribs for her heart. It grew too fast and threatened to break her open. She couldn't understand how anyone who looked like Peter, so classically and unnaturally beautiful, would say anything so wonderful and sincere about *her*. Not only did he say nice things, but he was so kind and generous. He remembered the things she said and cared when she talked. Sybil wanted to let herself fall into his love, but she kept waiting for the other shoe to drop. It wasn't fair that his biggest fault was living on the wrong continent.

"You can't say shit like that. You're going to make me fall in love with you."

"That's the point."

Chapter Fifteen
Crane Cove, Oregon

THE CALL that the production schedule had shifted for the day came five minutes before Sybil's alarm went off. Apparently the weather wouldn't be sufficiently gloomy or drizzly enough to film until the afternoon.

So, until her noon call time, she spent the insufficiently gloomy and drizzly morning at Stardust, helping with the morning rush and catching up on administrative tasks. It was relaxing to be back in the chaos of the coffee shop, a place where she knew who she was and what she was supposed to do. No one paid her a lot of attention behind the bar and she liked it that way.

During the mid-morning dead time, she sent both her baristas off on their breaks because she missed the peace and quiet she normally had. Any other week, she would have been the only one on duty anyway, because the second opener would have left and the afternoon shift wouldn't have arrived yet.

The damn movie had her turned upside down and around.

At least one thing remained consistent: her flower delivery. This week's arrangement was gothic, with burgundy, purple, and even black flowers in a black vase. The note read: *Casual* –

PAPG. She'd rolled her eyes, smiled, and tucked the note into her pocket before anyone else saw it.

Sybil was doing inventory when the bell above the front door jingled. The supply order would have to wait another ten minutes.

The person contemplating the menu had to be from the movie. They were too confident to be a tourist, and they definitely weren't a local. She knew practically everyone in Crane Cove, and if she didn't know them, she'd at least seen them around. And she'd have remembered someone who dressed like they'd time-traveled out of the '90s grunge scene in Seattle.

"Do you know what you want to order?" Sybil asked, setting her clipboard down next to the till before picking up the marker they used to write on cups.

They sighed heavily. "Yeah. It's kind of a big order. Do you have drink carriers?"

Sybil kicked herself internally for sending both baristas on break at the same time. "Be pretty stupid if we didn't."

"Perfect. Can I get a quad-shot iced dirty chai, a big black coffee, a large iced decaf soy sugar-free caramel macchiato, a flat white, and"—they paused to sigh again and adopted a look of true contrition—"Peter said you'd know his order. I told him that was unlikely, so if you want to make him something truly disgusting to teach him a lesson, I'll look the other way."

"Unfortunately, I know exactly what he's talking about." Sybil wrote *Pain In The Ass* on his cup and set it to the side. She took the credit card, which belonged to Peter, and ran it. "I'll have the drinks at the end of the bar."

"Can you make the dirty chai first? It's mine, and I'm greedy."

Sybil nodded and got to work. There was a flow and a rhythm to her job, and after so many years making coffee, she had it down to an art and a science.

"Oh, so this is where the flowers go." The person at the end of the bar was admiring that week's arrangement with a smile. "I'm Dempsey. Peter's assistant. Are you the one who gets the flowers?"

For a moment, she considered lying, but then couldn't find the point.

"Believe it or not, yes." She mixed the chai, espresso, and milk. "Do you order the flowers, or does Peter order the flowers?"

"Peter does, actually. It's one of the few things I don't oversee. All I did was find him a flower shop."

Sybil put Dempsey's drink on the end of the bar. "Did he say why he needed a flower shop?"

"No, but he gets wild hares often enough that for my own sanity I don't ask too many questions unless it might be illegal or dangerous. Do you know why my boss is sending you flowers every week?"

"Because he enjoys wasting his money?"

Dempsey chuckled. "Not going to argue with you there. Did he inquire about you catering a coffee cart for the production?"

"He did. Is there a problem?" Was that why Peter had sent his assistant instead of coming himself? He'd changed his mind again and once again couldn't be bothered to tell her himself.

"No. I'm just doing what I always do and making sure he did the thing he swore up and down he was going to do. Not that he's unreliable, he's just...Peter." They shrugged and tried their coffee. Sybil watched from the corner of her eye. Someone taking their first sip of her coffee was one of her favorite things in the world. Dempsey didn't disappoint. Their eyes grew big, and they stared at the plastic cup. "Holy shit. This is incredible."

"Maybe that's why Peter sends me flowers every week."

"I might start sending you flowers every week. This is going to be so bad for Peter's wallet."

Sybil laughed. Dempsey could stick around as far as she was concerned. "If you want another one, I'll bring it to set later."

"You do delivery?"

"I'm Madelyn's double somehow. I guess we have the same ass or something?" She shrugged. "But I'll be there anyway, so I'll bring you another coffee."

"You're an angel from heaven, and I worship at your feet."

"So you know Peter pretty well," Sybil began nonchalantly, keeping her eyes on the coffee she was making so she seemed very disinterested.

"I'm going to stop you before we end up in an awkward situation," Dempsey said. "Because one, I have a signed NDA I'm not interested in breaking, and two, even if I didn't have an NDA, this job is too good to lose over gossip. So if you read it in a tabloid, it's probably false, except for that one set fire which was absolutely his fault. If the quote comes from anyone other than Peter or his rep, it's likely not true. Peter doesn't have any close sources. He's friends with everyone, but only actually close to a few people. Did that answer your question?"

The hot blush didn't creep up, it slapped her in the face. It was for the best Dempsey had cut her off. She hadn't found a tactful, non-interested way to ask if Dempsey had to oil the hinges on the revolving door to Peter's bedroom.

"Basically," she mumbled, and secured the lid to Arthur's black coffee. On a whim, she grabbed her marker and wrote his name with a little heart next to it, then put it in the carrier. "Peter's a good boss?"

"If you tell him I said this, I'll deny it, but he's the best boss." They took the full drink carrier. "I'll see you later, Sybil."

It wasn't until after they'd left that Sybil remembered she'd never told them her name.

. . .

"Cut!"

Charlotte's shout from the director's chair startled Sybil and she almost dropped her book. This had become a pattern that would have been hilarious if it was happening to anyone else.

At exactly noon, Sybil had shown up at the hotel, been fussed over by hair and makeup, stuffed into a costume, and then she'd been packed into a van and driven to a wooded area to film. Except for the original lighting adjustment, her presence had so far been superfluous. Madelyn hadn't needed her to step in, which was fine with Sybil because the fake corpse they had for the scene was terrifyingly lifelike and she didn't mind staying as far away as possible.

From her seat at the back of the pop-up tent that housed the monitors, the director's chair, chairs for the various department heads, and chairs at the very back if the principal actors wanted a seat, Sybil watched the merry band of PAs leave the tent and rush forward with umbrellas. A few of the PAs put puffy winter parkas over Peter and Madelyn's shoulders to keep them warm.

The weather was truly miserable: cold, gloomy, and drizzly. And if that hadn't been enough, there was a fog machine for extra ambiance.

She reopened the book and shifted to try and find a more comfortable position in the chair. The three pages she'd managed to read so far were very good, but between the activity on set and the small annotations Peter had written in the margins, it was taking her a lot longer than normal to make progress.

"Sybil, they need you."

"For what?" she asked, and saw Charlotte had gone out to talk to Peter and Madelyn. "Oh, right. That."

She left the book in the chair and carefully walked around

the crime scene. They'd already had to redo shots because some-one, usually a jumpsuit-clad background actor, had kicked over one of the yellow markers. She didn't want to be the cause of another slowdown.

Madelyn looked downright apologetic when she reached them.

"I'm sorry." She put a hand on her stomach. "My tummy doesn't feel very good. I just need to sit down for a little while until this passes."

Sybil shrugged. "It's fine. This is what they're paying me for."

Madelyn gave her a small, grateful smile and took the path Sybil had used back to the tents.

"Should she see a doctor? This doesn't seem normal."

Peter and Charlotte exchanged a look.

"She'll be fine," Charlotte said. "Let's get Peter's shots done while she rests. For the first one, you're going to crouch on either side of the body."

Sybil's stomach turned. "I have to go near that thing?"

"It's not real," Charlotte promised.

"Props did a great job," Peter chimed in, and Sybil narrowed her eyes at him. He grinned.

Charlotte left to go tell the crew the plan, and Peter shrugged off his parka. He handed it to one of the umbrella-holding PAs, thanked them for their service, and indicated that they could leave.

"So, I'm a pain in the ass, hm?" He tried to look stern and disappointed, but the twitch in the corner of his mouth gave him away.

"What would you rather I have written? 'Smarmy bastard'? 'Attention whore'? 'Cocky asshole'?"

He pondered those suggestions with irritating calmness,

then said, "'Love of my life'? 'Light of my day'? Your phone number?"

"Places, please," Charlotte barked from the tent.

"My phone number is in the phone book," she said as they carefully made their way through the set to the body. She couldn't look at the pale, plastic corpse as she edged around it to be on the opposite side from Peter.

"I guess I'll have to find a phone book," he said and crouched down next to the body. "Is your cell number in there, too?"

Sybil crouched too, but didn't get to answer him because Charlotte began her countdown instructions and then shouted, "Action!"

Peter delivered his lines flawlessly. Or at least she thought he did. She didn't know what his lines were supposed to be, but the way he said them was captivating. Instead of looking at the body, Sybil watched his mouth. It wasn't hard to remember how his lips had felt against hers yesterday, and any anxious doubts she'd had about asking him to be casual faded away.

"Cut! Good job."

"I have another question," Peter said, standing and stretching. "Why did my dad get a heart on his cup and I didn't?"

"You have to earn the heart. Arthur has put in the hours."

"How do I put in the hours?"

The flutter in her chest was as delicate as a butterfly's wings. Hopefully he would think the blush that warmed her cheeks was from the cold air.

"Sybil, you can come out. Madelyn is coming back in."

She didn't need to be told twice. The quicker she got away from the body, the better.

"The back of your head did a great job," Madelyn told her.

"Thanks. The back of my head tries its best," Sybil replied.

Sybil spent the rest of the shoot in the chair reading Peter's book. She found a pen buried in the bottom of her purse and began to add her own annotations. Then she was packed back into a van with some other background actors and shuttled back to the hotel. She turned her costume in to wardrobe, picked up her call sheet for the next day, and groaned at the early call time. Early mornings were her stock and trade, but at least at Stardust she didn't have to interact with anyone for the first half hour.

She folded her call sheet, put it in her purse, and went outside where she wavered on the sidewalk, torn between going to her car and looking for Peter.

She wanted to ask him to come over. To spend time with her at her house, to make good on all the unspoken promises his lips had made when he kissed her. She wanted to start being casual with him. But how could she get him alone? And what if he said no? It was unlikely, but a possibility. Was having him over and luring him to her bed even a good idea?

She squeezed the book in her hands to ground herself with something solid. It gave her an idea. She went inside and marched up to the front desk.

"Hello, Kevin," she said and rummaged for the pen in her purse. She opened the book to the title page, wrote her cell phone number, and below that *Tonight?* She could let fate decide if Peter was supposed to come to her house.

"Are you defacing a book?" Kevin asked, trying to loom over the counter to get a look at what she was writing.

She closed the book. "Could you give this to Peter Green for me? It's his."

"What's Peter's?" a vaguely familiar voice asked from behind her.

Sybil turned, still holding the book, and Dempsey was behind her.

"Peter let me borrow his book. Could you give it back to him and tell him I enjoyed his annotations?"

Better to give it to Dempsey than Kevin. Kevin was a snoop and a gossip.

"Sure." They took the book. "Thanks for leaving the coffee here. I had a lot of work to catch up on, and it was the only thing that kept me going. What do I owe you?"

"That one is on the house. We can call it a book delivery fee."

"I am completely willing to exchange menial errands for caffeine." Dempsey grinned. "Also, Peter was very smug that you remembered his coffee order."

"Oh, that's easy. It's how he takes his tea."

The factoid slipped out before it even had time to register as something she shouldn't have shared. Dempsey's head tilted ever so slightly. It wasn't much of a reaction, but they probably had a lot of practice keeping a straight face around Peter. Still, it was enough that Sybil knew she'd fucked up.

The best course of action was to quickly exit stage left before she said anything else stupid.

"Well, I should go make sure my business hasn't burned down. No rest for the wicked."

Sybil took a few backwards steps, then turned and hurried out the door.

Chapter Sixteen

IT WAS the curse of his life to always be a few minutes behind Sybil.

Peter had wanted to climb into the van Sybil got in to leave the set in the woods. He'd have double buckled with her if he needed to. But his mother had requested he and Madelyn hang back and ride with her to the hotel so they could go over some notes and talk about the next day's schedule. Which was fine, the movie was his job—but it was hard not to feel like a dog watching from the window as its owner pulled out of the driveway.

When they finally got to the hotel, he hustled to wardrobe because he hoped to catch her there. But her costume had already been checked in for the day.

Her next logical destination was the production office to pick up her call sheet. So he speed-walked through the halls to see Velda and Verna, but she wasn't there. And the twist of the knife in his heart was that she'd already picked up her call sheet. Dejected and disappointed, he accepted his with a mumbled thank you and shuffled out the door.

At least they had the same call time in the morning. That

was worth the horrendously early wake-up call he'd need to schedule.

"I was just coming to get that." Dempsey walked down the hall toward him. "I didn't think you knew where the production office was."

"You did leave me to my own devices for a week," Peter reminded them, handing over the call sheet for safe keeping. "I came dangerously close to becoming a responsible adult."

"I'll believe that when I see it. I've got your book." They held out the copy of *Night Watch* he'd loaned Sybil. "I'm supposed to tell you she's enjoyed the annotations."

He took the book, turning it over in his hands. "When did you get this?"

"A couple of minutes ago? Sybil was on her way out the door."

Peter held in a sigh. He hadn't expected her to hang around and wait for him, but hope caused heartache.

"Do you have anything else for me?" he asked.

"Nope. You are free and clear until tomorrow. Did you want to figure out your own dinner or have me send something up?"

"Could you send something up? I'm going to go sit in silence for a while."

Peter took the stairs, not in much of a mood to chat at the elevators. The book was heavy in his hand. He'd seen her reading it, but the last time he'd caught a glimpse of her, it didn't look like she was very far into the story. Why had she given it back so quickly?

He patted himself down until he found his room key, and then once he was in his room, tossed it onto the nightstand. Peter turned the water on hot, stripped down, then took an efficient shower to warm himself up and tried not to think about how much colder those outside shoots would be.

His cozy clothes, a pair of sweatpants, and a T-shirt were

still on the floor where he'd left them, and he put them back on before falling into bed.

A series of polite knocks on his door woke him up. Peter frowned, unable to remember nodding off, and groaned when the clock on the nightstand told him he'd have a very hard time falling asleep at bedtime.

He stumbled to the door, still getting his bearings back, and opened it. A uniformed hotel staff member was there.

"Room service," he said, holding out a tray.

Peter took it, thanked him, and shut the door. He wasn't particularly hungry, but he knew if he didn't eat now, his food would be cold when he was starving, and then he wouldn't want it because it was cold. So, he sat down at the desk and removed the lid.

Salmon, roasted root vegetables, and a side salad.

Very healthy, and nothing like the greasy cheeseburger and French fries he would have ordered for himself. He stabbed a few vegetables, skewered some salad, and took a bite. Absolutely delicious, and it probably wouldn't give him the same tummy trouble the cheeseburger and fries would have. This was exactly why he let Dempsey do things the way they saw fit.

As his grogginess wore off like a morning fog, the boredom crept in. He shifted in his chair. He made every possible combination of bites from the food available on his plate. He leaned back in his chair until it almost tipped over and he caught himself by the slimmest of margins. Peter looked around for something to occupy his mind before he accidentally hurt himself in his quest for stimulation.

The book he'd loaned Sybil piqued his curiosity. Why had she returned it so fast? She couldn't possibly be done, could she? When had she had time to read it all? Had she stayed up late reading in her bed, fingers lovingly caressing his scribbles in the margins?

That might be a stretch.

Peter noticed the faintest edge of something peeking out from the bottom of the book, about a quarter of the way through. Gingerly, he pinched it between his thumb and forefinger and drew it out the tiniest bit. Receipt paper. He flipped through the pages until he found the receipt.

It was an old grocery store receipt, slightly crumbled and worn, like it had taken a long ride in her purse before being repurposed as a bookmark. He studied it like an archeologist would look at a piece of pottery, searching for clues about an ancient civilization. A frozen pizza, a bag of salad, a few apples, Fresca, and, surprisingly, salt and vinegar potato chips. She hadn't liked those twelve years ago. The memory of her scrunched nose and puckered lips still popped up every time he grabbed himself a bag.

Peter was about to shut the book with more questions than answers when an annotation caught his eye. It wasn't one of his. For starters, it was in blue ink instead of black.

You would think this was funny

Heart racing, he thumbed through the earlier pages. She'd been responding to his annotations. And Dempsey had said something about the annotations when they'd handed him the book. What clue was he supposed to be finding?

Dinner forgotten, Peter poured over small notes in the margins, desperately searching for whatever it was Sybil wanted him to find. There were no randomly capitalized letters, no single words underlined. For a woman who'd torn through detective novels by the bucketful, she wasn't giving him anything to go on.

"Blast and damn," he muttered when he reached the first page. Maybe there wasn't anything to find.

Pages slipped from under his thumb and there it was, written in blue ink on the title page:

(541)555-3167
Tonight!

Peter jumped up. Somewhere in the world, someone had just won a life-changing sum of money, and they weren't even half as elated as he was to see those ten numbers and seven letters.

His feet had him to the door before his brain chimed in that shoes were a necessity, as were car keys and maybe a jacket. And while his brain had control, it took the opportunity to remind him that it had been twelve long years since he'd been intimate with someone in a non-simulated situation, and that he'd come in his pants just from kissing her.

He sat on the foot of his bed, overwhelmed with thoughts and scenarios, all of them ending in horrifically embarrassing ways where Sybil never wanted to see him again, let alone let him worship her body. He didn't know if he wanted to talk to empty his brain or if he wanted advice, but he needed someone who was a good listener and knew a lot about sex.

He needed Sam.

Sam picked up on the fourth ring. "Hey, what's up?"

Peter took a deep breath and forced himself to speak calmly. "Remember last year when we were having brunch and I told you that thing?"

Silence resonated on the other end of the call, and then, "Peter, you tell me a lot of things. You're going to need to be way more specific."

He cringed. "About how I haven't had sex in a really long time and I'm worried I'll be awful at it."

"Oh! That." Sam chuckled in a relaxed, good-natured way that put Peter's teeth on edge. "Are you still working on reconnecting?"

"She invited me over and I have no idea what she's expecting. The last time we kissed I might have gotten a little overexcited and..." He trailed off, unable to bring himself to admit what had happened.

Unfortunately, Sam could fill in the blanks. "Oh no. How did she react?"

"I don't think she noticed. She left shortly after it happened."

"So what kind of advice are you looking for? Because if you're worried about finishing before the party starts, you've got options," Sam said. "You could jack off before you go over there, recite one of your plays in your head, relive all of your cringiest moments, but my personal favorite when I'm concerned about premature ejaculation is to focus a lot on my partner and make sure they've gotten off at least once before they reciprocate. Is that what you're worried about?"

Peter flopped back on the bed and ran a hand down his face. "Kind of? I'm worried if I disappoint her, she'll never give me another chance."

Another moment of silence, and then Sam asked, "Is she, by any chance, a certain redhead we both know and slightly fear?"

"I'm not afraid of her and I don't see how that's relevant to this conversation," Peter answered.

Sam snorted. "Look, whoever she is, you didn't disappoint her before. Allegedly. So there's no reason to believe that you're going to disappoint her this time. And, unfortunately, you're never going to know unless you get off your ass and go over there. If you were giving me advice, what would you say?"

"That the kind of chemistry you shared doesn't diminish

over time," Peter grumbled. "That if she's worth having, she'll be understanding if things don't go perfectly."

"Do you feel any better?"

"No."

"Great. Go get her, champ."

Peter frowned. "What an inspiring pep talk."

"You don't need a pep talk. You need to get your ass over to her house before she thinks you're not coming," Sam said.

They said their usual goodbye, with Peter requesting his love be passed along to Sam's wife Lacey and their dog Daisy, and then he was alone with his thoughts again. He didn't feel particularly lighter, happier, or more confident, but Sam was right: he needed to get over there before Sybil thought he wasn't coming.

With clumsy thumbs he added her number to his contacts. It was strange to finally see her name in his phone after all these years. He'd wanted it there for so long, and there it was, waiting for him to use it.

PETER

I found your number, clever girl. If you still want me, I can be over any time.

A watched pot never boiled, but that didn't stop him from staring at his phone until those three dots appeared, signaling that she was typing.

SYBIL

You're a terrible detective. I thought you would have figured it out hours ago.

I'm leaving Stardust. Be at my house in fifteen minutes? Park down the street so no one sees your car.

Putting on my shoes. See you soon.

Reinvigorated, Peter sprung out of bed and wandered around his room to find where he'd taken off his shoes. There was no point in changing out of his sweats; it was late and his clothes weren't going to impress her anyway. But if they were really going to sneak around, a dark hoodie and a hat wouldn't be out of place. The less recognizable he was, the better.

How long did it take to get to Sybil's house from the hotel? More than fifteen minutes? Less than fifteen minutes? If he left now and it only took ten minutes, would she be mad that he was early?

All of his worrying was moot because first he needed to find his keys.

Chapter Seventeen

Sʏʙɪʟ sʜᴏᴠᴇᴅ her phone in her back pocket and peeked out the backdoor of Stardust. The black-and-white cat had been eating from the bowl she'd put out, but darted back behind the dumpster when the door creaked. She shut the door and locked it. She might not be any good at catching cats, but she'd managed to lure Peter to her house. Except that was hardly an accomplishment. If she'd blinked "house" to him in Morse code, he would have shown up on her doorstep.

As she locked up for the night, she wracked her brain trying to remember the state of her house. She wasn't a messy person, but she hadn't had a lot of free time to clean lately. Would he care? Did it matter? Could she shove him upstairs so he wouldn't notice the dishes in the sink? When had she last done laundry? Was her hamper overflowing?

The butterflies in her stomach raced back and forth as she speed-walked to her car. Maybe she should have told him more than fifteen minutes.

Her hand froze as she put the key in the ignition.

When had she last shaved her legs?

Sybil cursed under her breath as her car rumbled to life. Too late now. Of course there was always the chance she was putting the horse before the cart. Maybe Peter didn't want to fuck. Maybe he wanted to talk instead.

The thought made her shudder. She didn't want to talk. The entire point of casual was *not* talking.

Crane Cove had sparse traffic during the day, and at night the streets were empty. It helped that a larger-than-the-nation-wide-average number of residents couldn't drive after dark. So Sybil let her foot rest heavily on the gas, confidently rolled through stop signs, and made it to her street in record time.

She slowed to a crawl after she made her turn because something was wrong. Sure, she couldn't remember if she'd washed her sheets in the last two weeks, but she did know she hadn't left the TV on because she rarely used it. There was no reason the screen should be lighting up her front window.

Did she have a very bold burglar?

No, she had a sister who came home with no warning at the most inconvenient time. Mallory's car was parked in the driveway, so she had to park on the street next to the mailbox.

"Shit, shit, shit, shit," Sybil cursed, digging through her purse for her phone, then emptying the contents on her passenger seat before she remembered it was in her pocket. If Mallory was home, she couldn't have Peter over. Depending on her level of jet lag, Mallory wouldn't go to sleep for hours, so Sybil couldn't even postpone the visit.

She hoped like hell he hadn't left the hotel yet.

SYBIL

Abort. Abort. Abort. Do not come.

She hit send and waited for the tiny clock below her message to turn into a check mark to confirm it had been sent.

"Please go through," she pleaded with her phone.

The clock turned into a check mark, and she sighed. Peter

was chronically late. He probably hadn't even made it to the lobby yet. As long as he was using the hotel's Wi-Fi on his phone, he should get her message before he left.

As a precaution, she copied the message and sent it three more times.

Sybil shoved everything back into her purse and slammed her car door shut. Long-simmering frustrations sparked into a blaze. Mallory got to come and go as she pleased. She never gave Sybil a heads-up about when she was coming home. Not a call, not a text, not even an email. Hell, most of the time Sybil didn't even know where in the world her sister was. Weeks or months would go by, and then one day her sister would be home. It must be nice to have no responsibilities and heaps of wasted potential. Sybil was using all of her potential, and it was exhausting.

"You parked in my spot," Sybil said as she crossed the threshold.

Mallory leaned her head over the back of the couch to look at her. "Did the extra few feet from the curb kill you?"

"Would they have killed you?" She glared at the TV. "What are you watching?"

"*My Cousin Vinny*," Mallory answered and turned her attention back to her movie. "Want to watch? I made popcorn."

Sybil didn't want to watch, but she could see the front walk from the couch, and if Peter didn't get her messages, she could hopefully intercept him before he got to the door.

"Sure." She picked a spot with a good view of the street and pretended like she was interested in the movie. Every minute or so, she'd glance out the window. No sign of Peter yet.

"Marisa Tomei won an Oscar for this," Mallory pointed out.

Sybil checked her phone. No response. Three hundred and sixty-four days of the year she loved living in a town with shitty cell phone service. Today was the exception.

"Sybil?"

Mallory's forceful tone made her head snap up.

"What?"

"I asked if you wanted some popcorn." Mallory held out the bowl.

"Oh." Sybil helped herself to a small handful. "Thanks."

They watched in silence for a few minutes. How had the bad guy from *Home Alone* landed Marisa Tomei in any universe?

"When did you get in?" Sybil asked, reaching for the bowl.

Mallory shrugged and held it out again. "About two hours ago?"

"And you didn't come find me to tell me you were home?"

"What's the point? You were going to be home soon anyway. Me being home doesn't change your life."

Except this time, it did.

Movement on the front walk caught her eye, and every curse word Sybil knew flashed through her mind. Peter, hood up and hat on, was more than halfway to the door.

"Mal, I had a really long day. Could you go get me some water?" Sybil tried to sound pathetic and it worked, because her sister paused the movie and got up.

As soon as Mallory disappeared into the kitchen, Sybil began to wave her arms, hoping the movement would get Peter's attention. If Mallory hadn't paused the movie, she could have opened the door and told him to go away.

He looked her way and her heart leapt. She had his attention. Then he gave her a crooked grin and this time her heart did a somersault. Of all the nights for Mallory to come back to town, she had to pick this one.

Sybil tried to shoo him away, but he cocked his head and frowned. Instead of retreating to the street, he came up to the bushes that were planted in front of the porch.

"Go. Away," she mouthed, and tried to wave him off. He didn't budge. But he squinted. Crap. She was backlit by the TV. Sybil tried again, this time sweeping her hand from left to right rapidly. Peter looked to the right and then walked out of her sightline.

"What are you doing?" Mallory asked.

Sybil camouflaged her startled jump by turning around on the couch. "I heard a fly. I think I got it."

"Okay, Mr. Miyagi," she said, and handed Sybil a glass of ice water. Mallory took up her former position on the couch and started the movie.

Disappointment filled every available nook and cranny inside of Sybil. So much for her night of fun. She'd text him later to explain what had happened and he'd probably understand. Peter was sweet like that.

Thump!

They both looked at the ceiling. The muffled sound had come from upstairs.

"What was that?" Mallory asked.

"Something probably fell," Sybil said and stood up. "I'll go look."

"Do you want me to come with you?"

Sybil shook her head. "No. Watch your movie."

If the new shelf she'd hung in her room, the one she'd bragged to Connor she hadn't needed his help with, had fallen off the wall, she was never going to hear the end of it. Then again, she didn't *have* to tell Connor it had fallen. But Mallory probably would. There were a lot of books on that shelf. Should she have used longer screws?

She got to the top of the stairs and heard a noise from her bedroom, like her window being closed. The hairs on her arms stood on end and her skin prickled.

Slowly, carefully, quietly, she crept down the hall.

Had she remembered to close her window before she left? She needed to install screens on the old windows before there was a repeat of the bird incident. If there was a wild animal in her room, she was calling the police. She'd had enough of being a strong, independent woman for one day.

Cautiously, Sybil wrapped her hand around her doorknob and eased the door open. Nothing scurried into the hall. She opened the door wider and saw her bookshelf was still on the wall, overburdened with books she didn't have any space for but wanted to keep. The final extension of her arm revealed the source of the noise.

Peter had his back to the door, inspecting the small collection of photos she kept by her dresser. There was one of her, Mallory, and the McMahon boys at Thanksgiving seven or eight years ago, overfilling a couch and smiling widely. A picture of her in the old Stardust Coffee cart from when she'd started the business; she was scowling because she'd told Mallory *not* to take the picture. Then there was the trio of photos from Graham and Eloise's wedding: her and Eloise, the bridesmaids plus Connor, and then the entire bridal party.

All the things she cared most about in the world, preserved on film and kept safe in frames.

"What are you doing?" she hissed, stepping inside and closing the door quietly behind her. "I said go away! Not break into my house."

Peter turned, confused instead of contrite. "I thought you wanted me to climb the tree."

"Why would I want you to climb the tree? That's so dangerous. What if the branch broke or you missed the roof and fell?" A horrible image of his broken body on her lawn flashed through her mind and a nauseating shiver ran down her spine.

"Because we talked about the tree," he reminded her. "You

were pointing to the tree so I thought this was a fantasy you wanted to act out."

Sybil groaned. "I wasn't pointing to the tree. I was trying to tell you to shoo!" She went to the window and peered out the glass. The tree looked far away and flimsy when she tried to imagine how Peter had managed to get himself onto the roof and into her window. The nausea returned, and she shook her head. "*Never* do that again. And we will *never* be charades partners."

Peter drew her back against him, his strong arms wrapped around her middle. "I'm fine," he murmured in her ear, the brim of his baseball cap bumping her face.

"And why are you dressed like a cut-rate burglar?" she bristled and pushed his hat off his head.

Peter chuckled. "They're my sneaking-around clothes. I'm trying to be stealthy."

His arms tightened around her, the pressure oddly soothing. Sybil relaxed a little.

"Why did you want me to go away? Did you change your mind?"

The tension returned twofold. It had taken him all of thirty seconds to make her forget that her sister was downstairs.

"Mallory came home unexpectedly. There's no good reason for you to be here at this time of night." She frowned. "I don't know how I'm going to sneak you out of here while she's awake."

"Then you'll have to be very"—his lips brushed her neck and her pulse jumped—"*very*" —his teeth scraped her jaw— "quiet."

A pathetic, needy whimper bubbled up and escaped as Peter slowly, torturously kissed her neck and jaw, hitting every tender spot he'd discovered ages ago. All the reasons she should say no and push him away went up in smoke and were blown away by a desperate, greedy wind.

"What makes you think I want this?" she asked while putting one of his hands on her breast and the other at the waistband of her pants. She didn't want him to stop, but she wasn't ready to beg yet.

"I can stop," he offered and tried to withdraw his hands. Hers clamped down on them and held them in place. His suppressed laugh rumbled against her back. "That's what I thought."

"Could you shut the fuck up and kiss me already?"

Peter had always taken direction well. He caught her mouth in the hungrier sequel of the kiss they'd shared on set. His tongue plunged into her mouth, stealing her appreciative moans for himself. The hand at her waistband slipped beneath the fabric, and Sybil congratulated herself on choosing comfort that morning because the lack of buttons and zippers made it easy for his fingers to explore. When the tip of his middle finger brushed her clit, a shudder like an earthquake rolled through her body. Seemingly encouraged, his hand went deeper into her pants and she tilted her hips as if it would make things easier.

"Fuck," he moaned into her mouth as he ran two fingers up and down the length of her opening, spreading around the wetness that was rapidly growing. "I missed this."

She wanted to snort. Peter had probably been up to his eyeballs in pussy the last dozen years. But any contempt died when his lubricated fingers began to rub her clit in firm circles.

Yes, she'd missed this too.

"Hey!" The exclamation came out louder than she'd intended when he withdrew his hand from her pants. Any further protest was tabled when he licked his fingers clean, his eyes fluttering closed like he was tasting decadent chocolate.

"Mmm...More."

She didn't know if it was a demand or a request, but either

way she wasn't going to argue. Sybil took his hand and tried to guide it back to her pants, but he resisted.

"No, I want to taste you direct from the source." He intertwined their fingers and squeezed. "Please."

The pleading in his blue eyes seemed like it was for something a lot deeper than sex. She needed to check her life insurance policy because he was going to make her heart explode before he left.

"Okay," she whispered and led him the few feet to her bed.

Sybil had been with men since Peter. The number was sparse, but it wasn't zero. So why did she feel like a virgin all over again, like she'd never done this before? Did she undress? Did she let him undress her? Or did she keep it business like and just take off her pants?

And did she pay any attention to his *very* obvious erection attempting to bust out through his sweatpants?

Thankfully, Peter made the choice for her. He backed her into the bed until she had no choice but to sit down, then he hooked his fingers into the waistband of her leggings.

"Lift your hips," he requested and she complied. Underwear and leggings were peeled off simultaneously and discarded off to the side.

"That's better," he sighed, sinking to the ground to kneel next to the bed. Firm but gentle hands pressed on her inner thighs and pushed her legs open wide, exposing her to him completely. "So much better."

There was very little preamble. A few perfunctory kisses to her inner thighs, then Peter began to eat her pussy with the same enthusiasm and dedication she remembered so well. He licked and sucked, paying particular attention to her clit, flicking his tongue over it in firm, quick circles, because of course he remembered exactly how she liked it. She'd have been annoyed at his perfection if he hadn't been making her feel so damn good.

So damn good, but something was missing. She needed...

Peter slid two fingers inside of her, and Sybil's arms, which she'd been using to prop herself up to watch him work his magic, lost all structural integrity. She flopped back on the bed with a strangled moan and bit the side of her hand to try and muffle a small scream as he found the really good spot inside.

It was pathetic how close she was already. Pressure built and twisted inside of her, and she wanted it to go on forever as much as she craved sweet release. One of her hands squeezed her breast, while the other tangled in Peter's hair to hold him in place. But given the blissful noises he was making, there wasn't much threat of him stopping anytime soon.

The finish line was so close she wanted to cry. It drew closer, then got a little farther away, then close again, in that frustrating ebb and flow orgasms had when she was on the precipice of one.

Almost...there...

Sybil arched her back to see if a change in position would help, and opened her eyes.

Her bedroom door was open. Mallory and Crane Cove's night watchman Willis stood there, eyes wide, mouths open in shock.

"Oh my god!"

Chapter Eighteen

"GET OUT!" Sybil shrieked.

Her knee connected solidly with Peter's temple as she scrambled to get off the bed. She slid off the side, hiding next to Peter—who was clutching his head—like it was a bedroom-set foxhole.

"Are you okay?" Mallory asked.

"Get. Out!"

The door clicked shut, and Sybil put her head in her hands and groaned.

"This can't be happening," she said into her palms.

"It's okay," Peter soothed, and squeezed her knee.

"No, it's not," she insisted. "I am not an exhibitionist. I do not have discovery fantasies. It would've been bad if it had *just* been Mallory but—" She shuddered at the memory of Willis's shocked and mortified expression. She could relate. "I may never be horny ever again."

"Were you close? Because I don't think they're coming back," Peter began, then trailed off when she glared at him. "Never mind."

She had been close. So. Very. Close.

Bone-melting embarrassment made space for fury. Why was Mallory letting a cop into her house and then barging into her room?

Sybil hunted for her leggings, and after a few frustrating, fruitless tries to put them on and getting her feet stuck, she grabbed a pair of baggy fleece pajama pants from her hamper and shoved her legs into them.

She yanked the door open and marched out. "Mallory!"

Mallory and Willis weren't loitering in the hall. Sybil raced down the stairs, skipped the last two, and skidded across the wood floor when physics worked against her.

The front door was open and Mallory had been in the process of ushering Willis out, but they both stared at her as she regained her footing and stalked toward them.

"What the actual hell?" It wasn't a question but a demand for an answer.

"There was a call—" Willis began, but Mallory cut him off.

"Edith saw someone in a hoodie and hat walk down the street, hide in our bushes, peer through the front window, then climb the tree and enter through your window. She called the cops, and Willis came to check it out. I was telling him that we'd heard something upstairs and you went to check it out when we heard you kind of scream, but it was muffled and we thought maybe you were being attacked by a burglar."

Edith Nelson was Sybil's across-the-street neighbor and Crane Cove's reigning busybody. Who needed a neighborhood watch or a security system with Edith peeking through her curtains?

"If you breathe a word of this to anyone—" Sybil pointed a menacing finger at Willis, and he held his hands up in surrender. He looked awfully scared for someone carrying a gun.

"My lips are sealed," he promised. "Can I go tell Mrs. Nelson there wasn't anything to worry about?"

"What are you going to say if she asks what *was* happening?" Sybil crossed her arms.

Willis fumbled for an answer. Mallory came to his rescue.

"Tell her it was one of the McMahon boys playing a prank," she said and put a gentle hand on Willis's back. If she hadn't been so mad, Sybil would have thought it was comical, tiny Mallory comforting the looming, giraffe-like Willis. "And that they're very sorry that they scared her. Have a good night, Willis."

Her sister nudged Willis out onto the porch and closed the door.

"You thought I was being attacked by a burglar?" Sybil asked dubiously.

"Yes, I did," Mallory said with a sigh. "You went upstairs and I didn't hear anything, and then I *did* start to hear some weird noises and I was about to go check on you when Willis showed up and said Edith had seen someone lurking and breaking in. So, yes, Sybil, I thought you were being attacked by a burglar. It never occurred to me that the burglar was after pussy and not plunder."

"Plunder? Is he supposed to be a pirate?"

"I liked the alliteration, so sue me." Mallory rolled her eyes. "Why is your paramour peeking through the panes instead of coming to the door?"

Footsteps on the stairs made them both turn their heads. Peter descended, a sheepish look on his face, and gave Mallory a small, awkward wave.

"Hey, Mallory."

Mallory's eyes widened. She looked from Peter, to Sybil, back to Peter, and then Sybil again.

So she hadn't noticed the *who*, just the *what* when she'd barged in. Sybil should've told Peter to stay put.

"You"—Mallory pointed to Sybil—"and you"—she pointed

to Peter—"are...?" She made a circle with one hand and inserted her pointer finger into the circle rapidly.

"No," Sybil said at the same time Peter said, "Yes."

"Ah. Schrödinger's hookup."

"Except the box is open and the cat is dead," Sybil said and went to the front door to open it for Peter, but she thought better of it and changed directions to head for the back door. Edith wouldn't stop snooping even if Willis gave her the all-clear. She snagged Peter's wrist as she passed him, and he followed as dutifully as a dog.

She unlocked the backdoor, wrenched it open because it stuck, and motioned for him to exit.

"Are you really kicking me out?" he asked, an amused smile gracing his gorgeous face. He stepped outside and down the first step, but stopped, turned, and added, "Your sister already knows I'm here. I could stay."

She shook her head, but followed him out to stand on the small back porch. Peter didn't loom over her so much this way, and they were nearly eye to eye.

"I am definitely not horny anymore."

"We don't have to fool around." He touched her arm, caressing her from elbow to wrist. The goosebumps that rose on her skin had nothing to do with the cold night air. "We could snuggle. Talk."

"We're not talking. We're not even fucking," she told him.

Peter smiled softly, like he knew something she didn't, then kissed her forehead, then her nose, then finally her lips. The kiss was gentle, so featherlight that her heart clutched and she instinctively pressed into him, wanting more. He cradled her face in one hand, the other held her hip, and kissed her in a deep, unhurried way that made time stretch. He'd always been good at making her feel like a precious, perfect, ephemeral yet everlong treasure. Like he couldn't believe he got to hold her, to touch her. Which was ridiculous, but she wasn't going to correct him right then when she could still taste herself on his tongue.

The sound of Willis's patrol car starting broke the spell, and Sybil pulled back.

"Okay, we're not fucking tonight," she said in a daze.

"But another time?"

"We'll see."

Peter walked backwards down the steps. "Despite how it ended, I had a great time tonight."

Sybil shook her head but couldn't help but smile. "Go back to your hotel. Make sure to stay in the shadows this time."

"Lock your window. You never know who's going to climb in."

She stood on the back porch until he rounded the corner of the house and was out of sight.

Chapter Nineteen

As INSTRUCTED, Peter had parked his car on the next street over from Sybil's to avoid being seen, though in light of recent events, it seemed pointless. All he had to show for the subterfuge was blue balls, an erection that refused to entirely deflate, and the taste of Sybil's pussy in his mouth.

That last item had been worth climbing the tree, even if upon a second, more reasonable assessment, the distance from the tree to the roof was borderline inadvisable.

Still worth it.

Tomorrow he'd work on convincing Sybil that Mallory knowing they were trying to hook up was a good thing because she was one less person they had to sneak around. A critical person too, since they lived together. Maybe he'd buy Mallory some nice, noise-canceling headphones, though if he remembered correctly, she worked at the hotel bar, the brewery, and a dive bar. Those late-night shifts could work in his favor.

Peter made it to his car without being descended upon by the neighborhood watch, vigilante senior citizens, or the Crane Cove police department. The street he'd parked on was dead quiet. No wonder the old lady across the street had been concerned. This had to be why Graham admitted to forgetting to lock his doors.

He hadn't actually been gone from the hotel for that long, but he'd still lost his prime parking spot. After circling the parking lot twice, he settled for a spot in the back corner of the lot, almost as far away from the entrance as he could get.

Still worth it.

Peter knew he should be disappointed and frustrated with how his night had gone, but there was a spring in his step as he traversed the parking lot. So much had gone *right*. They'd kissed, he'd touched her, he'd tasted her, and despite needing to recall *King Lear*, he hadn't come in his pants this time. Was there a significant amount of precum clinging to the hair on his thigh? Yes. But it wasn't a full ejaculation, and he was taking his wins where he could get them.

The lobby was empty except for a few people passing through. No one was lounging in the high-back chairs by the fire or lingering to have conversations under the gigantic showpiece chandelier. Peter tipped an invisible hat to Clarence the skeleton bellhop as he passed. The elevators were in sight, his clandestine mission nearly complete.

Kiki floated out of the manager's office and locked eyes with him.

"What are you doing out and about at this time of night?" she asked loudly so her voice carried across the lobby.

His heart rate momentarily spiked before he remembered that Kiki didn't know where he'd been or what he'd been up to, and she was just asking an innocent question. He focused on calming his breathing and smoothing his face into a neutral expression.

"Do I have a curfew?" he asked, striding over to the front desk where Kiki had set up shop for the night.

She held up a thick stack of papers. "I'm about to log all the wake-up call requests. I've seen the times. You should definitely be in bed."

"I was headed that way. I accidentally took a late nap so I haven't been very sleepy."

Kiki winced sympathetically. "I won't keep you, then. If you still can't sleep, you can call me or come back down and hang out. I'll be here all night." She gave him a jaunty two-fingered salute, which he returned.

The elevator opened moments after he pressed the call button, and once the doors slid shut, he relaxed against one of the wood-paneled walls. Not a close call at all, but his body acted like it had been. Or maybe that was all the pent-up sexual frustration simmering just under the surface of his skin.

He pressed the heel of his hand against the semi-engorged shaft of his cock. There wouldn't be any possibility of sleep until he took care of himself.

The elevator dinged its arrival to his floor, and the doors slid open. Peter reached into his pants pocket for his keycard. It wasn't there. He checked the other pocket. Nothing. The keycard wasn't in either of his sweatshirt pockets. With a heavy sigh, he pushed the button for the lobby.

"Back so soon?" Kiki asked within seconds of the elevator doors opening.

"I either lost or forgot my keycard," Peter admitted.

She unlocked a drawer, grabbed a new plastic card, and placed it on the little machine that programmed the keys.

"Can we keep this between us? There was a pool on how long it would take you to lose your first key and today wasn't my day."

"Whose day was it?"

"Graham's."

"Then we can definitely keep this between us," Peter

promised and crossed his heart before putting a finger to his lips.

New key in hand, Peter retreated to the elevators, then back to his room. It was just how he left it, which was somehow in a much greater state of disarray than he remembered, but he knew himself well enough to know that he was the culprit. He put the half-eaten dinner tray in the hall to be collected, then made an attempt at tidying the room. Dirty clothes went in a pile on the floor so he could ask Dempsey about getting them laundered, and clothes that had been worn but weren't necessarily "dirty" moved to the desk chair.

The book caught his eye, and he picked it up, thumbing through the pages. If Sybil was reading his annotations, maybe he needed to leave her more to read.

He had to search the room for a pen. The one that had been by the phone when he checked in had migrated to the TV stand; he couldn't remember why. Peter took a step toward the desk, then saw all the clothes he'd just piled onto the chair and detoured to the bed.

He laid down, propping himself into a half-sitting position with all the pillows, then tapped the pen against his lips, trying to decide what to write. Did he try to fit a dozen years of love and longing into the tight margins?

No, that was impossible. He'd need a much bigger book.

Instead, Peter scribbled small notes of adoration. *You're wonderful. You're brilliant. You're beautiful. I love you.* On the last page, he found space to write her a short love note.

He put the book aside and checked the time. Far past his bedtime and the wake-up call would come quicker than he'd like, but he was still restless, unspent energy crackling under his skin like electricity.

Peter sighed and pushed his pants down off his hips. If this didn't relax him, he was going to sneak into the kitchen and knock himself in the head with a frying pan to get some sleep.

There was a hidden folder on his phone filled with pictures of Sybil. Some were copies of Polaroids from their time in London, but most were photos from Graham and Eloise's wedding and—he was ashamed to admit this—sneaky photos he'd taken during Thanksgiving last year. If Sybil ever found this folder, she'd probably file a restraining order. He didn't necessarily need the photos because his memories were good enough, but the visual helped.

A new memory, the one of her gripping his hair and holding his face to her pussy like he'd ever make the mistake of leaving, immediately sprang to the forefront of his mind, and he settled into it. It wasn't hard to imagine what could have happened if they hadn't been interrupted. Her inner walls would have clenched around his fingers while her back arched, then he would have covered her body with his—no, he'd have liked her better on top, where he could watch her better. Sybil riding him, taking her pleasure from him.

His cock had swollen back to life and Peter worked it roughly in his fist. All the lingering desire worked in his favor. Within moments his muscles tightened and cum splashed on his T-shirt. He melted into the mattress, contentment trickling through his veins like warm honey.

Peter luxuriated in the glow of post-orgasmic bliss for a minute, then got up, carefully removed his shirt so he wouldn't end up with cum in his hair, put it in the dirty clothes pile, considered the state of his underwear and added those too, then got ready for bed.

When he finally settled into bed, he avoided looking at the clock. What he didn't know couldn't hurt him.

His wake-up call did hurt. The sharp trilling of the phone was offensive to his soul. But Kiki, doing a Boris and Natasha impression that was so bad it was good, helped soften the blow. An accidental lukewarm shower did not. It would have been nice to be awake before he'd incorrectly adjusted the water temperature, but he couldn't argue with the results.

Peter ate breakfast on autopilot, only vaguely tasting the breakfast burrito Dempsey handed him. People talked to him, he nodded, but the words didn't penetrate the fog surrounding his brain. If any of it was important, he hoped they'd told Dempsey too.

His phone buzzed once in his pocket. He took it out and the name on the screen woke him the rest of the way up.

SYBIL

Do you want coffee?

He scrambled to reply.

PETER

Yes please. Could you bring Dempsey one too?

Way ahead of you.

I want the book back. Don't forget it.

Way ahead of you.

In a miraculous turn of events, he hadn't forgotten the book in his room. At least not after he'd done a U-turn in the hallway to go back and retrieve it from his room.

"Who got you smiling like that?" Dempsey asked when they handed him his script for the day.

"No one," he lied, and put his phone face down.

"Ask Sybil to bring me a coffee."

Peter's cheeks warmed. "Is it that obvious?"

"You forget that I know everything about your life." Dempsey opened the lid on a yogurt parfait. "And I figured out she's who you've been sending flowers to this whole time. Logically, it should be her, and I'd have been mad if it wasn't."

Peter put down his breakfast burrito. He wasn't full, but he was bored with it.

"So you like her?"

Dempsey nodded. "A lot. If you weren't borderline obsessed, I'd have made a move."

"There's nothing borderline about it," Peter said. He paused a moment before adding, "Can I ask your advice?"

Dempsey grinned. "I thought you'd never ask."

He tried to pick his words carefully. "Obviously I'm enamored, but things aren't moving forward as quickly as I'd like them to. Granted, a year ago she wouldn't speak more than two words to me and those two words were 'go' and 'away,' but I feel stuck. I'm walking on eggshells, afraid that if I sneeze wrong, she's going to call it off."

"What happened?"

"I don't have a definitive answer." He sighed. "I have some theories and probable reasons, but she refuses to talk about it, so I don't know. I can't even bring it up."

Dempsey stared at him with a neutral expression on their face, like they didn't believe him.

"Peter," they said slowly, "I cannot help you if you won't tell me what happened."

"It's kind of a long story."

"Make it shorter."

If looks could kill, his glare didn't even graze Dempsey.

"We dated," he explained, "before my career got going. She

was doing a semester abroad in London, I was living in an absolutely rubbish flat with multiple roommates. The first time I saw her, I just knew. Then I had to kind of stand still long enough for her to catch up."

"I'm not seeing what the problem is," Dempsey commented.

"She couldn't stay in London forever. I got a role that required me to stay. She didn't want to do long distance so we sort of broke up."

Dempsey frowned. "Sort of broke up? You either are or you aren't. Which was it?"

"We—"

Madelyn sat down next to Peter. "Yesterday, all I wanted was oatmeal, and today I can't even look at it. It's a miracle the human race has survived this long." She eyed Dempsey's yogurt parfait. "And yogurt made me gag when I tried to eat it."

"Have you asked my mom about her pregnancy? Apparently I was a menace in the womb," Peter said.

"In the womb? I don't think anything changed upon your eviction," Dempsey countered. "What are you able to eat, Madelyn?"

"I've been craving apples and Chex Mix," she said. "Which is fine, but I need protein too."

"Peanut butter," Dempsey and Peter suggested at the same time.

"I'm allergic," Madelyn reminded them.

"I think right now whatever you can keep down is good enough," Peter said. "Have you told Kitty yet?"

She shook her head. "No. I want to be sure of what I want to do before I talk to him. Like, if I want the baby and he doesn't, I need to be prepared to be a single mother. Or if I don't and he does, I need to be firm that I'm not an incubator. I can't just go along with whatever he wants, right?"

Peter put one of his hands over hers. "Mads, you need to

talk to Kitty. The decision is ultimately yours, but I think knowing what he thinks would help you make that decision."

She nodded, but frowned. "I know, but I'm scared. What if he gets really mad and breaks up with me?"

"That's a joke, right?" Dempsey asked. "If he gets mad at you and breaks up with you because he filled you up with baby batter and didn't like that it made a cake, then he's a piece of human garbage."

Peter nodded in agreement. "So when are you going to tell him?"

Madelyn put her head in her hands and groaned. "I don't know."

Peter put a comforting hand on her back. "You're never going to know how he feels until you talk to him."

A PA came to take Madelyn to get ready for the day. As soon as she was gone, Dempsey gave him a look so pointed it hurt.

"Have you ever considered taking your own advice?" they asked. "That maybe, oh, I don't know, having the hard uncomfortable conversation might benefit you, even if you don't like the answer?"

Peter slumped in his chair and considered hiding under the table.

"Look." Dempsey moderated their tone so it was gentle. "Sybil doesn't strike me as the kind of person to lead someone on, so if she's entertaining your shenanigans, I think it's worth finding out why." They shrugged. "But what do I know? I'm just the help."

"She said she wants to keep things casual."

Dempsey cackled. "You don't have a casual bone in your body."

"Well, *she* doesn't need to know that."

"Oh, I bet she does, and she's as delusional as you are." They tittered, still amused. "What a pair."

A smart reply died on Peter's tongue when he spied red hair from the corner of his eye. Sybil had arrived, a cardboard drink carrier in her hand, and she was looking around. Then their eyes locked and her cheeks turned pink. Was she thinking about what they'd done last night? He hoped so. He wanted to do that again, minus the stuff better left to stunt people.

Sybil made her way over to them and sat down in the chair Madelyn had vacated.

"One super-caffeinated dirty chai," she said, handing it to Dempsey. "Yours." She gave Peter a hot cup with a Stardust-branded sleeve on it.

"Thank you," he said, their fingers brushing when he took the cup.

Sybil focused her attention on Dempsey, and he might have been offended, but the color in her cheeks was more vivid and that mollified him.

"Do you know if we're doing what was on the call sheet?" she asked Dempsey. "You seem like the kind of person who knows everything."

Dempsey preened. "I am, and we are. Why?"

"Because the location isn't super far from my house, so I'd like to drive myself if that's allowed."

"Wardrobe might have a problem with it—"

"It'll be fine," Peter interrupted. "Can I ride with you?"

"I guess," she said with a small, confused frown. "Dempsey, did you want a ride too?"

"No, they were going to stay behind and get caught up on some work," he interjected quickly before Dempsey had a chance to respond and ruin his rapidly forming plan. Ten minutes alone in a car with Sybil was the most privacy they were likely to get all day.

And bless Dempsey, they went along with it. "Yeah, I'm still catching up from being on vacation," they lied.

He countered the subtle narrowing of Sybil's eyes with an innocent smile.

"If you don't want to ride in whatever kind of fancy car they've got for you, I guess you can ride with me," she said.

Dempsey checked the time and pushed back their chair. "You should both go see if wardrobe is ready for you. I'll let the powers that be know that Peter is riding with you, Sybil."

Peter stood and gestured for Sybil to go first. Once they were in the hall, he handed her the book.

"Before I forget," he said.

"Did you mean to give me a book where the main character's wife is Sybil?" she asked, tucking the book into her purse.

"Not particularly. I actually forgot that was her name until I started reading."

"I'm shocked you haven't called it fate yet."

"You have to give me time. I was working up to it for dramatic effect."

"I had a good time last night," Sybil said quietly. "If you promise not to climb the tree, I might even let you come over later."

"Might?"

"Mallory gets home from work at two." She sipped her coffee casually.

They arrived at wardrobe and went their separate ways. The very possibility of being alone with Sybil in her house had his blood buzzing. It was hard to concentrate, but he kept telling himself that the quicker they got the day done, the sooner he could spend time with Sybil. So he looked over his lines, familiarizing himself with the words, while the hair and makeup team worked on him.

He waited for Sybil in the lobby, making notes in his script while sitting in one of the high back chairs. He'd look up occasionally to see if she was done yet, then back to his script when he saw she wasn't. Right around the time he'd started to get concerned that she'd left without him, he heard her voice... followed by Madelyn's.

"There you are," Madelyn said with a smile when she saw him. "We were looking for you."

It was so strange to see them side-by-side, wearing identical outfits, with identical hair and makeup. They looked like fraternal twins.

"I was waiting for you," Sybil explained, "and Madelyn offered to help me find you. She's riding into town with us."

"She is?" He hoped the crushing disappointment and borderline frustration he felt didn't leak into his voice.

"Sybil kindly offered when I told her I wanted to go over some ideas with you," Madelyn said. "And maybe we can get a quick rehearsal in before we get to set."

The universe gave, and the universe took away.

Sybil's car smelled strongly of roasted coffee. Peter had a brief glimmer of hope that the smell would make Madelyn queasy and she'd decide to catch a ride with someone from the production, but coffee seemed to be one of the few smells she could stand.

The day's filming location was an empty office building that had been transformed into a police station and an FBI office. If the weather continued to be unfavorable, they would be at this location for the next several days, unless Mother Nature cooperated and then they'd film the exterior scenes when they could.

The parking lot was packed with equipment trucks and crew members.

"I think I'm going to have to park down the street," Sybil remarked.

"Can you let me out here?" Madelyn asked.

After Madelyn got out, Sybil drove down the street and around the corner, parking away from the chaos.

"When I offered to give her a ride, I didn't expect her to take me up on it," Sybil said as she turned off the car and unbuckled her seatbelt.

"So you weren't trying to avoid being alone with me?"

She shook her head, and relief filled him to bursting. Peter unbuckled then leaned over the center console and kissed her tenderly. She sighed softly as she kissed him back.

He broke the kiss and rested his forehead against hers. "We need to talk soon."

"We are talking."

"About us."

Sybil stiffened then retreated to her side of the car where he couldn't reach her without crawling over the console.

"Peter—"

"I know what you said," he interrupted, "but I think we need to clear the air. I can't live the rest of my life not under-standing why you're mad at me. Even if this ends when filming wraps, we're still going to see each other. Our best friends are married, they're going to have kids, and I plan on being an obnoxiously involved uncle. I don't want them asking me why Aunt Sybil glares at me all the time."

"I do not glare at you all the time," she argued.

"Not since we kissed, but you did."

Sybil glowered. It wasn't quite a glare, but it was skirting around the edge of one.

"We're not talking about this right now," she insisted.

He nodded his agreement. "I know, but I would like to later."

"More than you want to have sex with me?"

War broke out inside Peter's brain. The base half screamed at the mature half that he could be torpedoing his only chance to have sex with Sybil again. That he'd waited twelve years for this moment, and he was considering throwing it away for a *conversation?*

"Not more, but I think it's more important," he said, though every word hurt.

He couldn't breathe while she thought, but finally she said, "Okay. We can talk tonight. I guess I want some answers too."

Chapter Twenty
Twelve Years Ago, London

"PETER, I am supposed to be studying for finals, and I can't do that if you're kissing my neck."

Sybil squirmed, but didn't move away while Peter kissed her neck in an attempt to distract her from studying. It was working. She should've stayed at her own flat, where she could lock the door and focus, but the days they had left together could be counted on one hand and she was trying to soak up every spare minute she could.

Peter's flat was cozy, in a very low-rent, cobbled together from charity shops, starving artist kind of way. It felt more like home than her pre-furnished university accommodations. Plus, his double bed offered slightly more space than her single, though either way they ended up tangled together like two shipwreck victims holding on for dear life.

"Fail and stay for the re-sit," he said, and placed a shiver-inducing kiss on the tender spot behind her ear.

"I have to leave at the end of the week no matter what, so if I fail this exam, I'll have wasted a lot of money." Sybil caught his mouth with hers and kissed him until his bones became useless and he melted into the mattress, dragging her on top of him.

"You didn't waste your money. You had really good sex," he reminded her, nipping at her bottom lip.

"I think that makes you the world's most expensive whore." She forced herself into a sitting position to create some distance, though she was still straddling his hips. The solid ridge of his cock nestled between her lips and pressed against her clit. If she rocked back and forth, she could probably get off this way.

"I've been looking at places in Los Angeles," Peter said.

That tossed a cold bucket of water over her.

He propped himself up on his elbows. "I get that it's still long distance, but we'd be on the same continent. In the same time zone, even. Less than three hours of flight time and we could see each other."

"Peter, we've been over this." She smoothed his hair back from his beautiful, earnest face. "I don't want to do long distance of any kind. I'll drive myself nuts thinking you're out meeting more interesting girls and forgetting about me. And you can't uproot your life for me. We haven't known each other long enough. We're not old enough for that kind of commitment."

"I've been in love with you since I met you. Being older or knowing you longer isn't going to change my mind about that. What's long enough? What's old enough?"

"I don't know!" Sybil threw her hands up. "Twenty-five? Thirty? Not twenty. If you follow me back to the States, you couldn't go out and drink. No more pub quizzes."

"I would happily be sober to be with you."

She groaned in frustration. "What about your career?"

"Because no one has ever been able to act in Los Angeles," he responded sardonically. "It's not like I'm giving up some great job if I leave here. I've been auditioning, but I haven't heard back from anyone."

"You had those callbacks," she reminded him.

"That doesn't mean I've booked it," he pointed out. "Why are you so resistant to me moving?"

Sybil hesitated. "Because if things don't work out, between us or with your career or both, you're going to resent me. And that's a lot of pressure on a relationship. I can't be that scared all the time, Peter."

He pushed himself up into a fully seated position so they were nose to nose, forehead to forehead.

"I'm never going to resent you. Ever. I don't want to be somewhere you're not, and if I have to be, I don't know if I could sleep knowing you're not mine anymore."

It was hard not to crack and nearly impossible not to cry, but she'd had a lot of practice pushing down her hurts. So she squared her jaw and swallowed the lump in her throat.

"You can't know that you're never going to resent me. If you're going to move, it needs to be because it's the right move for your career, not because you want to stay close to me. You don't see me putting my life on hold to keep snuggling in this piece of crap." She looked around his room. "Let's enjoy the time we have left, okay?"

Two days later, Sybil walked out of her final exam feeling light as a feather. She was confident she had done well, and now she could enjoy her last few days in London unencumbered by school.

Peter had come with her to the exam because they were going to do some Christmas shopping once she was done. But when she got to the bench where she'd left him, he wasn't there. Sybil turned in a slow circle, searching for him. Had he gone to the bathroom?

She waited awkwardly outside the men's toilet for a few

minutes, and when he didn't appear, she opened the door and called his name. No answer.

Cold, sinking dread washed over her. He'd left without saying goodbye. She'd pushed him too hard and—

"Darling, what are you doing hanging around the men's?"

She whirled around. There was Peter. Relief flooded her, until she registered the grim expression on his face.

"I was looking for you," she explained and frowned. "Is something wrong?"

"My agent rang," he began, and looked up at the ceiling. Their voices echoed in the empty hall. "Let's get going."

Hand in hand, they exited into the chilly December air.

"What did your agent want?" Sybil asked as they walked in the direction of the shops.

"Turns out the reason there's been a delay in hearing about any of those jobs I've auditioned for is that I got one, and then she went around and used that job as leverage to hear back about some others I was more interested in and—" He stopped so abruptly that Sybil was yanked backward when she didn't stop, too. "She's managed to book me for the next year and a half."

"Peter! That's incredible." She threw her arms around him and hugged him. He didn't hug her back. Frowning, she took a step back. "Why aren't you excited about this?"

"Because all the jobs are here or involve travel. If I take them, I won't be able to move to Los Angeles for a while."

Her heart sank like a stone. Despite all her protestations, Peter had held firm that he would move to Los Angeles, and secretly, she'd started to come around to the idea.

"So you're going to stay here."

"I don't have to—"

"Yes, you do," Sybil insisted. "You have multiple job offers on the table. Walking away from those would be giving up on yourself and your career. If you did that, I'd never forgive you."

"How could I ever forgive myself if I walked away from you?" His voice caught on the last word.

Sybil closed her eyes because she couldn't bear to look into his.

"We're at a point in our lives where we need to prioritize ourselves and our careers. We're never going to go and accomplish all the things we want to accomplish if we're twisting ourselves into knots trying to make this work." She put her head on his chest and pressed her ear against his sternum, like she could memorize the beat of his heart. "If you ever wanted a sign from the universe, this is it. You're supposed to stay here."

The tube ride to Heathrow was silent. There was plenty of noise around them. Fellow travelers with luggage of all shapes and sizes strategizing their journeys home, families going to collect loved ones buzzing with excitement, and somewhere on the other end of their car, a baby crying. But Peter and Sybil rode in silence, sitting shoulder to shoulder with Sybil's luggage bumping against their knees and shins.

Overhead, the speakers announced their arrival at Heathrow and advised riders to wait on the platform for a different train to take them to the terminals. Peter took possession of her large suitcase, she grabbed her carryon, and they exited the train, minding the gap as they'd been told.

The anxiety that had twisted her chest tighter and tighter with every stop threatened to grind her into dust as they waited on the platform. She couldn't breathe. There wasn't any room left for her lungs to expand. Tears pricked her eyes to the point of pain.

"You have to leave me here," she blurted.

Peter looked at her with a blank, uncomprehending stare. "What?"

"You have to leave me here," she repeated, "because if you go with me to the terminal, I'm going to beg you to get on that plane with me. And you'll say yes because you love me and then I'll hate myself for ruining your life." Her chin trembled while her bottom lip quivered. "So you have to leave me here because I'm not strong enough to do the right thing if you go with me any further."

"What if I want to get on the plane with you?" he asked softly, and she shook her head.

"That's not an option."

"So this is goodbye?"

The pain in her chest spread through her body like her veins were filled with pins and needles. Could she bleed out without a physical injury?

"Five years." She didn't know where she got the number, but saying it eased a smidgen of the tension inside of her. "If we still want this in five years, we go back to where we started. We can go be our own people and do our own things, and if in five years this still feels like it matters as much as it does right now, we try to find a way to make it work."

Peter wrapped his arms around her and crushed her against him. She didn't mind. If he broke all the bones in her body, she could stay a little longer.

"You expect me to survive five years without you?" he said against her hair, and she felt one of his hot tears slide down the shell of her ear.

"I expect you to be brilliant."

He squeezed her tighter, and she clung to him in return. Somewhere in the outside world she heard the train to the terminal arrive and depart without her, but it didn't matter.

Finally his hold on her slackened, but only so he could take her face in his hands. His thumbs caressed her cheeks, and a few tears slid down his own.

"I'm going to miss your stardust," he whispered, and she suspected that was as loud as his voice would go at the moment. "How else will I get to hold a galaxy in my arms?"

"They're just freckles," she reminded him.

"They're perfect. You're perfect."

Soft lips brushed hers, once, twice, three times before she gripped his jacket and rose on her tiptoes for a proper goodbye kiss. For the last time, his fingers sank into the hair at the base of her skull and they both tried to pour all the young, hopeless love they had leftover, all the love they didn't have enough words or time to say, into that kiss.

Overhead, the arrival of the train to Terminal 5 was announced, and Sybil lowered her heels to the ground and released Peter's jacket.

"It's time," she said around the unmovable lump in her throat.

"Five years," he reminded her. "I'm coming to get you in five years."

The train pulled into the station, and Sybil grabbed her bags and hurried aboard, not looking back. She couldn't stand to see him alone on the platform, and she wouldn't survive watching the train pull away from him.

She checked her large suitcase and had her passport verified, then she made her way through security. On the other side, she filled her water bottle, bought some overpriced snacks, and found her gate. She picked a seat as far away from her future planemates as she could, sat down, and opened her backpack.

Red wool spilled out the top.

She shouldn't have taken it, but during the weeks she'd spent with Peter, it had practically become hers. Selfishly, she'd wanted to keep as much of him with her as she could.

Sybil took the sweater out of her backpack and slipped her arms through the sleeves. Something else red caught her eye. She reached into the depths of her backpack and took out the copy of *Emma* she'd allowed Peter to have the day they'd met. There was a yellow sticky note affixed to the cover.

You should have this.
All my love,
Peter

Chapter Twenty-One
Crane Cove, Oregon

"Oh, no."

The kitchen was a mess. Sybil hadn't noticed the chaos she'd caused while trying to create order in her pantry and cabinets until she'd taken a break to go to the bathroom and came back to the shocking reality that everything in her kitchen was on the counters or the floor.

Cans, bags, and boxes of food were strewn in half-finished categories in front of the pantry. Baking dishes, serving dishes, cookie sheets, and small appliances cluttered the counters.

Thank god she hadn't started on the fridge.

All the nervous energy that had spurred this ill-advised bout of organization drained from her body, leaving her with only dread and an adrenaline hangover.

How the hell was she supposed to put all of this back before he got to her house?

Why the fuck had she agreed to have him over?

Well, she knew the answer to that one. Peter still had a magic mouth and magic hands, and she wondered if the rest of his talents had stayed the same. She'd wondered until she couldn't sleep and then screamed into her pillow while her vibrator made her come.

Why had she agreed to *talk* to him? What was there to even say? *"You broke my heart and made me cry but gave me the best sex of my life, so yes, my bedroom is up the stairs, last door, thank you."*

The stovetop clock caught her eye. She hadn't given Peter a precise arrival time, but it was after the time she told him he was allowed to show up.

"Fuck, fuck, fuck," she cursed and started cramming dishes back into cabinets.

A knock at the back door almost made her drop her vintage Pyrex. The door creaked when it opened, and Peter paused halfway through and stared at the mess she'd created.

"Trying to pack up and skip town?" he asked, eyes darting around the room.

Sybil gently set the Pyrex on the counter. If that broke, she'd never forgive herself.

"More like trying to fix the mess inside my head by making a mess in my house," she said ruefully, surveying the damage again with more critical eyes. "And I need to oil the hinges on that door."

"Are you sure? Makes a great burglar alarm." He closed the door behind him, the hinges illustrating his point. "Do you want help cleaning up or help ignoring the problem?"

Sybil laced her fingers on top of her head and did a slow turn to assess the situation.

"I need help cleaning," she admitted.

"Good thing I'm very good at taking directions." Peter kissed her cheek and shed his coat.

Warmth spread through her body, and she stooped to pick something off the ground so he wouldn't see the blush she was positive was on her face.

"Why did you come in through the back door?"

"Because you said I wasn't allowed to climb in through the window," he answered, pushing his sleeves up to his elbows.

"But you could've come in through the front door," she pointed out, trying and failing to ignore the muscles in his forearms that flexed when he hefted her crockpot off the counter.

"Are we not sneaking around anymore?"

"We are, but my nosey neighbor might think you're a burglar if you come in through the back door after dark." She assessed her empty pantry for a moment. "God, I should've waited for Eloise to help me with this."

"Probably," he agreed. "I'm not known for my organizational prowess. Where did you want this...thing?"

"The crockpot?" Sybil tilted her head. "Peter, do you not know what a crockpot is?"

"I know what a crockpot is," he said, "I just didn't know that's what it was called."

She laughed. "Put it down. I think I want to tackle the pantry first."

They worked in relative silence for a while. Occasionally Sybil would ask Peter to hand her something, or he'd ask her if she wanted to keep something close to or just past its expiration date. The conversation, or lack thereof, was in the no-man's-land between awkward and comfortable. It was a relief when he finally said, "Do you think we could have that talk now?"

"I don't really know what there is to talk about," she said, stacking cans like she worked at a grocery store.

"I don't understand what happened. I don't understand why you're so upset with me."

He sounded so sincere that she had to laugh.

"You don't understand?" she mocked. "You have *no* idea why I might be upset with you? Not the tiniest little inkling of a clue?"

"If I knew, I would have apologized by now. I will happily crawl over broken glass if you point me in the right direction."

Sybil gripped the can she was holding so tightly that the label tore.

"You never showed up."

London, Seven Years Ago (October)

In five years, the bookstore hadn't changed much. The gold lettering on the window and the door was more chipped, but the cat still napped in the display, trying to catch errant rays of sunshine amidst the London gloom. It still smelled the same too, like dust, groundwood paper, and old wood.

Sybil trailed her fingers along the spines as she browsed the shelves. In five years no one had established a better cataloging system, either. Books had been added not by genre or author, but by wherever space could be found at the time. What had Peter called it?

A treasure hunt.

She yawned. Jet lag was a bitch. Sleep had eluded her on the flight from Portland to Heathrow, and she tried to hit the ground running once she landed in London, but she was dead tired by six in the evening. Her little nap turned into her waking up at one in the morning, and she never got back to sleep. So she turned up at the bookshop as soon as it opened because she had nothing else to do.

The antique clock by the register announced the passing of another hour with twelve chimes.

Doubt seeped into the cracks of her anxious excitement. Where was he? The Peter she'd known would have camped outside the bookshop all night so he couldn't possibly miss her arrival. But the shop had opened three hours ago and there still wasn't any sign of him.

At least the employee babysitting the register was ignoring her. He couldn't ask her if she needed help finding anything because there wasn't any possible way he could know where anything was located. But he'd started looking her way more frequently over the last hour, so she pulled a book from the shelf and pretended to read the back cover.

The cat from the window wound its way between her feet, rubbing against her legs in search of affection. She crouched down and scratched it behind the ears, then under the chin. The cat purred, chirped, then trotted to a faded green velvet chair shoved into a corner. It looked at Sybil and meowed.

She could take a hint.

Book in hand, Sybil sat in the chair, and the cat jumped into her lap and curled itself into a warm, purring ball of fur. She was trapped now, because it felt like bad luck to move a cat, so she opened the book she'd grabbed and started reading.

The Light Below was a serial killer mystery thriller that followed Honor Gardner, an FBI agent, as she returned to the small town she'd grown up in to investigate a string of mysterious killings. It had a stronger romantic B-plot than most books in the same genre, since her local law enforcement counterpart was her ex-boyfriend.

The clock chimed the hours as they passed, each *ting* becoming more and more mocking as the day wore on. Her heart sank lower and lower, and by four in the afternoon, it was somewhere under the floorboards.

Peter wasn't coming.

Sybil didn't know why she'd assumed the narrative arc of her life would change. In the last five years, she'd watched Peter's life play out in pictures in magazines and online. He was famous enough, or spent time with people famous enough, to have his picture bought and sold. His life had outgrown her exponentially. She couldn't compete with the gorgeous actresses and musicians he spent time with these days. After college she'd moved back to her small, quiet hometown and started a business. Stardust Coffee was popular enough that she'd signed a long-term lease for a storefront in the heart of downtown Crane Cove, and soon she'd be able to retire the cart she'd been using for good. She was proud; she'd started with nothing and clawed her way to success by sheer grit and determination. But when she held it side by side to Peter's life, it looked small and insignificant.

For five years she'd lived her life as fully as she could. She'd casually dated a few lackluster guys, had sex—some good, some bad—but she couldn't shake the golden-haired boy with the sparkling blue eyes who, for a few eternal weeks, had meant everything to her. Hope had driven her to buy the plane ticket to fulfill the promise they'd made to each other on the train platform, and hope proved yet again that all it did was crush her.

"We're closing soon," the man behind the register shouted from his post.

The cat jumped off her lap, and Sybil knew it was time to go. The Peter she'd known five years ago never would have made her wait all day.

She put the book back on a shelf. It was a good book, but she didn't need or want a memento from this day.

The bell over the door jingled, and her heart leapt into her throat.

A short, squat woman wiped her shoes on the doormat, and Sybil's heart broke a little bit more.

And even though hope was a spiteful bitch, Sybil still looked up and down the street when she left the bookshop, because a little of Peter's silly romanticism had rubbed off on her, and maybe, just maybe, he'd be sprinting down the street to try and arrive before the bookshop closed.

Maybe she'd come back tomorrow, just in case.

Sleep didn't come any easier her second night in London. Sybil lay awake, hoping Peter was okay while also hoping something horrible had happened to him that had kept him away. Maybe he'd been hit by a car and was in the hospital. That was a comforting possibility. He'd have been there, except his leg was broken in two places and he was in traction.

At three in the morning, she opened her laptop, connected to the hotel Wi-Fi, and searched Peter's name. If something had happened to him, a news outlet would have picked it up.

Under Top Stories, there were pictures and small headlines about him being spotted around London with actress Sasha St. Jaine, a striking ingenue he'd recently filmed a romantic movie with, at least according to the short article detailing their day out. Sybil checked the date.

She slammed her laptop shut.

The bastard was in London.

Chapter Twenty-Two
Crane Cove, Oregon

"You never showed up."

The words rattled around Peter's brain, but refused to sink in.

"I waited at the bookshop all day, and you never showed up," Sybil continued, her voice growing tighter and tighter with emotion as she talked. "I actually hoped that you'd been hit by a car because at least being in the hospital was a good excuse standing me up. But you weren't. You were galivanting around London with Sasha St. Jaine. And I've been really angry with you for a long time, Peter. Really, really angry. Because you made me believe in love, and you made me believe that I was loveable. You said we were soulmates. I spent that first year we were apart thinking you'd show up at any minute, that you'd find me and throw pebbles at my window until I let you in. Because you made me believe in that kind of rom-com bullshit. I did my best to live my life in a way that when I went back to London, I'd have no regrets. But you didn't show up and you broke my heart. So I've been angry with you, but I've never been able to hate you, and goddammit, I've *wanted* to hate you. If I could hate you—

really *hate* you—maybe I could stop loving you. But I couldn't —I can't..."

Sybil put her fist in front of her mouth, like that would somehow hide the tears that were leaking out of her eyes. She took a shaky breath.

"Do you see now why I don't want to talk about this?"

Peter was stunned.

"You're angry with me because you still love me?"

"*That's* what you got from all of that?" She threw her hands into the air in frustration.

He crawled across the few feet separating them, pushing aside cans and boxes of pasta, until their knees touched when he sat back on his heels. He put his hands on her shoulders and contorted his torso so she couldn't avoid his eyes.

"I love you too."

"Peter," she groaned, overflowing with frustration.

"I have loved you from the moment I first laid eyes on your broken knockoff Doc Martins, the first time you glared at me, since that very first hint of a smile. I have loved you with every breath since the day I met you, Sybil."

She sniffled and wiped vigorously at her eyes. "You've got a funny way of showing it swanning around London with Sasha St. Jaine instead of showing up at the bookshop. Not to mention all the others you've paraded through the papers."

It was hard not to smile. Once he'd played in a celebrity poker tournament to raise money for charity, and when he'd arranged his cards in order, he had a straight flush. This felt startlingly similar.

"Sasha is just a friend. They're all only friends. I can't control what delusional but creative pseudo-journalists choose to invent about my personal life based on a picture." He squeezed her shoulders. "Since there was you, it's only ever been you."

"So why weren't you there?"

"I was there," he insisted.

"Peter," she groaned again, exasperated. "I was there all day. You could not possibly have been there for more than two minutes without me seeing you."

"You went to the bookshop, right? The one with the gold lettering and the cat?"

"Yes. The one we met at. I was there five years to the day we met."

He had to laugh. Seven years of wondering had boiled down to this.

"I think we might have had a slight miscommunication."

London, Seven Years Ago (December)

Peter was surprised that the bookshop wasn't operating under holiday shopping hours since Christmas was less than two weeks away. Maybe he'd spent too much time in the States lately. He stamped his feet and blew into his hands while he waited for nine o'clock to come around and for someone to come unlock the door.

He had waited five years for this moment. How many times had he imagined what it would be like to see Sybil again? Thousands, maybe more. Would she still look the same? How would her face have changed? It didn't matter, he was just curious.

The last five years had passed at a crawl. He'd lasted one year before he broke down and tried to find Sybil, but she was no longer at the school she'd been attending when they'd been dating and no one he talked to at the school would tell him anything about her whereabouts. Peter would never forgive himself for not insisting that they stay in contact for the duration of their separation. Then again, if he'd had his way, he'd have been on the phone with her 24/7. When she went to class, she could have slipped him in her pocket and he would have listened to her lectures.

Finally, an employee came and unlocked the door. Peter rushed inside, grateful for the warmth and bowled over by the rush of memories brought on by the smell of dust, groundwood paper, and old wood.

Except for the Christmas decorations, the shop looked the same. Same chipped gold lettering, same cat in the window display, except instead of snoozing it was walking through the miniature Christmas village like a furry Godzilla. A quick assessment of the shelves confirmed that the organization method hadn't been updated in the last five years, either.

He looked at the door expectantly, but no one came inside. He wasn't worried. Sybil was probably jet-lagged and sleeping. There were still many hours left in the day.

Peter wandered up and down the aisles, casually searching for treasures. He'd never found another red copy of *Emma* since the day he'd met Sybil. Did she still have the one he'd given her?

The bell above the door jingled, and his heart leapt into his throat. But it was a young dad about his age, with a bundled-up baby strapped to his chest in a baby carrier.

"I'm looking for a gift for my wife. She likes to read," he told the clerk stationed behind the register.

The clerk waved his hand in the direction of the books. "Feel free to look."

The young man blinked in surprise, but headed for the shelves, looking for some kind of genre markers. Confusion quickly turned to dismay on his face.

Peter walked over to the man and smiled at the sleeping baby. "What does your wife like to read?"

"Books?" the man said. He looked hopeless but hopefully up at Peter, and frowned a little. "Has anyone ever told you that you look like that guy from that film? Peter...Something. Or Patrick."

Peter grinned. "You know, I get that all time. Back to your wife. Can you recall any of the books on her nightstand? Any titles or what the covers may have looked like?"

"Umm..."

"What kind of shows does she like to watch?"

His face brightened at that question. "She loves *Claymore Abbey*. And *Midsomer Murders*. Oh, and *Bake-Off*. Got a real thing for Paul Hollywood."

"Who doesn't?" Peter asked with a grin and held out his hand. "I'm Peter."

"John," the man replied, and they shook hands.

It took some hunting, but Peter found John's wife some historical romance novels, some murder mysteries, and one of Paul Hollywood's cookbooks. Relieved and grateful, John paid for the books and left the shop.

The shop cat wound its way between Peter's feet and leaned against his legs, begging for affection. He crouched down and scratched the cat behind the ears.

"Aren't you sweet? When I settle down, I'm going to get a cat."

The antique clock near the register chimed ten. Peter pulled a random book off the shelf and settled himself into the old, green velvet chair in the corner. The cat jumped onto his lap and immediately curled into a ball.

Hours passed. Peter read.

The book was good. *The Light Below* was exactly the kind of book his parents' production company was looking to adapt.

He specifically remembered his mother talking about wanting to do either a murder mystery or a thriller. It had a good chance of being made into a movie if he wrapped it up for Christmas and let her think it was her idea.

More time passed until the clerk finally hollered from the front of the store, "We're closing. You don't have to go home, but you can't stay here."

Peter checked his phone. Four fifty. Disappointment deflated his optimistic bubble. Sybil wasn't coming today.

He gently eased the slumbering cat off his lap and went to purchase the book he'd almost finished.

The clerk frowned at him. "Do you come in a lot? You look familiar."

Peter smiled and handed the man some cash for the book. "No, I just have one of those faces."

The clerk snorted. "No, you don't."

If the day had ever grown warmer, he'd missed it. The cold air bit his cheeks, nose, and ears as soon as he left the cozy bookshop.

He should be sad. He knew he should be sad. Five years ago exactly, he'd made plans with the love of his life to meet again back where they'd started and she hadn't shown up. But hope was stronger than any disappointment. This wasn't how their story would end. It was a small obstacle, a story they'd laugh over in the future.

Peter would see Sybil again when the time was right. He was certain of that.

Chapter Twenty-Three
Crane Cove, Oregon

"I was there in December," Peter explained. "When we said 'let's meet in five years,' I started counting from the day you left. You started counting from the day we met." A dreamy, but definitely smug, smile graced his lovely face. "That's rather romantic of you."

Sybil sniffled. She couldn't shake the feeling that snot was leaking out of her nose.

"I am not romantic," she protested flatly, wiping her nose on her sleeve. "I clearly said 'from the beginning.' We began in October. I don't see what's so complicated about that."

Except she could see what had been so complicated. They'd lost seven years because she'd been too emotional to be sensible and make sure they were on the same page about when and where they were supposed to meet.

"Okay," Peter conceded, scooting forward so his knee was wedged between hers and his lips brushed over hers when he spoke. "You're right. I should've hedged my bets and gone in October too. Now that we've cleared that up, will you let me love you?"

Her heart was so light she worried she'd float away like a balloon in a breeze.

"You're impossible," she told him with faux exasperation, and she absorbed his smile as he kissed her.

Peter cradled the back of her head as he kissed her, leaning into her until his weight gradually lowered her to the floor.

Something hard and unyielding dug into her back.

"Ow," Sybil said against his mouth, and reached behind her. She held up a can of refried beans. "Maybe not on the kitchen floor."

He hid his face in her neck and his shoulders shook with silent laughter.

"Maybe you're right," he agreed and got to his feet. He held out a hand to help her up. She took it, and he hauled her to her feet.

"My bed is more comfortable," she promised, intertwining their fingers and guiding him out of the minefield of cans.

"The couch is closer," he pointed out as she mounted the first step.

Sybil stopped and looked over her shoulder. "Peter. Do you really want the first time we have sex again to be on the *couch*?"

He looked at the living room. "It's a nice couch..."

"Peter."

"But the bed is better," he agreed and hurried up the stairs after her.

If she'd known that morning that Peter was going to be in her room again, Sybil would've bothered cleaning up. Or changing the sheets. But by the way he wrapped her up in his arms and kissed the living daylights out of her as soon as they crossed the threshold, Sybil guessed he didn't really mind the mess.

Stumbling steps took them to the bed because navigation was secondary to the need to not separate their bodies more than absolutely necessary. Sybil's legs folded involuntarily when they collided with her mattress, and they tumbled onto the bed. Fumbling fingers tried to remove clothing with little success because they kept getting in each other's way, until Sybil finally put a hand on his chest and pushed him back.

"I remove my clothes," she panted, "and you remove yours. Otherwise this is never going to work."

Peter scrambled into a position more conducive to stripping and then his shirt was off his body and flung across the room before she could marshal her limbs to twitch.

She stared.

Time hadn't been cruel to her, but it had been generous as fuck to Peter. Twelve years ago, he'd been rangy, still growing into his body as he exited adolescence. As a full-grown man, he was breathtaking. Well-defined muscles hid just under his skin, so she could see them bunch and flex as he moved, but he remained long and slender. As he shucked his pants, she noticed the faintest hint of definition from his hip to his groin, and she wanted to lick that subtle line. Absolutely mouthwatering.

"I think I'm going to have to turn out the lights before I take my clothes off."

The words that were supposed to be inside thoughts slipped out of her mouth, and Peter paused taking off his socks.

"Why?"

Too late to take it back now.

"Because." She gestured at his body with a sweep of her hand. "You look like *that*. And I can't say I've necessarily improved since you last saw me naked."

"Bodies change," Peter said. "I've been dying to see how yours has."

"Okay, but can you temper your expectations because my body doesn't look like it did when I was twenty."

"I know. Your boobs are bigger." When she stared at him,

wide-eyed, he added, "I noticed at the wedding. You looked really amazing."

It took a lot of effort not to preen. She had looked amazing. God bless Eloise for having impeccable, timeless taste that made her look like an Old Hollywood movie starlet. Too bad he'd missed the wedding rehearsal, because she'd thought the best revenge would be to look good and she'd looked fantastic.

"Are you going to leave your socks on?" Sybil asked, and Peter grinned, then nearly fell over taking them off.

She reclined, propping herself on her elbows, and watched him. No, life wasn't fair but she was certainly reaping the benefits. She was so caught up in studying the muscles on his back that she didn't notice he was watching her too.

"You're still dressed."

"Technically, so are you," she said and pointed to his underwear. Black boxer briefs. Some things never changed.

"These are my insurance policy," he told her, curling an arm around her waist and lowering her to the mattress. "You can't see my goods if I can't see yours."

Peter kissed her again in the slow, deep, thorough way that made her toes curl and her pussy clench in eager anticipation. Most of her reluctance melted away and she was about to tell him to get off so she could get undressed when he pulled back, his expression soft yet serious.

"If you want me to tell you that you haven't changed a bit since we were twenty, I can't do that. Because you have changed. I wish I'd been around to see it, because it would be a privilege to watch you grow older. But"—he interlaced their fingers and then brought her hand between them to assess the hard, hot length of his cock through straining cotton—"clearly I'm a big fan of you at every stage of life."

"Showing me this would've saved you a speech." Sybil squeezed him through the fabric, and his eyes rolled back into his head while a shudder traveled the length of his body. "But I like your sweet-talking. Now get off so I can get naked."

He moved quickly, rolling off her and scooting up to the head of her bed, where he reclined against her pillows. Nervousness rose in her like smoke, wispy but unavoidable. Did she start with her shirt or her pants?

Peter hooked his thumbs into the waistband of his underwear and pushed them off his hips, down his thighs, and once his legs were free, he tossed them aside. Then he wrapped a hand around the thick base of his cock and stroked it with long, slow motions, watching her expectantly.

Suddenly the order of removal didn't matter so much as long as her clothes came off.

She shed her pants, then her Cranberry Festival T-shirt, then her bra, then her underwear. All of it gone in under thirty seconds. Peter moaned his appreciation.

"Fuck, you're perfect," he said.

"No, that would be you," she countered, slinking up the bed and feeling like a cat about to pounce. She licked her lips as she spread his knees to give herself more room. This close she could see a bead of precum leak from the tip of his cock and slide down to pool against his fingers. "God, I want that."

"As much as I want you to have it, I'm afraid if you touch it, I'll explode."

"You say that like it's a bad thing." Sybil lightly raked her nails down his inner thighs, satisfaction and desire surging within her when his knees and balls drew up at the same time. "Is there a condom in your wallet? Because I'm going to be way too tempted to make stupid choices if we don't get it out and ready."

His hand paused mid-stroke, his gorgeous, cinematic face broadcasting distress.

"I forgot to bring one." His head fell back against her head-board with a painful sounding *thunk*. "Fuck. Do you have one?"

Sybil stretched her body across his as she reached her night-stand drawer. The insistent head of his cock prodded her belly, making her body ache with anticipation. Remembering the stretch and the fullness of him inside of her, hitting spots that made her lose her mind and beg for more, made her nipples tingle as they became harder.

She pulled open the drawer and dug around. When was the last time she'd even needed a condom? If she found one, would it have expired?

"Oh, fuck," she groaned, her eyelids fluttering as Peter rubbed her clit. She lifted her hips to give him a better angle, and pressed her cunt against his hand.

"Did you find one?" he asked, sliding two fingers inside of her and then using the abundance of wetness to lubricate his ministrations on her clit.

"N-no," she stuttered.

The horny part of her brain was getting louder and louder, daring her to make not-smart, and potentially unsafe, decisions, consequences be damned. Anything to end the perfect torture between her legs. It wouldn't be hard to straddle his hips, fit the tip of his cock in her pussy, then slide down the bare length of him. She was so wet she could probably glide down in one motion. And he'd fill her up so good too. So good, so hard, so full.

Sybil rocked against his hand and moaned loudly.

Peter's voice sounded tight when he asked, "Is there one in the bathroom?"

"If you want me to think, you have to stop touching me," she said, and when he stopped, she immediately protested with a high-pitched, whiny "Nooo."

"We need a condom," he reminded her. Sybil pouted at him

over her shoulder, and he relented a little by stroking her pussy, but he avoided her clit. "Is there one in your purse?"

"No. Men are aggravating, and one-night stands aren't fun for me." She wracked what little of her brain was still useful, trying to imagine where in the house there might possibly be a condom. "I'll go check Mal's room. She might have one."

The sprint from her room to Mallory's room was so impressive that if any nudists had spotted her, they'd have recruited her for the fifty-yard dash in the Naked Olympics. She tore through her sister's half-unpacked luggage, hoping Mallory wouldn't notice the difference between the original mess and her mess. Hope dwindled, and Sybil actually considered calling Eloise to see if she had any condoms left over from her years of baby prevention when she unzipped a small pink bag. Inside was a small vibrator and three condoms. Carefully, so as not to touch the vibrator, Sybil plucked a condom from the bag and raced back to her room, holding the packet above her head in triumph.

"I found one!"

Peter sagged against the pillows, slack with relief. She could relate. The idea of hunting down a condom in Crane Cove at any time was daunting, but when she had something at stake? Horrendous. She couldn't have abandoned the condoms if the cashier was a gossip, or if she spotted someone apt to give a shit what she did behind closed doors. And it wasn't like she could send Peter. Now that he'd released his cock, she didn't think they'd be able to stuff it back into his pants until it deflated again.

"Get over here," he beckoned. It was an invitation, not a command. Peter was a fantastic actor and could turn on bossy if she wanted him to, but at his core he was a considerate pleaser.

At some point during his stay, she would ask him to be bossy, if only because the illusion of barely bridled danger kept in check by steely control was thrilling. Or maybe it was thrilling because it was so out of character for him. She would need to experiment a lot to pinpoint exactly what about him got her motor going.

Sybil joined him on the bed and straddled his thighs, condom still held between her fingers. "How do you want me?"

If brains were like computers, Peter's crashed, his face becoming the human equivalent of the blue screen of death.

"On my back? On my knees? On top, riding you for all I'm worth?"

He continued to stare, but he was finally able to coax out a hoarse "Yes."

"There were options, Peter. Yes to what?"

"All of it," he croaked, then cleared his throat. "I want you every way I can have you. Any way I can have you."

She grinned. "What about right now?"

"Right now, I want to finish what I started yesterday and taste you while you come."

Anticipation flooded her body, and if she hadn't thought she'd need to wash her bedding before, she would after that.

"I think that can be arranged," she said in a poor attempt at being coy. "Do you want me exactly like I was last night? Or I could sit on your face..."

Between them, his cock pulsed so hard it jumped. Peter groaned and squeezed her hips tightly, his fingertips digging into her flesh.

"That. I want you on my face. Please."

Like she could—or would—deny him *that*. Sybil put a hand on top of his head and pushed down.

"Get to work."

The way he slid under her reminded her of a mechanic rolling under a car. It was quick and fluid. One moment he was sitting up, the next she could feel his breath against her hypersensitive clit. And, bless him, he took "get to work" to heart. He licked and suckled her clit like it was his one mission on Earth, squeezing and kneading her hips and ass while he did so. Her core strength gave out and her hands smacked against the wall as she caught herself.

"Oh, *fuck*," she moaned. She left one palm plastered on the wall, and her other hand threaded through his thick blond hair, gripping it near its roots, and she hung on for dear life.

Pleasure rolled through her like the foreshocks of an earthquake, with the promise of something big on the horizon. She ground her pussy against his mouth, desperate to make something happen so she could find some relief. He somehow managed to redouble his efforts, and her eyes rolled back in her head. Her hand slipped down the wall, and she grabbed a hold of the headboard to steady herself.

"Peter," she whined, her fist tightening around his hair. "Fuck, I wanna come so bad. Please. I wanna come so bad—oh, god, *yes*. That. Keep doing that. Oh, fuck, fuck, fuck."

His tongue moved rapidly across her clit and the pressure inside of her grew more intense, twisting and tightening until she broke, shattering with a breathless shriek. Her whole body convulsed in unison with her pussy, which was constricting around nothing.

As the aftershocks passed, Sybil loosened her grip on his hair, then let go. She slumped forward, letting the headboard hold her up so she didn't smother Peter.

Heavy contentment settled over her body, leaving her feeling fuzzy around the edges. Moving to a different position seemed impossible, so if Peter wanted to fuck her, he was going to have to get behind her and do all the work.

"Fuck, that was amazing." Even speaking took a lot of effort. "You're—"

A firm swipe of his tongue stole the words from her mouth.

She tried to say "Oh, god," but no sound came out. Another swipe, a swirl, and his determined tongue went to work on her again. With every touch heightened, it took no time at all for another, smaller orgasm to pass through her body.

Sybil barely found the strength to tap the side of his head to get his attention.

"Stop, stop, stop," she begged. "It's too much."

With a final kiss, Peter wiggled back up onto the pillows and Sybil collapsed on top of him, her bones melted like chocolate on a hot summer day.

His hair was a wreck and his nose, lips, and chin were so wet they glistened.

"Did I do good?" he asked, stroking her back, his fingers bumping over each vertebrae in her spine.

"I might chain you to the bed so you can never leave," she told him, her voice so languid that she sounded drunk to her own ears.

"I don't have any objections to that, except that the chains aren't necessary."

She chuckled weakly. "You might have done *too* good. I don't know if I can move."

"Does that mean you want a raincheck on the sex?"

"If you don't fuck me with that huge cock, we're going to have a problem."

His laugh rumbled against her cheek, and she smiled. This was what she'd missed. Life-altering orgasms and the comfortable afterglow camaraderie.

Peter curled an arm around her and rolled them so she was on her back under him.

"Great view," she commented. He grabbed the condom and sat back on his heels to roll the latex sheath down his length. Sybil pushed herself up on her elbows to watch, and added, "Really great view."

An adorable blush colored Peter's cheeks. The rosy glow looked good on him, but everything looked good on him. Sybil knew she shouldn't look a gift horse in the mouth, but she would never stop being baffled as to why he'd chosen *her* of all people to become hyperfixated on. She wasn't anything special.

But when Peter lowered himself so he could kiss her again, the tangy taste of her body still heavy on his tongue, she felt special.

She gasped, inhaling sharply like she was trying to steal the breath from his lungs, as he pushed into her, his girth stretching her open. It felt so good to be filled that she wanted to weep from relief.

"Oh, god," she moaned.

Chapter Twenty-Four

"Oh, god."

Sybil's moan traveled like lightning from his ears, down his spine, through his balls, up his shaft, and straight to the tip of his dick. He was barely inside her warm, welcoming body and the desire to come was almost too strong to be tenable.

One of her hands gripped his shoulder while the fingers on her other hand threaded through his hair, and her legs wrapped around his hips, trying to draw him deeper, faster as he worked his length into her with each roll of his hips.

"Fuck, I've missed this," Sybil sighed, tilting her hips to deepen his thrust. "You feel so good."

If she wanted this to be over before they really got started, she was doing a great job. Peter caught her mouth and kissed her deeply to shut her up before her words obliterated the thin thread of self-control holding him together. Except the slide of his tongue against hers made her inner walls tighten around him and his toes curled in response.

Peter tried to distract himself with condom safety facts, like if it was safe to unload his balls twice in the same condom. If he came immediately, he could probably shoot off a second time without her noticing the first, but it was likely inadvisable.

Sybil's needy whimper focused his attention back on her.

"More," she begged, rocking her hips against his.

His next thrust had him firmly seated inside of her, his balls touching her ass. Sybil arched her back like a woman possessed. And he might have enjoyed the moment more if he wasn't ready to rip her pillow apart to distract himself so that wouldn't be his last thrust.

"Peter? Are you okay?"

The gentle sweetness in her voice, tinged with trepidation, cut through him like a knife.

"You feel too good," he admitted, nipping her shoulder. "I'm barely hanging on."

"I already came twice. You can let go," she told him. "I want to feel you come inside me."

"You can't say shit like that when I'm on the edge," he groaned, and buried his face in the crook of her neck.

"Fuck me. Come for me."

She'd asked for it, and Peter had never been able to deny her anything.

The bedframe creaked as he chased his own pleasure, and the headboard thumped against the wall rhythmically, punctuated by Sybil's squeaks and breathless moans. She'd called it fucking, but to him it was making love, showing her how desperately he'd wanted and needed her all the years they'd been apart.

His muscles tightened, taut with anticipation, as he rapidly approached the finish line. Some almost-forgotten instinct had him slip his thumb between their bodies to find her clit, and he rubbed it rapidly.

"*Shit!*"

Sybil's body contracted around his violently and that was

enough. He came with equal ferocity, blinded by the sweet rapture of release. Shudders rolled through his body in wonderful waves. When the pulsing in his cock subsided, exhaustion hit him like a tsunami, and he collapsed on top of Sybil, his arms drained of their strength.

His balls were drained too.

"Are you okay up there?" Sybil asked, her hands gently stroking his back.

"I'm dead," Peter mumbled against her neck. "I went to heaven, so I must be dead."

She laughed and wiggled under him until he got the hint to roll off her.

"You're dramatic." She sat up, and he was too hypnotized by her breasts to protest the characterization. "So you had a good time?"

"The best time," he promised, and kissed her freckled shoulder.

The cleanup process was as awkward as it always had been. Or it was for him. Sybil showed him the upstairs bathroom, where he disposed of the used condom by wrapping it in toilet paper and throwing it in the little trash can. Then they switched spots and he lingered awkwardly outside the door, naked, for a moment before it occurred to him that if he stayed there, it would look like he'd been trying to listen to her pee. He decided to wait for her in bed instead.

He faintly heard the toilet flush down the hall as he snuggled himself under Sybil's blankets. The flannel pillowcases were infused with her scent, and he turned his face to inhale deeply. Could he smuggle one of these home with him without her noticing?

"What are you doing?" Sybil asked from the doorway, her face a mixture of surprise, confusion, and amusement.

There was no use denying the obvious.

"Smelling your pillow."

"I mean, why are you in my bed? I thought you'd be half dressed already."

He frowned. "Why would I be dressed?"

"So you could leave."

His heart sank, and he struggled to keep his face close to neutral. "Did you want me to leave?"

Sybil shook her head, then wordlessly crawled into bed next to him and nestled herself against him, one arm across his stomach and her cheek on his chest.

The rush of dopamine made him dizzy, and he was so happy his heart hurt. This was all he had wanted for the last twelve years.

"Don't fall asleep," Sybil mumbled, sounding like she was about to do exactly that. "You can't sleep here."

An amused grin tickled the corner of his mouth.

"Why is that?"

"I heard from Graham how this works. If I let you sleep here, you'll never stop sleeping here. You'll move in when my back is turned." She yawned. "That was really good sex."

"I think I could do better next time."

"You could start by coming prepared. I can't believe you didn't remember to bring a condom."

"I haven't purchased condoms in years, so it completely slipped my mind."

All the lovely, languid sleepiness in Sybil's body vanished, and she sat up, as if propelled by a spring. "Please tell me you've been using condoms."

A vivid blush spread from his neck all the way to his forehead and the tips of his ears.

"I haven't needed to," he said.

"You haven't been using condoms?" she admonished. "Seriously, Peter?"

"It's not like that—"

"You're not some exception to the rule. STDs don't care who you are— Oh, god, do you have kids you're hiding?"

"No!" He sat bolt upright and reached for her, but she shrank back, putting a protective arm over her bare breasts. "It's not like that at all. It's...I haven't needed condoms because I haven't had sex with anyone since you."

Sybil stared at him like she didn't believe him. Peter hadn't expected her to, which was why he was hoping they could go the rest of their lives without her ever finding out about his self-imposed celibacy.

"You expect me to believe that?"

He sighed. "Sybil, if I was lying, wouldn't I have come up with a better lie than that? I know it sounds implausible—"

"Impossible," she corrected.

"But it's true. You're the last person I had sex with. Outside of work, I haven't even kissed anyone else. It felt wrong to even consider it, like I was cheating on you."

Her disbelieving expression didn't even flicker.

"You expect me to believe that someone who looks like you" —she gestured from his head to where the sheets had pooled around his hips—"hasn't had sex or even *kissed* anyone you weren't being paid to kiss in *twelve years*? No one hangs on that long."

"You hung on to my sweater that long," he pointed out, "even though you claim to have borderline hated me the entire time."

"That's a sweater," Sybil countered, exasperated. "I have a box of stuff I hung on to. That's stuff. I didn't deny myself for over a decade because of some over inflated sense of duty or self-flagellation. You don't get a good conduct medal for waiting, Peter."

By the time she was finished, her voice had risen and the

flush from her cheeks had spread to her chest, like an angry sunrise. To anyone else, he knew she would have seemed cross, but he'd spent his life obsessively studying facial expressions to use in his craft, and his favorite subject had always been Sybil. The almost imperceptible pinch between her eyes and the slight downward turn to her hard-set mouth told him that she felt guilty, maybe even ashamed. She wasn't mad at him, at least not more than she was mad at herself.

Peter kissed the lovely slope of her shoulder, right where it dropped off to her arm. "I never expected you to wait. That would've been unreasonable. I only fervently hoped you'd still be available."

She let out a heavy, exaggerated sigh. "Why do you have to be so understanding? It's infuriating."

He grinned and laid back against the pillows, pulling her with him. She went, unresisting. When he put his arms around her, she melted against him.

"Tell me more about this box."

It was a plain shoebox, tucked into the corner on the high shelf in her closet. There wasn't any writing on the box, no indication that it was full of memories or who they were associated with. Only a shoebox that rattled conspicuously when she took it down. She handed it to him, then shoved her fists into the pockets of his sweatshirt that she'd grabbed off the floor. The sweatshirt grazed the tops of her thighs, and he tried not to get distracted when he frequently remembered it was the only thing she was wearing.

Peter placed the box reverentially in front of him on the bed, adjusting the sheets so they were a little higher up his waist, then lifted the lid.

It was filled with scraps of paper, ticket stubs, programs, trinkets, and photos. He lifted out each memory carefully.

The first love note he'd ever written her before he'd told her he loved her, so every word was laced with saccharine adoration without ever using the word "love."

The program of a play he'd done for free to help a friend who was trying to become a playwright. That friend had become an award-winning playwright, but they hadn't been then. Sybil had suffered valiantly through three performances of that wretched play.

Ticket stubs from all the films they'd seen at the discount cinema, trying to cobble together dates on a shoestring budget.

He should take her on a date. Maybe to the cinema. Maybe to that nice restaurant Graham had taken Eloise to on their first date. It didn't matter what or where, as long as they were together.

Then came the photos, proof of how young they'd been and how deliriously in love he'd been with her. Every candid photo someone had taken of them, he was looking at her like the besotted dolt he had been and continued to be. Every posed shot he was smiling so widely it looked like his face would break from happiness. And there were candid shots of just him, ones she'd taken when he wasn't looking.

He held up a photo strip from a photo booth. "I still have my copy."

Sybil stopped anxiously nibbling on her thumbnail. "You do?"

"Check my wallet. It's in my pants."

With a soft, uncertain frown, she went and picked up his pants and located his wallet. She opened the brown leather billfold and took out his well-worn copy of the photobooth pictures. It curved in the middle from the years it had spent in his back pocket. If he'd had any true talent at art, he could have drawn the four stacked photos with his eyes closed.

"Why?" she asked, passing her thumb over the photo where he kissed her while she laughed, like she could feel the moment.

"Because I never stopped loving you." He picked out a post-card sized watercolor of a fox he'd bought for her at a market. "Why did you keep all of this?"

"So I'd know it happened."

"Were you afraid you'd forget?"

She shook her head. "No, but sometimes I felt like I'd made it all up, or that part of my life was one of those stupid movies you made me watch where the character wakes up and it was all a dream."

Her voice cracked on the last syllable, and she clenched her teeth so hard he saw her jaw muscles flex. Determined as always to ignore any seemingly "weak" emotions, she focused on replacing the photo strip in his wallet, and then his wallet to his pants. She held them out to him.

"You really can't spend the night," she reminded him.

He ignored his pants and grabbed her instead, bringing her back onto the mattress and close to his body.

"I know you keep saying I can't spend the night, but that doesn't mean I have to leave right this second. I haven't had a proper cuddle yet."

And for good measure, he stuck out his bottom lip and looked up at her through his eyelashes, doing his best orphaned puppy act.

Sybil groaned, rolled her eyes, but wrapped herself around him like an octopus, and squeezed him tightly.

"You're so damn needy."

"You like being needed."

Chapter Twenty-Five

Peter didn't spend the night, but he came close. The contentment of having him in her arms and being in his was as good as a strong sedative for Sybil. While he stroked his fingers up and down her spine, her eyelids grew too heavy to keep open and sleep came swiftly once they closed. And she probably would've slept the whole night through, tangled up with Peter, but at about 2:30 in the morning, Mallory came home from her shift at Moonie's bar and tripped over the mess in the kitchen.

There was no shame in Peter's walk when he left her house. It might have been her tired eyes, but Sybil could've sworn he was strutting like a peacock. He unabashedly said hello to Mallory and would have struck up a conversation if Sybil hadn't shoved him out the door and locked it behind him.

"You've got sex hair," Mallory said, perching on the back on the couch with a suggestive grin on her face.

There was no use denying it. Mallory would dig through the trash cans for the evidence if she did deny it.

"That's because I had sex," Sybil said bluntly, putting her hands in the pockets of Peter's hoodie to make herself look more casual than she felt. "You're out of condoms."

Mallory threw back her head to laugh and tipped backwards with a yelp of surprise, tumbling ass over head onto the couch.

"Serves you right," Sybil grumbled and headed for the kitchen to clean up the aftermath of her earlier anxiety.

"I have questions!" Mallory called from the living room, her voice growing closer as her sentence progressed.

Sybil picked up some scattered cans from the floor. "If you're going to ask questions, you have to help clean."

Mallory scooped up a few more of the scattered cans. "Tell me everything."

"That's a demand, not a question."

Sybil could feel the eye roll that happened behind her back.

"Was that the first time?"

The truthful answer sprang into her mouth and died on her tongue. Mallory didn't need to know about their past. It was a precious secret she'd guard close to her chest.

"Yes," Sybil lied. "You managed to come home *after* the grand finale this time."

"I guess you're welcome," Mallory said, stacking cans in categories that surprisingly didn't annoy Sybil. "Moonie offered to cut me early because we were slow and I decided to stay."

"How magnanimous of you."

"So is this a thing? Are you seeing each other?"

"I manage to see him every day whether I want to or not," Sybil replied, transferring Mallory's stacks onto the shelves of the pantry.

"If you're going to give me bullshit answers, I'm not going to help," Mallory warned coldly.

"We're not dating. It's casual. Ish."

"What does *ish* mean?"

Sybil looked to the ceiling like she was praying to the single light bulb in the pantry for strength.

"It means..." She struggled to define those three devilish

letters. They were infinitely problematic. "It means ish. Peter's mildly incapable of being truly casual, but it's not going anywhere."

"Mildly incapable." Mallory snorted. "Understatement of the decade."

"Oh, you know him super well?" Sybil snapped, much harsher than she'd intended.

"Do you?" Mallory bit back.

"You know what, I can do this myself. Go to bed."

"No." Mallory shoved a can into her hand. "You can't always push people away when you're uncomfortable." She set her jaw into an unyielding line. "I'm not scared of you like everyone else is."

"Is it time for you to leave again yet?"

"Maybe I'll stay to spite you," Mallory responded, but retreated to the other side of the kitchen to work on the kitchenware.

They worked, unspeaking, for twenty minutes and went upstairs in tense silence once the kitchen was back in order. They shut their doors on the opposite sides of the hall firmly with choreography they'd perfected over a lifetime of conflict.

No matter how late she went to bed, Sybil's alarm still trilled bright and early, rudely interrupting a fantastic dream where she was in a bookstore with Peter after it had closed for the night. He was on his knees in front of her, her legs hooked over his shoulders, her back against the shelves, and his hot breath igniting fire on her flesh while he recited poetry in between long, luxurious licks of her pussy. She couldn't remember if it was Shakespeare or Neruda or someone she'd heard once and long since forgotten, but those reverent recitations had curled her toes and made her pant. The details of the dream rapidly slipped away, but the aching and the wetness remained.

Her frustrated growl echoed in the early morning stillness.

There was no time for relief. She wasn't needed on set until the afternoon, and because production was scheduled to be near downtown all day, she wanted to spend the first half of the day at Stardust. And if she was going to open like she'd told her staff she would, she needed to pry herself out of bed and get ready for the day ahead.

Sybil saw several production assistants during the morning rush, coming to collect coffees for various departments. She couldn't remember the last time they'd gone through so many gray cardboard drink carriers. Before the end of the week she might even need to re-order those along with a lot of other supplies.

Guilt tainted the elation she felt when she got a moment to add the receipts from the week so far to her spreadsheet. Stardust was making a healthy profit, especially compared to what they usually made this time of year, but she hated that she was leaving her employees by themselves during the unexpectedly busy time.

There was an almost timid knock on the doorframe of the office. Lorna, one of her longest serving employees and de facto assistant manager, opened her mouth and hesitated.

"What's up?" Sybil prompted.

"I don't know how to say this," Lorna admitted, and Sybil's stomach clenched. "This isn't exactly my two weeks, but I wanted to let you know that Nicky got a job in Boise, so we're going to be moving soon."

Inwardly, Sybil cursed. Outwardly, she said, "How soon is soon?"

"We're supposed to be in Boise on the first of November."

"Fuck," she swore, and then remembered this was a good thing for Lorna. "I mean, this is a huge step forward and exciting for you two, but I am really going to miss you around here. I'm happy to write you a glowing recommendation letter or be a reference."

"Thank you. With Nicky's new job, we might be able to afford for me to go back to school to get my nursing degree."

"You mean you lied on your résumé and making coffee isn't your lifelong passion?" Sybil teased with mock indignation.

"Thanks for being so understanding. I was really nervous about telling you."

Mallory's words from the night before flashed through her mind, but Sybil pushed them aside.

"Stop yapping and go clean something."

Lorna grinned and disappeared from the doorway. Sybil counted to twenty before she put her head in her hands and groaned. She didn't need to add hiring and training to her impossibly long list of things to do. Any other year she would have absorbed the slack and figured it out later, but Lorna would be leaving before the end of production. With the increased business and Sybil's inability to be in two places at once, it felt like a recipe for disaster.

"Goddammit," she muttered under her breath.

A confident knock in a silly syncopation scared her half to death. She whipped her head up to castigate the intruder, and was only slightly mollified to see Peter's gorgeous, smiling face.

"What are you doing here?" she asked, her exhaustion leaking into her words along with her discouragement.

"I popped in to say hi," he answered innocently. "They waved me back."

Sybil doubted anyone had waved him back. Knowing Peter, he'd darted back when Lorna's back was turned.

"Aren't you supposed to be at work?" She pointed to his

costume. It had to be a costume, because she doubted Peter owned any flannel and no sane person would have handed him a real badge and gun.

He shrugged and leaned against the doorframe. "We're taking a break."

Her eyes narrowed. "The kind of break where you're allowed to wander off-set?"

"We're not far, and I wanted to see you."

Sybil sighed. "We need to talk."

Peter frowned. "About what?"

"Not here." She pushed back from her desk and stood. "The walls have ears."

She took him to the back door, looking up and down the alley before pulling him outside.

"I meant what I said at Eloise and Graham's. This can only be casual, and you sneaking off set to say hi to me when you know I'm going to be there later is *not* casual." She crossed her arms.

"But last night you said you still loved me."

"I know," Sybil admitted, cursing her past emotional self. "It doesn't matter. Our lives aren't compatible, and I don't think it's smart to try and delude ourselves into thinking we'll ever work again."

"I'm not following."

"Your life is big and mine is small," she said, using hand gestures for emphasis. "Everywhere you go, people are excited to meet you. They want to take a picture with you so they can show their friends that they met you. Outside of Crane Cove, no one knows or cares who I am. And that's fine with me. Everything and everyone I care about could fit inside this coffee shop. But our lives are too different. So it's casual or nothing at all because I already know how this ends and I don't want it."

There. She said it. All of the racing, looping thoughts that had plagued her since the very glimmer of a possibility of Peter being in her life again had arisen.

"What if I want to be here? What if I want a smaller life?"

"What we—what *you* want—what you *think* you want is on the opposite side of reality from what's practical, Peter. Do you really want to live in a place with god-awful cell phone reception and a newspaper that comes out weekly? Not daily. *Weekly*. The fundraisers we have around here aren't to cure cancer, but to buy new uniforms for the marching band, and it's not black tie, it's barbeque."

"That doesn't sound bad. I think I'd enjoy that."

"What about your career? If you want to keep working, you'll never be here. That's not much of a relationship."

"Our friends have made it work," Peter reminded her.

"Graham sold his company and moved here full-time to run the hotel with Eloise. Annie moved to Los Angeles for Jordy. Sam and Lacey travel together because their careers can intersect." For every example, Sybil held up a finger. "If you quit acting and moved here, I don't know what you'd do. You'd be miserable because you love your job." She put down her first finger. "I'm not moving to Los Angeles or New York or London or wherever you happen to be at the time." She put down her second finger. "I can't travel with you because my business is here, and it's not mobile." Sybil put down her final finger. "We're not them."

"I could live here. I could scale back my schedule. I could—"

"Casual or nothing."

Peter put his hands on his hips and looked at the sky, his mouth setting into a hard line. He let out a heavy, almost weary, sigh.

"Are you saying that because it's what you want, or because you're scared again that I'm going to resent you?" He looked down and leveled her with a soul-searching stare. "Because I think twelve years is long enough for me to know that anything I accomplish doesn't mean anything to me without being able to share it with you. I want this—I want *us*, no matter what it takes, no matter what it looks like."

His words reached into her chest, grabbed her heart, and squeezed so hard they crushed that vital organ like an overripe tomato. Never go against an actor when the future is on the line because they have too much experience delivering emotional speeches. Her resolve wavered.

Sybil tore her eyes away from his and looked at their feet, hoping to regroup and stiffen her backbone. All attempts to be stronger vanished when she saw that the black-and-white cat she'd been feeding had wandered between them unnoticed and was rubbing vigorously against Peter's legs, looking for attention.

Peter must have looked down too, because he said, "Oh, hello," in a delighted tone, and then crouched to pet the stray cat. She almost warned him not to, that it would run away, but the traitorous cat she'd been trying so hard to befriend arched its body to follow his scratches, and pushed its head under his hand for more.

"You've got to be fucking kidding me," she fumed. "I've been trying to get that cat to come to me for months, and it waltzes up to you like you're a fucking Disney princess."

He smiled up at her. "You know, I actually did voice a—"

"I know!"

Peter scooped up the cat, cradling it like a little baby, and stood. She could hear the cat purring while he scratched its chest.

"Did you stuff catnip in your pockets?" she asked accusingly, but reached out to scratch the cat behind the ears. "You're a smart kitty, going to the one that could keep you in wet food and treats."

"I've never had a pet," Peter admitted. "I've always wanted one, but it's never been a possibility because of my travel schedule."

It amazed her that he didn't see the irony.

"So does that mean you're going to keep her?"

He sighed. "I shouldn't." He scratched the cat under the chin, then, before Sybil could tell him not to, put the cat on the ground.

"Don't—" But it was too late. The cat bolted away like someone had lit its tail on fire. "...let go of the cat."

Peter's face was the picture of innocent horror and regret.

"I didn't know I was supposed to hang on to it," he said, and looked half ready to chase the cat down the alley.

The back door opened a little, and Lorna stuck her head out.

"Um, there's someone named Dempsey here looking for—" Her eyes landed on Peter, and her cheeks turned red. "Oh, hi."

"Busted," Sybil said. "Lorna, this is Peter, and he was just leaving."

"Hello, Lorna," Peter said warmly, putting a bright smile on his face and extending a hand. She took it, dazed. "Wonderful to meet you."

"Dempsey is plotting your murder," Sybil reminded him before he could try to make Lorna his new best friend. It wouldn't have taken any effort judging by the look on her face.

"Lorna, could you tell my assistant I will be with them shortly? Thank you." He waited until Lorna had disappeared back inside the building before turning his attention back to Sybil.

"I want you any way I can have you, so if casual is all you have to give right now, then I can be casual. I'd rather have a little of you than nothing at all." He cupped her face and stroked her cheek with his thumb. It took every ounce of self-control she had not to push into his touch like the cat had. "But I'm not going to give up trying to change your mind."

"That's not very casual of you," she pointed out.

Peter brushed his lips against hers, and her heart fluttered between her legs.

"You have your definition, I have mine."

"Dempsey. Murder."

Even the potential threat of bodily harm didn't stop Peter from giving her the kind of goodbye kiss reserved for soldiers going off to war. By the time he was done with her, Sybil was hanging on to his broad shoulders for dear life.

"I'll see you in a few hours," he said, and went inside like he hadn't attempted to alter her brain chemistry via her mouth.

Sybil leaned against the cool exterior of the building and took some deep, calming breaths. The way her heart raced was absolutely, completely, one hundred percent casual.

Chapter Twenty-Six

PETER CROSSED the threshold of the Crane Hotel and yawned. It was like his body knew that this was where his bed was and if it hinted hard enough, maybe he'd listen and get some rest.

Last night had been magnificent, but the opposite of restful. Sybil had fallen asleep so easily in his arms, but he'd forced his eyes to stay open as long as possible to soak the moment in. He re-counted the freckles on her nose and noted there were some new additions, and was fascinated by the few strands of silvery white hair on her head. There were six, and it looked like someone had dropped tinsel on her head. Sleep had only just overtaken him when Mallory came home and Sybil kicked him out.

It had been worth the hazy headache he'd had all day.

A good night's sleep—unless Sybil invited him over again, in which case, fuck sleep—and he could tackle his newest project: convince Sybil he could fit into her life.

"Peter!"

Graham's voice cut through the fog of concentration, and Peter looked around for his best friend. Graham smiled at him from behind the front desk, a look of bemused confusion on his face.

"Are you okay?" he asked after Peter arrived at the desk. "I said hi a few times, and you looked like you were somewhere else."

"Just being me," Peter said. "Off in la-la land. How are you? Any luck on the...?" He let the question hang in the air for Graham to fill in the blank.

"No, but I'm having fun trying. Or trying to have fun trying." Graham clipped a few sheets of paper together. "I was going to head out soon. Are you coming to barbecue night?"

Peter frowned quizzically. "What is that?"

"Practically a Crane Cove institution. Every Thursday night is barbecue night at Cranberry Brothers. Do you want me to save you a seat?"

"I will be there."

A Crane Cove community activity had fallen right into his lap. Fate had to be on his side.

Peter returned his costume, went to his room to wash the last vestiges of his character Glenn off his body, and worried over what to wear while he towel-dried his hair. He settled on a very comfortable and extremely casual outfit: jeans, a soft dark blue T-shirt, and his remaining zip-up hoodie. Dressing up for dinner felt very LA, and this outfit said, "I can be a very regular normal person."

Cranberry Brothers Brewing wasn't far from Sybil's coffee shop, which meant it had a sub-optimal parking situation. The parking spots nearest the brewery were full, and he ended up parked on a side street a few blocks away. Thankfully, it was a dry night, so he arrived without looking like he was starring in a pirate film.

Peter had never been to the brewery before, though he knew of it from his friends. Cranberry Brothers Brewing was owned and operated by Connor's twin brothers, Chase and Cole. From Sam, Peter knew that Cole was an excellent and meticulous cook, and from Jordy, he'd heard that Chase should've played professional sports. Graham complained that they were aging him in dog years ever since he moved to town and the twins had decided that he was going to be their best friend. The way Graham described it, they made up the cast of *Up*, with Graham obviously being the old man.

He didn't know what kind of crowds the brewery drew other nights of the week, but the place was packed when he stepped inside. A chalkboard said, "We give up. Find your own seat." Peter chuckled and craned his neck to see if he could spot Graham. And maybe he would have, if he hadn't seen a red ponytail at the bar. His heart leapt, and he squeezed his way through the crowd as quickly as he could, adopting a serpentine quality to his movement as he dodged bodies.

"Hello there," he said, putting a gentle hand on Sybil's lower back. "You made it here quickly."

She looked up at him, and he realized part of the reason she'd made it to the brewery so quickly was that she was still wearing her makeup from the movie.

"If you don't get here early, it's hard to get a seat."

"Connor doesn't make his brothers save him a table?"

"Connor can't make his brothers do anything. He's tried. They're immune to his disapproving glares."

"I'm very familiar with those," Peter said.

Sybil dropped her voice to a level he could barely hear. "You should stop touching me. People will get ideas."

"But I like touching you," he whispered back.

"Save it for later."

Electric anticipation zinged through his body and his blood

crackled. Any lingering fatigue disappeared and he decided he could sleep when he was dead.

Peter put his hands in his pockets.

"I've got beers— Hey, Pete!" A giant McMahon—Chase, because his blond hair was short and he didn't have a beard—put two pint glasses on the bar and held out his hand.

Peter didn't point out that no one called him Pete because he didn't want to accidentally offend Sybil. He took Chase's hand and got yanked halfway across the bar into what was universally known as the "bro hug." After three chest-rattling pats on the back, he was pretty sure a rib had been knocked loose.

"Good to see you. What can I get for you?" Chase asked after he'd released Peter.

"Umm..." The options were overwhelming, especially for someone who didn't drink a lot of beer.

"Do you want me to pick? I'm a pretty good guesser," Chase offered.

"Yes, please."

Chase grabbed a glass and went down the row of taps, stopping to consider a few, before settling on one near the end. He filled the glass with a golden beer, much lighter than the dark brown and amber beers in the glasses he'd handed Sybil, and came back.

"This is a golden Belgian ale made with local apples. I think you'll like it."

Peter picked up the glass and took a cautious sip. It was delicious. Dry, fruity, and the carbonation danced on his tongue.

"Wow. That is really good."

Chase beamed. "Glad you like it. Did you want to order any food while you're up here?"

Peter looked down at Sybil for help answering that question. She rolled her eyes and sighed.

"Can you add another plate to our table? I think that'll be easier."

"I'll let the kitchen know," Chase said, and bustled off.

"What am I getting to eat?" Peter asked as he followed Sybil through the crowd.

"Does it matter? It's food. You'll eat it."

They arrived at a small rectangular table that had benches instead of chairs. One bench was filled with Kiki, Graham, and Eloise. The three of them were having what sounded like an impromptu hotel staff meeting, probably so they could write the meal off on their taxes. Connor sat on the other bench, a blank, half-listening look on his face, his eyes following something in the direction of the bar. When they interrupted his sight line, Connor's shoulders tensed and his eyes narrowed. He slid from the left side of the bench right into the middle, presumably trying to create an immovable barrier between Peter and Sybil.

The joke was on him, because that was exactly where Peter wanted him for phase one of Operation Crane Cove. The name needed work, but that was a problem for when he had more than three working brain cells.

Sybil set the dark beer in front of Connor and lowered herself onto the bench. No sooner had her butt touched the wood than Connor asked, "Where's the popcorn?"

"Damnit." She started to rise.

"I can get it," Peter offered quickly.

She shook her head. "No. I'll get it. You'll never make it back, and I'll have to wrest the scraps of your broken body from your adoring fans."

Confused, he looked to Graham for an answer after she'd headed back to the bar.

"I don't understand. No one's bothered me at all here."

"You haven't really spent a lot of time out and about," Graham pointed out. "You've been too busy with the movie."

"And you were with Sybil, and people are scared of her," Kiki chimed in, delighted to add her tidbit to the explanation.

"People aren't scared of Sybil—" Eloise began charitably, but stopped when everyone but Peter stared at her pointedly. She sighed and amended, "There's an abundance of cautious respect for her in the community."

Kiki cackled.

"Speaking of the community..." Peter turned to Connor. "Is there a drama club at the high school? Or a local children's or community theater?"

Connor frowned suspiciously. "Why?"

"It's customary for productions to give back to the communities they're involved with," Peter said. He was pretty sure that was the truth, though he'd never experienced it firsthand. "I'd like to talk to some aspiring young actors. Give them some tips or advice. Or maybe I could come to your class and talk about plays and the theater."

Connor pursed his lips and his eyebrows drew together.

"That would be amazing," Eloise gushed. "Maybe you could bring your dad too. Arthur has done plays with the Royal Shakespeare Company, Connor. What an incredible opportunity for the students to hear from award-winning actors about how the things they're learning in your class are used in the real world."

"I don't know if I'd call acting the real world," Connor mumbled under his breath.

"Maybe seeing the notes on Peter's scripts could help them with their close reading skills," Eloise continued. "Or maybe how Charlotte does it as a director."

"That's an idea," Connor said and sipped his beer.

Sybil returned with two metal bowls of popcorn and set them down on the table before retaking her seat on the other side of Connor.

"I found out today that Lorna is leaving," she began as

Mallory arrived with a stack of six plates. "So, if anyone has any leads on a replacement, I'm all ears."

"I could do it," Mallory offered quickly.

"I need someone who isn't planning on leaving in a few weeks to a few months," Sybil pointed out coolly. "Then I've got the same problem all over again. Plus, you're a bartender, not a barista."

"I could learn."

"We're not talking about this right now," Sybil said, taking the plates and distributing them around the table.

Peter didn't understand. He'd seen Mallory work before, and she was fantastic. She struck the perfect balance of efficient and personable with patrons, somehow making everyone feel like her best friend. As far as he could see, she would be a wonderful addition to the Stardust staff and someone Sybil could lean on to get her through the interim period finding a new Lorna, or as a permanent replacement.

But the storm-on-the-horizon look on her face told him this wasn't the time or place to bring up his opinions.

Cole, Connor's younger brother and Chase's hulking twin, appeared at the side of the table, a large, round serving tray filled with food held at shoulder height. His curly blond hair was pulled into a bun near the top of his head and he'd cut his ginger-tinged beard closer to his face since the last time Peter had seen him at last year's Thanksgiving. He lowered the tray so Mallory could reach the platters, which she put on the table.

Chase came over as Mallory finished unburdening Cole's tray, and the twins exchanged a suspiciously meaningful look.

"So, Peter," Cole began after Chase elbowed him in the side, "we don't know if you've noticed any of the flyers around town, but the closest Saturday to Halloween we host a benefit here—"

"We call it the Boo-wery," Chase interjected helpfully.

"Yes. We have a silent auction that benefits the animal shelter," Cole continued. "So we were going through our list of generous donations, and we were wondering if you and/or the movie would be interested in making a donation to the auction."

Chase nodded. "It doesn't have to be anything over the top. Last year Sam donated a guitar lesson."

"That I bid on so he wouldn't actually have to do it," Graham interrupted. "I'm not rescuing you if you donate something like that."

"If you choose to donate," Chase clarified, his voice and face full of the kind of hope children have on Christmas Eve.

"I don't see why not," Peter said. "I'll talk to my parents to see what the production wants to do. I'm sure some of the other cast members would be happy to donate something too."

The twins relaxed in unison.

"Thank you so much," Cole said. "It really doesn't have to be anything big or extravagant."

Sybil put a slab of brisket on his plate. "Put Cole's meat in your mouth before they get you to agree to anything else."

The problem with the golden ale that Chase had given him was that it was too good. By the time people at their table started to make excuses for why they needed to leave and over exaggerated yawns, Peter was tipsy and on the downhill slide toward being drunk. Connor left first, then Graham and Eloise, and finally, Kiki. He dug into his back pocket for his wallet and put a bill on the table, then looked to Sybil.

"Do you think that's enough to cover it?"

She was fighting a losing battle against a smile. "How much do you think beer is here?"

He looked at what he'd taken out of his wallet. "Is a hundred not enough?"

She rolled her eyes. "You need to walk this off before you drive back to the hotel." She slipped her arms into her coat and grabbed her purse from the hook under the table. "Let's go get you some coffee."

"At your place?" he asked hopefully, trailing after her like a puppy, but he had to double back to get his coat.

"My place of business," Sybil clarified and held the door open for him. It was still dry outside, but the air smelled like coming rain. "I don't know if it's right for me to take advantage of you in your current state."

"Please take advantage of me."

Her laugh sounded like a sky full of twinkling stars, and he smiled, falling into step with her as they crossed the empty street.

"I love you," he sighed, and stuck his hand in her coat pocket to find her hand. She allowed him to awkwardly lace his fingers with hers.

"You might be drunker than I thought."

"I will concede that I shouldn't drive for a bit, but I am not drunk."

"Then what are you?"

"Enamored with you."

"You're horrible at being casual, Peter," she said.

"Is this not how casual people behave?"

She shook her head. "Nope."

"Hmmm..." He pursed his lips in faux thought. "I guess we'll have to spend more time together so I can practice being casual. Can I casually kiss you?"

"Putting the word 'casual' in front of something doesn't make it casual," Sybil pointed out, but diverted their path toward the alley next to Stardust.

The alley was dark, and in a different city with less alcohol in his system, it might have made him nervous. But this was

Crane Cove, and the worst thing that might be in that alley was a raccoon.

In the darkest part of the alley, where the shadows cast by lights on either end converged, Sybil rested her back against the wall and pulled him to her. She curled a hand around the back of his neck, and it took only a featherlight pressure to bring his mouth to hers. Bitter hops lingered on her tongue, mixed with a sweetness that was all her, and Peter wondered if Chase could bottle the taste. He'd buy the entire stock.

Sybil's teeth scraped his bottom lip and a deep sound rumbled in the back of his throat, somewhere between a moan and a growl. He pressed his body into hers, pinning her against the wall, and she made a noise that was a softer, more delicate version of the one he'd made.

Peter knew he wasn't drunk. He was in control of his body, and he knew what was going on around him. But his impulse control, which was low on a good day, had hit rock bottom and found a drill. His hands roamed her body, exploring her curves through her clothes, and paused at the waistband of her pants. He ran his fingers just under the edge of the fabric.

"I want to touch you so bad," he murmured against her mouth. He trailed his lips along her jaw, down to her neck. "I want to make you feel so good." He tugged at the button on her jeans. "Please?"

"Peter," Sybil whispered, even as she tilted her neck and raised her hips to give him better access. "We're outside. What if someone caught us?"

"No one is going to catch us," he reassured her, and sucked gently on her neck until she shuddered. "It's dark and you'd be sure to be very, very quiet, hm?"

He nuzzled her pulse and finally worked the button through the denim hole. As he lowered her zipper, he nipped her collarbone, then raised his head. Their noses brushed as he slid his hand into her pants.

The jingle of a bell made Sybil tense, and she grabbed his wrist. From the end of the alley where the street was, the sound of laughter and goodbyes filtered toward them. Was that why they were outside in an alley instead of in her office, where he might have been able to already have her bent over her desk, moaning his name while he fucked her from behind? Because her employees had still been inside Stardust?

Soft pressure on his shins made him look down.

The cat from earlier was rubbing against his legs again.

"Get the cat," Sybil hissed.

Peter hurried to obey, which was likely his downfall. He swooped down to grab the cat, who was startled by his sudden movement and tried to bolt. In his slightly inebriated state, Peter lost all spatial awareness and lunged. His hands clamped down on the furry body at the same time his head collided with the wall.

The sound registered before the pain did. The hollow thud, a delay of a second or two, then sharp pain that spread through his skull like fingers of lightning.

But he had the cat.

He staggered as he straightened, and turned to show Sybil his triumph.

"Peter!" She stretched on her tiptoes to try and examine him. He liked her fussing over him. "Are you okay? Do you have a concussion? How do we know if you have a concussion?"

He shrugged. "Ask Jordy?" He held up the cat. "I got the cat."

"Yes, you did," she said soothingly, and buttoned her pants. "Let's get you some ice."

. . .

Sybil unlocked the front door to Stardust, led him by the elbow to the office, sat him down in the chair, and ordered him to stay put.

"You're sexy when you're bossy," he said with a goofy grin.

She rolled her eyes and left.

He scratched the cat behind the ears and under the chin. The cat purred and followed his fingers every time he tried to stop.

"You're a sweet kitty," he cooed.

Sybil returned with a bag of ice and gingerly placed it on his head. He winced. The miniscule weight of the bag stung.

"I'm sorry," she said. "If I'd known you were going to take your cat-catching duties so enthusiastically, I would've done it myself."

"I take everything you want seriously."

She kissed his forehead, and his heart fluttered. He'd head-butt a thousand walls if she'd brush her lips against his skin.

"You're a little *too* good at taking directions," Sybil teased. "How are you feeling?"

"A lot like Wile E. Coyote."

"Got an urge to chase roadrunners?"

"Get me an ACME catalog and my credit card."

"Beep-beep." She grinned when he laughed. "Let me grab the cat carrier and we can go back to my house. I want to keep an eye on you for a little bit longer."

"I'd be happy to let you keep an eye on me for the rest of my life," Peter called after her as she left the room again. He looked at the cat, who was looking up at him with peridot eyes. "One of these days, that's going to work, and you'll have a two-parent household."

The cat responded with a doubtful meow.

Sybil returned with a small, soft-sided pet carrier, the kind he usually saw on airplanes.

"I ordered this a while ago," she explained. "I never thought it would take this long to catch the cat."

Peter lowered the cat inside, and Sybil quickly zipped it before the cat could escape. It yowled in protest.

The vocal complaints continued the entire walk to Sybil's house. He convinced her that she needed to hold his hand so he could cross the street and managed to distract her so she didn't drop it when they reached the other side.

Sybil didn't lock her front door. It took a moment to register that she'd opened the front door without inserting a key first, and the brief panic was waylaid when he remembered Graham didn't bother much with home security either and his big house was a much more attractive target for a burglar than Sybil's Craftsman bungalow.

They took the cat to a small laundry room, and Sybil unpacked cat supplies hidden in a cupboard. She really had been preparing for a cat. Litter was emptied into a litter box, dry food was scooped into a small bowl, and wet food was left on a little plate. She left briefly to fill up a water dish. The whole time he stood there holding the cat carrier with the ungrateful cat inside.

"I don't know when I'm going to find the time to take her to see Chris tomorrow," Sybil said after they'd left the cat in the laundry room.

"Dempsey could do it," Peter offered. "I don't send them on enough errands."

"Would they mind?"

"It's part of their job description...I think. They could have rewritten their job description when I wasn't looking." A thought from earlier tickled the forefront of his mind. "Why won't you let Mallory work for you?"

"Because she's immature, irresponsible, and flighty." She walked to the kitchen, and he followed. "There's no point in me training her since she's going to leave whenever she feels like it, and then I'll have to find someone new."

"Graham seems to like having her as an employee," Peter pointed out while Sybil got him a glass of water. "No one has ever accused him of being an easy person to impress."

"That's different."

"Not really. A lot of those skills she uses as a bartender seem transferable to me. Would it really be so bad to give her a shot?"

"Yes, it would." She crossed her arms. "It's all good and fine for Graham, and Moonie, and the twins to have someone who pops in and out, but I need someone that's going to stick around."

"You won't even consider her as a stop-gap option?"

If looks could kill, he'd be a cloud of dust. Peter held up his hands in surrender, and a little water sloshed out of the glass and onto his wrist.

"Forget I said anything. It's not my business."

"You're right. It's not your business." Her eyes flicked to his glass. "Drink your water."

Chapter Twenty-Seven

Sybil considered throwing her phone across the room when her alarm rudely interrupted the dream she'd been having. Peter had another starring role, but the details dissipated like smoke in the wind before she could luxuriate in the afterglow.

She stretched her body toward her nightstand and silenced the alarm. Another day, another dol—

A warm arm curled around her midsection and attempted to drag her backwards. Adrenaline shot through her nervous system and her body jolted into action. Except her brain wasn't fully functioning yet, so her limbs flung themselves erratically and ineffectively, except for her elbow, which caught something soft that made her assailant go "Oomph."

"Ow," the voice behind her croaked hoarsely. Peter.

When it should have been time to send him back to the hotel, she didn't have the heart to kick him out. It was dark and cold, and what if he got lost walking back to the brewery? She couldn't have a head injury *and* hypothermia on her conscience. Plus, she'd been far too comfortable with her head on his chest and his arms wrapped around her. *Just another ten minutes,* she'd told herself over and over until she'd drifted off to sleep.

Too bad she hadn't remembered any of that until after she'd assaulted him.

Peter had curled himself into a protective ball, a pained grimace contorting his gorgeous face.

"I forgot you were here! I'm so sorry." She put a gentle hand on his shoulder. "Are you okay?"

"You didn't hit anything vital. Just my kidneys or my liver." He groaned, but relaxed his body. "I think you're going to be hell on my insurance premiums."

"For your own good, I'm going to have to wrap you in bubble wrap," she told him, stroking his face. "Would it help if I kissed it better?"

His eyebrows jumped. That had caught his interest.

"Could you be persuaded to move the medicinal kiss about seven or eight inches lower?"

If he was making hopeful requests, he couldn't be too injured. Then again, Peter could have a limb hanging by a single blood vessel and he'd probably still try his luck at getting in her pants.

Sybil's hand stole under the covers and cupped his balls, squeezing gently. Peter's eyes rolled back and his lips parted.

"Hmmm..." She slid her hand along his growing shaft and squeezed the hard length through the thin cotton of his underwear. When had he taken off his pants? "It does feel like you might need some *particular* attention in this area. A very *thorough* examination. For safety. It would be negligent if I didn't check for further injuries."

Down the bed she went, situating herself between Peter's thighs. She kissed the bend of his knee, falling a little bit in love with the small creases there. He squirmed.

"This seems fine." She kissed the spot on his inner thigh where his boxer briefs ended. "All good here." The head of his cock strained against its cotton confines. She clicked her tongue and shook her head. "Oh dear. This doesn't look good at all."

Her "sexy medical professional" character needed a lot of work, but Peter the professional actor hung on every word.

Sybil licked the tip of his cock through his underwear, and then drew it into her mouth and sucked the best she could. The taste of laundry detergent and salty precum coated her tongue. Peter's choked moan made her pussy throb.

"Relax, and this will all be over soon," she soothed, pulling his underwear off his hips in torturously slow inches. The elastic waistband caught on the tip, so when she freed his cock, it flew out like it was spring-loaded and slapped against his stomach. She widened her eyes like it was her first time seeing it. "Is it always this big?"

Peter shook his head. "Sometimes bigger."

Sybil nodded, but frowned like she was considering a grave problem.

"I need to stimulate blood flow to make sure everything is functioning properly. This is best achieved by manual and oral stimulation."

She grasped the base of his cock and squeezed, then worked her hand up and down his shaft a few times to demonstrate.

"That's manual stimulation," she explained, then brought his cock to her mouth and wrapped her lips around the tip and sucked. Peter whimpered and gripped the sheets. "That's oral stimulation. A combination of the two usually produces results. Should I proceed?"

"*Fuck* yes."

The breathy, wonderstruck way he said those words was dangerous. It made her feel desirable and sublime, like no one had ever made him feel like this before and no one ever would again. She could get addicted to that kind of feeling.

She took him deeper in her mouth this time, and continued to take him deeper with each bob of her head until he hit the back of her throat. She swallowed against her gag reflex and Peter's entire body tensed.

"Bloody hell," he cursed rapturously. She swallowed again and his mouth fell open while his eyes fluttered shut. Strong fingers sank into her hair and squeezed the roots. "Cheeky minx."

Her pussy ached to be filled. It continued to get wetter and wetter, as if a lack of lubrication was the only thing preventing Sybil from taking Peter's cock out of her mouth and putting it in a different hole. She rocked against the bed since both of her hands were busy. One hand was wrapped around the base of his cock as a stopper so she wouldn't accidentally go too far down his shaft and do more than tickle her gag reflex. The other hand played with his balls, rolling them in her palms like a pair of baoding balls.

"I–I'm close," Peter warned.

Sybil worked his shaft with her mouth a few more times, then pulled off, rapidly stroking him with her hand until he gasped, tensed, and came on his stomach. Some of it even managed to hit his chest.

Peter collapsed against the pillows, panting like he'd crossed the finish line at a marathon.

"I think I'm cured," he finally said, dazed.

"We'll be asking you to fill out a customer satisfaction survey."

Sybil got up, crept to the bathroom for a washcloth, and made it back to her room without hearing so much as a snore from Mallory's room.

She tossed the rag at Peter, and it landed on his face. He grabbed it and started to mop himself up.

"So are there any follow-up appointments?"

"Were you planning on getting injured again?"

"I would play in traffic if you'd do that again with even half the effort."

Peter tried to stay.

He dillyed. He dallyed. He took a hell of a long time acting like he couldn't find his socks. But in the end, Sybil managed to shove him unceremoniously through the front door, locking it behind him so he couldn't scamper back in.

She sagged against the door and smiled.

It was a good thing that production took weekends off, because she was in legitimate danger of wanting him around all the time. A nice little break to remember what peace and quiet felt like would solve that.

She went into the kitchen to make breakfast and jumped when she saw Mallory standing in front of the open refrigerator.

"You're up early," Sybil said, trying to inject cool casualness into her voice instead of sounding like a child who'd been caught with their hand in the cookie jar.

"Peter's voice carries." Mallory yawned and took out the carton of eggs. "Are you hungry?"

Sybil's stomach answered for her with a loud growl.

"I was going to have eggs and toast. Do we have bread?" Mallory opened a cupboard.

"Bread got moldy. We have tortillas. There's some leftover fajita veggies in the fridge if we want to make breakfast burritos."

"Always a problem solver." Mallory climbed onto the counter to get the tortillas.

Sybil started the coffee pot while Mallory cracked a few eggs into a bowl. Soon the only sounds in the kitchen were eggs being whisked and coffee dripping. The silence between them wasn't exactly awkward, but it wasn't comfortable. Or maybe it was just Sybil that felt that way, because she didn't see a trace of worry on her sister's face.

"So, I was thinking," Sybil began as Mallory poured the eggs into a pan. "Maybe you could try working for me on a trial basis."

Mallory's eyebrows rose. "Hell has frozen over. What changed your mind?"

Truthfully, it had been Peter. But she was never going to admit that.

"I'm dusting off the old coffee cart for the movie and could use some help running it. At least if you screw up there, you won't piss off my existing customers."

Mallory rolled her eyes and moved the eggs around the pan with a spatula. "Don't let the weight of your confidence in me break your back."

"Do you want the job or not?"

"Do I get to keep the tips?"

"We'll split them."

Mallory frowned. "Don't you have a job on this movie? How is it fair to split the tips if I'm doing more of the work?"

"Fine. We'll split them 60/40."

"Still doesn't seem fair."

"There's an education surcharge." Sybil took two coffee cups from the cupboard. "If the coffee cart goes well, maybe you can pick up some shifts at Stardust and we can go from there. But you're not replacing Lorna."

"How are you planning on training me?" Mallory asked,

sprinkling some salt over the eggs, which were exiting their runny stage.

"Can you go in with me before we open tomorrow?"

Mallory shook her head. "I'm closing at Moonie's tonight. I won't be home until close to three."

Sybil frowned. "I thought you did weekends at the hotel?"

Mallory sighed. "I'm doing both. I'm at the hotel until nine when things kind of die off there, and then I go to Moonie's to finish the night because that's when things pick up there. The goal is to maximize my tip potential."

"When were you planning on working for me? Because you've got shifts at Cranberry Brothers too."

"Mid-day. Come in between ten and four, which covers your mid-morning crowd that's meeting for coffee and your mid-afternoon crowd that needs a pick me up to survive the rest of the day." Mallory moved the pan off the burner. "Then I'd go to the hotel or Cranberry Brothers, work a shift there, and then Moonie's to finish the night. Do you want me to pan-fry your burrito?"

"Um, yes, please."

"I saw something where someone sprinkled the cheese on the *outside*." Mallory wiggled her eyebrows enticingly, and an unexpected laugh bubbled out of Sybil. "I knew you liked it cheesy."

Even though that wasn't necessarily about him, Peter jumped to the forefront of her mind. The man was cheesy as hell, and she did in fact like it. And as much as she hated it, he was probably right about giving Mallory a chance. If she was as effortlessly good at making coffee as she was at everything else she'd ever tried, she might even admit to his face that he'd been right.

"If you can find time to pencil me into your incredibly busy schedule, I could find time to teach you."

Mallory scooped scrambled eggs onto a tortilla. "It's a date."

There was a plaintive yowl from the laundry room, and Sybil splashed coffee on the counter. "Oh my god! I forgot about the cat!"

"We have a cat?" Mallory shouted after her.

Chapter Twenty-Eight

PETER HAD three new text messages when he stepped out of
the shower.

SYBIL

Mallory offered to take the cat to the vet so
Dempsey is off the hook

PETER

Our cat needs a name. We can't keep referring
to it as "the cat"

He was surprised when he got a swift text back.

My cat, even if it likes you better. And "Cat"
worked just fine for Holly Golightly

Don't try and use Audrey Hepburn against me.
We could do Sherlock for a boy or Agatha for a
girl. Mystery theme.

It's only a theme if there's more than one cat.

Peter had just started typing when another message came
through.

> Do not get me a second cat.

He laughed. She knew him too well, because he'd been about to ask if she wanted him to find her a second cat.

> Fine. No second cat. Love you.

> Casual.

The next unread message was from Sam.

SAM

> Lacey wants to know how my sex advice worked for you.

Lacey really was the most perfect person in the world for Sam. He had a tendency to clam up, but she was a blunt instrument designed to crack him open.

> Good enough that I don't want to leave a paper trail.

Finally, he opened Jordy's thread.

JORDY

> Call me.

Jordy answered on the third ring.

"Hey, bud. What's up?"

"You told me to call you, remember?" He put the phone on speaker and laid it on the counter so he could get ready. "What's up with you?"

"Yeah, I can talk," Jordy said with exaggerated casualness, then Peter heard him loudly whisper, "I'm going to take this outside."

"You'd make a terrible actor," Peter told him.

"Good thing I have no plans to enter the dramatic arts."

There was a soft breeze in the background, and Jordy grunted, so Peter assumed he'd lowered himself into a chair. "I think I might have a plan for proposing, but I need your help."

"Do I need to get a fireworks permit?"

"No." Jordy chuckled. "I've been stuck for days trying to figure this out, and last night Annie and I were talking and it all just came together."

Peter picked up his phone and wandered into the bedroom area to get dressed. "The suspense is killing me."

"We were talking about how much we miss everyone and how we don't think we want to raise our kids in LA—"

"Kids? Is Annie pregnant?"

"No...I don't think she is..." There was a confused lilt to Jordy's voice and Peter could imagine the small frown on his face. "Anyway, she brought up maybe moving to Oregon. Both state universities are only about two hours from Crane Cove, which is kind of perfect. I suggested we go visit while you're in town, maybe go look at some properties between the universities. She loved the idea."

"So where do I fit into this plan?"

"Can you hold onto the ring? I don't want her accidentally finding it."

"Of course I can! When are you going to come up?"

"We're still figuring that out, but definitely before you wrap." Jordy let out a shaky breath. "I'm so nervous. I want this to be perfect."

"I think no matter what happens, Annie is going to think it's perfect because she loves you," Peter said. "But I'll have Dempsey source a bunch of those little battery-operated candles, just in case."

"Why battery-operated?"

"So they won't blow out, burn out, or start a fire."

"Oh, that's smart."

Peter buttoned his pants. "I'm becoming really practical as I get older."

———

Cell service in Crane Crave was fucking abysmal. Peter took small steps, holding his phone at face height, trying to find the signal he'd somehow lost so he could purchase the multi-level cat tree he'd found for Agatha. Their cat was a girl, and he was chuffed that Sybil had used the name he'd suggested. He'd already managed to order an automatic litter box, a water fountain, and some cat toys between takes.

Would Agatha like a catnip plant? Was it okay for cats to have access to kitty weed? If he got her one, would she become a kitty stoner and nap in the sun all day, high out of her little mind?

"That's a wrap," his mom shouted into her megaphone. "Great work, everyone. Enjoy your weekend."

It had been perfectly overcast all day, but the predicted rain had started half an hour earlier than the weather man had called for. Crew members hurried to strike the equipment, partly to protect it from the elements, and partly so they could get their weekend started. People who lived in Portland and the surrounding areas would drive home, and those staying behind started making plans. He scanned the moving people for Sybil and saw her headed for her car.

He'd order the cat tree later.

"So what are we doing this weekend?" Peter asked when he'd caught up to her.

"I don't know what you're doing, but I have things to do," Sybil said and opened her car door.

"What kinds of things?" He got into the passenger seat before she could object.

She sighed and started the car. "I'm helping Connor with his cross-country meet tomorrow morning, then I'm working at Stardust, and I've got to get the coffee cart ready so it actually works."

"I could help with that," he offered.

"With what?"

"All of it. Any of it. As long as I get to spend time with you, I don't really care what we're doing."

Sybil snorted. "You're only saying that because you've never stood in the rain for hours waiting for teenagers to finish jogging through the woods."

"I guess I'll find out what that's like tomorrow."

Peter really didn't care what they were doing as long as they were together, but helping Connor at the same time was a bonus. He needed Sybil's best friend on his side if he had any hope of convincing her in a few weeks that continuing their relationship was feasible. Eloise would be on his side, but Peter had a sinking feeling that Connor's probable dissenting opinion would hold more weight.

"You have to be there by seven," she warned.

"You know what might make this easier?" Peter began, covering the hand that was casually resting on her thigh with his own and twining their fingers together. "If I spent the night at your place. Then you can make sure I'm there on time."

Sybil laughed, so he decided to keep pressing his luck.

"And I don't want poor, sweet Agatha to think I've abandoned her. I could help with her transition from alley cat to house cat."

"God, I hope Mallory put her back in the laundry room and didn't let her roam the house," Sybil muttered as she turned on to the road that would take them back to the hotel.

"So was that a yes or a no to me spending the night?"

"I'll think about it."

But she squeezed his hand, so he felt pretty good about his chances.

Rain drummed on the roof of Sybil's covered porch and the fat drops splashed on the pavement, miniature droplets spraying the bottom step. Peter sat on the top step, the toes of his shoes slowly growing damp from the residual mist.

He could have let himself into the house and waited for Sybil in there where it was warm and he could have snuggled with the cat. The door was unlocked. But as he'd been opening the door it had occurred to him that letting himself into Sybil's house was *not* a good idea. So he sat on the porch, watching the street for her to come home, his fingers worrying a leaf from the bouquet of flowers he'd bought for her. All cat-safe, in case Agatha got into them. He'd interrogated the florist.

A car turned into the driveway, and once the headlights weren't in his eyes, Peter confirmed it was Sybil's car and an ounce of the nervous tension in his shoulders leaked away.

"I'm surprised you're not in the house," she said as she headed toward the porch.

Peter stood, grabbing the bottle of wine he'd brought by the neck, and held out the flowers as she reached the bottom step.

"I decided to follow vampire rules. Can I come in?"

Sybil took the flowers and lifted her head for a kiss, which he gladly gave her.

"You're terrible at being casual," she murmured against his lips.

"I'm being very casual. I haven't asked you to marry me yet."

She rolled her eyes, but there was a smile playing in the corners of her mouth.

"Where's your stuff? I know you didn't show up with flowers and a bottle of wine without an ulterior motive."

Peter looked at his backpack, which was hidden behind a flower pot, and Sybil's gaze followed his.

"Is the wine red or white?"

"Red, of course."

Sybil opened her front door. "Good answer."

Irritated meows could be heard from the back of the house. Agatha did not enjoy her confinement.

Peter left his backpack near the door, slid out of his shoes, and followed Sybil to the kitchen.

"Will you let Agatha out?" she asked, taking a vase out from a low cupboard.

The cat was thrilled to see him. Her yowls changed to delighted chirps when he opened the laundry room door, and she rubbed against his legs, purring loudly.

"Is your girlfriend happy to see you?" Sybil asked, already opening the bottle of wine when he returned to the kitchen, cradling Agatha like a baby.

"I ordered her some stuff today," Peter confessed, scratching the cat on the chin while she tried to contort her body so he could pet her head at the same time.

Sybil poured two hefty glasses of wine and handed one to him. "You've got a sugar daddy, Agatha."

"Do you think a catnip plant is a good idea or a bad idea?"

They wandered back to the velvet couch, and he sat right next to Sybil, their thighs touching. Agatha, in an effort to be cute and garner more attention, wiggled, rolled, and got herself trapped in the seam where their legs met, like a turtle that had landed on its shell instead of its feet.

"Tale as old as time." Sybil shook her head and *tsked* her tongue disapprovingly. "A normally very intelligent girl makes an absolute fool of herself for the attention of a good-looking man."

Peter draped his free arm around her shoulders. "You think I'm good-looking?"

"You're fishing for compliments." Sybil tapped the end of his nose with her index finger. "Weren't you on the Sexiest Man Alive list?"

"The compliments mean more when they come from you."

"I will never understand you," she confessed, brushing a few humidity-induced curls off his forehead.

"You don't have to understand it, just accept it."

He waited for her to try the wine and then leaned forward and kissed her, enjoying the warmth of the grapes from her tongue. She sighed lightly, relaxing into his attention like it was all she'd been waiting for all day. Agatha pawed his side, but he ignored her.

"That's good wine," he said when Sybil finally broke their kiss.

"You should try it again," she suggested and took another drink.

Peter relieved her of her wine glass and put both glasses on the coffee table, then sank his fingers into the hair at the base of her skull and kissed her again, slow and deep, savoring her. Shivers flooded his body as her tongue slid against his, and he swallowed the tiny, whimpering moan that escaped her.

Agatha meowed.

"Should we go upstairs?" Peter asked. "We could drink our wine without any interruptions."

"Mallory is closing at Moonie's tonight. She won't be home until after two."

"I meant the cat."

"Worried your girlfriend is going to get jealous?" Sybil teased.

"I am. I want to continue to be her favorite. Plus, I don't want to scare her when I start begging to eat your pussy."

Sybil deposited Agatha on the floor and hopped up from the couch, grabbing her wine glass and walking quickly toward the stairs. Peter didn't need to be told to follow. He snatched his glass of wine and hurried after her, catching her on the third step and curling an arm around her waist.

"So can I eat your pussy? Please?" Peter asked, kissing the sensitive spot behind her ear.

Sybil let out a heavy, dramatic sigh. "If you must."

He grinned and released her, but the swat he'd intended for her rear missed as she bolted up the stairs as fast as she could without spilling her wine.

Peter got to her room a mere footfall after she did, and quickly shut the door behind him as he heard the pitter-patter of little paws on the stairs.

Sybil set her wine on the nightstand and started undressing.

"Please tell me you brought condoms this time."

He froze, his wine glass halfway to his mouth. *That* was what he had meant to get at the store. Condoms.

"You are so lucky I'm responsible," Sybil said as she opened her nightstand drawer. A fresh box of condoms, still sealed in plastic. "Otherwise you'd have spent the night eating my pussy over and over again as an apology."

"Don't threaten me with a good time." Peter took a hefty swallow of wine then set the glass next to Sybil's so he could undress too.

His shirt was halfway off when Sybil took off her top and his brain short-circuited so violently he got stuck with his arms around his ears.

When they'd been dating in London, she'd once told him that she didn't see the point of lingerie because it was impractically constructed and coming off in thirty seconds anyway. So the last thing he'd expected was for her to be wearing a sheer black bra with red flowers embroidered along the top half of the cup. He didn't understand the physics of how a bra that insubstantial managed to make her breasts look that full and perky, but the effect made him dizzy from lack of blood flow to his brain.

"Oh fuck," he moaned. "What...when...how..."

No, there was definitely no blood left for his brain. It was all flowing into his dick, which was almost hard enough to dent steel.

"What? This?" Sybil touched the black straps coquettishly. "Oh gosh...a few years? Eloise was shopping for her honeymoon, and I got inspired." She shrugged nonchalantly and unbuttoned her jeans. As she parted the zipper, black lace peeked out.

"You're trying to kill me, aren't you?"

"You don't think you're already in heaven?"

Peter awkwardly tugged his shirt off and tossed it behind him, then fumbled with his belt, trying to catch up to her.

"Have you been wearing those all day?"

She shook her head. "I came home after I dropped you off to check on the cat and thought, why not?" She trailed a finger along the top edge of the bra, following the outlines of the flowers, and he'd never been so jealous of a digit before. "Do you like it, or should I take it off?"

"Yes."

"There were two questions," she reminded him.

"I know, and the answer is still a very enthusiastic yes." Peter shucked his pants and underwear at the same time, leaving him standing in his socks. "I like it *very* much"—he indicated his penis, which was standing straight out from his body—"and I would like it off...eventually."

"Eventually?" She frowned. "What does that mean?"

He stepped into her space and slid his hands into the gaping waistband of her jeans, squeezing her ass, and running his hands over her skin to learn where the lace ended and she began.

"You're perfect," he murmured and tipped her backwards onto the bed.

He knelt before her and peeled off her jeans like wrapping paper he wanted to save, kissing her skin like the gift it was as it was exposed to him. Sybil went to take off her underwear, her fingers already in the waistband before he grabbed her wrists to stop her. He used his shoulders to part her thighs, then guided one of her hands to the crotch of her panties and helped her pull them to one side.

Then he feasted.

Every day felt long when Sybil was near and he couldn't touch her whenever he wanted, but today had lasted a lifetime. He couldn't get her mind-blowing blowjob out of his head, and every second that ticked by he regretted not returning the favor. Going down on her wasn't a favor, it was a privilege. It didn't matter that the hard floor was biting his knees, or that his jaw started to ache when he pressed on because he thought she might be close; he was exactly where he wanted to be.

Her fingers tangled in his hair and gripped tightly, holding his face in place, like there was a chance he might give up and move on. A bomb couldn't have shifted him. Her scent, her taste, and her voice filled his senses, all urging him on until her thighs tensed and her body tightened.

Her chest and cheeks were flushed when he crawled up next to her on the bed. She reached out and wiped some of her wetness off his chin with her thumb.

"You kept your fancy knickers on for more than thirty seconds after I saw them. Still think they're silly?"

"If they're going to get me those kinds of results, I'll wear them all the time," she said. "But I think you'd be just as happy if I was wearing cotton."

He licked his lips and smiled. "Guilty."

Sybil put a hand in the center of his chest and pushed him onto his back, then swung a leg over him, mounting his hips like he was a horse. His cock was safely nestled against her ass crack, so he had no objections.

"This was your favorite position, wasn't it?" she asked him, lowering her torso so her nipples grazed his chest through the thin material of her bra. They inhaled sharply in unison. "You liked watching me ride you? Fucking you so good until you couldn't stand it anymore and you begged me to let you come?" She rocked her hips back, grinding her wet pussy against his rock-hard shaft, the soaked lace tickling his sensitive skin. The head of his cock pressed against her opening, barred from penetrating her only by her delicate panties. It would be so easy to pull that scrap of fabric to the side and impale her on his bare cock. "Mmm...do you want me to make myself come on your cock?"

It was a miracle he didn't come then and there.

"Y-yes, please." His breathless plea caught in his throat when her teeth grazed his racing pulse.

Sybil dismounted and he missed her warmth so acutely that he whimpered. She smirked, and took the box of condoms from her nightstand, piercing the shrink-wrap with her nails and tearing the box open. She tore a condom off the edge of the strip and tossed it on his chest.

"Put that on."

Peter scrambled to do her bidding. While he rolled the latex sheath down his length, she stepped out of her lacy underwear and dangled them from the tip of her finger. Once his task was complete, she straddled him again, trapping his erection between their bodies.

"Say 'ahh,'" she commanded, opening her mouth wide to demonstrate.

He opened his mouth and she stuffed her panties inside. He moaned, sucking the taste of her from the fabric.

"Good boy."

She sank onto his cock, working him in slowly, her eyes half closed and her lips slightly parted. Peter fought to keep his eyes from rolling back in his head as she enveloped him in her tight warmth. He didn't want to miss a second, but it felt so good he thought he'd die. Nothing this good happened to anyone who had another sixty years or so to live.

"Oh fuck," Sybil whined when she'd taken in three-quarters of him. "You're so big, you stretch me so good— *Oh fuck*, you feel so, *so* good."

She rolled her hips, rocking back and forth, and he didn't dare move for fear of ruining the rhythm she was building for herself. Her fingers dug into his chest and he focused on the slight pain to distract himself from the intense pressure of his building orgasm.

"Rub my clit," she begged, and he jumped at the chance to be useful.

His thumb found her clit, and he started touching it the way that seemed to get the best results. Sybil gasped and her body clamped around his, her pussy trying to milk his cock for all it was worth. Her motion faltered, so he grabbed her hips and wrung every last drop from her orgasm.

Sybil collapsed on his chest, panting.

"Did you come?" she asked.

Peter removed her underwear from his mouth and dropped them onto the floor. "Not yet. Are you all done?"

She nodded. "Come for me."

He gripped her hips, pressed his feet into the mattress, and fucked her from below, his cock pistoning in and out of her as he chased his own bliss.

"Oh fuck, *yes*," she moaned, and he lost it.

His muscles tightened as he exploded in the condom, coming like he hadn't relieved himself in days instead of just that morning. His mind shattered and slowly came back together, golden happiness repairing the cracks.

His bones felt like they weighed a ton as he wrapped his arms around Sybil, their breath slowly falling into sync.

"I am definitely in heaven," he said against her hair, and kissed the top of her head.

"I don't want to move. I don't know if I can move," she mumbled.

Outside the door, Agatha yowled. They both chuckled, too spent to find the energy for a real laugh.

"We should clean up," Sybil said, slowly disconnecting their bodies. She pushed herself off the bed and went to the door. She'd barely opened it a crack when Agatha darted in and dove under the bed. "Someone doesn't want to be kicked out."

"I understand how she feels." Peter forced himself to sit up. "If I go under the bed, can I stay too?"

Chapter Twenty-Nine

Sʏʙɪʟ ᴡᴏᴋᴇ ᴜᴘ ʙʏ ʜᴇʀꜱᴇʟꜰ.

Any other day, this wouldn't have been strange, but when she'd fallen asleep Peter was in her bed and so was the cat, who'd apparently lost all interest in her once Peter left. She would've bet her meager retirement savings that nothing short of a natural disaster could have gotten him out of her bed.

Bleary-eyed and yawning, she made her way downstairs to start a pot of coffee before she took a shower. A strange smell hit her as she reached the bottom step. It was like a cacophony of burnt foods: burnt eggs, burnt bread, burnt bacon.

Had Mallory been cooking after work?

Except Mallory *could* cook. She did occasionally burn things, but they were few and far between.

Wasn't smelling toast a stroke symptom?

Sybil turned into the kitchen and froze. She'd discovered the source of the smell and he was loading bread into the toaster, despite the charred evidence on the counter that he didn't understand how the appliance worked.

"What are you doing?"

Peter's hand stilled, and he looked over his shoulder at her. "I'm making breakfast."

She'd heard stories of Peter's culinary adventures from Graham, Sam, and even Eloise, and she was thankful there hadn't been a fire.

"Step away from the toaster," she said, and came to the stove to inspect the damage. "How are those eggs raw and burned?"

"They're sunny side up," he explained.

She picked up a piece of black bacon from a plate and it crumbled in her fingers.

"Do you like extra crispy bacon?"

Peter winced. "I kind of forgot about it and then there wasn't any more for me to try again."

She glanced at the sad eggs that were crispy around the edges but still raw on top.

"How many times did you make the eggs?"

"We might need to go to the store later."

Sybil sighed and pushed down her annoyance at the mess and the smell. The intention had been good, even if the results weren't edible.

"I can make us some oatmeal after I shower," she said and patted his cheek as she passed him to get to the coffee maker, which he miraculously hadn't managed to touch yet.

"Shower?" Peter repeated hopefully. "I could use a shower."

Sybil checked the clock on the stove. "There isn't enough time for us to both take one."

"We could shower together," he suggested. "It would save time and water."

She measured coffee into a filter. "How would showering together save time when I can guarantee you'll spend the entire time feeling me up under the guise of 'making sure I didn't miss a spot'?"

"I promise I will be on my best behavior." He crossed his heart. "If we shower together, we don't have to wait for the other person to finish and we can start getting ready to go at the same time."

"This still feels like a trap."

Sybil's hair was still damp and the granola bar she'd had for breakfast while she drove to the high school hadn't even taken the edge off her hunger. In the passenger seat, Peter searched his empty wrapper for more crumbs.

"I'm still hungry," he complained.

"Whose fault is that?"

Apparently Peter's version of "being on his best behavior" included a thorough tongue bath for her pussy. His time-saving shared shower idea had left Sybil with almost no time to dry her hair, and because she didn't even trust him with the microwave after what she'd seen him do with a toaster, no time for breakfast.

"You weren't complaining while I was—"

"I know! I know. I was there." She pulled into a parking spot reserved for volunteers. "You know you don't have to do this, right? You could wait in the car. It's boring, and I don't think those glasses are doing for you what they do for Superman."

Peter adjusted the fake glasses he'd pilfered from the movie. "I think they're giving a certain Clark Kent Effect. The hat helps too." He tapped the bill of his baseball cap.

"You look like a celebrity trying to be incognito."

"That's only because you know it's me. Maybe if you'd let me wear the mustache..."

"The mustache took the disguise in a direction you did not want to go at a youth sporting event."

Peter spotted the concession stand as soon as they got near the football field where the race would start and end.

"Are we going to be working in there? That doesn't seem too bad. Maybe not super warm, but it's dry."

"I don't think you were listening when I said you'd be standing in the rain."

"I was hoping you weren't serious."

Sybil spied Connor tying a string of colorful flags to the poles that made the finishing chute. He looked up, made eye contact with her, frowned, and tapped his watch. His frown deepened to a glare when he noticed Peter walking beside her.

"You're late," Connor said when they reached him.

"Only by a few minutes," she pointed out.

Connor looked Peter up and down suspiciously. "What's he doing here?"

"He's here to volunteer," Sybil told him. "You're always complaining you need more help, so I brought a warm body capable of following directions. Where do you want us?"

Connor looked towards the concessions shed.

"He's not allowed to work concessions for health and safety reasons," Sybil said, guessing that Connor wanted to stick Peter somewhere he didn't have to see him. "Unless you wanted to call the fire department today."

Connor glowered. "He can be a course monitor. He can't bother anyone out in the woods."

"Okay. Where are we going to be stationed?" Sybil put her hands on her hips and looked up at Connor defiantly. "Or he can be a chute monitor, and you can keep me here to do what I always do and pass out the numbers."

"Fine," Connor snarled.

Peter's gaze strayed to the concessions stand. "Is that open yet?"

"I bet if you go ask the moms nicely, one of them will take

pity on you," Sybil said. Peter wandered off in the direction of the concession stand.

As soon as he was out of earshot, Sybil smacked Connor's shoulder with the back of her hand. "I can't believe *I'm* the one saying this, but be nice."

"Ow." Connor rubbed his shoulder. "I am being nice. I didn't say any of the things I was thinking."

"Your face is pretty loud."

"Why did you bring him?"

"Because he wanted to come." Sybil shrugged and dug at a piece of loose soil with the toe of her shoe.

"You're not falling for him, are you?"

"Of course not. I'm horny, not stupid," she half-lied. She was definitely horny, but when it came to Peter, she was also incredibly stupid. "I did try to talk him out of it, but he insisted. Maybe if you were nicer to him, he wouldn't be trying so hard to make you like him."

"Maybe if he wasn't trying so hard to make me like him, I would be nicer to him."

"Is this what it's like trying to talk to me? Because if it is, I'm starting to understand why I'm not the most popular person in town."

Peter trotted back across the field with his hands full of snacks. An apple, a banana, a plastic baggie of orange slices, granola bars, and some fruit leathers overflowed his fingers.

"How did you get all that? Did you pretend you had a gun?" Sybil asked as she examined his bounty.

Peter shook his head. "I just said hi and asked if they had any snacks they could spare."

She exchanged a look with Connor. It didn't surprise her that strangers had outfitted Peter with provisions like he was setting out on the Oregon Trail. He had pretty person privilege, and the only reasons she didn't resent him for it were because he seemed oblivious to it and it benefited her.

Sybil relieved him of the apple. "Has anyone ever told you no?"

"You do all the time," he reminded her, stuffing the granola bars and fruit leathers into his pockets for later.

Connor handed Sybil the remaining bunting. "Finish hanging this," he told her, "and you need to talk to my parents because Dad wants to know when you're borrowing the truck, and Mom wants to know if you're coming for dinner tomorrow."

"I'll call them later," she promised.

Connor nodded, glared at Peter one more time for good measure, then headed toward the school.

"What's happening tomorrow?" Peter asked, following her to the end of the chute.

"I need to go out to the McMahon farm to get my old coffee cart ready. I store it out there." She tied the string around the last stake and moved forward to do the same to the next stake. "Greg lets me borrow one of his trucks to haul it." She studied the bunting across the chute so she could match the tension between the stakes. "Plus, on Sundays, Bitsy does a big family dinner, so I'll get fed."

"Do you want help tomorrow? I'm free," Peter offered.

It was how he phrased the question that made all the difference. Want versus need. Did she need his help? No, not particularly. Did she want his help? Did she want him around while she cleaned and organized?

"That would be great."

A giant smile that warmed her like summer sunshine spread across his face.

. . .

Halfway through the morning, Sybil realized she was in trouble.

Contrary to what Peter believed, it was obvious to her that everyone knew who he was. Luckily, everyone who had approached him had been very respectful and hadn't let on that they were in on the secret. The first few people to approach him had set her nerves on edge and she'd been prepared to run them off at the slightest provocation, but they'd only wanted to talk. And Peter could talk. A lot. He talked to anyone and everyone that came up to him, like his calling in life was idle small-town chitchat. Hell, he fit in better than she did.

How could she keep telling him that he wouldn't like living in a small town when he looked so damn happy standing in the rain at a youth sporting event?

Guilt curled around her insides like a prickly vine. She could never reciprocate his level of enthusiasm and ease at one of his events. Walking a red carpet, having people shout at her to look at them while cameras flashed all around her, was the kind of nightmare she'd wake up from in a cold sweat.

Then he'd look her way, like he was checking to make sure she was still there, that she was okay, and she'd give him a tiny smile to reassure him, and he'd flash her one of his award-winning grins, and she *knew* she was in trouble because her heart did a triple backflip every single time.

"Did you get your name on the ballot for mayor?" she asked as they walked back to her car after the runners had gone home and the course had been cleaned up.

Peter took her hand and laced their fingers together. "The current mayor still has two years left on her term, plus I think she's pretty popular. I think I could poach a city council seat, though."

"If you keep Mitch Appleton from ascending the throne, I will personally sponsor your campaign."

"Who's Mitch Appleton?"

"Local asshole," she explained. "He's the jerk who made Lacey's life hell here."

"Then I wouldn't worry about fundraising for my campaign. Sam will bankroll me in a heartbeat."

"Don't tell him I said this, but I think Graham should run."

Peter opened her driver's side door for her. "Why don't you want me to tell him you said that?"

"Because then he'd know I think he's a competent businessman and a semi-decent human being with a good head on his shoulders." Sybil shuddered dramatically, which made Peter laugh.

"You don't think letting him marry your best friend already went to his head?"

"I didn't *let* Eloise marry him. She's stubborn and ungovernable. Don't let that sweet facade fool you."

Sybil glanced around the parking lot. There were a few lingering vehicles, but none of them were running and she didn't see anyone walking to any of them. She stretched up on her tiptoes and gave him a quick kiss on the lips.

"What was that for?" he asked quietly, a little stunned.

"To say thanks for being such a good sport today. This can't have been your ideal way to spend a Saturday."

"No, it wasn't, but that's just because my ideal Saturday is being naked in bed with you. A very close second is literally any other activity with you." He caressed her cheek with a cold hand, and she pressed her face into his touch. "We do still have some Saturday left. We could go back to your house and snuggle with Agatha."

Sybil sighed. "Why would you suggest something so

wonderful? I need to go to work. I've hardly been there all week."

"We can do my thing second. Maybe I can make you dinner too." Peter walked around to the passenger side and got into the car.

Panic shot through her nervous system as visions of his failed breakfast attempt flashed before her eyes.

"Your kitchen privileges have been revoked until I have a signed note from Sam that your skills are up to his standards," she said as she sat down in her seat and started the car.

Peter looked crestfallen. "That's impossible."

It was impossible, but it was the only way to keep her kitchen safe. She patted his thigh reassuringly.

"Nothing's impossible if you put your mind to it."

Chapter Thirty

ONE OF THE things Peter loved most about his brain was, when properly interested and incentivized, he could focus unwaveringly for hours. It also helped if he was trying to complete a task for someone else and not himself. Helping Sybil clean and reorganize the trailer she'd used to start her business was the perfect job for him. The task was Sybil-centric, so he was adequately interested and incentivized, and it required little to no actual thinking. Any idiot could wipe down counters.

So far it had been his idea of a perfect weekend because he'd spent it with Sybil doing normal, everyday life things.

After volunteering at the cross-country meet, they'd gone to Stardust because Sybil had a lot of work to catch up on. He sat in the office with her while she did her bookkeeping and ordering, then tucked himself into a corner table while she made coffee, pretending to read a book the entire time, though he spent a lot more time watching her than reading. He couldn't help himself. He had twelve years of gazing at her to catch up on.

They picked up a pizza on the way home and drank the bottle of wine they'd opened and barely touched Friday night.

Then they sat on the couch and talked about nothing important, Agatha wedged between them, proving the theory that cats were actually liquid, purring blissfully. It was cozy, domestic, and he was so damn happy he thought he'd explode in a shower of glitter and rainbows.

Eventually Sybil yawned, and Peter solemnly told her that it was probably in his best interest to spend the night again because he didn't want to risk being late to help her on Sunday. When she'd pointed out that he needed to go back to his hotel for a change of clothes, he told her he'd packed a second change of clothes, just in case. She'd rolled her eyes, but didn't make him go back to the hotel.

The McMahon farm was located a little over twenty minutes outside of town, on a quiet stretch of road dotted with other small farms. Peter wasn't sure what exactly categorized a piece of property as a farm, but he'd seen some livestock, so he assumed they were farms.

The McMahons were cranberry farmers, which was a fruit he'd never given a lot of thought. If Sybil hadn't pointed out the bogs, he wouldn't have noticed them. It wasn't like an apple orchard or a vineyard. The cranberry bushes were low to the ground and incredibly nondescript. Everything he knew about cranberries came from cranberry juice commercials, so he was surprised when he found out they didn't grow in water, they were just harvested that way.

A knock on the doorframe disturbed their companionable silence.

"It's dinner time," Connor said, and sighed when he saw Peter.

Apparently volunteer hours weren't the way to win him over.

"We'll be in in a minute," Sybil said, replacing a part on the espresso machine.

Connor disappeared.

"How long do you think it's going to take for him to like me?" Peter asked.

"I don't know why you're so worried about it."

"Because he's important to you."

"That doesn't mean you need to make him your best friend too," Sybil said, crossing the small space and putting her hands on his hips. "I know it's hard for you when people don't like you, but the good news is, I like you and that's a much harder get."

Peter perked up a little. "You like me?"

"Don't push it." She rose on her toes and kissed his cheek. "Let's go eat."

The McMahons lived in a large white farmhouse. On the drive, Sybil had pointed out a smaller yellow house that belonged to Grandpa Beau, who still worked with his son Greg on the farm, even though he was in his late eighties. According to Sybil, the twins and Chris lived in the house with their parents, all saving money and paying off loans. Connor had moved out when Chris had moved back in after finishing school, deciding that living in his fixer-upper on Lilac Lane was better than reliving his childhood sharing a bathroom with his brothers. There was a fifth brother, Clark, but he didn't live in town so Peter didn't waste brain space remembering any details about him.

The closer they got to the house, the faster his heart beat. Peter surreptitiously wiped his sweaty palms on his jeans. Why was he so nervous? He liked meeting new people. He was *good* at meeting new people.

Was it because Sybil had called this a family dinner?

"Do you come out here most Sundays?" he asked.

"I do. Bitsy likes to see all her kids once a week. She wishes she saw three of them a lot less often, but I know she'll miss having them underfoot when they're gone."

"So you're close?"

Sybil nodded. "Very close. Bitsy is a better mom to me than my mom ever was."

She'd never mentioned much of anything about her family, so Peter wanted to dive into that more, but Sybil pulled open the back door and stepped to the side.

The thundering of paws and the scratching of nails trying to find purchase on a hard, slippery surface reached his ears a little too late for him to move out of the way. Four excited dogs swarmed his legs, almost knocking him over. They were a mass of wiggling, prancing, jumping bodies, inspecting him and vying for his attention.

"Hello...hello—oh, that is my butt!" Peter craned his head over his shoulder to see a hound dog with its nose firmly in his rear end.

"Copper, that's not polite." Sybil moved the dog's nose away from Peter's butt just as another dog shoved its snout into his crotch. "Gizmo, no." She hooked her fingers into the border collie's collar and pried the dog away. "Christ on a cracker...*Christopher!*"

Moments later, the friendly veterinarian and second-oldest McMahon brother loped outside.

"Sorry, sorry," Chris said. "They're excited. They love new people."

"Are they all yours?" Peter asked.

Chris blushed a little. "Yeah. This is Copper"—he pointed to the gingerbread-colored hound dog that had sniffed Peter's butt—"Gizmo"—the black-and-white border collie that was a budding urologist—"Pebbles"—a mid-sized spotted mutt whose tail propelled its entire body—"and Ziggy."

Ziggy was the smallest of the pack and had situated its pint-sized body between Copper's front legs and was barking ceaselessly. Chris stooped and scooped up Ziggy, scratching the dog behind its silky blond ears.

"I know. You're so tough and so scary," he cooed to his dog, "but he's our friend." Chris smiled sheepishly at Peter. "The smaller the dog, the tougher they think they are. Copper and Pebbles would let anyone rob the house as long as they got a belly rub and a treat."

"What about Gizmo?" Peter asked, cautiously moving forward as the black-and-white dog paced behind him.

"Gizmo would try to herd them."

Sybil absentmindedly scratched Copper's head as they moved inside. "I can't believe your mom didn't make you put the dogs up."

"Well, I was about to when you opened the door and distracted them."

Chris beckoned the dogs, and they all followed him like he was the Pied Piper.

Sybil paused by a pile of large shoes to take hers off. They looked like children's shoes in comparison.

"I should warn you that Bitsy is a bit of a fan," she said, "and I told her I might be bringing a friend to dinner, but I didn't say who in case you flaked. Just be prepared for some squealing and some fawning."

"Don't worry about it." Peter took off his shoes, too. "I'm used to it."

Hopefully Bitsy would be the domino effect he needed to start getting Connor on his side.

Peter inhaled deeply. The house smelled heavenly. He'd have bet his bank account that the savory scent was a pot roast, and his mouth began to water. There weren't a lot of home-cooked meals in his life. Craft services and restaurants were fine, but there was something about eating a meal someone hadn't yelled at anyone else to get on the table.

"Stop eating the roast!" A woman's voice roared from what Peter assumed was the direction of the kitchen. "Chase Beauregard, you are not too old for me to smack you with this spoon."

Maybe there was some yelling, but it was family and barely counted.

"Ow!"

When they reached the kitchen, Chase was nursing his knuckles. A tall blonde woman that had to be the McMahon matriarch was pointing a wooden spoon at him menacingly.

For a woman named Bitsy, she was very tall. Peter would have guessed somewhere around 5'10". She was still inches shorter than her sons, but that didn't stop her from being an imposing figure.

"Bitsy," Sybil said gently. "This is my friend, Peter."

Bitsy turned around. Her eyes became wide, and there was a three-second delay before she shrieked. The wooden spoon flew out of her hand, bounced off the ceiling, and almost hit Chase in the head.

"Hello, Mrs. McMahon," he said, opting for ultra polite and deferential, like he was meeting the Queen of England again. "It's nice to finally meet you. I've heard so much about you."

Bitsy put a hand on her chest, though it was hard to tell if it was to remind herself to breathe or to calm her breathing.

"You...you...you've heard of me?"

Peter nodded. "I have. Cole made your cranberry sauce for Thanksgiving last year, and it was *magnificent*. Did you have a smooth recovery from your appendectomy?"

"Um...yes, I did," she stammered, her cheeks turning apple red. "You...had my cranberry sauce?"

"I did, and I loved every drop. Tried to lick the bowl, but Graham wouldn't let me."

"Do you want the recipe?"

It was like a record scratch had played over a stadium-sized loudspeaker because the entire house froze. Not even the floor-boards dared to creak. Chase stared at his mother, agog and dumbfounded.

Sybil shattered the silence.

"Oh, no. Peter isn't allowed in the kitchen," she said.

"You told me that recipe would leave this house over your dead body," Chase said, still teeming with disbelief. "That you *might* consider giving it to our wives one day, but you'd have to see if they could be trusted first."

"With the exception of Heidi and Eloise, you have incredibly terrible taste in women, Chase," Bitsy told him. "And poor judgment, since you let both of them slip through your fingers."

Chase threw up his hands and stomped out of the kitchen.

"That was a little below the belt," Sybil said cautiously.

"Someone has to tell him. He's not getting any younger." Bitsy shook her head. "I don't understand where I went wrong with any of them. They can cook, clean, do laundry...and not one of them is married."

"The Mrs. Bennett Problem," Peter chimed in. "A surplus of children and no suitors."

"He understands."

"If you taught me to cook, clean, and do laundry, I could probably get married," Peter offered, not even needing to glance Sybil's way because he could feel her eyes burning holes in the side of his face.

Bitsy flushed. "Oh, I doubt you'd need my help finding someone to marry you. You've probably got a line of hopefuls around the block."

"The finding part was easy. It's the convincing."

"Convincing?" Bitsy was aghast. "Sybil, can you imagine anyone saying no to this man?"

"Very easily," Sybil mumbled, but Bitsy didn't seem to hear her.

"If I'd known you were coming, I would have made something fancier. It's just pot roast."

"It smells amazing," Peter assured her. "No one ever makes me pot roast." He went in for the kill and put his arm around Bitsy's shoulders and squeezed. "I'm very excited."

Bitsy piled more food on Peter's plate than he could possibly eat. And the dogs were banned from the dining room, so he couldn't slip bits and pieces under the table to them.

He whispered in Sybil's ear, "I don't know how I'm going to finish all of this."

"There's dessert after too," she whispered back, a devilish twinkle in her eye. She enjoyed his misery. "Connor made pie."

Peter bit down on a whimper.

The McMahons' dinner table was big, and they were all still shoulder to shoulder. Which, given the average size of a McMahon's shoulders, didn't take a lot of effort. Peter was wedged between Sybil and Chase, and he wondered if he could sneak some of his food onto Chase's plate without him noticing.

"So, Peter, how did you meet our Sybil?"

The question came from across the table. Grandpa Beau looked like he'd wandered off a movie set because any costume designer worth their salt would have dressed an old farmer the exact same way: yellow flannel shirt and well-worn blue-jean overalls with a red handkerchief poking out of the bib pocket. For a man his age, he was remarkably spry. Peter never would have guessed Grandpa Beau was a year older than his own grandmother.

"I met Sybil at a bookshop in London when she was studying abroad." He glanced at Sybil, who was acting very interested in her pot roast. "We lost touch, so us both ending up here feels a bit like magic."

"It's interesting that she's never mentioned her very famous friend," Connor said frostily, then winced. Sybil had probably kicked him under the table.

"I wasn't famous when we met. I lived in a truly wretched flat with a few friends."

"But your parents are rich," Connor pressed.

"*They* are. I was not at the time. My mother never wanted me to go into acting, so she told me if I wanted to pursue the profession, I'd have to go it my own way. No money, no introductions, no contacts. It wasn't that people in the industry didn't know who I was, but my parents weren't actively greasing the wheels for me."

It was a story he'd told about a hundred times in various interviews. He always played it a little sheepish and very humble.

"How does your mother feel about your career now that you're established?" Chris asked with genuine curiosity.

"She's still not happy about it. I'm only able to do this film because men are incapable of keeping their horrid opinions to themselves and she was out of options. If you were wondering what the bottom of the barrel looks like." He pointed to himself.

A door at the front of the house creaked, and the dogs went nuts barking. A few moments later, Mallory stepped into the dining room.

"Sorry I'm late. My shift at the hotel ran long."

She hugged Bitsy, then Greg, and hugged Grandpa Beau the longest before kissing the old man on his cheek.

"We're just glad you're here, sunshine," Grandpa Beau told her, beaming at her.

Mallory dropped into the open seat between Connor and Chris. "It smells amazing. I'm starving."

She loaded up her plate with as much food, if not more, than Bitsy had put on Peter's plate. He didn't know where she was planning on putting it since she was about a foot shorter than he was. If she'd displaced Chase, maybe he could've shuffled some of his food onto her plate.

"What did I miss?" Mallory asked, looking around the table. "Oh, hey, Peter."

Next to him, Sybil tensed. Gently, he tapped his knee against hers, and she relaxed a fraction.

"We were just discussing my super-secret past that's been used as clickbait for about a decade," he said and took a sip from his water glass. "Sadly, the truth isn't very scandalous."

"Peter and Sybil met in London," Connor pointed out, and Mallory's eyebrows rose. "At a bookshop."

"London?" Mallory repeated, then leaned forward to try to make eye contact with her sister, though Sybil was very invested in cutting a carrot as small as she could with her fork. "You met a movie star on your vacation, and you didn't say anything?"

"It was before he was famous," Sybil said tersely. "I did my study abroad in London, but you probably don't remember that because it didn't revolve around you."

The temperature in the room dropped ten degrees, and Peter mentally scrambled for a different topic to steer away from potential disaster.

Grandpa Beau beat him to it.

"Isn't your grandmother Estelle Whitman?"

The entire table exhaled in unison.

"She is, and yes, she is as drunk in real life as she's appeared on every award show and interview you've ever seen."

The collective chuckle thawed the room. Grandpa Beau continued to pepper Peter with questions about his grandmother, some of them borderline inappropriate, but apt considering some of her more titillating roles, until Peter finally said, "I'd give you her phone number, but she'd eat you alive on the first date."

"Kind of like a praying mantis," Chase said.

Grandpa Beau grinned. "But what a hell of a way to go, eh? She was my hall pass. That is what you kids call it, right?" He looked to his son for confirmation, though for a man well into middle age, Greg looked as mortified by his father as any teenager. "Peggy would be tickled pink to know I had dinner with Estelle Whitman's grandson."

The conversation moved along as Grandpa Beau asked Connor about the cross-country meet. Peter leaned over and whispered in Sybil's ear, "Who is Peggy?"

"Grandma McMahon," she whispered back. "She died ten years ago."

Peter's heart ached for everyone at the table. Estelle was the only grandparent he'd ever known, and while he recognized her comedic value as martini-swilling matriarch, they didn't have a heartwarming relationship. If the late Peggy was even half as warm and welcoming as Grandpa Beau, her death must have been a catastrophic loss.

Sybil's knee tapped against his, and her eyebrows scrunched together in a silent question. *Are you okay?*

He flicked his eye in a casual upward diagonal like an ocular shrug. *You know me.*

Her mouth twitched downward into a frown, and under the table, she squeezed his thigh.

Heaven and hell help him if he lost this woman again because he loved her more than he could bear.

"That was fun," Peter said, turning the ice pack on his forehead to the colder side. "I've never played a game of Pictionary with casualties before."

"You shouldn't have sat between Connor and Mallory."

Sybil turned on her bright lights. The road was dark and empty.

"Why not?" he asked.

"Because they're so absurdly competitive that there's an unofficial town ordinance that requires they be on the same team for any team activity because otherwise people get hurt in the crossfire."

"My forehead would like to point out that they were on the same team for Pictionary and I got hurt."

"It's worse when they play against each other."

Peter chuckled. "I had fun, though. I'd like to do that again. We should have a game night, the four of us."

"That is the worst idea you've ever had."

"Why? It would be fun. We could have some wine, a little charcutcric board. Maybc Connor would go from hating my living guts to benign dislike."

"I think it's going to take more than one game night for that to ha— *Oh shit!*"

A deer darted into the road, its hooves scrambling for purchase on the asphalt. Sybil slammed on her breaks, throwing both of them forward against their seatbelts, but it didn't matter. The deer had entered the road too close to her car, and the resulting *thud* was much louder than he would have guessed, like a giant taking a baseball bat to the front of the car.

"Fuck!" Sybil threw the car in park and jabbed the triangular hazard lights button with her finger before springing out of the car to inspect the damage.

Peter didn't know if it was a good sign or a bad sign that the airbags hadn't gone off.

The deer was definitely dead. Its brown eyes were open and unblinking. He tried to focus on the damage to the car instead of the animal. The hood was crumpled up and in, and there was a faint tendril of smoke in the cold night air. It was like the deer said, "If I'm going down, you're going down with me."

"Do you have a signal?" Sybil asked, holding her phone in the air to search for reception, a frustrated scowl on her face. "I need to call the tow truck."

Peter checked his phone. "I might? The bars don't always update."

He handed it to her, and she dialed, then waited.

"Hello? Jody, can you hear me? It's Sybil Morgan."

Sybil explained to the tow truck driver where they were and what had happened, then she hung up.

"Jody will be here in about thirty or forty minutes." She handed Peter back his phone, then looked at the deer. "Goddammit."

"What do we do with it?" he asked.

"Move it off the road. Nature will take care of it."

Together, they moved the deer off the road and into the ditch. It was somehow lighter and heavier than Peter had expected, not that he thought about deer a lot.

Sybil kicked shards of a broken headlight into the ditch.

"Will your car insurance cover this?"

"I don't know." Her voice was thin and tense, like a string about to snap. "But this couldn't have happened at a worse fucking time. I mean, I guess it could have, but... Fuck! I finally get a little ahead, and I hit a fucking deer." She looked at him. "Do you know how long it takes to save two thousand dollars?"

"Um, no." He didn't dare add that he didn't know because he hadn't tried to save money since she'd known him in London. Even then he wasn't particularly good at it. "Why two thousand?"

"That's my car insurance deductible. I wanted a low monthly payment to free up cash month to month. I thought, hey, I'm a good driver. I live in a safe, small town. What could happen?" She laughed mirthlessly. "I forgot about the fucking wildlife."

"I can pay for your car to get fixed—"

"No." She shook her head. "I take care of myself. I have the money, it's just..." Her chin wobbled, and her lower lip quivered. "I'm going to lose it again. I thought I had it this time, and it's going to slip through my fingers again."

Peter took a step towards her to comfort her, but Sybil stepped back in equal measure.

"Lose what? What are you losing?" he asked, making his voice as soft and gentle as he could.

Sybil wrapped her arms around herself and stared at the damage again.

"You know the empty storefront next to Stardust? I've always wanted to turn it into a bookstore. Everything seemed like it was lining up. The space was available. I was getting an influx of cash from the movie stuff. And then..." She thrust her hands in the direction of her car like she was showing it off on a game show. "I can't win. I can't..."

Her voice caught, and she clamped her mouth shut. The light from the headlights made the tears that filled her eyes glisten. Then Sybil turned and started to walk down the road. She walked until she was almost out of the reach of her headlights, then she stopped and screamed.

It was the guttural yell of someone who'd been pushed and pushed and had nowhere left to go but over a cliff. Sybil screamed at the top of her lungs, hands balled into fists at her sides, until she was out of breath, then she inhaled deeply and screamed some more. The sound was eaten up by inky night, pushed away in a thoughtless breeze.

When she came back, she marched up to him and put her head on his chest. This assignment he understood, and he wrapped his arms tightly around her and swayed gently side to side until she moved her arms like a rusted robot and hugged him back.

"I'm paying to fix your car," he said into her hair as he kissed the top of her head. She tensed, and he cut off her argument at the pass. "I'm not taking no for an answer. I know you're perfectly capable of taking care of yourself, but goddammit, Sybil, I can take care of you, too." He squeezed her tighter. "And before you start feeling guilty or resentful about my generosity, this isn't altruistic. I'm going to have to sleep at your place so you have a ride to set, or so you can take me and borrow the car for the day. It's a sacrifice, but it's one I'm willing to make."

Sybil's watery laugh bubbled up like a mountain spring, and the sound soothed his peripheral anxiety.

She sniffled a few times, then rose up on her tiptoes for a simple, lingering kiss.

"Thank you."

Chapter Thirty-One

Sybil hated making schedules. One day, she was going to invest in one of those programs that made the schedule, but in the meantime, she was stuck doing it by hand, the old-fashioned way.

The phone next to the computer rang.

"Stardust Coffee, this is Sybil."

"Hi, Sybil. This is Gary from Haney's Auto Body. Do you have a minute to talk?"

Her stomach sank. After the collision with the deer, she'd had her car towed to the mechanic in town, who then referred her to an auto body shop in Florence. They said they'd call her when they had an estimate.

"I do. What's the damage?"

"With our current workload, we'll have the car back to you next week. As for cost—"

"Please don't tell me how much it's going to cost. My boyfriend said he'd cover it, and I don't want to know."

Boyfriend. The word fell out of her mouth, completely bypassing her brain. Was Peter her boyfriend? If she asked him, he'd say yes before she finished the question. *"Are you my—"*

"Yes." The possessive *"my"* would be enough to get him nodding rapidly.

He'd certainly surpassed the Boyfriend Residency Requirements since it would be his fifth night in a row sleeping in her bed, with another seven nights on the horizon if he continued to insist on room and board for his chauffeur services.

But those nine letters didn't bring her joy or peace. They were the harbingers of anxiety. Acknowledging and labeling their relationship meant she had to admit that it wasn't casual, and if it wasn't casual, she'd opened herself up to an entire world of heartache.

Gary's voice yanked her back to the present.

"Since you're not going through insurance, we do require a forty percent deposit to start the work. Is your boyfriend around so we can set that up?"

"Yeah, I'll go get him."

She'd left Peter at the table usually occupied by his father while she did her office work, not trusting him or herself with a door that locked. One massive perk of allowing him to spend the night was that every night he'd been at her house she'd had an assisted orgasm. But when she exited the office and looked toward the table, Peter was gone.

A warm, rich, rolling Southern Welsh voice resonated from the side room where the romance book club was meeting. The only reason that Sybil knew that was because she'd made the very entertaining mistake of asking Peter about his father's accent. Arthur was from the Cotswolds. But simply telling her that wasn't good enough for him. He had to take her on a vocal tour of the United Kingdom to demonstrate the differences.

Peter had infiltrated book club. Whether he'd been invited or had invited himself, she didn't know, but he was sitting in the circle reading a passage from the historical romance the group had read that month.

"I do not want you to be my wife in name only, Honoria. I do not wish for you to lie back and think of England when I come to your bed. I was selfish when we married and you have borne that as I never could. I thought only of my title and your money when we wed. But you've blazed across my life like one of those comets you told me about and lit up the corners of my dark soul. I love you, Honoria, my wife. I am begging you not to go to the continent. Please give me another chance, and I shall endeavor with every beat of my heart to deserve you."

A gasping sob from one of the women in the group broke the delicate spell Peter had woven over the room. He looked up from the book, and his eyes met Sybil's. The corner of his mouth quirked upward in a lopsided grin. Her heart stuttered, and she ignored the warmth that flooded her cheeks.

Sybil curled her finger and beckoned him to her. Without a word, he handed the borrowed book to the woman sitting next to him and crossed the room. She stepped out of earshot.

"The auto body shop wants to talk to you," she told him.

Peter frowned. "Me? But it's your car."

"But it's your money," she reminded him. "They're on hold in my office."

"Are you going to be in your office?" He wiggled his eyebrows suggestively.

She rolled her eyes. "No, besides you already pounced on me this morning."

"But what about second pouncings? And elevenses?"

"Go."

He grinned at her, making her nerves hum like a live wire, and ducked into her office.

Oh, yes, she was definitely in danger of getting her heart absolutely shattered again, label or no label.

Sybil sent her closers on their breaks, confident she could handle the light evening crowd. While she was restocking the cups, Peter popped out of the office, checked for witnesses in the exaggerated way he could, then kissed her on the cheek before scurrying back to his table before she could smack him with the towel she'd tossed over her shoulder.

The bell above the door jingled and she looked up. Marianne Warner, coach of the high school cheerleading squad, entered. If "Most Likely To Peak In High School" had been a superlative in the yearbook, Marianne would've won in a landslide. Instead, she'd won "Most Talkative," which unfortunately didn't have a substance requirement, because Marianne had only ever been full of spite and hot air. It was karmically fitting that she'd finally started to date Mitch Appleton after more than a decade of hot pursuit on her part. They really deserved each other.

"Iced, non-fat, sugar free hazelnut macchiato, light on the ice, no whip."

Marianne's voice never failed to rake across Sybil's skin like claws. She bristled and took three calming breaths before walking up to the register to slowly tap in Marianne's order.

"Macchiatos don't come with whip."

"I didn't want to risk you making a mistake." Marianne checked her cell phone. "Mitch will be here soon. Make him a decaf, sugar-free caramel latte. And make *sure* it's decaf. I don't want him up all night."

Sybil didn't point out that Mitch never ordered decaf or sugar-free. If Marianne was controlling his sleep habits, she was probably trying to rein in his weight gain. Sybil might have felt sorry for him if he hadn't been such an unmitigated asshole the entire time she'd known him.

Marianne paid for the drinks and then stood at the end of the bar to watch Sybil make them.

"Oh my god. Is that Peter Green?" she stage-whispered, unfortunately audible over the hiss of the steamer.

Sybil flicked her eyes in the direction of Peter's little corner table. He was reading his book again, either oblivious to the conversation happening at the counter, or doing a very good job of acting like he wasn't listening.

"Yes, it is. Don't bother him."

Ignoring things she didn't want to hear had always been a strong suit of Marianne's. She strode over to Peter's table like she'd been invited, but before Sybil could do anything to stop her, the romance book club started to file out of the side room, meandering toward the door and making it hard to hear what was happening across the room.

There was the usual humble smile and head nod he did when he thanked someone for being a fan. He graciously took a photo. And then it seemed like he tried to say goodbye to Marianne, but she didn't leave. She touched his arm, and he subtly moved it away. When she scooted closer, he pretended to look for something on the floor and slid further along the bench.

Peter normally talked enough to make strangers regret ever saying hello to him, so the fact that he was trying to get away from Marianne meant that he had *some* survival instincts, except he was too polite. His smiles became tighter and his body looked so tense she knew he'd *twang* if she tapped him with a fork.

Marianne touched his arm again, and any restraint left in Sybil's body vanished.

"Hey!" Sybil barked, and the entire room froze. "He's too nice to say it, but I'm not. Back. The. Fuck. Off."

All eyes turned on Marianne, who sputtered, "I'm not doing anything—"

Sybil kept her tone cold and even, so it could not for one second be interpreted as a friendly request. "I told you not to bother him, and you did. Either get away from him right now, or get the fuck out."

Marianne's eyes darted around the room as she tried to calculate how much support she'd get if she stayed right where she was and cried harassment. Her brain was working so hard that Sybil could practically see steam coming out of her ears from the effort.

By some miracle, Marianne was able to read the room. She snatched her purse from the bench and stomped out of Stardust, intercepting Mitch on the sidewalk and dragging him with her.

The collective gaze of the romance book club fell on Sybil, and she felt the hot blush crawling from her chest up her neck to her face.

"What?" she snapped, and threw Mitch and Marianne's half made drinks into the garbage as the end punctuation to the interaction.

Like a video catching up after lag, the room sped through their usual goodbyes and hustled out the door. Sybil noted that those that said goodbye to Peter and thanked him for reading were extra polite and brief.

Once Stardust had emptied out of everyone except for her and Peter, she took a deep breath, expanding her lungs as far as her ribs would allow, then let it out slowly through her lips. Her heart was pounding and she was jittery, like she'd eaten a bowl of espresso beans for breakfast.

"Have you ever considered a second career as a bodyguard?" Peter asked. "I'd hire you."

"I don't think anyone outside of Crane Cove would take me seriously as a threat," she said, lacing her fingers together on top of her head, something she'd seen Connor tell his runners to do after a race.

"I don't know. I was pretty intimidated by you when we met."

"Really? I couldn't tell by the way you wouldn't leave me

alone." She took another deep breath. "You need to stand up for yourself when someone is making you uncomfortable."

"It's not that easy."

"Yes, it is."

Peter slid his bookmark into his book and gently shut it. "No, it's not. If I'm short with someone, or if I decline an interaction, I'm labeled as rude. People are always looking for a reason to label me as another problematic, spoiled nepo baby."

"Why do you care what people think? Your safety and comfort matter more than what ignorant people call you in the comment section. You're allowed to have boundaries. Sam doesn't have an issue telling people to get the fuck out of his bubble."

"It's different for Sam. There are only so many jobs out there for an actor. If I'm considered difficult, my phone doesn't ring. I don't work. He can be a pill and then write an album about it, and people will say 'Oh, he's so misunderstood' and buy it. He doesn't have to wait to be booked."

"I think your peace of mind and bodily autonomy are more important than being perceived as a nice guy."

Peter looked down and toyed with the slightly bent corner of the cover of his book. Sybil's mounting frustration dissipated like steam escaping a hot kettle, and she went and sat next to him, resting her head on his shoulder.

"Anyone who's met you for even fifteen seconds would never, ever say that you're rude," she said gently, squeezing his forearm. "You are the kindest, most generous person I've ever known, and if someone whose knowledge of you only extends as far as your pedigree wants to talk shit, fuck 'em. Don't sacrifice your peace and put yourself in potential danger so strangers who don't matter will call you nice."

"This is why you can't leave me again. Who else is going to tell me this?"

Sybil began to tick off names on her fingers. "Graham, Sam, Dempsey—"

"Okay, okay, yes, them. But none of them look as pretty as you do when they say it." He kissed her forehead. "I love you so much."

Sybil pressed her face into his neck, like she could hide from the way those words cracked her open and overwhelmed her.

"I need to finish the schedule," she mumbled.

"I can watch the front," he offered.

"Do not, under any circumstances, touch my espresso machine."

Chapter Thirty-Two

THE DOOR of Connor's classroom was covered in blue and yellow butcher paper, festooned with glittery winged shoes, and phrases of encouragement for the cross-country team written in sharpie.

Crane Cove High School was bigger than he'd expected, but still much smaller than any of the schools he'd shot in in Los Angeles. Connor's classroom was at the end of a hallway and, at a glance, was across from a math class. He could feel the misery exiting the room in waves.

Connor's door was open and his room was empty, just like Mallory said it would be at this time.

Peter knocked on the doorframe carefully so he wouldn't spill the coffee he'd brought as a peace offering.

Connor looked up from the papers he was grading and frowned. "What are you doing here?"

"Bringing you coffee," Peter said innocently, holding up the cup as proof. "Can I interrupt your prep period?"

"You already did." Connor put down his red pen and motioned for Peter to come inside. "What do you need?"

"Who said I needed anything?"

Connor gave Peter a look that possibly worked on rowdy teenagers but definitely worked on him. He put the coffee he'd brought on the corner of his desk, then boosted himself onto the top of a student desk.

There wasn't any point in beating around the bush, so Peter laid it out, plain and simple.

"You don't like me, and I want to know why."

Connor popped the lid off the coffee and peeked inside before taking a cautious sip. Satisfied with the contents, he took a longer drink, keeping one eye on Peter the entire time, like he'd vandalize the classroom while Connor was distracted.

"You really want to know why I don't like you?"

"Wouldn't bother asking if I didn't."

Connor sighed and leaned back in his desk chair. "Because you're going to end up breaking Sybil's heart."

Peter opened his mouth to protest, and Connor held up a hand to silence him. It worked, because he closed his mouth to listen. No one ever scored points by arguing with the person they were trying to win over.

"You don't see what I see. You don't see how she looks at you when you're not looking. I've known Sybil since we were seventeen, and I have never once seen her look at someone the way she looks at you. And maybe you won't mean to hurt her, but you will. You'll leave her alone in a room full of people she doesn't know. You'll give her cause to doubt your faithfulness, and that will be splashed across the pages of a magazine for everyone to see. Sybil is a very private person, and you're very... loud." Connor pursed his lips. "The doubt, the worry, the fear that she's not enough for your oversized life will eat at her day by day until she's nothing. She's the strongest person I know, but even strong people have their breaking points, and I see you being hers."

"That's it?" Peter asked.

Connor's eyebrows raised.

"You don't think I'm cruel, dishonest, manipulative, or abusive. I can handle you thinking I'm feckless because I know that's not true and eventually you'll believe me. Truthfully, I'm worried I'm not enough for her. She's smart, ambitious, resourceful, loyal. I can't even cook eggs. I've been staying at her place, and sometimes I fight sleep because I'm scared she'll realize I don't bring anything to the table except for unwavering devotion and she'll leave me in the middle of the night."

"She wouldn't leave her own house," Connor assured him. "She'd kick you out."

And for the first time, he grinned at Peter.

"I still don't like you."

"That's fine. You'll get there. Drink your coffee."

Connor took a sip. "Did Sybil tell you my order?"

"Actually, no. I got it from Mallory. Same with when your free period was and where your classroom was. Speaking of Mallory, I've planned a game night tonight, and I'm inviting you. Really quiet. You, me, Sybil, and Mallory."

Connor's cup stalled halfway to his mouth.

"It'll be fun. You'll hardly notice I'm there."

"Yeah, that's a bad idea."

"Why?"

"Remember how Sybil is very private? If you don't know, then it's not my dirty laundry to put on the line, but trust me."

Peter hopped off the desk. "I've got wine and Sam drew me a diagram for a charcuterie board since that doesn't involve heating anything up, so I will see you at seven."

"Are you just going to ignore my warning?" Connor asked.

"Like a group of teenagers stopping at a creepy gas station in a horror movie."

"That's a lot of meat for four people," Sybil said, stealing a piece of salami from the tray Peter was arranging.

"That's something you'd never hear in porn." Peter shooed her hand away when she tried to snag another piece. "Stop trying to touch my meat."

"Definitely something you'd never hear in porn." She grinned at him, and while he was distracted by the dazzling glimmer in her eyes, she poached another piece of salami.

"Thief!"

She put a hand on his chest and tilted her head to the side, looking at him from under her lashes. "If you cancel this game night right now, I'll put your meat in my mouth later."

He was sorely tempted.

"Mallory and Connor are already setting up the board."

Sybil rolled her eyes and backed away. From the floor, Agatha chirped, like she couldn't understand how both of her humans could be in one room and neither of them were petting her. Sybil scooped her up and scratched her behind the ear.

"Your daddy doesn't have the sense he was born with," she cooed to the cat. "He even picked Monopoly."

"It's the only board game you own."

"Only because I forgot I had it, otherwise I would've thrown it out." Sybil kissed the top of Agatha's furry head and headed for the front room, where Mallory and Connor were supposed to be setting up the Monopoly board.

And they were, in a way. If setting up the Monopoly board involved repeated games of rock-paper-scissors over who got to be the car, they were absolutely setting up the board.

"Ah-ha!" Mallory raised her hands above her head, triumphant.

"That doesn't count. You shot early. Redo."

"I won the best of twelve," Mallory said.

"Seven. You won seven of twelve," Connor rebutted. "That's basically a tie."

Sybil reached between them and plucked the car from the tray. "My house, I pick first. Now neither of you get the car."

"I call banker!" they shouted at the same time.

Sybil looked up at the ceiling, like she was gathering strength from on high.

"Peter will be the banker, since he's the closest thing we have to a neutral party in this house," Sybil declared, and put Agatha in her cat tree, which dominated a corner of the room.

Peter put the charcuterie board down. "Is this a bad time to mention that I was homeschooled and *not* because I was a genius who needed to work at a faster pace?"

"There's a calculator on your phone," Sybil reminded him. She sat down and started to divide the colored paper bills into everyone's starting stacks of fake cash.

It looked like he was banker in name only. He could handle being the bank's figurehead.

Peter picked up the dog piece while Connor and Mallory picked up the hat and train, respectively. Then, they went around the group and rolled the dice to determine who got to move first. Mallory won, which made Sybil and Connor frown deeply.

On her first roll, she got a five and landed on the first railroad, which she purchased without a second of hesitation.

"That's why I picked the train. I'm going to be the railroad baron."

An hour later, Peter was teetering on bankruptcy.

He'd spent the majority of the game in jail. The Morgan-McMahon Rules of Monopoly dictated that a player could either stay in jail for three turns, or roll doubles to be set free.

The catch was that if they rolled and didn't land doubles, they had to pay a fine.

Peter hadn't landed a double yet and was starting to think the dice were loaded.

Connor had a portfolio balanced between cash on hand and property. He'd managed to win a railroad out from under Mallory when, on one of his forays out of jail, Peter had landed on it and had decided against purchasing it because he had his eye on property further down the board that he had yet to land on. According to the Morgan-McMahon Rules of Monopoly, any property declined was then auctioned off to the other play-ers. He didn't know if it was a coordinated effort, but Connor and Sybil drove the price of the railroad to dizzying heights, but Connor hadn't been watching Mallory's purse close enough because she bowed out after Sybil did and left Connor on the hook.

Mallory was cash-poor but property-rich. If it wasn't for Connor's singular railroad, she would be the railroad baron. A few bad rolls by the rest of the group, and she'd have the cash she needed to start building on the cheap properties she'd been able to afford when she landed on them.

Sybil was sitting on a fat stack of cash. If Peter was a jail-bird, she was queen of the community chest. All of his misroll fines had ended up directly in her pocket. If she could roll a six, she'd land on Pennsylvania Avenue, complete her acquisition of the green properties, and then they were all screwed because she had the capital to do major building.

"Blow on them," Sybil said, holding the dice under Peter's chin. Then she glanced at his money and curled her fist around the dice. "Actually, never mind."

She jiggled the diced in her palm, then rolled them on the board.

A four and a two.

Mallory groaned. "You have all the fucking luck."

Sybil slid her car across the spaces to Pennsylvania Avenue. "It's not luck. It's strategy. Maybe if you managed your money better, you wouldn't have to rely on luck."

"At least I take risks. We've been playing for an hour, and you just purchased your third property."

"And how are your railroads working out for you?"

"I'd take advice from you, but when was the last time you won?" Mallory tilted her head and raised her eyebrows. Sybil didn't answer. "Exactly. You play it safe, and you lose."

If Peter had a time machine, he would have gone back to exactly that moment and intervened.

"Am I losing? I have a house, a business, and a retirement account. What do you have? Three part-time jobs and a passport?"

"At least I live my life," Mallory retorted. "You're so scared of making a mistake you won't move forward. You're so stuck in your fucking rut that you can't see a good thing right in front of you."

"I'm not moving forward with my life?" Sybil shouted. "You can't stick around long enough to acquire any grown-up responsibilities! And the ones you do have, I take care of!"

"I never asked you to do that!" Mallory shouted back.

"What was I supposed to do? Let the registration on your vehicle lapse six years ago? Because that's the last time *you* renewed your tabs."

"Yes! Because it was my problem. You didn't do it to be nice, you did it so you could lord it over me. 'Mallory fucked up again, I'm such a good person for saving her.' I'm so sick of being fodder for your savior complex. You think you know better than everyone, but you're full of shit."

"You gave me a savior complex because *someone* had to save you from yourself. Do you know how much easier my life would've been—*would be*—if I wasn't constantly worried about you?" Sybil threw her hands in the air. "I'm sorry making sure you didn't go to jail or die was such a fucking hardship *for you.*"

Sybil shoved herself to her feet and stormed out of the room, her steps pounding up the stairs. Mallory followed suit, but she marched out the front door, slamming it behind her.

Connor sighed, the sound heavy with disappointment and frustration.

"I *told you* this was a bad idea."

He got up, but instead of going up the stairs to comfort his best friend, he slipped on his shoes, grabbed his coat, then picked up Mallory's shoes before heading out the front door.

"Mal..."

A lot of information that had been uselessly floating around in the back of Peter's mind suddenly fitted together.

Connor had feelings for Mallory.

"Oh...shit..." Peter breathed, blinking a few times as he assimilated the information.

At least if Connor ever tried to convince Sybil to leave him, it wouldn't be to take his place.

Peter knocked tentatively on Sybil's door frame. Her door was three-quarters shut, like she'd run out of rage-fueled steam before she was able to slam the door.

"Go away," she whispered.

Peter ignored her and slipped inside. Maybe he wasn't so good at following directions.

Sybil sat on her bed, back to the door, her shoulders sagged, like her entire body was frowning. She sniffed and wiped at her eyes with her sleeve.

"I thought I told you to go away."

Peter sat next to her and wrapped an arm around her sad shoulders. "I'm not going to do that."

Sybil melted into him, her body conforming to his edges. "Sorry we ruined your game night."

"If I'd known it was going to be the start of a very cathartic family therapy session, I would have catered differently," he joked and squeezed her shoulders. "Can you explain what just happened so I don't accidentally trigger the minefield again?"

She sighed, curling inwards on herself more. "We had a really shitty childhood. I don't know if Mallory understands how shitty because I've always done my best to protect her. She's my little sister. That's my job." She sniffed, then wiped her nose on her sleeve. "Our mom—"

Her voice cracked on "mom," and it would have hurt less if she'd driven a knife through one of his ribs to stab him in the heart.

"Our mom wasn't a stable person. Nothing was ever good enough for her. *We* were never good enough for her. I don't know what her vision of motherhood looked like, but we weren't it, so she mostly ignored us. I figured out a lot faster than Mallory that she didn't give a shit. Mallory tried *so* hard all through elementary school to make her proud. Student of the month, spelling bee champion, academic awards. None of it mattered. Whatever boyfriend she had at the time was more important." Sybil's hollow laugh sent icy shivers down his spine. "She hoed for a home. Lots of stepdaddies. But she was never satisfied with her life, so we moved a lot. Fresh city, fresh start, fresh dating pool."

She pushed her face into his neck, and he felt her hot tears slide silently into the collar of his shirt. The quietness filled the space while he waited patiently for Sybil to gather herself together to continue, all the while stroking her shoulder.

"We got harder to ignore as we got older. Or Mallory got

harder to ignore. I was happy to fly under the radar and be left alone. But Mallory liked to see how hard she had to push to get a reaction. I think the only reason she didn't fail classes on purpose was because she liked doing sports. I really think if we hadn't come here, Mallory would've ended up in juvie."

"Which stepdaddy brought you here?" Peter asked, finally daring to speak.

"None of them, actually. The last guy before we came here was a little too interested in me and Mallory. I refused to give him the time of day, but sometimes Mallory would flirt to annoy our mom. And one night, I was in the kitchen making myself a sandwich because I'd been sent to my room without dinner, and I heard footsteps in the hall. I don't know why I grabbed the big knife, but I had a bad feeling. And I caught him at Mallory's door, trying to pick the lock. I told her to lock her door at night, and for once she fucking listened. I held the tip of the knife against his dick and told him if he so much as blinked in my sister's direction again, I'd cut off all his favorite body parts, starting with that one."

This time when she laughed, it had a manic edge.

"He peed his pants."

Her laugh dissolved into a singular sob.

"He kicked us out. And for once, our mom didn't have an exit strategy, so we came here to live with her sister, who we'd never met. There was a moment when we were carrying our clothes inside that I thought maybe this time, without a man, she'd finally be happy." She sighed. "Two weeks into living here, we came home from school and she'd left a note on the fridge giving Aunt Faye custody of us. I don't think you could get away with that now, but you could then. She didn't even stick around to say goodbye or explain herself."

Peter didn't think his heart could break anymore for the women he loved, but the shards shattered into dust.

"I'm so sorry. That's awful."

Sybil shook her head. "No—I mean, it is fucking awful because who fucking does that? But with some distance I can see now it was the best thing she could have done for us. Aunt Faye never wanted to be a mother either, she didn't know what to fucking do with us, but she at least *tried*. And we got Bitsy and Greg, who treated us like their own kids. I just...I just wish Mallory saw me differently. I wish she liked me more. I wish she knew that when she thinks I'm nagging her, it's because I love her and I want what's best for her and I'm so fucking frustrated watching her waste her potential."

Peter pressed his lips against the top of her head. "I knew that you were brave and strong, but fuck." He wrapped his other arm around her and hugged her tightly, afraid she'd try and slip away to avoid her own vulnerability. "I don't have any siblings, so I can't pretend to know how any of this feels, but have you tried talking to her about any of this?"

"We'd just end up fighting again. I don't know how to talk to her anymore without it ending like this." Sybil picked at a loose string on her sleeve.

"Do you want advice, or do you want me to be silently supportive?"

A watery laugh escaped her lips. "You don't know how to be silent."

"It might kill me, but I'd do it for you."

She laughed again, then hiccupped. "What advice do you have?"

"Well, after years of therapy to keep my head on straight, I feel like you've got some options. You both wave the white flag, sit down, and have an open, honest, vulnerable conversation with each other about how you feel and what you want. *Or* you put on some headgear and boxing gloves, get in a ring, and wail on each other until you're too tired to shout, and then talk."

"Is there a third option?"

"Yes. You do nothing, nothing changes, and you feel like this for the rest of your life."

She groaned. "I don't like any of those."

"My personal favorite is door number one."

She looked up at him and narrowed her eyes.

"You don't have to do it tonight," Peter said, "but you should do it soon. This only gets worse if you keep letting it fester."

She huffed and pouted. "I don't like it when you're right."

Chapter Thirty-Three

Sybil couldn't sleep. There were a few times she thought she'd drifted off, but then she'd wake up, check the time, and it had been five minutes or less.

Peter hadn't had any trouble falling asleep. Annoyingly, he could close his eyes and three deep breaths later, he'd be asleep. She couldn't understand it. It wasn't fair.

So, at three in the morning, she got out of bed as quietly as she could so she wouldn't wake Peter or Agatha, who was curled up against his side. Neither one of them so much as twitched.

The house was so quiet that she skipped the third stair from the bottom because it creaked. Even opening the fridge seemed impossibly loud as she rooted around for a snack.

"Hey." Mallory's quiet salutation startled her, and baby carrots flung into the air and spilled across the floor.

Sybil pressed a hand to her chest to keep her heart in her ribcage. "Fuck. You need a bell." She stooped and started picking up carrots. "What are you doing up?"

"I couldn't sleep." Mallory crouched next to Sybil and helped her gather the cold, slippery carrots. "What are you doing up?"

"Working on my Bugs Bunny impression." Sybil chomped on the end of a carrot. Mallory chuckled. "I couldn't sleep either."

They piled the carrots on the counter and stared at them, neither of them sure if the kitchen floor was clean enough to implement the Five Second Rule.

"We could wash them?" Mallory suggested.

Sybil found the colander and put the carrots inside to wash them off. While the water ran over them, she said, "Can we talk about what happened earlier?"

Mallory leaned back against the counter and crossed her arms. "What's there to talk about?"

The familiar annoyance rose like a toxic river after a heavy rain, and Sybil took a deep breath, suppressing the urge to snap.

"A lot, actually." She shut off the water and left the colander to drain in the sink, then wiped her hands off on a dish towel. "I don't know the right way to do this, but I'm sorry."

Mallory sighed. "Me too."

The only way out was through, so Sybil plunged headfirst into the conversation she'd been avoiding her entire life.

"I know you think I'm overly critical and that I hate everything you do, but I worry about you. I feel responsible for you."

"Why? You're not my mom."

"I know that—"

"Do you?" Mallory raised her eyebrows. "You're the one who came to my parent-teacher conferences even though you're barely a year older than I am."

"Who else was going to show up?"

"Who showed up for you?" Mallory let that question hang in the air between them before saying, "I didn't want you to be my mom, Sybil. I wanted you to be my sister."

Tears stung Sybil's eyes, and her throat was so tight she

could barely squeak out, "I don't know if I know how to do that anymore."

Mallory wrapped her arms around her and hugged her sister for the first time in years. It broke the dam of sadness inside of Sybil, and she clung to her little sister so she wouldn't drown in her own tears.

"I know you're legally obligated to love me because I'm your sister," Sybil hiccupped, "but I'm scared you don't like me."

Mallory squeezed her tightly, her blonde curls tickling Sybil's cheek. "What the fuck are you talking about? I *love* you, you idiot. I thought that you hated my guts because my life looks different from yours."

"I don't like that you leave me here," Sybil wept, barely getting the words out around her sobs. "I worry about you. I miss you. And I don't hate your guts because your life looks different from mine. I get frustrated because you're fucking brilliant and you have so much potential and I don't understand what your plan is. I don't want you to regret a second of your life."

"I don't want *you* to regret anything," Mallory said, her voice cracking as she started crying, too. "I wish you'd take more chances, push yourself, do something really risky." She glanced up at the ceiling and grinned. "Well, besides the guy upstairs who's stupid in love with you. I'm really proud of you for that."

Sybil tried to roll her eyes and accidentally pushed more tears out. "Shut up."

"And..." Mallory hesitated for a moment. "I don't know if you'll need to miss me too much longer. I...I think I want to stick around for a while. I meant it when I said I wanted to work with you at the coffee shop. I'm getting too old for hostels."

"I think I was born too old for hostels," Sybil joked, using the dish rag to dry her face because her hands weren't cutting it.

"You really want to work for me? You're not scared you're going to get bored?"

"I've never been bored. That's not why I leave."

Peter yawned loudly from the entrance to the kitchen. He stretched, and Sybil could see every glorious muscle flex because he had wandered downstairs in his underwear.

"Whyaren'tyouinbed?" he mumbled, rubbing an eye with the heel of a hand.

Mallory let out a low whistle. "I have never been more proud of you than I am right now, Syb."

Sybil gently backhanded her sister's shoulder. "Stop looking at him."

"That's like asking me not to look at the *Mona Lisa* or the *David*. You don't turn your eyes away from art."

"You do from this art." Sybil put her hands on Mallory's shoulders and turned her around so she was facing the fridge. "Peter, go back to bed, love."

He mumbled something unintelligible, but turned and shuffled back toward the stairs.

"Do you want to learn to make coffee tomorrow?" Sybil asked Mallory.

"I'd love that."

***

Sybil had never realized how much energy it took to walk on jagged eggshells until she wasn't anymore. The days that followed her cathartic kitchen cry with her sister were the lightest she'd ever known. That didn't mean that she and Mallory didn't step on each other's toes, but there weren't decades of resentment buried under the words.

Training Mallory to make coffee wasn't half as hard as she'd expected it to be, but was exactly as frustrating as she'd imagined. Mallory had all the confidence of a mediocre man, and even though she picked it up quickly, she would try to jump ahead or she'd skip part of a process because she was trying to break some kind of barista speed record.

Sybil had said "Dump it out and do it again" so many times that she finally wrote it on a piece of paper, taped it to a coffee stirrer, and held it up the next time Mallory made a mistake.

But she didn't yell or say anything that made Mallory snap back at her with equal venom, even if she did have to walk away a few times to take a few deep breaths. It was progress.

She planned with Peter, Dempsey, and production to have the coffee cart be available on a day when they'd be filming at Connor's house. Dempsey had turned into the main point of contact for the project because as the script got heavier, Peter's focus was more divided. Sybil didn't mind having to liaise with Dempsey; they were fantastically organized and thorough. She'd never felt so prepared going into an event.

Peter was still sleeping in her bed every night, which meant Agatha was too. Sybil liked falling asleep to the sound of Agatha's blissful purrs. Mallory had tried to lure Agatha into her bedroom to sleep with her, but the cat had a preference order: Peter at the top, then way down the list was Sybil, followed by Mallory, who had heavily bribed her way onto the list.

They'd settled into cohabitation with an ease that made Sybil's stomach twist if she dwelled on it for more than a minute or two. It was already hard to imagine life without Peter as her shadow, and every hour she spent with him added to the weight of the inevitable goodbye. She'd learned from Dempsey that once production wrapped, he would travel to London to start rehearsals for a top-secret project. So he'd be leaving soon, on to the next shiny thing, and she'd be here, waiting to see if he'd really come back this time.

. . .

"Why the fuck is it so cold in here?" Mallory complained as she turned on the lights inside of the coffee cart.

"Because it's late October," Sybil reminded her, the fog from her breath hanging in the air. "It'll warm up."

Getting Mallory out of bed had taken an act of God, and Sybil was glad she'd gotten the coffee cart from the McMahon farm the night before and had the foresight to set it up. Even though they were late by Sybil's standards, they weren't going to be late by production's standards.

"Why did I let you talk me into this?"

Sybil turned on the espresso machine. "I didn't. You begged *me*, remember?"

Mallory glared at her, but there wasn't any malice in her narrowed eyes. "Don't go trying to distract me with your facts."

"I'll make you a quad shot," Sybil promised.

"Can I have six?"

Sybil looked her sister up and down, which didn't take a lot of eye movement because Mallory was short. "Six shots of espresso will *literally* explode your baby bird-sized heart."

"That's a risk I'm willing to take."

"Maybe at the end of the day when I don't need you anymore we can do that little science experiment, but for now, your limit is four." Sybil pulled out a folded piece of paper from her jacket pocket. "Peter's assistant Dempsey, who is a literal angel, already went around and got pre-orders from people who wanted coffee first thing, so let's get going on those and then some PAs will do deliveries."

Mallory studied the paper. "Wow. This is grouped by department, location on set, when it should be delivered, and has allergy alerts. Has Graham seen this? Because he'd faint."

"No, but if things ever get stale between him and Eloise, I'll show him this."

Mallory played music from her phone while they made the first batch of orders. It wasn't what Sybil normally would have listened to, but she could admit that Jenna Fox had some great songs.

When they were done, two PAs appeared like magic and took the grey cardboard drink carriers away, and they started on the second batch of orders. When those were done, the PAs materialized again and then disappeared with their charges. Sybil wished it was always this easy. No small talk, just a list of what she needed to do and people who didn't say a word.

The door of the trailer opened, and Dempsey stuck their head inside.

"Is Peter here?" they asked.

Sybil secured a lid on a cup. "No. Last I saw him, he was complaining to our cat about how early it was."

Dempsey frowned. "He didn't bring you to work today?"

Sybil shook her head. "No. My house is only a few streets over so we walked so we wouldn't have to deal with parking. Is he not here?"

"I can't find him, and I can't find any reliable cell phone service to call him."

"Do you want to go to my house and check?" Sybil rattled off her address, gave directions, and described her lawn decorations if there was any confusion about which house was hers.

Dempsey left, muttering, "I love my job, I love my job, I love my job..."

"'Our' cat, huh?" Mallory teased.

"Shut up."

"Peter and Sybil sitting in a tree, k-i-s-s-i-n-g—"

Sybil threw a piece of ice at her sister. It bounced harmlessly off the wall.

There was another knock, but this time from the window, which was shut. Sybil opened her mouth to tell whoever was out there to read the sign that said they'd be open in twenty minutes, but she spied Arthur through the plexiglass.

"Did you not put in your order with Dempsey?" she asked after she slid the window open.

Arthur put a dramatic hand to his chest. "No one ever thinks of us poor producers."

Mallory squeezed herself next to Sybil, and studied Arthur for a second. "I'm going to guess by your watch that 'poor' was more of an emotional state than an economic one."

"This timepiece was a gift from my wife for my seventieth birthday," Arthur said proudly. "I think she did a rather good job picking it out, don't you?"

"Do you want your usual?" Sybil asked, and Arthur flashed her a debonair smile.

"If it wouldn't be too much bother."

While she prepared Arthur's coffee, Mallory leaned out the window to talk to him.

"So, you're Peter's dad?"

"I am. And I would bet that you are Mallory, the infamous sister. Peter told me you travel a lot. Have you ever been to South Africa?"

"Yes. I love Cape Town."

"What about—"

Sybil reached over Mallory's head and handed Arthur his coffee. "You're distracting my help, Arthur."

"We'll have to compare passport stamps later," Arthur said with a conspiratorial wink. Then he dug into his pocket and put some money into their tip jar before heading off to do whatever mysterious work a producer did.

"Peter's dad is adorable. Please marry into that family so

he'll show me his slides and narrate them like my own personal *Planet Earth* special."

"How do you know he has slides?"

"Sybil. He looked like he wandered out of a magazine about English country living. There is no way that man doesn't have slides from the seventies and eighties."

Sybil rolled her eyes but gave up arguing. If Mallory wanted to make up elaborate but completely innocent fantasies about Arthur, so be it.

They'd almost finished the pre-orders when the trailer door opened again and Peter stepped inside.

"Did Dempsey find you?" Sybil asked, and lined a cold cup with caramel sauce.

"Dempsey was looking for me?"

"They said they couldn't find you anywhere." She noticed his clothes, which were his and not his costume. "When did you leave the house?"

Peter became very interested in reading what Mallory had scrawled on the side of a cup.

"Peter." Sybil snapped to get his attention. "You're late. Go check in."

"Can I get a coffee and a kiss first?"

"*Peter.*"

He held up his hands in surrender. "I'm going, I'm going."

Chapter Thirty-Four

THE SUMMONS from his mother to see her after they wrapped for the day felt like he'd been summoned to the gallows.

It had been a rough week so it wasn't an unexpected request, but that didn't make the walk to her hotel room any easier. His stomach rolled and twisted with every step down the hallway.

Charlotte had propped the door to her room open, and even though he'd been expressly invited, he still knocked.

"Come in and shut the door behind you," she instructed coolly.

His mother was sitting at the desk, her perpetually lost pair of glasses on top of her head, and her backup pair on her face. She looked like she'd been reviewing material for the next day, highlighters and sticky notes at the ready.

"Have a seat," she said and closed the binder she'd been marking.

Peter took the armchair in the corner and studied his mother. She looked tired, like the last few weeks had sucked the remaining youth from the marrow in her bones. On set, she wasn't exactly energetic, but she didn't look quite so hollow.

"I don't know if I'm asking this as your mother or your director—probably both—but I've noticed a concerning shift recently, so I need to know if you're okay." She pushed her backup glasses up on top of her head and her eyes widened when she felt her preferred pair already there.

"You should put those on a chain," he told her.

"No. That would make me look like an old lady." She took both pairs off her head and laid them on the desk. "Are you okay, Peter?"

He opened his mouth to answer but the answer wasn't there. He frowned and closed his mouth. Was he okay? His time in Crane Cove, at least this stint, was coming to a close. The time when he'd have to leave Sybil was speeding toward him like a train and he was tied to the tracks, helpless to change anything.

He shrugged.

"I don't understand. You were so excited about this project. But lately you've been showing up late, unprepared, and distracted. You were my one-take wonder until two weeks ago. Do you need to talk to the therapist? I know the material is a bit heavy..." She trailed off, her mouth drawn down into a tight frown. "It's okay not to be okay."

"I'm..." He couldn't bring himself to say that he was okay because he wasn't. "It's not the movie. That's not what's eating at me. I...Do you ever think you made the wrong choice being in this industry?"

"I think about that so often that it's the white noise I fall asleep to," she said. "You know I never wanted this life for you. You were such a happy child. You...sparkled. Everyone who met you loved you instantly. You were curious, creative, and had such a big, tender heart. I never wanted anyone to take those things away from you. Which is why I was so against you becoming an actor. This industry takes wonderful, excited, creative people and grinds them down, reduces them to parts instead of whole people. And you were always going to get it coming and going because of who your parents are. I knew it wouldn't matter how hard you worked or how fantastic you were—and you are *fantastic*—people would always say that you only got to where you are because of who's in your family tree. The same thing happened to me. I held you off for so long because I thought you'd find something else. Maybe you'd be a teacher, or a therapist, or a writer. But you wanted this so, so badly. You've always been so sure. What changed?"

He tried to swallow and couldn't.

His mother brought her chair over to his and sat, the toes of their shoes touching, and took his hands in hers. Her skin was soft and he could faintly smell the hand cream she'd been using his entire life, the scent of camellia, shea butter, and iris transporting him to childhood. She'd always been there, even when she was working, doing her best to be a pillar of strength and a soft place for him to land. He was too old and too large to curl up in her lap, but he ached to be rocked again.

"Nothing..." He groaned. "Everything. I've had so many years to imagine how this would go, and I never once imagined feeling this lost and trapped. I thought it would be easy, like it was for you and Dad, but it's not. I have to leave soon because I have contracts and commitments, but if I leave, I don't know if she'll still love me when I come back. She's been left too much, and it makes me sick that I have to add myself to that list. So I don't want to leave, but I can't stay, and I don't want to give up my career because I love my career, but I love her too and—"

"Peter," Charlotte interrupted gently, "who are you talking about?"

He blinked at her, momentarily mute while his brain caught up with his mouth.

"Sybil," he answered like it should have been obvious.

"The woman who owns the coffee shop? Maddy's double?"

"Of course."

It was Charlotte's turn to be stunned. Finally, she asked, "Since when?"

"About twelve years." His mouth curled into a sad smile. "She's the one. She's always been the one since the moment I met her, and I've been trying to show her for weeks how I can fit myself into her life so she'll give us a chance."

His mother's expression softened. "You were never meant to live a small life, sweetheart."

"Being here isn't a small life."

"But trying to wedge yourself into a box that wasn't meant for you is. When you find the person you want to spend the rest of your life with, it stops being your life and their life. You have to create a new normal together. You need to know what you're willing to give up, what you're not willing to give up, and what you're willing to modify or reduce. It's a lot of compromise. And it seems like it's easy for your father and me because we had those tough conversations before you were born. All you've ever seen is the product of years of open, honest, thoughtful communication."

"Were you ever scared you were going to fuck everything up?"

Charlotte laughed. "Of course I was. Look at the example I had growing up. You didn't think Grandma Estelle was a paragon, did you? Whatever the opposite of a saint is, that was my mother. And I'd already made so many awful choices by the time your father and I got together that I don't think I took a deep breath the entire first year of our marriage. I was so scared I'd ruin both of our lives." She squeezed his hands tightly. "It's okay to be scared, but don't let that fear dictate your choices."

"So what do I do?" he asked, his voice unable to go above a whisper.

She shrugged. "I have no idea. It's not my life."

"Mom—"

"No one else has as much at stake with your life as you do. I could tell you to do things I would never do myself because in the end, it doesn't affect me. Only you can know what the right decision for your life is." She smiled softly. "Trust yourself. You've got a good head on your shoulders, even if I'm not certain it's always attached."

She let go of his hands, stood, and opened her arms. Peter sank into her hug, letting her hold the weight of his worries for a few minutes.

She squeezed him tightly. "Get some sleep, and come prepared next week. We're in the final stretch. Have your existential crisis on someone else's time."

Peter parked his rental car next to the curb in front of Graham's house and let it idle, unable to rouse the strength to turn it off and go inside. The insurmountable gravity of the decisions he needed to make pinned him to the seat.

The two things he wanted most in life could not be so opposed to each other. He wanted to be with Sybil, to live a slow, quiet life in Crane Cove where they sat on her velvet couch, drank tea, and read books while rain drummed against the house. But he wanted his career, where he got to breathe life into people who only existed on a piece of paper, and made audiences who had never known them feel deeply about their struggles and triumphs.

Could he have both things? Or would he constantly be sacrificing one for the other?

The clock on the dash told him that he'd gone from late to very late, and he forced himself to turn off the engine and unbuckle his seatbelt.

Headlights flooded his rearview mirror and then turned off. He checked the reflection and saw that it was Sybil's car.

"I thought you'd already be inside," she said after they both got out of their vehicles, then frowned. "Is everything okay?"

"Yeah, everything's fine," he lied. "Where are you coming from?"

"Stardust. I wanted to grab the deposit before I came over."

She closed the miniscule distance between them and stretched up on her tiptoes. Automatically, he lowered himself to accept her tender kiss, and it cracked his hurting heart. How many of these sweet kisses did he have left?

"You sure you're okay?" she asked, cupping his face in her hands.

"It's just been a long, heavy week at work. I'll be okay."

Sybil looked ready to argue, but it never materialized.

"Knock, knock!" Peter shouted as he opened Graham and Eloise's front door.

They were met with the jingling of identification tags and the scrabble and pounding of paws on hardwood as Daisy barreled across the house to greet them.

"Daisy?" Peter's heart leapt at the sight of the dog. If Daisy was here, that meant...

Sam came trotting down the hall after his dog, a smug smirk on his face. Peter had known that Jordy and Annie were coming to visit for the weekend, allegedly to look at a few properties closer to Eugene and Corvallis, but no one had told him that Sam was coming.

"Oh god, don't cry," Sam begged when he saw the tears welling up in Peter's eyes.

Peter pulled him into a crushing hug. "I can't help it, I *missed* you."

"Can't. Breathe."

"If you can talk, you can breathe," Peter countered,

squeezing harder. Finally, he released Sam and held him at arm's length. "What are you doing here?"

"Well, Jordy told me about how he and Annie were coming to look at property, and Lacey and I have a little break, so we went in on a plane and came for the weekend. Plus, we needed to check on the cabin."

The unspoken words Sam hadn't said were that he knew what Jordy was planning on doing and wanted to be around to celebrate with his best friend. In their group of four, Jordy and Sam had always been closer to each other than they were to Peter and Graham, which was okay because the same was true of Peter and Graham's friendship.

"Graham and Jordy are building a fire in the backyard," Sam said, then looked at Sybil. "Eloise, Annie, and Lacey are in the den."

"I hope they have a bottle of wine open," Sybil said, slipping off her shoes and coat. As she passed, she squeezed Peter's arm, then disappeared down the hall.

Sam waited until she was out of sight, then raised his eyebrows at Peter. "What was that?"

"What was what?"

"Sybil just..." He mimed a squeezing motion. "Touchy-touchy." His eyes grew wide. "So it *was* Sybil you were asking me for advice about. How long have you two been fucking each other?"

"Shhh."

Sam laughed. "Do Graham and Jordy know?"

"No."

Sam beckoned for Daisy to follow him, not that it would have taken any prompting if he'd started walking away, and they made their way to the backyard. Graham and Jordy were arranging the wood in the fire pit with meticulous care, but when Jordy heard the back door open he looked up and dropped the piece of wood he was holding, demolishing their carefully built structure.

"Peter!"

They crashed into each other, stumbling around while they embraced until they got their footing, and then held each other tighter.

"I can't believe you're getting married," Peter gasped, because Jordy was squeezing him so tightly it was crushing his lungs.

"She hasn't said yes yet," Jordy pointed out.

"No one thinks she's saying no. People on the street who haven't met you two would put money on her saying yes."

"Is everything ready for tomorrow night?" Jordy asked.

Peter froze. His heart stopped, and ice filled his veins. Jordy's proposal. He'd forgotten that he was supposed to organize Jordy's proposal. Flowers, candle lights... He'd fucking forgotten.

"Uh-huh," he said weakly.

"Do you want to see the ring?" Jordy didn't wait for an answer. He dug into his jacket pocket and pulled out a small, black leather box. "I've been so freaked out she'd find this since I picked it up from the jeweler."

He lifted the lid. Inside was a pale purple oval gem, set in a delicate gold band that looked like a vine, each leaf studded with a tiny, glittering diamond.

"Oh, wow," Peter whispered. "That's beautiful."

"Would you mind holding on to it for me until tomorrow night? I don't want to have gotten this far only to have Annie find it in the final twenty-four hours." Jordy closed the box and held it out to Peter.

"Why me?"

"Because I'm scared she'll find it if I hide it in the house, and Sam and Lacey are going with us to look at properties tomorrow since Sam has built a home recently and has some insight into the process." Jordy smiled and offered him the box again. "Please? It'll be safe with you."

Peter took the box and slid it into his pocket, the guilt making the small box weigh his pocket down like a lead weight.

When they turned around, Graham had lit the fire and was setting out three crystal rocks glasses and a bottle of very fancy sparkling water for Sam. He held up an expensive bottle of whiskey.

"So I bought this in the spring, because I was convinced that Jordy was going to propose when he and Annie came up for their anniversary trip." He shot Jordy a glare. "But since that didn't happen, I've been holding on to it." He poured two fingers full into each glass.

"How come I didn't get a toast?" Sam asked.

"Because you eloped without telling us," Graham said, and passed out the glasses. He held his glass up. "Jordy, two years ago, I never would have guessed this day would come. But you and Annie are perfect for each other and I'm so excited that, technically, we'll be family now."

"Cousins-in-law seems like a bit of a stretch," Sam muttered, opening his sparkling water.

"To Jordy and Annie," Graham said, ignoring Sam's snark.

The four men clinked their drinks together.

Chapter Thirty-Five

THERE WAS NOT an open bottle of wine.

Eloise and Annie both claimed headaches, and Lacey said she wasn't interested in drinking that night. So Sybil couldn't manipulate the chemicals in her brain to slow down her racing mind because being the only person in a group drinking was awful.

Something was wrong with Peter. Or he had something on his mind. It had been a heavy week on set, like he said. One night he came home looking broken, and she'd taken him to the couch and laid his head in her lap and stroked his hair while they listened to Otis Redding and Sam Cooke. They'd stayed like that for more than an hour until his eyes started staying closed longer with every blink, then she took him upstairs to bed and held him until he fell asleep.

When they left Graham and Eloise's, Peter didn't seem much lighter or happier after spending time with his best friends. He seemed distracted. And when she asked if she'd see him at the house, he hesitated before saying yes.

Had he lost interest in her? Once the chase had slowed, was she not exciting enough to hold his attention?

Her stomach tied itself into a complicated knot in the two minutes it took her to drive home.

"I'm going to head to bed," Peter said, hanging his coat on the coat rack. He leaned down and kissed her forehead. "I've got a lot to do tomorrow."

"I'm going to clean the kitchen. I'll be up soon." Sybil gave him a small smile, and he went upstairs without questioning why it didn't reach her eyes.

She scrubbed the stove top until it sparkled, convinced that if she could rid her life of the ring of burned water from Peter boiling spaghetti, she'd rid herself of the anxiety that was crushing her lungs. In the end, the stove top looked new and she still couldn't take a full breath.

The bell on Agatha's collar jingled wildly in the other room as she darted around, getting out her nighttime zoomies. Sybil headed for the stairs just in time to watch Agatha skid into the coat rack and knock it over.

"Goddammit, cat," she muttered and went to pick up the coats off the floor. "We bring you inside, feed you, give you an automatic litter box so you never even have to see your own poops, and this is how you repay us?"

She picked Peter's coat up and it felt oddly...heavy. Did he leave his phone in his pocket again? She stuck her hand inside the right pocket and felt something unexpected: a leather box.

Sybil's heart jumped into her throat. This couldn't be a... there was no way...he wouldn't...

Carefully, like she was handling a sensitive bomb, she drew the box out of his pocket and, with trembling fingers, opened the lid.

"Oh fuck," she breathed.

In the morning, Sybil did two things she almost never did: she called off work and then she went back to sleep and slept until nine a.m.

It was disorienting to wake up hours after she normally did. And because it was a beautiful, sunny Saturday, the sun was shining through her window onto her bed. Sybil hissed at it like a vampire.

She reached for Peter to see if he was awake, but he wasn't there. The spot where he slept was cold.

Where was he?

The ring jumped to the forefront of her mind. Peter had been working hard learning to make pancakes the last few weekends. Was he downstairs trying to make her a romantic breakfast and he was going to propose over potentially edible pancakes?

The thought made her nauseous, and not just because some of his first attempts had been spectacularly inedible. It shouldn't be possible for a pancake to be burnt on the outside and so raw that it was runny on the inside.

It was too much too soon, and the worst part was...a very vocal part of her wanted to say yes. She wanted to spend the rest of her life being smothered in adoration. She wanted those beautiful blue eyes to sparkle at her when he smiled. She wanted Peter to be her husband.

But what she wanted and what she needed to do were on opposite sides of reality.

Sybil crept down the stairs, taking a long step to avoid the creaky one. It didn't smell like breakfast. She glanced toward the door. Peter's coat was still there, and so were his shoes.

"Hi, my name is Peter. I order flowers from you every week?...Yes, that Peter."

She froze. He sounded like he was in the kitchen.

"I know it's very last minute, but how many small, romantic

bouquets could you make me before four o'clock this afternoon? Not terribly picky about the contents, and price isn't an object... They're for a proposal...You can? Fantastic. One last thing—do you know where I could get a lot of electric candles? Or some tall vases where the wicks won't burn out if it's windy? You do? You are a *lifesaver*."

Sybil's mouth went dry and her heart pounded against her ribs. How the fuck was she supposed to gently dissuade him from proposing when he'd already called the florist?

"Oh hey. You're awake."

She jumped. Peter had appeared in the archway that separated the front of the house from the back of the house.

"Sorry I can't stick around for you to get ready, but I have a lot of things to do today, and I'm somehow already behind schedule." He closed the space between them and stooped to kiss her forehead. The soft brush of his lips squeezed her heart in a painful vice. "I need you to come with me to the lighthouse later for a surprise."

"I can't marry you!" The words burst out of her. Peter took a few steps back, his forehead creased in a deep frown. "I found the ring in your pocket last night, and it's beautiful, but it's too soon."

"Sybil—"

Panic rose like a flood and she flailed like a drowning person. "Why couldn't you listen to what I wanted? Why do you have to push, and push, and push? I'm not ready for this kind of commitment, Peter. I can't even wrap my head around how we could possibly move this relationship forward when you leave next week and you went out and bought a fucking *ring*. Without talking to me about it! Because if you'd asked, I would have said no. I would have told you that I don't think we're there and I don't know if we'll ever be there. I don't even understand how you leapt from 'let's be casual' to 'let's get married.'"

Peter was silent for a few frantic beats of her heart, and then asked, "Can I speak now?"

She waved a hand.

"It's not my ring. It's Jordy's ring. Jordy is proposing to Annie today, and I said I'd help him set up something romantic at the lighthouse since they're looking at properties today. That was the surprise." His explanation was so calm it chilled her to the bone. "Do you not see a future between us?"

"I'm not there yet."

"Well, I am. I've been there, and I don't know what else I have to do to convince you to meet me at least halfway." It was as close to a yell as she'd ever heard his voice, and she took a few steps back. His face fell and he looked at the floor and shook his head. "Maybe I don't know how this works either. If you don't want me to push, then I won't."

Peter turned and walked to the door. He put on his shoes and his coat and picked up his rental car keys. He didn't look back before he opened the door and left.

Mallory's ready smile turned into a frown when Sybil walked through the front door of Stardust.

"What are you doing here? I thought you weren't feeling well?"

Sybil stepped behind the counter and grabbed an apron, tying it around her waist roughly.

"I'm fine. What are you doing here?"

"You put me on the schedule, remember?" Mallory narrowed her eyes. "Are you sure you're okay? Your eyes are kind of—"

"Just let me work!" Sybil snapped. She knew what her eyes looked like. They were red and puffy because a few minutes after Peter left, she'd started crying and hadn't been able to stop.

Going to Stardust was the only thing she knew to do. If she could keep moving until he came home that evening, she'd be okay.

"No. Absolutely not. You're not yelling at me today." Mallory grabbed her elbow and marched her into the office, shutting the door for privacy. "You either have pinkeye or you've been crying. Which is it?"

The flimsy wall she'd built around her emotions crumbled like a sandcastle against the incoming tide. Her eyes welled up again, and Mallory's stern expression disappeared.

"Oh, no." Mallory wrapped her arms around Sybil and hugged her sister tightly. "What happened?"

"Peter...and I...had a fight," she sobbed, pressing her face into her sister's shoulder.

"I didn't think Peter was capable of fighting," Mallory said, rubbing her back. "Do you want to tell me what it was about?"

Sybil took a few shuddering breaths, trying to calm herself enough to speak.

"I thought he was going to p-p-propose and I freaked out and then he left."

"He just needs to go cool off," Mallory promised. "Give him some time. He'll come back."

"What if he doesn't? What if I fucked up too much this time?"

"He loves you. I don't think one fight is going to change his mind."

Sybil stayed at Stardust until close, dreading going home while simultaneously jumping every time someone entered the coffee shop, thinking it was Peter coming to talk to her once he'd calmed down.

She pushed open the front door she never locked and was

greeted by Agatha, who very loudly vocalized her displeasure at being left alone.

"I bet Daddy already gave you dinner," she said, hanging up her coat and taking off her shoes. "Is he upstairs, Aggie? Let's go see if you're trying to con me."

She climbed the stairs, reminding herself to breathe with every ascending step.

Her bedroom door was open, and the light was off. A shaking finger pushed the switch.

It took a moment for her brain to register what was different in the room. The items he'd been squirreling away in her room, like his book on the nightstand and his sweatpants on the floor, like she wouldn't notice he was slowly moving in were gone.

She went to the closet and yanked the doors open.

His shirts and hoodies were missing.

The realization rocked her like an earthquake. He'd left. While she'd been at Stardust, he'd taken all of his stuff out of her house in one fell swoop so he wouldn't have to come back.

She stumbled to the bed in a daze and collapsed on what had become his side. The co-mingled smells of his hair products and his cologne filled her senses and she sobbed into his pillow until she fell asleep.

Chapter Thirty-Six

Peter's gin and tonic tasted like sadness and regret. But all gin and tonics had a certain edge of melancholy. He'd never met anyone whose drink of choice was a gin and tonic that wasn't on or should be on an antidepressant.

"I've just come from your mother, and you are officially wrapped," his father said, sliding onto the barstool next to his. He caught the bartender's eye. "Scotch, please. Neat." Arthur folded his hands on the top of the bar and studied Peter for a second. "You don't look very happy for a man who just finished work three days early."

Peter drained the remainder of his gin and tonic and pushed it toward the bartender for another one.

He wasn't happy. He was somewhere at the bottom of a pit of sadness that he felt he'd never be able to crawl out of. Everything after Saturday morning replayed as hazy memories. He'd been wandering through life in a daze, barely having the presence of mind to ask if he could push and wrap his scenes early so he could go to London. His mother wouldn't outright agree to it, but she did say when she was satisfied they'd gotten good enough footage for his last pages, she'd release him. So he'd funneled what little energy he had into finishing work so he could get the hell out of Crane Cove.

"I'm tired."

It wasn't a lie, but there was a mountain of omission hanging in the air. Peter hadn't slept much since Saturday. His hotel bed was too big, too foreign, and didn't smell anything like Sybil. He'd taken all of his stuff from her house on an impulse. If she'd been home, he would have taken it as a sign they were supposed to talk it out, but she wasn't, so he loaded his clothes, his book, and his toothbrush into his rental car.

He hadn't heard from her since Saturday, either. She hadn't been on set Monday or today, which was fine for production because Maddy had been feeling better and needed Sybil less lately, but was hell on his nerves. As much as he wanted to reach out, he couldn't keep crossing oceans for her if she wouldn't cross town for him.

The bartender passed Arthur his scotch and replaced Peter's drink with a fresh one. Arthur picked up his glass, sniffed, and then sipped.

"A weary heart will make you feel that way," Arthur said with all the wisdom of a smelly hermit who lives on top of a mountain and has a concerning amount of devotees.

"I don't want to be weary, I want to be happy. I thought—" Peter cut himself off and sighed.

Arthur nudged him in the side. "You're forgetting that you're talking to the former president of the Abject Piners Club. Tell me what's on your mind. Burdens are easier when shared."

"Jordy proposed to his girlfriend this weekend." He took the lime from the rim of the glass and squeezed it into his drink until it was rind and pulverized flesh, then he dropped its corpse into the glass. "I was holding on to the ring for him because he was worried Annie would find it, except Sybil found it, thought it was for her, freaked out, said I don't respect her boundaries, that I push too hard, and she didn't know if she saw a future with me." He sipped his drink and winced as the piney liquor bit him. "It hurt like hell and it caught me off guard and I walked out."

"Do you see a future with her?" Arthur asked gently.

Peter watched the carbonation from the tonic water latch onto the lime like bubbly parasites while he contemplated a question he already knew the answer to.

"I want a future with her. I want to grow old with her. But if she doesn't want that...I don't know what to do."

"From the time I met your mother until we got together, it was about—" Arthur squinted as he tried to remember dates more than thirty years in the past and do the appropriate math. "Fourteen years? Or maybe fifteen? She wasn't ready for the kind of forever I wanted with her when we met. The hardest thing I've ever had to do was to wait for her to catch up to me. But, if I'd pushed, if I'd tried to force her into what I wanted before she was ready, we would have failed spectacularly." He put a hand on Peter's shoulder and squeezed. "My two cents, if my opinion is even worth that, is you give her the time and space she needs. If you want to wait from afar, let her know, but you need to let her figure out what she wants so when she decides, it's her choice alone without any pressure from you."

"I don't know if I can face her without begging her to love me."

"You don't have to face her. Write her a letter. Probably a better idea anyway. Gives you both space to process your emotions."

The weight of his misery was too much, and he leaned against his father, resting his head on the shoulder that had borne so many of his tears.

"Fifteen years?" Peter asked quietly. "It's already been twelve. I only have to survive another three."

The early November wind bit at Sybil's tear-stained cheeks and tangled her hair. In her hands she held two checks that represented enough money to sign the lease on the empty storefront in front of her. Her dream had never been so close and mattered so little.

"Is there a reason you've been standing here for the last twenty minutes?" Mallory asked, standing next to her. She pulled her coat tight around her and rubbed her arms. "It's fucking freezing."

"I can't even tell," Sybil said weakly and handed her the checks. "I don't know what to do with these anymore."

Mallory took the checks and let out a low whistle. "Wow. That is a chunk of change, babe. What do you mean you don't know what to do with this?"

Sybil sniffed and gestured to the empty storefront. "I wanted to connect this space to Stardust and open a bookstore. But I don't know anymore. I can't get excited about finding the money to do the renovations, to buy stock. It's so much work, and I'm so tired."

"How long have you been thinking about this?"

"Since I opened Stardust. The timing has never been quite right. Either the space hasn't been available, or I didn't have the money because something expensive always happens when I think it's time." She wiped her nose on her sleeve. "I still don't have all the money, but I thought if I could sign the lease, at least the space wouldn't disappear from under me while I figured out the whole loan process."

Mallory was quiet for a few moments, then asked, "How much money were you going to take out as a loan?"

"I haven't crunched the numbers in a while, but somewhere around twenty or thirty thousand."

Mallory nodded and studied the empty storefront. A strong gust whipped down the street, rustling the checks in her hands and blowing a leaf into her curly blond hair.

"What if," Mallory began slowly, turning her head to look at Sybil, "I gave you the money?"

The wind must have distorted what she'd heard.

"Give me the money? What money?" Sybil asked. "You don't have that kind of money."

"Actually, I do. I have this older sister who nags me a lot about saving my money and she doesn't think I listen to her, but I do. She also told me that I'm wasting my potential and she's not wrong." Mallory handed her back the checks. "I've saved about twenty-seven thousand dollars. I want to invest twenty thousand of that into our business."

"*Our* business?"

"Yes, *our* business," Mallory confirmed, mocking Sybil's tone. "If I'm going to put twenty down, I'm going to be a partner in this. And not a silent partner, either. You know I'm very loud."

"It's a lot of responsibility," Sybil warned her.

"I'm ready to give responsibility a try." Mallory's giant smile faltered when Sybil didn't return it. "Is something else wrong?"

The sadness welled up inside her again and her bottom lip quivered as she tried to stop it from spilling over.

"He's gone. He left."

Sybil had planned on talking to Peter when she went to pick up her check from production. After five days of almost nonstop crying, she was ready and willing to admit that she had overreacted and she didn't mean a lot of what she'd said. But when she'd arrived at the payroll office, there was a second check waiting for her from Peter: the balance of the coffee cart.

When she'd asked why he'd left it for her there, payroll told her that Peter had finished filming on Tuesday and had already left for London. He wanted to be sure she got her money, so he'd left it with them for her to pick up since he knew she'd be coming by for her other check.

"Oh, Sybil." Mallory wrapped her arms around her sister and hugged her tightly. "Did he say anything?"

"No." The first sob slipped out. "I f-fucked this up s-s-so bad, Mal. It's all my—" Her words got stuck in her throat, trapped by the boulder of emotion blocking the way. She was finally able to force out, "Fault."

"Let's take you home before anyone catches you sobbing on the sidewalk," Mallory said, curling an arm around Sybil's waist and guiding her toward the parking area at the end of the street. "You have a reputation to uphold. Scary bitches don't cry."

The front door of the house was unlocked. Mallory ushered Sybil inside and hung her car keys next to the door.

Sybil took off her shoes, avoiding looking at the coat rack, like it was solely responsible for the last five miserable days of her life. She wanted to go up to her room to see if any weak whiffs of Peter's scent could be pulled from his pillow.

Flowers on the coffee table caught her eye.

"Did you put those there?" she asked Mallory and pointed at the red roses.

Mallory shook her head. "They weren't there when I left."

Like she was moving through quicksand, Sybil slowly walked over to the coffee table, each step making her stomach sink lower.

There was an envelope tucked under the vase with her name written on it in a mix of print and cursive she was extremely familiar with.

"Is it from Peter?"

Sybil nodded. She sat on the couch before opening the

envelope, not having any faith in her legs to support her through the letter.

> Sybil,
>
> By the time you read this, I'll be on my way to London. I'm sorry I didn't say goodbye in person, but I'm trying to be less pushy and give you the space you need to process what happened on Saturday.
>
> Even though I'm leaving, I don't want to stay away forever. I love you, without hope or expectation. If I have to wait for you for the rest of my life, that's fine. I can do that. It's always been you since the first instant I saw you in that dusty bookshop, and I don't see that changing. When I'm with you, my heart knows it can rest and I feel, for the first time, calm.
>
> I know you're worried that we can't work. That my life is so big that you'll get lost in it. That I'll get bored of you once the chase is over, that I'll want to move on when the butterflies are gone and I find out that you sleep with your mouth open (you do, by the way). But my idea of a perfect day is one where we curl up on the couch with cups of coffee and our books, and listen to the rain while we read. I would take a million of those slow, quiet days if you'd give them to me.
>
> I love you. I want to figure out how we can make a future together work. I am willing to stand still and wait for you to catch up if you're willing to close the distance.
>
> Whenever you're ready, I'm waiting.
>
> All my love,

Peter

Tears fell on the letter like raindrops, the ink spreading outward in circles. Her chest was tight, and her heart felt like it was being used as a professional boxer's speed bag.

"What does it say?" Mallory asked.

Sybil handed her the letter, fighting for breath while her body fought to cry.

"I hate this. Being in love *hurts*. How do people walk around like this every day? I feel like I'm having a fucking heart attack."

Mallory didn't answer her question. Instead she snapped her fingers in front of Sybil's face.

"Snap out of it. I need your attention. And I need you to not think about your answers. Just whatever you want to say, say it. Do you love Peter?"

"Yes."

"Do you want to be with him?"

"Yes."

"When do you want to fix the mess you made?"

"Right now."

"Fantastic." Mallory set the letter down on the coffee table and pulled her phone out of her pocket.

Sybil used a throw blanket as a tissue. "What are you doing?"

"Trying to figure out what flight he's on to London...Fuck. It's taking off in thirty minutes. Is there another flight tonight?" She touched her screen a few more times. "Okay, so if you want to leave before tomorrow, there's a few flights with connections, but I'm personally a bigger fan of a nonstop because it's less hassle. There is one out of Portland, but it doesn't leave until tomorrow."

"Slow down...What?"

Mallory tapped her screen, not bothering to look up. "I'm booking you a flight. You're going to London to get your man back."

"Mal—"

Her sister tossed her phone down and held her hands up. "Too late. It's done. And you can't tell me it's too much money, because I have a *lot* of miles." She jumped to her feet and started toward the stairs. "Where's your passport? It's still valid, right?"

"Shouldn't you have asked that *before* you booked the ticket?" Sybil shouted after her, running to catch up.

"There's such a thing as emergency passport services. There's an office in Seattle. We could make it work."

"Who's going to run Stardust? I can't drop everything." Sybil followed Mallory into her room. "Are you listening to me?"

Mallory dug out a suitcase from under her bed. "I can take care of Stardust. We're partners now, remember? And you won't be gone for more than a few days. It'll be fine."

"Oh my god." Sybil sat down on the edge of the bed, her head swimming. "I'm going to London."

Chapter Thirty-Seven

"Did you really need me to run errands with you?" Peter asked, plodding two steps behind Dempsey as his assistant speed-walked down the sidewalk.

"I'm shopping for a birthday present, and you're good at presents. Considering how much I do for you, I think you can help me with this," Dempsey said.

"I pay you for that," Peter reminded them. "Why couldn't you have left me in bed to rot?"

"Because you're the closest thing I have to a pet, and it would be irresponsible of me not to make sure you get a walk in the fresh air once a day."

Peter sniffed the air. There was a faint odor of curry from a takeaway shop, petrol, and the putrid smell of someone's sick in the gutter.

"I wouldn't say fresh."

Dempsey paused their road march to look around, stopping so suddenly that Peter bumped into them.

"Give me two hours," Dempsey said, "and then I will let you draw your curtains and burrow under your covers until tomorrow."

They looked both ways, then darted across the street. Peter had to jog to catch up.

There was something familiar about the street. He glanced in a shop window and saw a cat sleeping amongst several stacked books.

"You're not looking for a book, are you?"

Dempsey pulled open the blue door roughly since it stuck, and some of the flaking gold lettering on the door quivered.

"I am. Come on."

They'd taken one step inside when Peter balked and said, "I can't."

Dempsey grabbed his wrist and tugged. "Yes. You. Can."

He tried not to breathe, tried not to let his sense of smell dig up all those memories, but the dust in the air tickled his nose and he sneezed. When he inhaled, the scent of dust, groundwood paper, and wood almost buckled his knees.

"How do you find anything in here?" Dempsey asked, having already discovered management's lack of organization.

"You just—" He thought he saw a flash of red from the corner of his eye. "Have to look for it."

His words trailed off as he edged toward where he thought he'd seen the flash of color. It would end up being nothing, and then his heart would break all over again. He had to stop thinking every bit of red he saw might be Sybil, no matter how much he missed her.

He poked his head around the shelves. No one was there, and besides the books, not a hint of red to be seen.

If he had it to do all over, he wouldn't have left Crane Cove. He would have grabbed a bucket full of pebbles and tossed them at Sybil's window until she'd talked to him. He missed her too much to care about anything else.

Peter wandered, hands in his pockets, down the aisle,

glancing up and down the shelves. There had to be something here. There was always something.

Of course, it was hard to find a needle in a haystack when he didn't know what kind of needle was looking for.

He turned to take the scenic route to where he'd seen Dempsey go, and froze.

Red wool sweater. Red hair bunched into a messy bun. Stretching up on her tiptoes to reach a book.

It couldn't be...

Her fingers grasped the spine and she pulled the book free from its shelf, and put her weight back on her heels. Then she looked at him and smiled timidly, but there was hope glimmering in her brown eyes.

"Hello, Peter," Sybil said softly.

"What are you doing here?"

Sybil took a few slow, cautious steps towards him. Peter didn't dare to even blink in case this was a hallucination that would disappear if he closed his eyes.

"I came to see if you still wanted to sit on my couch while we read books and listen to the rain." She pressed the book she'd pulled from the shelf into his hands. "Sorry it took me so long to get here. I had to catch up."

Peter looked down at the book in his hands. *Wyrd Sisters* by Terry Pratchett.

"I was hoping you'd read it and write in the margins for me," Sybil said.

He closed his eyes. When he opened them, she was still there, the line of worry between her eyebrows growing deeper with every passing heartbeat.

"You're actually here," he whispered, staggered by his own disbelief.

The book landed on the uneven wood floor with a *thump* and then Peter had Sybil in his arms again, his lips pressed against hers. She clung to him, her fingers twisting around the fabric of his clothes, and kissed him back like she never thought she'd see him again.

The world ceased to spin. The dust motes, stirred up when he dropped the book on the floor, froze in midair. It was a singularly perfect moment, and Peter was determined to memorize every part of it. The softness of the well-loved wool under his palms. How Sybil's scent mixed with the aroma of the bookshop. The pounding of his heart in his ears. All of it was precious.

When they finally parted, though only enough to speak, Sybil quickly said, "I love you. I don't know what this is going to look like or how we're going to make it work, but I want this. I want *us*."

"You're sure?" He touched his forehead to hers, and their noses bumped against each other. "I don't want to push—"

"Peter, I flew almost ten hours to get to you. I chased you across an ocean. You're not pushing."

"I really get to keep you?"

Sybil nodded, a watery smile stretching across her face.

"Not to break up this touching reunion, but you are in public and cell phones have cameras," Dempsey reminded them, standing where they might have blocked someone's shot if they were taller.

Peter took a step back from Sybil, but kept his hands on her arms. "I'm so sorry I got distracted. Did you find a book for your friend?"

Dempsey and Sybil exchanged a look of barely contained amusement and smugness.

"There was never a friend," Sybil explained. "I called Dempsey yesterday, explained my plan, and asked them to lure you here under whatever false pretenses were necessary."

Peter narrowed his eyes at his long-time assistant. "You

sneaky little—" He engulfed them in a hug. "I actually thought you meant the pet comment."

"I did." Dempsey's voice was muffled by Peter's chest. "You also qualify as a complicated, emotional houseplant I have to keep hydrated."

"Should we get out of here?" Sybil suggested, bending down to pick up the Terry Pratchett book he'd dropped.

"Where do you want to go?" Peter asked and took Sybil's hand, intertwining their fingers.

She squeezed his hand. "Anywhere I can take a nap. I was so anxious that I didn't sleep at all on the plane."

"I'm renting a flat between Grosvenor Square and Bond Street, if you want to go back there."

"Isn't that in Mayfair? Somebody's moved up in the world."

The flat Peter had rented for his stay in London wasn't very large. In terms of square footage, it was roughly the size of the shitty flat he'd rented twelve years ago when he'd met Sybil, except instead of four bedrooms and one bathroom, this flat had two bedrooms and two and a half bathrooms, and he couldn't hear his neighbors through the walls. It was cozy and bright, and Sybil immediately gravitated toward the window seat.

"The view is a lot shittier than I imagined," she said, peering out the window, which looked directly into the building next door.

"I rented it for comfort, not for the view. And the view isn't that bad. There isn't a dying neon sign in sight."

Sybil stifled a yawn with her hand. "Sorry. Jet lag."

"Do you want to see my bedroom?" he offered, not thinking about how that sounded until she chuckled.

"You've had me here for two minutes, and you're already

trying to get me into bed." She rested her head against the window. "Could we talk first?"

"Of course." Peter joined her on the window seat, which was not meant for two people, so their sides were pressed tightly together. "What did you want to talk about?"

Sybil closed her eyes. "I wanted to say that I'm sorry for how I reacted when I thought you were going to propose to me."

"You don't have to—"

"Please, just let me say this. If you interrupt me, I'll lose my nerve." She took a deep breath. "I freaked out because when I found the ring, I wanted to say yes. That really scared me because we're not ready. We haven't figured out how to merge our lives yet. So I knew I'd have to say no. And I guess I hated that you were ready to make that leap and I wasn't and I needed some way to make it not all my fault and...I'm sorry."

Peter knew there was some important stuff he should have heard, but his brain was stuck on one thing.

"You want to marry me?"

Sybil put her hand over his and squeezed. "Someday. Not yet."

"You know this means I'm going to start asking so I'll catch you the moment you're ready, right?"

She groaned, but there was a smile on her face. "Oh god, what have I done?"

"Sybil, will you marry me?"

"No." She laughed and then cupped his cheek, her brown eyes warm and soft. "Not yet."

She kissed him, tenderly at first, and then her tongue swiped his bottom lip, asking for entry. He opened to her, kissing her back with growing fervor, his blood humming, and his dick hardening and growing the best it could against the confines of his pants until she suddenly pulled back.

"I don't think I'm very sleepy anymore." She bit her bottom lip and smiled.

Peter jumped up. "I have to run to the chemist."

Sybil frowned. "Why?"

"I don't have any condoms."

"Hold on." She held up a hand for him to wait, then opened her purse, dug around for a second, and held one up. "There's probably six more in here. Mallory hid them like Easter eggs in my luggage. TSA had a really good laugh at my expense."

"I am buying her the biggest Christmas gift this year," Peter said. He grabbed Sybil's hand and tugged her towards his bedroom. "You said you had six more?"

"You think we're going to have sex six times?"

"How long are you here for?"

"Three days."

"We could make that happen."

As soon as they crossed the threshold, Peter tugged off his shirt and undid his belt, then sat on the end of his bed to take off his pants so he didn't get tangled in the legs and fall. A trip to Accident and Emergency would definitely put a damper on their reunion.

Sybil straddled him, her knees hugging his hips, and started kissing him again. Her tongue slipped into his mouth and his cock twitched roughly, like it could push through the thin cotton of his boxer briefs.

"I missed you," he moaned against her mouth.

"It's been less than a week," she pointed out, and scraped his bottom lip with her teeth.

Shivers tickled his body. "Worst, longest week of my life." He slid his hands under the hem of her shirt so he could feel her skin again. "I miss you when you go to the bathroom."

"If you quote me on this, I'll deny it, but I hope you always want me this much."

"As you wish."

Taking off Sybil's clothes gave him the same thrill as unwrapping every Christmas present he'd ever gotten as a child all at the same time. She was a gift.

"Sorry it's not sexy lingerie," she said as she struggled out of her sports bra. "I was going for comfort over fashion."

"You can wear whatever you want, as long as it comes off."

Sybil's boobs bounced when she finally succeeded in getting her bra off. His eyes followed their motion up then down. He licked his lips.

"I am the luckiest man alive," he muttered.

"My eyes are up here."

"They're beautiful eyes too, but your tits are in my face and I want them."

Sybil's laugh melted into a moan as he drew her nipple into his mouth and flicked his tongue over the sensitive tip. She arched her back, pressing her chest closer to him, and he cupped her other breast, circling her nipple with his thumb.

"F-fuck," she whined, threading her fingers through his hair. "More."

He sucked until she whimpered, and then he released her breast from his mouth with a *pop* before moving to the other side and giving it the same treatment.

Sybil tried to grind against him, but by the sound of her frustrated groan it wasn't helping. Peter wrapped his arms tightly around her middle and twisted his body, rolling them so she was on her back and he was between her thighs. Her brown eyes were wide with surprise and her cheeks flushed.

He bent over her, sucking each nipple once more before kissing a winding path down her body until he reached the waistband of her pants. He rolled the stretchy material down her hips and her thighs, kissing her newly exposed skin as it was revealed to him, and once he'd eased them over her feet, he threw them toward the corner of the room.

Peter grasped her thighs behind her knees and pushed her legs apart, opening her pussy to him. She was already so wet that she glistened.

"That's better," he murmured, then kissed the hollow where her leg met her hip.

Then he feasted.

There was no teasing preamble. He hadn't tasted her in too many days and he was starved. He dipped his tongue inside her pussy and moaned loudly as her sweet, salty wetness coated his tongue. Sybil gasped, and sank her fingers into his hair, holding his head firmly against her body. He continued to lick and suck until her legs tensed under his palms and her grip on his hair became borderline painful.

Peter didn't bother wiping his chin when he sat back on his heels.

"Condom?" he asked, and Sybil pointed at the nightstand.

He helped her scoot up to the head of the bed and settled her among the pillows before he tore open the packet and slid the latex sheath over his length. Then he settled himself back between her thighs and kissed her deeply.

"Mmm...you taste like me," Sybil murmured when she pulled back. There was a tender smile on her lips and she curled a hand around the back of his neck. "Make love to me?"

"I've only ever made love to you."

He fit the head of his cock against her slick opening and pushed, sliding in by small degrees so he didn't accidentally hurt her. She locked her legs around his waist and he rolled his hips, thrusting in and out while he kept his gaze locked on hers.

There was no race to the finish line. They moved slowly, taking time to kiss and luxuriate in every sensation. The pressure built gradually in his cock until he thought he couldn't hold it back any longer.

"That's it," Sybil encouraged. "Come for me."

He shuddered, his body contracting as he came. Her body tightened around his and faintly he thought he heard her gasp. With a final shiver, his arms gave out and he laid on top of Sybil, spent.

"Will you marry me?" he asked, his words muffled against her skin.

"Not yet," she said, stroking his back. "But someday."

Epilogue

A warm April sunshine had dried the lawn at the Crane Hotel in the nick of time. It had rained all week, threatening Annie's vision of an outdoor wedding, and Sybil had her hands full keeping two normally levelheaded women from dissolving into hysterics.

It made her question if she ever wanted to be pregnant.

But the sun had come out Friday morning, followed by unseasonably warm temperatures, which meant it reached a balmy seventy degrees instead of fifty-five. The perfect weather for an outdoor wedding. Plus, it was springtime, so the birds were adding their own joyful chorus to the occasion.

Sybil didn't know how she'd ended up as a bridesmaid in Annie and Jordy's wedding. She didn't think they were that close. If she had to guess, it had a lot to do with the stunningly handsome blond groomsman across from her who was doing his best to keep his crying dignified and undistracting.

The wedding party was made up of the Brunch Bros and their wives. Well, wives plus her. True to his word, Peter asked her to marry him at least once a week, but she hadn't given in yet.

The last six months had been hard. They'd been doing long distance while Peter worked, and every phone call or video chat filled her heart only to break it when they had to hang up. He was slowly scaling back his workload as he was able, trying to create a better balance for them, but that took time since he'd filled his schedule before they'd decided to give it a go again. She missed him fiercely. But that was ending, at least for a few weeks. Peter was taking her to Italy between projects.

It had taken a lot of work to convince her to go. It wasn't that she didn't want to go on vacation with Peter and eat pasta and gelato until she couldn't button her pants, but after a lot of setbacks and delays with the bookstore, she had been apprehensive about taking off during the final weeks before they opened. But Mallory and Peter combined into an unstoppable force of persuasion.

Her suitcase, chock full of condoms thanks to Mallory, was packed and ready to leave first thing in the morning.

She caught Peter's eye from across the aisle.

"I love you," he mouthed.

"I love you too," she mouthed back.

The dance floor was full as the band played "These Arms of Mine." Sybil surveyed the dance floor, her eyes settling on Annie and Jordy. They were in their own little blissful world, so wrapped up in each other their guests could have left en masse and they wouldn't have noticed. Jordy kissed his wife's forehead and put his hand on her pregnant belly. The many colored flowers embroidered on her flowing wedding dress, and the flowers woven into her hair, made her look like a fertility goddess.

"Do you think Annie and Eloise planned to get pregnant at

the same time?" Sybil mused as she swayed back and forth with Peter.

"I think it was fate," Peter replied. "And the inevitable consequence of too much unprotected sex."

Her head fell back as she laughed.

"Will you marry me?" he asked.

"You can't propose at someone else's wedding," she said.

Peter shrugged. "It was worth a shot."

"Someday you're going to ask and I'm going to say yes and you're going to be upset that I said yes at a gas station."

"Why would I be upset? You finally said yes."

"Because you're a hopeful romantic and a gas station isn't romantic. Your brand of ridiculousness is why I picked the bookshop for our reunion."

Peter frowned slightly. "Isn't it hopeless romantic?"

"Yes, but you never give up. Hopeful."

"That was a beautiful wedding." Peter clinked his champagne flute against Jordy's.

The four friends sat at an empty table at the nearly empty reception, watching the last few stalwart partiers on the dancefloor. Most of the people left were Jordy's former teammates from the Los Angeles Phantoms, trying to milk every last drop from the open bar.

Across the dancefloor he saw Maddy, her fiancé's gigantic suit coat draped across her shoulders, talking to Eloise, Annie, Lacey, and Sybil. Given the amount of gesturing towards various body parts, and the mildly horrified looks on Lacey and Sybil's faces, the three pregnant women were complaining about their various aches and pains, bonded in their shared misery.

"You're next," Jordy told him with a wide grin.

Sam snorted. "Sybil ducked when Annie threw the bouquet. Did you see it hit the woman standing behind her?"

"Right in the face." Graham shook his head and sipped his champagne. "It might be a while until we get to do this again."

"I'm doing my best," Peter said. "I ask her to marry me at least once a week."

Graham, Jordy, and Sam turned their heads in unison to stare at him.

"You do what?" Graham asked.

Peter didn't get a chance to explain because Lacey appeared and plopped herself down on Sam's lap.

"Well, that conversation really solidified my decision to never, ever be pregnant." She put a hand on Sam's chest and looked deep into his eyes. "You went to the follow-up appointment for your vasectomy, right? No chance any of those swimmers breached the dam?"

"I definitely went to my follow-up appointment. But you're making me want to call the urologist to get a follow-up to the follow-up."

"We should make it a tradition. Yearly trip to the urologist to calm our paranoia."

They high fived.

There really was someone out there for everyone.

Graham divided the remains of the champagne bottle between his glass and Jordy's, then asked, "So, Peter, how long are you and Sybil going to be in Italy?"

"A few weeks. I wanted to take advantage of these few weeks before the summer season starts. I've booked us some cooking classes, but other than that, we're focused on relaxing and reconnecting."

The last six months had been hard on Peter. He hated, with every strand of his DNA, being away from Sybil. No amount of voice or video calls made up for not being able to hold her in his arms. But there was an end in sight. Within the next year he'd have wrapped all the projects he had on his books and then he was going to take a break from working. Not forever, because he loved his job, but instead of saying yes to everything, he was going to be much choosier about his projects. It would have to be something special to pull him away from Sybil.

Deciding to scale back his workload had been an incredibly freeing experience. Peter had expected to feel an incredible anxiety the first time he said no, that he'd panic about never getting called again, or be tossed into a spiral where he'd obsessively check the internet to see if there was an article calling him a spoiled, entitled brat, but instead he felt relieved. Saying no to that role meant he got to say yes to more time with Sybil, or possibly yes to a project that really excited him.

"What's after Italy?" Jordy drained his champagne flute like Graham hadn't just refilled it.

"About a month and a half filming in Atlanta, and then I will be reporting for uncle duty."

Jordy and Graham looked at each other and gestured back and forth, like they were trying to figure out who Peter was talking about. Their wives were due within two weeks of each other.

"I'm coming back to Crane Cove," he clarified. "I'm going to live here."

"There goes the neighborhood," Sam said and grinned when Peter glared at him.

"You know," Graham said, his voice slow and contemplative, "it took a few years, but once Annie and Jordy move to their Oregon house, we'll all be together again. We won't have to go months without seeing each other anymore."

"Our kids can grow up together," Jordy pointed out, then

looked at Sam and Lacey and said, "You should get a puppy to join in on the baby boom."

Lacey shook her head. "I don't think Daisy is ready to give up being an only child yet."

"Not to pry," Graham said to Peter, "but since you're asking Sybil to marry you every week, have you two talked about the future beyond that?"

"You mean have we talked about having kids?" Peter shrugged. "A little bit. She's on the fence, so we'll see."

The upside to a long distance relationship was that they'd been able to have a lot of long discussions about what their future would look like and what they wanted out of life. Sybil was unsure if she wanted children, but her uncertainty centered around her fear that she wouldn't be a good mother because she hadn't had a good mother. Peter was fine either way. If they had no children or five children, he'd be happy as long as Sybil was happy.

If they did have children, he wouldn't be surprised if his parents announced a very sudden retirement and bought a house on their street. Even if they didn't have children his parents would probably buy a vacation house in Crane Cove because they adored Sybil so much. It had been the shock of his life to learn that they called her every week *and she answered.*

A slow song started to clear the dance floor of the rowdy guests, and the band announced it would be the last song.

Peter pushed back his chair and stood. He caught Sybil's eye across the dance floor and she met him halfway, relief flashing on her face like neon letters once she was in his arms.

"I should have bailed on that conversation when Lacey did," she said, and shuddered. "Pregnant women have no filters."

"Misery loves company," he reminded her.

"Next time I'd like to be left off the guest list."

Peter chuckled and kissed her forehead. "I love you. We should get married."

"Twice in one night?" Sybil raised a suspicious eyebrow. "Is all the love in the air getting to you?"

"I mean, it's hard not to wonder what our wedding will be like..."

"Small. I know you know every person on the planet, but I'd break out in hives if that many people were staring at me. Not Vegas, though. No offense to Sam and Lacey, but that also isn't my thing—why are you smiling like that?"

"Because you're planning our wedding."

Sybil blushed a perfect shade of rose and rolled her eyes to try and dispel any appearance of sentimentality on her part.

"Well, you asked."

"Actually, I didn't. I made a statement." He kissed her quickly before she could argue with him. "And I'm fine having a small wedding. We could self-solemnize in Colorado as long as I get to marry you."

"We're not getting married yet."

Peter grinned. "Not yet. But I can be patient. You're worth the wait."

Acknowledgments

Writing is, for the most part, a very solitary exercise. But this book and this series could not have happened without the love and support of the people I've surrounded myself with.

Erin, I literally don't know what I would do without you. I could not have done this without you. You're my favorite thing about landing after midnight or having to go to work at my real job at four in the morning because I know you're up, an ocean away. Thank you for never giving up on me, even when I wanted to give up on myself. Thank you for getting up before the crack of dawn to make sure I was writing and for constantly telling me I was doing a good job so I wouldn't stop writing. Thank you for all the marketing material you make because I would literally drown in all the tasks without you. I love you and absolutely considered dedicating this book to you like I did with Fret.

Mom Camp—Katie, Lara, and Emma. My sweet angels. The best damn Disney crew there has ever been. If I win the lottery, I want to build a compound so we can throw rocks at each other's houses and have mimosas every day. Thank you for supporting me as a writer, a mother, and a person. You make me feel seen and heard every day.

Esther, my Canadian exit plan. We had to be placed on opposite sides of North America because we'd be insufferable and unstoppable if we lived any closer. I mean, are you even friends if you don't get mistaken for a quaint queer couple?

Thank you for saying "yes, do" every time I send you an UNHINGED idea (especially for a spicy scene). I love you.

Danielle, Kae, Nicole, Julie, Jenn, thank you all for being early readers. I truly do need a cheerleading squad to get through a draft and all your DMs kept me going.

My lovely editor Sarah. Somehow you always know what I'm thinking. Sorry if I destroyed your search history at some point. I'll forever be planting tiny Taylor Swift references for you to find.

If you've ever slid into my DMs, shared something I've posted, or told a friend or stranger about my books, thank you. From the bottom of my heart. All of the friends I've gained along the way have been the BEST part about publishing these books. I'd do it all over again, all the late nights, the stress, the tears, to be able to know you.

Finally, thank you to my real life romance hero, Daniel. You have no clue what I'm doing but you are enthusiastically supportive and always ready to help with research. Thank you for holding down the fort during deadline days. You're the best thing that's ever been mine.

Also by Sarah Estep

Brunch Bros

Keyed Up

So Flocked

Fret Me Not

About the Author

Sarah is a Pacific Northwest based romance writer who would call herself "indoorsy". When she isn't traipsing around the country for work, Sarah enjoys buying more books than she can ever read, drinking an irresponsible amount of coffee, and not respecting her bedtime.

Find her on social media @remarkablysarah
www.sarahestep.com